Praise for the Dave Gurney Series

"Verdon's stellar eighth mystery featuring retired NYPD detective Gurney captivates from the first page . . . [The Viper] cements Verdon's reputation as one of the best contemporary fair play mystery novelists at work." —*Publishers Weekly* (starred review)

"Moral dilemmas, great characters, and twisty, propulsive plotting make John Verdon's *The Viper* a winner. You'll want to get your hands on this one." —Connor Sullivan, author of *Wolf Trap*

"John Verdon writes grown-up detective novels, by which I mean stories with intelligent plots, well-developed characters and crimes that have social consequences." —*The New York Times Book Review*

"John Verdon has written another tightly wound, intelligent mystery that keeps you guessing until the very end."
—Heather Young, author of *The Lost Girls* and *The Distant Dead*

"John Verdon is a master at crafting Sherlockian stories, each more mind-bending than the last." —J. Todd Scott, author of *The Flock*

"Verdon is masterly at keeping Gurney a step ahead of the reader."
—*The New York Times*

"For anyone who loves a good puzzle, John Verdon . . . is the easy answer." —CNN

"[Verdon has] brought back crimes of impossibility." —*Salon*

"Inventive and entertaining . . . The hard-edged characters and gritty plot recall Chandler's 'm   uzzles laid before Verdon's detective r   e grey cells' of Hercule Poirot."   shington Post

T0182672

THE VIPER

THE
VIPER

A DAVE GURNEY NOVEL

JOHN VERDON

COUNTERPOINT
CALIFORNIA

First Counterpoint edition: 2023
First paperback edition: 2024

The Library of Congress has cataloged the hardcover edition as follows:
Names: Verdon, John, author.
Title: The viper / John Verdon.
Description: First Counterpoint edition. | Berkeley : Counterpoint, 2023. | Series: Dave Gurney series
Identifiers: LCCN 2022060988 | ISBN 9781640095854 (hardcover) | ISBN 9781640095861 (ebook)
Subjects: LCGFT: Detective and mystery fiction. | Novels.
Classification: LCC PS3622.E736 V57 2023 | DDC 813/.6—dc23/eng/20230104
LC record available at https://lccn.loc.gov/2022060988

Paperback ISBN: 978-1-64009-649-3

Cover design by Nicole Caputo
Cover photograph © iStock / Christian Besliu
Book design by Laura Berry

COUNTERPOINT
Los Angeles and San Francisco, CA
www.counterpointpress.com

Printed in the United States of America

10 9 8 7 6 5 4 3 2 1

For Naomi

All that we forgot we saw
forever lives in what we see.

—ANONYMOUS

PROLOGUE

HE WAS AFRAID TO GO NEAR THE BIG HOUSE AT THE END of the quiet, tree-lined street.

The stories whispered about the man who lived there kept people at a respectful distance. There was no doubt that he'd had men killed. The number was guessed at in hushed tones, as was the number he'd executed with his own hands. It was a known fact that people entered that house and were never seen again. But such was the man's power—and the dread he inspired in potential witnesses—that he'd never been convicted of any crime at all.

Walking up the man's driveway that day in the autumn chill would have been unthinkable a short time ago, but everything was different now. As the heavy front door swung open and an ageless, stone-faced woman led him down an unlit hall into a windowless den, his trepidation was suppressed by a desperate hope.

The man sat in semi-darkness behind an ebony desk, massaging his temples. It was rumored that he suffered from migraines. He wore tinted glasses, a sign of his sensitivity to light. His hair was gray and thinning, his skin sallow. The air in the room was humid with a faint odor of tropical decay. There was only one object on the ebony desk—a small gold sculpture of a coiled snake, head raised, fangs exposed.

"So," the man said in a soft voice, lips hardly moving. "What can I do for you?"

The words came rushing out, not at all as he'd rehearsed them ever since calling for this appointment, this audience, but in a stuttering jumble. Even as he made his request with its peculiar requirement—especially with its peculiar requirement—he realized how idiotic it all sounded.

In a surge of regret, he wished to God he hadn't come. It felt like the worst mistake he had ever made in a life full of mistakes. But it was too late. Fear grabbed his heart. His hands trembled.

The man regarded him through his tinted glasses with morose, unblinking eyes for what seemed like a very long time. He finally gestured toward the only other chair in the room.

"Sit down. Relax. Talk slow."

He did as he was told. Afterward, he could remember almost nothing of what he said—only the man's response and the look in his eyes.

"The story you tell me is full of misery. Your son's disrespect has poisoned your life. What you want to do now is quite unusual. The favor you ask of me is something I would not normally grant. But because I know well the stabbing pain you have described, I will consider your request. If I agree to do what you ask, in return you must do what I ask. I will describe this to you when the time comes. But there is one thing you need to know from the beginning. If you accept my terms, there will be no turning back, no second thoughts. Our agreement will be unbreakable. You understand what this means?"

"I do."

The man's lips twitched in what appeared to be a fleeting smile. Behind the tinted glasses, his eyes, as impassive as death itself, were focused on a plan taking shape.

PART I

DAMNING EVIDENCE

1

SUMMER SLOWLY DECLINED AS IF IN THE GRIP OF A
wasting disease, then the orange flare of autumn swept by in the
blink of an eye, leaving the western Catskill Mountains a dull brown.
November arrived with a windy chill that never let up and a long succession of shortening days that passed with no sign of the sun.

On a raw, gusty afternoon Dave and Madeleine Gurney were
hard at work outside their farmhouse, high in the hills outside the
village of Walnut Crossing. Autumn leaves skittered across the patio
they were reshaping. Dave eased an unwieldy slab of bluestone into
its new position. Still lean and strong in his early fifties, he welcomed
the exercise.

Madeleine carefully set down a wheelbarrow full of fresh sod
next to him. "Did you call your son?"

He blinked. "What?"

"Today is his birthday."

"Oh. Yes. Right. I'll give him a call after dinner."

For the past week, they'd been changing the contours of the old
stone patio that lay between the house and the chicken coop. The
previous spring's Harrow Hill murder case had reached its bloody
conclusion on this patio, and the intervening months had done so
little to free Madeleine from the images of that dreadful night that
she still found it a challenge to step out through the French doors.

The work they were engaged in was an attempt to alter the look of the place in the hope of diluting the memory of what occurred there. Gurney hoped it might also dissipate the hard-to-define strain present in her expression more often than not these days.

The project was almost finished. He had completed most of the stonework and had broken up the hard Catskill earth for new planting beds. Madeleine had painted the chicken coop and its attached shed a cheerful yellow and planted dozens of tulip bulbs around the reconfigured patio.

As he leaned on his crowbar to adjust the position of the final slab of bluestone, the wind rose, and the first flakes of a promised snow shower swirled around him.

"I think we've done enough for today," said Madeleine, glancing at the slaty sky. "Besides, Emma should be arriving anytime now." She looked at him. "David, you're scowling."

"Maybe because you seem to know more about her visit than you're telling me."

"All I know is, she wants to talk to you about a murder case."

He laid his crowbar next to the wheelbarrow and took off his work gloves. "I doubt she's coming here just to talk."

Madeleine turned her strained face away from a gust of wind, started toward the French doors, and froze with a sharp little cry.

Gurney stepped quickly over to her. "What is it?"

She pointed at a spot on the ground just beyond the edge of the patio. He followed her terrified gaze.

"The leaves moved. A snake!"

Gurney approached the spot, his shovel at the ready. When he was within striking distance, a small gray creature darted from the leaves and disappeared under a nearby shrub.

"No snake," said Gurney. "Just a vole."

Madeleine breathed a shaky sigh of relief.

He was tempted to remind her that there were no snakes to be concerned about in their part of the Catskills. But he knew it would make no difference.

2

GURNEY STOOD WITH HIS BACK TO THE SHOWERHEAD. The warm, tingling spray massaged his neck and shoulders, gradually releasing the muscle tightness caused by hefting the patio stones, as well as the emotional tension of recalling what had happened on the patio six months earlier.

The soothing water was just beginning to accomplish its magic when Madeleine opened the bathroom door and announced Emma's arrival.

Gurney dried and dressed. He found Madeleine alone in their big farmhouse kitchen. She was peering through the French doors past the reconfigured patio and overgrown apple tree, to the figure of a woman facing the old pasture that sloped from the house to the barn. Her loose cape-like coat billowed sideways in the snowy wind.

"She told me she wanted to breathe in our pure mountain air," said Madeleine.

"Unusual day for it."

"There's nothing *usual* about Emma."

With the placid smile of someone enjoying a summer stroll, Emma turned and slowly returned to the house.

Gurney opened one of the glass-paned doors.

She stopped just outside, her blue-eyed gaze meeting his. "So beautiful here. The sound of the wind rushing through the trees, the earth breathing." She extended her hand. Her grip was strong, the palm calloused. "Thank you for taking time to see me."

"Nice to see you, Emma."

A little gust of snow blew in as she stepped inside. She looked smaller, thinner than he recalled, yet more intense, as if her diminished body had concentrated her energy. The gray-blond hair he remembered was now all gray. Its short style accentuated her cheekbones and the determined set of her mouth.

"I wish we had nicer weather for you," said Madeleine.

"This is perfect. I could inhale this air forever. It's detoxifying.

I've just come from Attica. What a pit of darkness and misery! The air there reeks of fear, hatred, despair."

"Not so unusual for a max-security facility," said Gurney.

"Our prison system is a machine that grinds souls into dust. It makes men smaller, harder, one insult away from explosion."

Her intensity led to a silence, broken by Madeleine's offer to take her coat. "Why don't you and Dave sit by the fireplace, and I'll get some tea going. Are you still a fan of lemon-ginger?"

"That would be nice," Emma said in a softened voice, slipping out of the loose coat.

Madeleine retreated to the kitchen end of the long room while Gurney and Emma settled into a facing pair of armchairs by the old fieldstone hearth.

"God judges our virtue by how we treat the damaged among us," Emma said in a tone more sad than angry. *"Show me your prisons, and I will know your heart."*

She paused before changing to a cooler, businesslike tone. "You're wondering why I'm here. How much has Madeleine already told you?"

"Nothing, beyond the fact that it has something to do with a murder case."

"The murder of Lenny Lerman. I can see the name means nothing to you. It meant nothing to me, either. Not until the conviction of his accused murderer. But I believe that Lerman is the key to the case."

The wind moaned in the chimney.

"I'm not following you."

"Lenny Lerman was a middle-aged, small-time criminal. He was murdered in a private Adirondack hunting preserve. His headless body was found in a shallow grave by a trespassing hunter three days later. The owner of the property—a rich young man with a terrible past—was arrested, tried, and convicted. The testimony of witnesses, physical evidence, fingerprints, DNA—all the available facts incriminated him, especially his lurid background. Are you familiar with the name Ziko Slade?"

"Something in the tabloids. Pro golfer gone bad? Drugs, violence, sex trafficking?"

"Tennis, actually. Great talent. Made the finals of all the big tournaments ten, twelve years ago when he was in his late teens. Handsome, charming, magnetic personality. Movie-star charisma. Became an instant fixture not only in the celebrity sports world, but in the art world, the fashion world, the money world, the drug-infested party world. Soon went on to became a drug supplier to the rich and famous. Rumors of money laundering, wild orgies, under-age girls. He put all that behind him, became a different person, but terrible reputations have a way of enduring—and giving life to new accusations."

"Like the murder of Lenny Lerman?"

"The prosecutor put together a compelling case. Motive, means, opportunity—all crystal clear. The jury took less than an hour to find Ziko guilty—close to a record, I'm told, for a major murder case. The judge polled them individually. Guilty, guilty, guilty—twelve times, guilty. He's just begun serving his sentence. Thirty years to life. In Attica."

She fell silent, her sharp gaze on Gurney.

"You didn't drive all the way from Attica just to tell me this story." Gurney said. "What am I missing?"

"I want you to solve the murder of Lenny Lerman."

"Sounds like that's already been done."

"The person they found guilty is innocent."

"Innocent? The Ziko Slade you just described to me—"

"That's the person he once was—a person he stopped being two years before the Lerman murder."

The eerie sound of the wind in the chimney grew louder.

"How do you mean, the person he stopped being?"

"Three years ago, his drug-addict wife stabbed him with an ice pick. Grazed his heart, puncturing his aorta. He was in intensive care for nine days. Face to face with death. In that position, he saw the wreckage of his life in a new way. The vision changed him."

"How do you know this?"

"When he was released from the hospital, the vision was still with him. He had clarity about his past but no idea what to do with it. He wanted help to understand who he could be—who he *should* be. In that state, the universe sometimes intervenes. Connections appear. Someone put him in touch with someone who put him in touch with me."

"You became his therapist?"

"I don't use that term. It creates a false impression of what I do."

Madeleine arrived with a tray holding two cups of tea, a plate of freshly baked scones, a small bowl of jam, spoons, and a butter knife for the jam. She set it on the low coffee table between the facing armchairs and stepped back.

"You're not joining us?" asked Emma.

"When it comes to murder cases, I'd rather—"

There was a loud thwack against a pane in one of the French doors. Madeleine winced, hurried over to it, peered down at the patio stones, and let out a sigh of relief. "Once in a while a bird flies into the glass. Sometimes the impact is so loud, you expect to find a little body on the ground. But whoever flew into the door just now managed to fly away." She shivered, began to speak, stopped, and returned to the kitchen end of the room.

After a brief silence, Gurney asked Emma, "Is there a term you prefer to 'therapist'?"

"There's no need for any term. I listen. I comment. I take no payment."

"And your listening sessions with Ziko Slade during the two years between his near-death revelation and the murder of Lerman have convinced you that the change in his character was so great that he couldn't have done what sworn witnesses and physical evidence convinced twelve jurors that he did?"

"Yes."

"When was he sentenced?"

"Just a week ago."

"You've spoken to him since then?"

"Most recently this morning."

"Did he have a competent attorney?"

"Marcus Thorne."

Gurney was impressed. "Big name. Must have been expensive."

"Ziko has money."

"Have you spoken to Thorne about the appeal process?"

"He believes it's a lost cause."

"Despite that, you have no doubt about Slade's innocence?"

"None."

Gurney took a sip of tea and gave her a long, appraising look. Unshakable certitude regarding a conclusion that seemed at variance with the available facts was not a rare trait. It was fairly common among egomaniacs, the emotionally unstable, and the deeply ignorant. Emma Martin was none of those things.

He cleared his throat. "So . . . what do you want me to do?"

"Discover the facts that prove his innocence."

"What if the facts prove his guilt?"

She smiled slightly. "Ziko has been betrayed by a legal system more interested in securing a conviction than uncovering the truth. I'm certain that you can find the facts that will exonerate him." She paused. "I know you're skeptical of my insight into Ziko's character. Let me add a more mundane observation. He's far too intelligent to have committed such a stupid crime."

"What was stupid about it?"

"According to the prosecutor, he was being blackmailed by Lenny Lerman over some dark secret in his past, and he killed Lerman rather than meet his financial demand."

Gurney shrugged. "A common enough solution."

"In general, but not in its details. According to the prosecutor, when Lerman arrived at Ziko's estate, Ziko knocked him unconscious, dragged his body to a shallow grave he'd already prepared in a pine thicket near the lodge, chopped off his head with an axe and cut off his fingers with a pruning clipper—supposedly to impede identification of

the body—covered the body with a scattering of dirt, left his fingerprints on the axe handle, left his DNA on a cigarette butt by the grave,
and did every other incriminating thing imaginable. The body, with a
few other parts chewed off by scavenging animals, was discovered—"

The clatter of a dropped plate in the sink drew Gurney's attention to the open kitchen area in time to see Madeleine hurrying from
the room.

Emma appeared chagrined. "Sorry. I shouldn't have been so
explicit."

"Not your fault. The Harrow Hill business has had some lingering effects."

"Of course. It must have traumatized you both."

Gurney responded with a small nod. "Please continue."

She regarded him with some concern before going on. "My point
is that Ziko has the financial resources to deal with a blackmail challenge in other ways. He would never have done what the prosecutor
says he did."

"Smart people can do stupid things under pressure."

"Suppose you planned to kill someone who was coming to visit
you. Would you dig a shallow grave out by your chicken coop and
bury the body under a couple of inches of dirt where coyotes and
vultures were sure to find it? You would not be so foolish, David,
and neither would Ziko."

Her steady gaze remained on Gurney. There were tiny droplets
of water in her hair, the glimmering remnants of melted snowflakes.

3

TWO HOURS LATER, GURNEY AND MADELEINE WERE FIN-
ishing a taciturn dinner of fettuccine bolognese left over from the
previous evening. Gurney's conversation with Emma and Madeleine's
emotional reaction to it hung over them, a silent presence.

Eventually, Madeleine laid down her fork, nudged her plate

toward the center of the table, and spoke in a conspicuously neutral tone. "What do you intend to do?"

"She wants me to reinvestigate a murder case that's been fully adjudicated—a case so strong that the jury returned an immediate guilty verdict, despite the defendant having a top-tier defense attorney."

"It wouldn't be the first time you took on a challenge like that."

"But there was always some apparent discrepancy, a crack that could be pried open. Emma's not offering me anything like that—just her total trust in a supposedly reformed slimeball."

"You're very good at discovering little discrepancies that aren't obvious at first."

"So . . . you're telling me I should get involved?"

"I'm not telling you that at all."

He stared at her. "I'm confused. You invited Emma Martin here. You just said I'd be very good at doing what she wants. That sure sounds like—"

She cut him off. "I didn't *invite* her. She called me out of the blue and asked if she could talk to you about a case she felt strongly about. Emma and I were close when we worked together in the city. She was a good friend. She provided guidance when I most needed it. So I couldn't say no, Emma, you can't come, you can't talk to my husband. Instead, I said fine, it'll be wonderful to see you again. But I had no idea she wanted you to jump head-first into the reinvestigation of a horrible murder."

"If you don't want me to do it, why are you telling me I'd be good at it?"

"Because I know what intrigues you, David. I know there's something in you that comes to life at the challenge of uncovering something that everyone else has overlooked. And if that's what you want to do—despite what happened here last year, despite both of us coming within an inch of being killed, despite that whole bloody nightmare I can't get out of my head—then let's get it out in the open."

Gurney sighed, placed his hands on the table, and slowly turned up his palms. "The truth is, Maddie, I have no idea what I want to do. God knows, I don't want to get sucked into something that ends up like . . ." His voice trailed off. He took a deep breath and continued, "Besides, I'm not crazy about the idea of getting involved with Emma."

"Oh?"

"Her assertiveness can be off-putting. And she's arrogant."

Madeleine sighed. "She's not arrogant. But I understand how she might seem that way to you. At the clinic, she was always at odds with the director. She made categorical statements about the mental status of clients that the director complained were unsupported by specific data. But the thing is, she was incredibly acute in her perceptions. She could see things instantly that could take other therapists a dozen sessions to get to."

"And she was always right?"

"I never knew her to be wrong."

"So, you're assuming she's right about this Slade character?"

"I'm not assuming anything."

"Are you pushing me toward this thing or away from it?"

The lines of tension at the corners of Madeleine's eyes had deepened. "Does it matter?"

Gurney said nothing.

"When I saw Emma out to her car, she said she'd left an envelope for you with information about the case. Looking at it might be the polite thing to do. You don't owe her anything more."

4

GURNEY SPENT A RESTLESS NIGHT. THE WINTRY WIND had grown stronger, seething through the trees outside the bedroom windows well into the wee hours of the morning. The shallow sleep he finally fell into just before dawn was disturbed by the recurrent nightmare he'd come to know as "the Danny dream."

It consisted of a weird, disjointed replay of the accident, long ago, that had killed his son a week before his fourth birthday—the only child he'd had with Madeleine.

On their way to the playground on a sunny day.

Danny walking in front of him.

Following a pigeon on the sidewalk.

Gurney only partly present.

Pondering a twist in a murder case he was working on.

Distracted by a bright idea, a possible solution.

The pigeon stepping off the curb into the street.

Danny following the pigeon.

The sickening, heart-stopping thump.

Danny's body tossed through the air, hitting the pavement, rolling.

Rolling.

The red BMW racing away.

Screeching around a corner.

Gone.

Gurney awoke in the same agony of grief the dream always produced. For twenty years, the dream had assaulted him at unpredictable intervals. The events, moment by moment, were always the same, always consistent with his memory. And the dreadful feeling in his heart was, as always, undiminished.

He got up, went to the bathroom, splashed cold water on his face; then put on jeans and a sweatshirt and went out to the kitchen. While his coffee brewed, he stood at the French doors and gazed out at the gray light of dawn over the eastern ridge. He opened one of the doors. The still air was damp and raw, but it attached him to the actual world around him.

There was just enough light to see the frost on the patio stones, frost on the grass beyond it, frost on the bird feeders. Soon the chickadees and nuthatches would be visiting, flitting back and forth from the apple tree. He began to shiver. He closed the door, got his coffee from the sink island, picked up the plain white envelope that Emma had left on the sideboard, and went into the den. In the light of his desk lamp, he opened the envelope and removed its single sheet of paper. On it were just two short items.

The first was the contact information for Ziko Slade's defense attorney, Marcus Thorne. Thorne, Gurney recalled, had achieved his initial notoriety by demolishing the seemingly airtight prosecution case against Simeon Lorzco (a.k.a. the Kindergarten Killer), who moments after his controversial acquittal was fatally shot by the mother of one of the murdered children. Below Thorne's phone number Emma had appended a handwritten comment: "He is still retained by Ziko and will answer any questions you have about the case."

The second item was a link to *New York State v. Slade* on the video archive of *Murder on Trial*, the division of RAM-TV that streamed sensational homicide trials.

Rather than go directly to the video, Gurney decided to look at the media coverage of Ziko Slade, past and present. If he had spent years as the sort of tabloid celebrity Emma described, jurors would have held preconceptions of Slade that might have slanted the verdict.

Typing "Slade Tennis Star" on his laptop brought up articles from *Sports Illustrated, Tennis Today,* and the sports sections of major newspapers. These articles—with headlines like "Hottest Teen in Tennis" and "Ziko-Mania"—covered Slade's career from ages fourteen to seventeen. The photos were action shots of him on the court—a graceful teenager with wavy hair, sinewy limbs, and an invincible grin.

The words "Slade Celebrity" led to articles covering his late teens and early twenties, a distinctly different phase of his life, in which the media's attention shifted to his romantic relationships with female pop stars, his frequenting of glitzy art openings, and extravagant promotional events for his "Z" brand of sportswear. In the photos taken in this period his eyes were more knowing, his grin more suggestive. An article titled "Sexiest Man in Tennis" caught Gurney's eye, mainly because of the writer's name—Connie Clarke.

Back when Gurney was given an award for a record number of

NYPD homicide arrests, Connie Clarke had written a piece about his career for *New York Magazine*. Its "Supercop" title and adulatory tone raised his department profile in ways he'd found endlessly embarrassing.

The search term "Slade Scandals" brought up stories revealing the dissolution of the twenty-three-year-old darling of society into a recklessly corrupt twenty-six-year-old. There were drug-related arrests, rumors of underage sex trafficking, accusations of statutory rape, links to disgraced politicians, and a succession of fashionable drug rehabs followed by spectacular public relapses.

An enlarged mugshot from this period showed his movie-star features marred by hard eyes and a smirking mouth. The final headline at the end of this chaotic time announced that he'd entered yet another recovery program—a private facility run by a controversial psychologist named Emma Martin. After that, the media lost interest in him, relegating him to the black hole reserved for troubled personalities no longer creating newsworthy trouble.

This period of invisibility ended explosively two years later with the news of his arrest for murder in what the tabloids were calling "The Case of the Headless Hunter."

A brief announcement had run in *The New York Times* the previous November.

CELEBRITY ATHLETE CHARGED WITH MURDER

Former tennis prodigy and society bad-boy Ziko Slade has been arrested in the upstate town of Rexton, New York, for the murder of Leonard Lerman, a sometime employee of the Beer Monster, a local beverage retailer. Rexton Police Chief Desmond Rickles provided the following statement:

"After a thorough investigation, we have arrested Ziko Slade and charged him with the premeditated commission of this heinous crime. Further details

*will be provided by the Office of the District Attor-
ney at the appropriate time."*

The reference to District Attorney Cam Stryker gave Gurney a
jolt. Although Rexton was a good sixty miles from Harrow Hill, it
was part of the same sprawling rural county that fell within Stryker's
jurisdiction. His recollection of the young, transparently ambitious
DA was mixed at best.

Now that he was up to speed on Slade's history, Gurney turned
to the trial itself. The link Emma provided brought up a flashy page
with a pulsating headline: MURDER ON TRIAL. A subhead read,
YOUR FRONT-ROW SEAT AT THE ULTIMATE CONTEST IN OUR
JUSTICE SYSTEM. In a blue banner were the words, NEW YORK
STATE V. ZIKO SLADE—FROM THE TRUE CRIME ARCHIVES
OF RAM-TV. Gurney adjusted the angle of his laptop screen, clicked
Play, and sat back in his chair.

The front of a courtroom appeared on the screen, centered on
the judge's raised bench. The Rexton courthouse managed to escape
the mid-twentieth-century modernization craze of blond furnishings
and fluorescent lights that made so many other courtrooms appear
shoddy and ephemeral. Dark mahogany covered every surface, from
the judge's bench to the witness box adjoining it and even the wall
paneling.

A small plaque identified the dour-faced judge as Harold Wartz.
He had unruly gray hair, brushed straight back, and thick features.
His heavy-lidded eyes were magnified by his glasses. His first words
were delivered in a voice as cheerless as his demeanor.

"Ms. Stryker, you may proceed with your opening statement."

A lean young woman in gray slacks and a dark blue blazer strode
from the prosecution table to a nearby lectern. Placing her hands on
it, she leaned slightly forward, making eye contact with each member
of the jury.

"Ladies and gentlemen, the crime I'm about to describe is sad
and horrifying. It involves a fatal confrontation between a pathetic

small-time criminal and a slick, ruthless murderer. It's the story of an ill-advised blackmail attempt that ended with the would-be blackmailer decapitated and buried behind the country lodge of the powerful man he'd targeted. That would-be blackmailer was Lenny Lerman—a high-school dropout who spent the next twenty-six years of his life in a succession of menial jobs interrupted by arrests for petty theft, possession of stolen property, and passing bad checks. A dreamer with no common sense, always on the lookout for the one big score that would change everything. And then he found it. Or he thought he did."

Stryker stepped from behind the lectern and approached the jury box.

"It all began when, in Lenny's own words, a former jail-mate passed along a piece of information involving something awful that had happened in Ziko Slade's wild, drug-using days. You'll hear from witnesses how obsessed Lenny became with using this information to get rich. He planned to offer Slade the 'exclusive rights' to the information for a million dollars. If Slade balked at this, Lenny figured he could threaten to sell what he knew to the highest bidder."

As Stryker went on, her angular features seemed to grow sharper and her voice flintier. "Perhaps because he had some inkling of the danger in this plan, Lenny purchased a million-dollar accidental death policy, with his son and daughter as beneficiaries. But, blinded by his dream of wealth, he failed to grasp how great the danger really was." Stryker sighed in sad amazement at this blindness.

"You'll hear testimony regarding the phone calls he made to set up a meeting with Slade at his remote Adirondack lodge. You'll see GPS data and DNA evidence that places Lenny Lerman at that lodge when Slade was also present—at the time the medical examiner has established for Lerman's death. There's just one reasonable conclusion: Ziko Slade murdered Lenny Lerman in a vicious, premeditated fashion." Stryker paused to let this sink in.

"Through witness testimony and forensic data, you'll be able to follow Lenny's movements on that final day of his life—as he drove from his little two-room apartment in Calliope Springs to the door of Slade's grand mountain lodge. From there you'll follow the evidence trail to the lonely spot in that cold November forest where he was beheaded and buried."

Stryker let that final image creep into the mind of each member of the jury before going on.

"Ziko Slade knew exactly when Lenny was coming. Slade was ready. When Lenny arrived, Slade let him talk. Let him make his proposition. Let him state his price. Then he killed him."

Stryker's voice rose to a high pitch of outrage. "Killed him with an axe and buried him. Coolly, calmly, without hesitation or remorse." She smiled sadly, her voice suddenly oozing sympathy. "Lenny Lerman was no saint. He'd committed crimes and paid for those crimes. Like many of us, he'd made some mistakes. But he didn't deserve to be murdered. He had a right to live, something that was stolen from him by Ziko Slade. Lenny Lerman has a right to justice. Justice that you, as members of the jury, can deliver. Thank you for your attention."

Wartz cleared his throat roughly. "Mr. Thorne, your turn."

At that moment, Gurney heard Madeleine coming across the hall toward the den, and he paused the video.

She hesitated in the doorway. "Sorry. Am I interrupting?"

"Emma left me a link to the trial video. l decided to take a quick look at it."

"And?"

"Judging from the DA's opening statement, the case against Slade is strong."

"Trying to create that impression is the purpose of an opening statement, right?"

"She succeeded. By the way, the 'she' is Cam Stryker."

Madeleine froze for a moment, then abruptly changed the subject.

"Gerry and I have the early shift at the Crisis Center. She'll be picking me up in a few minutes. I don't have time to deal with the chickens. Maybe you could check the feeder and make sure they have fresh water?"

He nodded with a conspicuous lack of enthusiasm.

"And," she went on, "you could give them some blueberries."

"*Blueberries?*"

"They're birds. Birds eat berries. I hear Gerry's car now. See you tonight."

"Doesn't the early shift end in the afternoon?"

"It does. But then we're meeting with our music group. I'll be home in time for dinner." She smiled tightly and departed.

Since the dreadful ending of the Harrow Hill case, the shadow it cast over their lives often made activities that were once normal feel strained. Madeleine seemed determined to maintain her external routine as if nothing had happened, but that determination itself added to the tension in the atmosphere. Occasionally, a small crack appeared in the facade, as it had the previous afternoon with the dropped dish and her retreat from the room, but soon enough the subject would always shift to something like snacks for the chickens or practice sessions with her string quartet. Gurney didn't see a solution. Conducting business as usual felt artificial, but perhaps there was no better alternative. Maybe the weirdness of it all was the way it needed to be.

More disturbing was his suspicion that the weirdness might be rooted in some central fact of their marriage, something he was unwilling or unable to confront.

For a long while, he stared out the den window at the high pasture. The pale morning sun was just beginning to creep above the eastern ridge, casting a cold light over the hillside's withered remnants of milkweed and goldenrod.

A slight movement at the top of the field caught his eye. Three deer were standing at the edge of the tree line, alert, ears twitching, as if they sensed that the hunting season—with all its random pain and death—was about to begin.

5

GURNEY MADE HIMSELF A GENEROUS BREAKFAST OF THREE
eggs, two slices of toast, and four slices of bacon. Madeleine didn't
approve of bacon, insisting it was full of carcinogens, which made
having it in her presence uncomfortable. It was a vice he preferred to
enjoy alone.

He finished eating and washed up. It occurred to him that he
should tend to the chickens, but that thought was nudged aside by an
urge to watch Marcus Thorne's opening statement. Returning to the
den, he resumed the paused trial video.

Thorne stood beside the defense table, facing the jury, his well-
fed features constricted in a way that conveyed something between
amazed disbelief and a reaction to an unpleasant odor. His voice was
cultured, a bit weary, and distinctly mid-Atlantic.

"Well, Ms. Stryker's statement was really something. I had to keep
reminding myself that she was talking about this case. Rarely have I
heard a prosecutor sound so sure about facts that are open to so many
interpretations. And rarely have I seen 'evidence' as inconclusive as
what the prosecution intends to present in this trial—evidence that
proves nothing beyond the fact that a murder was committed. I'll say
no more at this point. There'll be no windy introduction from me. I'm
sure you'll see through the prosecution's so-called logic, and your own
common sense will persuade you to acquit this innocent man."

He took his seat at the defense table next to his client.

This was Gurney's first clear sight of Ziko Slade. Three years
had elapsed since his descent from tennis star to dissolute druggie to
moral conversion and involvement with Emma Martin. The man's
face seemed to contain two opposing personalities. The mouth—
full-lipped, pouty, on the verge of a sneer—was that of a corrupt
Adonis, a mixture of creepiness and seductive charm. The eyes, however, radiated a calm intelligence and something almost ascetic. The
mixture of qualities struck Gurney as both unsettling and magnetic.

"Ms. Stryker," Judge Wartz said, speaking in a voice that sounded like it was coming from the bottom of a wet barrel. "Are you ready to proceed?"

She rose, straightening her blazer. "I call Thomas Cazo to the witness stand."

A bull-necked man in a silvery gray suit approached the witness box, sat down, and cleared his throat. The top two or three buttons of his shiny green shirt were open, revealing more hair on his chest than on his head.

In response to a question from Stryker, he stated that he was employed as a night manager at the Beer Monster in Calliope Springs Mall and that he had been Lenny Lerman's boss until Lerman quit at the beginning of the previous November. Stryker regarded him with respectful attention, conveying to the jury that this was a man worth listening to.

"So, when he quit," she said, "that would have been about three weeks before he was murdered?"

"Yeah."

"And that was your last conversation with Lenny?"

"Yeah."

"Would you please describe that conversation to the court."

Cazo cleared his throat again and wiped his mouth with the back of his hand. "He came into my office to tell me he was quitting. I asked him why. He said he was onto something real big, and he didn't need to be stacking cases of beer anymore."

"Did he tell you what that 'real big' thing was?"

"He said he had some facts worth a fucking fortune. Excuse my language, but I'm just saying what he said. *A fucking fortune.*"

"Did he tell you where he expected that fortune to come from?"

"From Ziko Slade."

"Did he tell you why Slade would be willing to pay him a fortune for these facts?"

"Because they were about him."

"About Slade?"

"Yeah."

"Did he tell you what these facts were?"

"About bad shit that went down with Slade a few years back. I told him all sorts of bad shit about Slade was already common knowledge. He said, not this. This was worse than what everybody knew about. This could get Slade put away for life."

Stryker nodded, her lips pressed together in a grim line. "Did you interpret what Lenny told you as a plan to extort money from Slade?"

"What else could it be?"

"Did you comment on his plan?"

Cazo grinned. "I told him he better watch his ass and keep away from Slade."

"Because you thought his plan was too dangerous?"

"Too dangerous for him."

"Thank you. I have no more questions."

Wartz peered at his watch. "Mr. Thorne?"

Thorne was already approaching the witness box. "Your name is Thomas Cazo?" He managed to inject some distaste into the name.

"Yeah."

"The same Thomas Cazo also known as Tommy Hooks?"

Cazo gave him a long hard look. "I might've heard somebody say something like that."

"Interesting nickname. How'd you get it?"

Cazo shrugged. "I used to be a boxer. I had a good left hook."

"Doesn't it also refer to your custom of using a meat hook to persuade people who owe you money to pay up?"

Stryker, who'd been on the edge of her chair during this exchange, leapt to her feet with an outraged cry. "Objection! That's a scurrilous smear! It has no relevance, no—"

Wartz cut her off. "Sustained. Defense counsel's comment is to be stricken from the record. Mr. Thorne, you're over the line."

"My apologies, Your Honor. I have no more questions."

"Mr. Cazo, you're excused. Ms. Stryker, call your next witness."

After a dramatic pause, she called Adrienne Lerman to the stand. A heavyset young woman in a loose-fitting earth-colored dress made her way to the witness box. She wore no makeup or jewelry. There was a dark mole above her upper lip.

Stryker's opening questions established that she was a twenty-four-year-old unmarried nurse who provided care to the terminally ill, that she was Lenny Lerman's daughter, and that she was sure she knew her father better than anyone else on earth.

Adrienne Lerman's tone sounded both sad and syrupy, worn-down and wistful. She struck Gurney as the sort of woman who believed in lighting candles rather than cursing the darkness, while fully expecting them to be blown out.

Stryker spoke softly, a good imitation of empathy. "Ms. Lerman, we've heard witness testimony that your father had a plan that he claimed would make him rich. Did he tell you about it?"

"He told us in a restaurant one night."

"By *us*, you mean you and your brother, Sonny?"

"That's right. We were at the Lakeshore Chop House." Adrienne frowned, as though making a distasteful admission.

"Not your favorite place?"

She lowered her voice. "It has a reputation for being mob-connected."

"That didn't bother your father?"

"He liked being close to that world. To him, those people were strong, impressive. He was like a little kid watching the big kids."

"He admired gangsters?"

She took a handkerchief out of her sleeve and dabbed at her nose. "He wanted to be accepted by them, seen as an equal. I think that's what trapped him in that awful plan."

Stryker nodded sympathetically. "What did he tell you about his plan?"

"That he'd got lucky and come by a big secret—a bombshell, he called it—that was going to turn our lives around."

"Your life as well as his?"

"Mine and Sonny's. He kept repeating how good it would be for Sonny and me. But he seemed more focused on Sonny, like he was trying to make up for something."

"Do you know what that *something* was?"

"The fact that he'd never made anything of himself. That he'd never earned Sonny's respect."

"Did your father tell you what he was actually going to do?"

"Yes. Sell some information he had to a famous rich guy with a dirty past."

"Did he tell you the rich guy's name?"

"Ziko Slade."

"He hoped to get a lot of money from Slade for this information?"

"Yes."

"Did you understand what that really meant?"

"I guess I did. Even though I didn't want to."

"Did the terms 'extortion' or 'blackmail' occur to you at the time?"

Adrienne bit her lower lip and stared down at her clasped fingers. "Yes."

Stryker glanced significantly at the jury before going on.

"You loved your father, didn't you?"

"Yes."

"And you believed he was doing this for you and your brother?"

"For Sonny, mainly."

Stryker smiled softly, as if contemplating the admirable motive behind Lenny Lerman's foolish plan.

"One more question, Adrienne. Did you get a call from your father on the evening he was killed?"

"He called me at seven o'clock. I was at a hospice patient's home, checking her meds. I found his message on my phone when I got home."

Stryker walked from the witness stand to the bailiff's desk and requested evidence item number AL-009. The bailiff sorted through a file box, removed a cellphone from a plastic bag, and handed it to her.

"Your Honor," said Stryker, "if it please the court, I'd like to play the message Lenny Lerman left for his daughter, Adrienne, at seven o'clock on November twenty-third of last year—the evening he was killed."

Wartz nodded. "Proceed."

After tapping a series of icons, Stryker laid the phone on the front railing of the witness box. Adrienne's eyes began filling with tears.

A tense male voice spoke from the phone. "Adie? Adie, are you there? It's me. Dad. Christ, I hope you get this. I'm here at Ziko Slade's. This is it. What it's all about, right?" Lerman's voice sounded like it was breaking. "For Sonny and you. Tell him this is to make up for everything. Whatever happens tonight . . . whatever happens. I wish I was talking to you both instead of some fucking machine. So . . . that's it. I'm going in." The voice on the phone let out a crazy, raspy laugh. "Like in the movies. I'm going in."

Adrienne was shaking. She pressed her handkerchief against her mouth, stifling sobs.

Stryker paused for a long ten seconds, then reached out and put her hand on Adrienne's arm. "If you feel you can answer, I have one last question."

Adrienne blew her nose and took a deep breath. "Go ahead."

"Are you certain that the voice in that phone message was your father's?"

"Yes."

"Thank you. That will be all. I'm so sorry we had to put you through that."

Sorry, my ass, thought Gurney. Stryker knew damn well that she had to humanize Lenny Lerman to make the jury care about his murder, and the combination of his paternal angst in that message and his daughter's tears accomplished the goal. On a prosecutorial success scale of one to ten, Lenny's words and Adrienne's reaction added up to a twelve.

Gurney paused the video and went to the kitchen for another cup of coffee. When it was ready, he carried it to the table by the French doors and took his habitual seat, the one that gave him a view out past the bluestone patio and the chicken coop, down over the low pasture to the barn and the pond.

His gaze drifted out to the rise on the far side of the pond. The trees were mostly bare now, except for isolated spruces whose summer greens had darkened into somber colorlessness. A few scattered oaks retained clumps of desiccated leaves. The muted color palette on the hillside was typical of a Catskill November—sepias, beiges, murky umbers. The still surface of the pond reminded him of a steel skillet. It wasn't a pleasant image. He picked up his coffee and returned to the den.

6

THE NEXT WITNESS WAS A SQUARE-JAWED MAN WITH A law-enforcement crew cut, light blue shirt, dark blue tie, and a gray sport jacket with a flag pin on the lapel. He projected the calm, attentive expression of a witness well acquainted with courtrooms. Stryker asked him to state his full name, rank, and connection to the case.

His voice was clear, confident, pleasant. "Detective Lieutenant Scott Derlick, Rexton Police Department. Chief investigating officer assigned to the Leonard Lerman homicide."

Stryker looked impressed. "You were personally involved in the case from start to finish?"

"Correct."

"Please take us back to the moment when your involvement began."

"We received a call from Adrienne Lerman at 9:00 a.m. on the Friday morning after Thanksgiving. She expressed concern about her father, whom she hadn't heard from since receiving a 7:00 p.m. phone message from him on Wednesday. She did not at that time divulge the full content of that message, nor did she mention his proposed visit to Ziko Slade."

"Did she give you any indication of where her father was when he called her?"

"She had the impression from something he said that he was somewhere north of Rexton, up near Garnet Lake."

"Was any action taken at that point?"

"As a courtesy, we gave our mobile units Mr. Lerman's physical description and vehicle data. However, unless there is evidence of foul play, an adult being out of contact with a family member is not a law-enforcement matter."

"So, when did this turn into a homicide investigation?"

"Approximately twenty-four hours after we heard from Ms. Lerman, we received a call from a hunter who came upon a partially buried body on a private estate not far from Garnet Lake. We were unable to immediately identify the body as Lenny Lerman's because the head and fingers had been removed. However, we found a DNA match on the state database of felons."

"When you informed Ms. Lerman of her father's death, was she then more forthcoming about his approach to Ziko Slade?"

"She was."

"Did she explain her earlier evasiveness?"

"She said she was scared that the truth would get her father into legal trouble. But now that he was beyond trouble, all that mattered was bringing his killer to justice."

"Please describe to the court exactly what you discovered when you arrived at the site of Lenny Lerman's body."

"The first thing I noticed was the smell. A decomposing corpse releases foul odors." Derlick paused as murmurs of disgust arose from the jury box. "As I got closer, I could see it had been buried in a shallow grave, covered with pine needles and loose soil, some of which had been scraped away. By coyotes, most likely."

Stryker grimaced. "I see. Please go on."

"As I mentioned, the corpse's most notable feature was the absence of the head and all ten fingers. The body was also dressed in hunting camos."

"Anything special about them?"

"They were too big for the size of the body. The sleeves and legs were too long. The pockets contained a box of 30-30 cartridges and a package of venison jerky."

"What was your initial interpretation of the scene?"

"That I was looking at a murdered hunter. But when we got a

positive ID on Lerman and I spoke again to his daughter, she told me her father never hunted, had no gun, no ammunition, no camo outfits."

"So, what did you make of that?"

"That I was looking at a smokescreen—a setup to point us in the wrong direction."

Stryker nodded in thoughtful agreement, giving the members of the jury the impression that she was just learning these important facts along with them.

Good actress, thought Gurney. She knew how to create that all-important bond with the people whose verdict she depended on.

Stryker continued. "Did you later discover a diary in Lenny Lerman's apartment—his own handwritten record of the events leading up to his death?"

"Yes—concealed under his mattress."

Stryker strode over to the bailiff's desk, picked up a small spiral notebook, and brought it to Derlick. "Please read the indicated passages aloud."

Derlick opened the diary to the first page and began reading.

"*October 24. Ran into Jingo at the Monster yesterday. Can't get what he told me out of my head. Question one—is it true? I'm thinking sure why not? Z getting rid of Sally Bones. I can see how that would happen. Question two. What's it worth? A hundred K? An even mil?*"

Derlick continued through the notebook, turning over a new page for each entry.

"*October 27. Do I or don't I? If I do, a mil. If I don't, nothing. Fucker has the cash. Cost of being a scumbag. Cost of Sally Bones. Need to work it out. One thing after another. Focus. Need sleep.*

"*November 2. Took A and S to the Lakeshore. Said hello to Pauly Bats at the bar. Big Pauly! Nobody fucks with Pauly Bats!! Explained the plan to A and S. Adie worries like always. What if? What if? What if? Like her mother. Sonny doesn't talk. But Sonny likes money. Now we'll have money. Serious money!*

"*November 5. Got Z's number and made the call. The asshole picked up. I asked him how much it was worth for me to forget everything I knew about Sally Bones. I told him to think about it. I made the scumbag worry.*

"*November 6. Talked to Tommy Hooks. Quit the fucking job. Breaking my hump for chump change. Goodbye to that shit!*

"*November 13. Called Z again. Told him I figured an even Mil was the right number—to save his evil fucking ass. In used twenties. Whining son of a bitch said that was like two suitcases. I told him so what, you worthless prick. What the fuck do I care about suitcases? You got ten days I told him.*

"*November 23. Called Z, told him his time was up, he better have the fucking Mil. He said he did. I told him to have it ready tonight, make sure he's alone. I walk with the Mil, or the whole fucking world hears about Sally Bones.*"

Derlick closed the diary. "That was the last entry."

"Thank you, Detective. By the way, were you able to verify the existence of the three phone calls Lenny described?"

"Yes. Phone company records show three calls from Lerman's number to Slade's number, corresponding to the entries in the diary."

Gurney paused the video.

He sat back in his chair. The likely effect of Lerman's diary on the jury was unclear. On the one hand, the entries supported earlier witness testimony regarding Lerman's extortion plan, which the prosecution alleged was Slade's obvious motive for killing him. In that respect, the entries were a plus for Stryker's narrative. On the other hand, their tone might have eroded whatever sympathy Adrienne's tears had generated for Lerman as a victim. However, the murder scene photos were yet to come, and they might have the power to regenerate that lost sympathy.

Gurney was reminded of the first time, early in his NYPD career, when he encountered the phenomenon of a serial killer recording his plans for attacking his victims—in a notebook not unlike Lerman's. A consulting psychologist on the case explained that putting such a plan in writing could serve several purposes. One was the desire to externalize an idea before executing it. Putting the plan on paper made it more real, more exciting. Another was the opportunity to place pejorative labels on the target individual—a way of blaming the victim for the intended crime.

Gurney went for another cup of coffee. While waiting for it to brew, he watched the amber ferns in the asparagus bed sway in an erratic breeze. His gaze wandered to the coop, and he remembered his promise to check the food and water. And bring the chickens some blueberries. He'd tend to all that as soon as he finished watching Scott Derlick's testimony.

He took his coffee back into the den and resumed the video.

Cam Stryker stood next to the witness box, addressing Derlick.

"Let's move on to the day of Lenny Lerman's last call to Slade—the day of his final journey from Calliope Springs to Slade's lodge in the mountains north of Rexton. What can you tell us about that trip?"

"We retrieved the GPS data that was transmitted continuously from Lerman's phone and transferred that data to an area map."

Stryker placed a large, stiff map on an easel.

In the typical meandering path of trips through hilly country, a bright red line followed a succession of secondary roads from the village of Calliope Springs in the lower left corner of the map to a point above Rexton in the upper right corner. There were four black stars along the route, with a time noted next to each star.

Derlick explained that the lower left star showed the location of Lerman's apartment, and the 4:25 p.m. notation next to it was the time Lerman departed. The star halfway up the red route line was a gas station where he stopped for sixteen minutes. Of the two stars close together at the top end of the line, the first indicated the location where the private road to Slade's lodge left the public road, and the second indicated the lodge itself.

"That star at the turnoff to Slade's place," said Derlick, "is where Lerman made the phone call to his daughter at 6:46 p.m. The next star, in front of the lodge, is the last spot from which Lerman's phone transmitted location data."

Stryker put her finger on the final star and turned to the jury. "For Lenny, that was the end of the line—in more ways than one."

7

STRYKER'S NEXT WITNESS—KYRA BARSTOW—STARTLED Gurney.

Barstow was the forensic supervisor on the Harrow Hill case. She was director of the local college's forensic sciences program and provided services to the local police department from time to time. Evidently Rexton enjoyed a similar arrangement.

She looked just as Gurney remembered—tall, athletically slim, with a quick intelligence behind striking gray eyes. Working with her had been a pleasure.

Stryker approached the witness box. "Ms. Barstow, please describe your involvement in the Lerman case."

"I received a call from Detective Derlick approximately fifteen minutes after his arrival at the scene. I was at the opposite end of the county, and it took me a little over an hour to get there. When I arrived, Detective Derlick was finishing his interview with the hunter who found the body."

Stryker nodded. "Detective Derlick just led us along Lerman's route from Calliope Springs to Ziko Slade's lodge. Can you lead us from that spot to the grave in the woods?"

"We found contact DNA from Lerman on the layer of pine needles in front of the lodge, plus traces of his blood," said Barstow. "The residual pressure deformation of the pine needles indicated that he'd either fallen there or been knocked down."

Stryker adopted at earnest frown. "But his body was found a hundred yards away in the woods. Can you tell us how it got there?"

"It's likely that Lerman was dragged, facedown. There was a trail of blood, bits of skin, clothing fibers."

"Fibers from the camo outfit the body was found in?"

"No. Fibers from the clothing he was wearing when he arrived at the lodge. We found a jacket, shirt, and pants with Lerman's DNA buried near the grave."

"Did the clothing switch take place before his head . . ." Stryker hesitated. "Before it was removed?"

"Yes. There were only a few drops of blood on the original clothing, on the back of the shirt collar, consistent with Lerman having received a blow to the back of the head prior to being dragged to the grave. That's where his clothing would have been switched. We also determined, in cooperation with the ME, that he was still alive at the time of his beheading."

"How do you know that?"

"The amount of blood in the grave indicated that his heart was still beating when the axe severed the arteries in his neck."

Stryker grimaced. "So Lenny Lerman was dragged through the woods, dragged into a waiting grave, and then . . . ?"

"Beheaded. Then his fingers were removed with a small pruning clipper. There was very little bleeding from the stumps—meaning the removals occurred postmortem."

Stifled sounds of revulsion came from several jury members. Stryker lowered her head and closed her eyes for a moment, as if sharing their distress. When she looked up, she turned to the jury box.

"This is the point when I have to show you photos of the crime scene. They're not easy to look at. But you need to see them."

She fetched several foam-core boards, leaned them against the prosecution table, and placed the top one on the easel. The color image on the board was of the back of a headless body in camo pants and jacket lying in a roughed-out hollow in the ground. The soil around the truncated neck was stained a brownish black. At the ends of the extended arms fingerless hands lay palms-down on the brown earth. Raw gouges were visible on the backs of the hands and on an exposed calf where the pants leg was torn. After pausing to let the jury's horror build, Stryker asked Barstow about the gouges.

"The large ones were made by the teeth of coyotes. The small lacerations suggest vultures. In another week there would have been nothing left. Perhaps some bones the coyotes hadn't carried off."

Stryker put the next photo on the easel—a full-size image of an axe and a pruning clipper. She asked Barstow if they were the implements used to kill and mutilate Lenny Lerman.

Barstow confirmed this, stating that though the tools had been washed after the murder, presumably by the perpetrator, traces of Lerman's blood remained at the point where the axe head joined the handle and at the pivot bolt in the center of the clipper.

"We found them both in the shed behind Slade's lodge," Barstow added in response to a follow-up question from Stryker. "Next to a shovel with soil traces matching the chemical composition of the soil at the grave."

"In addition to all these incriminating facts, did you discover any direct physical links between Ziko Slade and the body of Lenny Lerman?"

"Yes."

"And what were those links?"

"The jacket found on the body contained contact DNA from both Lenny Lerman and Ziko Slade. Ziko Slade's DNA was also recovered from a cigarette butt found near the grave."

"Thank you, Ms. Barstow. I have no more questions."

Marcus Thorne approached the witness box. "Ms. Barstow, were you able to identify the person who supposedly knocked Lerman down in front of the lodge and dragged him into the woods?"

"No."

"Or the person who dug the grave?"

"No."

"Did your tests reveal how Mr. Slade's DNA ended up on that camo jacket?"

"No."

"Or who may have placed that cigarette butt where you found it?"

"No."

"Thank you, Ms. Barstow. That'll be all."

For a moment, Stryker looked like she might opt for a redirect examination of Barstow to dilute the impact of those negative replies. Instead, she recalled Detective Lieutenant Scott Derlick to the stand.

"Detective, during your testimony you showed us Lenny Lerman's route from Calliope Springs to Ziko Slade's lodge. Did he make that trip in his own car?"

"Yes, a black 2004 Corolla—confirmed by video from two strip mall security cameras along the way."

"Did you find the car?"

"Yes. Three days later we received a call regarding a burnt-out vehicle in an abandoned quarry less than a mile from Slade's lodge. We were able to identify it via the VIN number on the chassis."

"You say it was burnt out?"

"Yes. An empty gas container was found at the site, suggesting arson."

"Did you find anything else of interest?"

"A key on the floor next to the driver's seat, where it probably fell from the pocket of whoever drove the Corolla to the quarry."

"What sort of key was it?"

"A padlock key."

"Were you able to match the key to any particular padlock?"

"Yes. The padlock on Ziko Slade's tool shed."

8

MARCUS THORNE ROSE AT THE DEFENSE TABLE.

"I'm curious about that padlock key, Detective," he said in an innocent, conversational tone. "Might it have been placed in the car on purpose rather than fallen out of someone's pocket?"

"There's zero evidence of that."

"Just as there's zero evidence that it dropped out of Mr. Slade's pocket?"

Derlick's mouth twitched, but he made no reply.

"In fact, Detective, I'm wondering if you have even a speck of real evidence that Mr. Slade emerged from his lodge at any time that day or night—much less that he killed anyone or drove that car to the quarry or set fire to it."

Derlick's jaw muscles tightened. "Based on the facts, those are the only reasonable conclusions."

"So, you have absolute certainty with zero proof. The sort of certainty that puts thousands of innocent people in prison every year."

Stryker rocketed out of her chair. "Objection! Counsel is inventing statistics and badgering the witness!"

"Sustained," said Wartz. "Mr. Thorne, your next inappropriate remark will have consequences."

Thorne smiled meekly and raised his palms in surrender. "Thank you, Your Honor. I'm finished with this witness." He made "witness" sound like species of rodent.

Wartz turned to Stryker. "You may proceed."

"The prosecution rests its case, Your Honor."

Wartz nodded and asked Thorne if he was ready to present the case for the defense.

"Your Honor, my client and I believe we have no need for a formal defense. We prefer to move directly to our closing argument."

Wartz's stolid features registered a touch of surprise—the same surprise Gurney felt, until he guessed that the reason was that Slade had no alibi and Thorne was afraid to put him on the stand.

Thorne approached the jury box. "Ladies and gentlemen, you and I have just witnessed a carefully orchestrated production in which random bits of dubious evidence were cleverly strung together to create a remarkable piece of fiction. The prosecution wins high marks for creativity. But when it comes to addressing the key questions in the case—all those sources of reasonable doubt—they failed miserably." He shook his head. "So many problems, it's hard to know where to begin. Take Lerman, for example. Was he a bumbling fool, broadcasting his dumb plan to the world? Or was he a calculating blackmailer? He couldn't have been both. But the prosecutor wants you to ignore that contradiction.

"We were shown a map with a dramatic red line highlighting his route—to prove what? That Lerman drove to Slade's property? But his drive has no bearing on the only question that matters: Who killed him after he arrived?

"In a desperate effort to link Mr. Slade to the murder, the prosecution came up with traces of contact DNA on a camo jacket and a cigarette butt. But key facts were conspicuously missing. We were told there was a match between DNA on the camo garment and Mr. Slade's DNA. What we didn't hear was the scientific confidence level attached to that match. Was it ninety percent? Eighty? Seventy? Less than that? We don't know because we weren't told. As for that cigarette butt, might not Mr. Slade have dropped numerous butts outside his lodge, and might not the real killer have picked one up and placed it by the grave—to create the sort of false impression the prosecution passed along to you today?"

"Objection!" cried Stryker. "That's a slanderous characterization of prosecution motives."

Wartz let out a heavy sigh. "Defense counsel is stretching the envelope to the breaking point. However, I am inclined to overrule the objection in this instance—in the interest of affording maximum leeway to closing arguments."

"I appreciate Your Honor's indulgence," said Thorne, turning back to the jury.

"In my long career as a trial attorney, rarely have I seen a case give rise to so many areas of reasonable doubt. Especially when you realize that the police failed to investigate other plausible scenarios for this murder. Did it not occur to them that Lerman's public bragging about his plan to extort money from Mr. Slade would provide the perfect cover for an enemy of Lerman's to follow him and kill him? What about Lerman's million-dollar life insurance policy? The prosecutor mentioned it in her opening statement, yet I didn't hear a word about that from Detective Derlick, even though 'follow the money' is a foundational principle of sound investigative procedure. So many stones left unturned. So many questions unanswered."

Thorne paused, making eye contact with each juror. "Faced with this mountain of reasonable doubt, the law demands that you acquit the defendant."

After a brief silence, Wartz addressed Stryker. "Are you prepared to proceed with your closing argument?"

"Yes, Your Honor." Taking a deep breath, she approached the jury.

"Reasonable doubt." She articulated the phrase with precision. "If I told you the sky was blue, I'm sure Mr. Thorne could conjure up a dozen reasons that you should doubt that simple fact. But none of them would be reasonable. Creating a smokescreen of doubt and confusion—making you wonder if the sky is really blue—is what defense attorneys are paid to do."

Thorne shook his head with exaggerated weariness. "Objection, Your Honor. This is scurrilous nonsense."

"Overruled," said Wartz. "I'm giving the prosecutor the same leeway I gave you."

Stryker shot a "gotcha" glance at Thorne before continuing. "The thing about *reasonable* doubt is that the doubt must actually be *reasonable*. Defense counsel's distracting questions and wild suppositions are far from reasonable. He waves the term 'doubt' around as though it were magic dust that could make evidence disappear."

Stryker paused before going on. "This is the moment in a trial when a prosecutor normally reviews all the key evidence and explains to the jury how it fits together. But I don't think you need to hear it all again. This is a very simple case. So simple that I can sum it up in one sentence: 'A poor man thought he could acquire a fortune from a rich man, but he had no idea how ruthless that rich man could be.'"

She took a step closer to the jury and spoke softly. "Lenny Lerman didn't know what Ziko Slade was capable of. But you do. You do, because you saw the photograph of Lenny's mutilated body—a sight none of us will ever forget—a sight that underscores your duty to find this defendant guilty of premeditated murder."

9

BY THE TIME MADELEINE RETURNED HOME FROM THE Mental Health Crisis Center that evening, Gurney had viewed the trial video twice, all the way through to the jury's concluding verdict: guilty of murder in the first degree.

After changing clothes, Madeleine asked about the chickens. Without admitting that he had forgotten about them, Gurney put on his barn jacket, picked up a sack of chickenfeed from the mudroom, and headed out through a chilling wind to the coop.

The five hens pecked at a scattering of cracked corn in the fenced run. Gurney entered the coop and found it acceptably clean. It smelled mainly of the straw spread across the floor and in the nesting boxes. He discovered two fresh brown eggs and slipped them into his jacket pockets. He refilled the feeders, then checked the watering device. It was half full and wouldn't need replenishing for another day or two. He returned to the house and brought the two eggs to the sink island in the kitchen, where Madeleine was rinsing lettuce in a colander.

"I thought we could have our salad first," she said, patting the lettuce dry with some paper towels. "Okay with you?"

"Fine."

"You set the table. I'll make the dressing."

He moved two books she was reading off the table—one on the history of the cello and the other on the lives of snails—to make room for the plates and silverware.

WHEN THEY WERE nearly done with their salads, Madeleine asked the question Gurney knew was coming: What did he think of the trial?

He laid his fork on the edge of his plate. "Impressive, on the prosecution's side. The evidence against Slade was overwhelming. Apart from inflicting a few minor dings, the defense wasn't able to dent it. In fact, no formal case for the defense was even presented."

"Any chance of an appeal?"

Gurney shook his head. "I'm surprised this even came to trial. Cases with such a one-sided weight of evidence and no credible defense generally result in a guilty plea in exchange for a reduced charge. I'm tempted to call Slade's lawyer and ask about it."

Madeleine frowned and pierced a grape with her fork.

"If his lawyer had even a scrap of exculpatory evidence," Gurney went on, "I can't imagine why he wouldn't have introduced it."

"Well," Madeleine said with some tightness in her voice, "I suppose, if you're that curious, you'll eventually make the call."

She stood up, cleared the table, then said she was tired and headed to bed.

After sitting alone for a few minutes, Gurney went into the den and called Marcus Thorne.

10

MARCUS THORNE LIVED IN THE LOW-PROFILE, HIGH-NET-worth village of Claiborne. His driveway led through several acres of mountain laurels, rhododendrons, and ancient oaks to a gravel parking area in front of a large white colonial house. Planting beds bordered the parking area and curved around both sides of the house.

As he stepped from his Outback, Gurney was surprised to hear his name called. He turned and saw a man waving to him from the corner of a stone cottage. Marcus Thorne wore a British-looking field jacket, brown corduroy slacks, and a Harris Tweed pub cap. All that was needed to complete the picture, thought Gurney, was a pricey shotgun and a dead pheasant.

Gurney crossed the wide expanse of freshly mown lawn.

"Thanks for meeting me on such short notice," Gurney said as he shook the shorter man's hand.

"My office away from the office," Thorne said, leading the way past a small pond. "I thought we'd be more comfortable chatting here than in the city."

The exterior of the cottage reminded Gurney of houses built in the eighteenth century, but the only visible remnants of that period inside were the rough-hewn ceiling beams of smoke-blackened oak, a fieldstone fireplace, and a wide-board pine floor. Everything else in the single-room ground floor was starkly modern, minimalist in design, and dominated by a wall of glass on the pond side of the building. The ornamental grasses surrounding the pond were various autumn shades of brown, rust, and ocher.

Thorne tossed his jacket and cap on the back of a couch facing the fireplace. He wore a russet flannel shirt that fit him so perfectly it suggested custom tailoring. Gurney left his light windbreaker on.

"Had ducks out there till a month ago." Thorne waved toward the pond. "Gone south now. But the damn geese stay. Wife feeds the filthy things. Have a seat."

He dropped onto a geometric object of black leather and chrome that only faintly resembled a chair. Gurney sat on a similar one at the opposite end of a gleaming glass slab that appeared to function as a coffee table.

"So, Mr. Gurney, illustrious detective, what can I do for you?" Thorne leaned back in his seat and steepled his fingers, the gesture of thoughtful attention at odds with the blasé look in his eyes.

On the two-hour drive from Walnut Crossing, Gurney considered several subtle ways of framing his questions, but Thorne's breezy attitude prompted a franker tone. "To begin with, you can tell me why your defense of Slade was such a disaster."

Thorne smiled a lawyer's empty smile. "If you're asking why the jury returned a guilty verdict, the answer is simple. They didn't like Slade."

"That doesn't tell me much."

Thorne's gaze drifted up to the beamed ceiling. "You might say we faced a perfect storm of unfortunate circumstances."

"Namely?"

"Born with a superabundance of talent, looks, and charm, nothing was difficult for the magical Ziko. Naturally, the jury hated him on sight. That fact alone assured his conviction. Hardly any need for—"

A soft musical tone interrupted him. He took a sleek phone out of his shirt pocket and peered at the screen. His expression became sharper, more attentive. He tapped out a short reply with an aggressive glint in his eye and slipped the phone back in his pocket, his expression reverting to its former nonchalance. "Where was I?"

"The jury hated Slade on sight."

"Indeed. But the particular difficulty of the case from our point of view was the fact that the primary witness against Slade was the murder victim. Lenny Lerman's extortion plan, about which he left no doubt, established the perfect motive for Slade to kill him. Lerman drove to Slade's lodge at a time that Slade was there by himself—with zero alibi. The physical evidence was simple and concrete. And Stryker's narrative was seamless."

"You couldn't come up with a competing narrative?"

Thorne shook his head. "If you're going to posit an alternate theory, you need facts, which we didn't have. Otherwise, its weakness enhances by comparison the strength of the prosecution's narrative. And, of course, Stryker had the bonus of the weapon. Juries love a bloody weapon." Thorne flashed a chilly grin. "And when it comes to bloody weapons, it's hard to beat an axe."

"Had you considered making the argument that Slade was too smart to have committed such a sloppy crime?"

Thorne emitted a high-pitched, metallic-sounding laugh. "That argument goes nowhere. Worse than nowhere. Smart is not an endearing quality. It doesn't conjure up thoughts of innocence. Now, if a defendant seemed too stupid to have engineered a particular crime, something could be made of that. Stupidity suggests harmlessness. Cleverness suggests danger."

"Why no character witnesses for the defense?"

"It would have let the prosecution bring in anti-character witnesses from Slade's past, and that would have been a horror show."

Gurney nodded. "Slade's mountain lodge—that's not his main residence, is it?"

"He has a horse farm in Dutchess County and an apartment in the city—which is where he spent most of his time before the murder last year, when he wasn't at Emma Martin's place."

"Why did he happen to be at the lodge the day of the murder?"

"It was the day before Thanksgiving. He went to the lodge that morning to start preparing a big dinner for the following day."

"Big dinner for who?"

"A group of Emma Martin's patients, clients, disciples—whatever she calls them."

"The dinner actually took place?"

"Indeed."

"You spoke to the guests?"

"Of course."

"How did they describe Slade's emotional state?"

"Calm, pleasant, untroubled, but that didn't help our case. A sharp prosecutor like Stryker could turn that around and convince the jury that Slade's serenity was the natural facade of a murdering psychopath."

Gurney couldn't argue with that. Juries hated calm killers. "Speaking of Stryker, do you know why she called Lerman's daughter, Adrienne, to the stand, but not her brother, Sonny?"

Thorne made a mirthless chuckling sound. "Daughter's an automatic jury favorite. Cuddly, emotional. Sonny, on the other hand, is an obvious piece of garbage. Did two years for assaulting a police officer. Currently on parole. Slimy like his father, and more explosive."

Gurney sat back in his seat and gazed out the wall-sized window. A late-season wasp, lethargic from the cold, was making its way across the glass. Thorne lifted his phone halfway out of his shirt pocket and glanced meaningfully at the time.

"Just a couple more questions," said Gurney. "Considering the case against your client, I assume you considered making a deal with the prosecutor?"

"I recommended it. Slade refused. Said he wouldn't plea to something he didn't do. Said he wasn't willing to lie. So, instead of fifteen-to-twenty, which I think I could have gotten him, he's doing thirty-to-life." Thorne's grin returned. "Principles. They can really fuck you." He paused. "What's your game, Mr. Gurney?"

"You mean, why did I get involved? Emma Martin asked me to find cracks in the case that could be pried open."

Thorne uttered a harsh little laugh and shook his head.

"You think I'm wasting my time?"

"Time billed at an appropriate hourly rate is never wasted. But as for finding cracks in the case? Cracks that could be leveraged into a successful appeal? Not likely. And even if an appeal did result in a retrial, you'd still be stuck with Slade's unsavory history."

He glanced again at his phone before going on. "Let me tell you a quick story about juries. Years ago, when I was practicing law in Southern California, a high-profile robbery-and-murder case came my way. A bonded precious-gems courier was intercepted in an underground parking lot and relieved of an attaché case containing emeralds worth roughly three mil. He gets a broken nose, the lot attendant gets shot dead, and the three-man heist team gets away with the emeralds. But, according to the courier, only the two who attacked him were wearing masks. The driver wasn't, and the courier ID'd him as a guy who'd been following him the previous week. He even gave the cops a picture he took of the guy on the street one day. On top of that, the courier got the plate number of the getaway car—which turned out to be registered to a scumbag rumored to be involved in jewelry fencing, money laundering, and sex trafficking. The scumbag had no alibi, and the guy the courier ID'd as the driver turned out to be one of the scumbag's trusted employees. The courier, by the way, was a retired cop with a spotless record and a strong resemblance to Tom Hanks. I was the scumbag's defense attorney."

Thorne paused, as if to verify Gurney was following, before going on. "Surprisingly, the DA offered my client a reasonable plea arrangement. Given the vulnerability of our situation, I strongly recommended that he accept it. He refused. He insisted a business rival, a guy by the name of Jimmy Peskin, was setting him up. He gave me a blank check to launch a private investigation to get to the truth, which I did."

Thorne produced a self-satisfied smile. "The real story began with the courier's son. The kid had landed a spot at a hot L.A. law firm. Problem was, he had a gambling, coke, and hooker addiction. His debts got him into deep shit—to the tune of four hundred grand—with a Vegas mob guy who was demanding payment or pictures would be posted on the internet that would end the kid's career. The kid went begging to Dad. Dad, the courier, approached a character whose reputation suggested he might be open to a certain kind of arrangement. The guy was Jimmy Peskin, business rival of my client. Dad proposed the jewel heist to Peskin with a fifty-fifty split of the proceeds. He even recommended that his own nose be broken to deflect any suspicion regarding his involvement. At first, Peskin wanted seventy percent, but he agreed to settle for fifty—providing that Dad incriminate my client by giving the police a false ID of the driver, a false plate number for the getaway car, a bullshit story about the driver having followed him, and a photo of the man on a busy street—which Peskin would provide. We couldn't prove any of this, it was all second-hand information, inadmissible hearsay, but it was *very* credible."

Thorne gave a Gurney a cagey look. "So how do you think our alternative narrative played out?"

Gurney shrugged. "Depends on how persuasively you presented it, and how adept the prosecutor was in undercutting it."

Thorne smiled without a hint of warmth. "Our presentation incorporated enough of what we discovered about Peskin to create a textbook example of reasonable doubt. In fact, court reporters and other observers found our case a hell of a lot more persuasive than the prosecutor's. It was a steel-trap indictment of Jimmy Peskin."

Gurney sensed what was coming. "However . . . ?"

"However, the jury found my client guilty on all counts. Guilty of armed robbery. Guilty of murder in the commission of a felony, due to the fatal shooting of the parking lot attendant. And guilty of half a dozen bullshit charges on top of those. You know why? It's simple. The greatest defense in the world doesn't matter if the jury hates your client."

"You're sure they reached the wrong verdict?"

"After my client was sent to prison, he proved his innocence by ordering a hit on Jimmy Peskin. Payback for the frame job."

After a moment of silence during which Thorne seemed to be savoring the impact of his story, he raised his palms in a gesture that said, *Are we finished here?*

"One final question. Do you have any bottom-line observations on Ziko Slade?"

Thorne took a long breath and let it out slowly. "I've never had an innocent client with so much evidence against him. On the other hand, I've never had a guilty client who seemed so forthcoming. For example, take the release he signed to make this conversation possible. It places no limits whatsoever on what I can share with you."

"So, the facts say he's a murderer, and his attitude says he's innocent?"

"Innocent or delusional. He's so damn unconcerned. When I visited him the other day in that hellhole of a prison, he made jokes about the tie I was wearing." Thorne checked his phone again, then rose from his chair with the conspicuous energy of a man who enjoyed looking busy. "Good luck with your search for those elusive cracks."

He started leading the way toward the door, then turned to Gurney with a cold sparkle in his eyes. "Let me know if you find Lerman's head in one of them."

11

AS GURNEY PASSED FROM THE RAREFIED ENVIRONS OF
Claiborne into the bleaker reality of upstate New York, he spotted a
Starbucks in a small strip mall. The sight triggered an instant desire
for a double espresso, and he pulled into the nearly empty parking
lot.

He checked his phone for messages as he waited to place his order. There weren't any, but checking reminded him that he forgot to
call Kyle for his birthday. Annoyed at himself, he knew he should
take care of it before it slipped his mind again. Instead, he decided to
make the call as soon as he got his coffee and something to snack on.

Back in his car, munching on a cinnamon bagel and sipping his
coffee, Gurney took out his phone. It rang in his hand, just as he
started looking up Kyle in his contact list. He didn't recognize the
incoming number, but he answered anyway.

"Gurney here."

"Are you finished with Marcus Thorne?"

It took him a few seconds to place the owner of the cool, even
voice.

"Hello, Emma. How did you know I was meeting with Thorne?"

"I'm psychic."

He didn't reply. He wasn't sure she was joking.

"Adrienne Lerman has agreed to meet with you."

"Excuse me?"

"She lives in Winston, not that far from Claiborne. You know
where it is?"

Gurney cleared his throat. "More or less, but—"

"Good. It's her day off. She'll be expecting you. I'm texting you
her address."

She disconnected. A minute later the text arrived: "5 Moray
Court, Apt B."

Gurney took another bite of his bagel and finished his coffee.
The bagel was less than half finished, but he tossed the rest in a small

garbage bag he kept under the glove compartment. The cinnamon was giving him heartburn.

WINSTON TURNED OUT to be one of those upstate towns endeavoring to survive the collapse of dairy farming by transforming itself into an antiques center—selling its mundane relics to weekend visitors who viewed rusted hay rakes and battered milk pails as objets d'art. Its main street was home to one precious emporium after another with names like the Heavenly Pig, the Blue Mallard, and the Smiling Cow.

Number 5 Moray Court was a large Victorian with two entrances, having been divided into an upstairs and downstairs apartment. Overgrown rhododendrons obscured the front porch, and two cars occupied the driveway. Gurney parked a few car lengths from number 5.

The first thing that struck him as he emerged from the Outback was the raw dampness in the air. The second was the acid-green Corvette farther down the street, conspicuous among the Subarus and Toyotas. The third was the tall, muscular young man walking in his direction. Despite the weather, he wasn't wearing a jacket—just a tight yellow tee shirt, silky beige slacks, and fancy loafers. His moussed hair was fashionably spiky, his eyes small and dark, his thick neck encircled with tattoos.

The rhythm of his stride put Gurney on guard. He subtly adjusted his balance and centered his attention on the man's solar plexus—not only as a potential target but as the best focal point from which he could sense either hostile hand or foot movements.

The man stopped just outside Gurney's personal space. "You want some friendly advice? Stay out of our business."

Gurney said nothing.

"You hear what I'm saying? You fucking deaf?" His voice was growing louder.

Gurney spoke softly. "I think you're making a mistake."

"You're the one making a fucking mistake. Keep your fucking nose out of our business."

That *our* confirmed Gurney's assumption that this was Sonny Lerman, brother of Adrienne. "You're in my way. Please step aside."

The dark little eyes widened with rage. "How about I step on your fucking face?"

Gurney sighed. "You don't really want to violate your parole, do you, Sonny? Get dumped back in the can for another year?"

"This is no goddamn violation. I'm just telling you, stay the fuck away from my sister. You stir shit up, you'll eat it, you nosy fuck."

A loud voice came from the direction of number 5. "Hey, fellas, what's going on here?"

A big, white-haired, red-faced man stood on the porch steps. He had the look of a retired cop. He held a nightstick partly concealed against the side of his leg.

Sonny Lerman stared at him uncertainly. "Nothing. No problem." He turned away abruptly and headed for the acid-green Corvette. He opened the door, then called back to Gurney, "You fuck with me, you got big fucking trouble. I got a relative you never wanna meet. Keep that thought in your head, asshole!"

12

GURNEY RANG THE BELL FOR APARTMENT B AND A MOMENT later was buzzed in. A drably carpeted staircase was lit by a single ceiling fixture.

"Come up. I'll be with you in a minute," a woman's voice called from somewhere on the second floor.

The stairs creaked underfoot. There was an unpleasant odor in the air.

From the top landing, he could see into an eat-in kitchen. To his right was a living room with bare wood floors. To his left, a hallway with three open doorways—a bathroom and two bedrooms, he guessed. From one of those rooms came the meowing of multiple cats. The source of the odor he noticed on the way up was likely a busy litter box.

"Are you a cat person, Mr. Gurney?"

A large, soft-looking woman in a gray sweat suit emerged from the hallway, pushing loose hairs back from her forehead. He recognized the same sad smile of repeatedly disappointed optimism on Adrienne Lerman's face that he had seen in the trial video.

"I'm not sure, but I do like watching them."

"I'm trying to find a permanent home for some kittens. If you know anyone who might be interested . . ." Her voice trailed off. "Come in, have a seat."

Gurney joined her at an old Formica-topped table.

"I saw what happened in the street. I'm really sorry. Sonny can be . . . excitable."

"You told him I was coming?"

"I try to be open about everything. I didn't expect him to react like that."

"Any idea why he did?"

She let out sharp little sound that might have been a humorless laugh. "All I told him was what Emma Martin told me—that you were reviewing the case to see if there might be a chance of an appeal. He didn't seem to have any reaction. But once Sonny starts thinking about something, you never know where it's going to go. Maybe his mind went back to that insurance company lawyer, Howard Manx, a very mean person, who was trying to keep us from getting the money in the first place. Money means a lot to Sonny. He sees it as the only thing he ever got from our father. It was like Manx was insinuating that we killed our own father for the insurance. What kind of person would kill their own father for money? How sick would you have to be to do that?" She closed her eyes and pressed the tips of her fingers against the lower part of her cheek.

"Are you alright?" asked Gurney.

"Bad tooth. Comes and goes." She opened her eyes and lowered her hand. "I should get to the dentist. Never seem to have the time. With hospice and the cats and Sonny . . ." She looked vaguely around the kitchen, before going on with a beleaguered smile.

"Most of my problems are gifts, not problems at all. To be busy is to be useful, right? To be useful is a blessing. So, it's all how you look at it." She forced a smile. "Emma said that you had some questions."

"I'll start with one that occurred to me while I was watching the video of the trial. Why do you think your father told his boss about his money-making scheme?"

She swallowed, and her eyes appeared on the verge of tearing up.

"That night in the restaurant when he talked about it to Sonny and me, I had no idea he was telling anyone else. I'm not even sure I believed what he was saying. But when the district attorney told me what he said to Mr. Cazo, I wasn't surprised. I knew Lenny liked having people think he was involved in something big, especially involving a celebrity like Ziko Slade. He always wanted respect. It was *so* important to him. He was obsessed with what people thought of him. He was always chasing acceptance in the wrong ways."

She shook her head sadly. "He was always trying to be whatever he thought the most powerful person in the room wanted him to be. It was like he had no weight, no center, no direction of his own. He was desperate for approval, especially from Sonny." A tear appeared and ran down her cheek. She took a napkin from wooden holder on the table, wiped her cheek, and blew her nose.

"Sorry," she said, "You have other questions?"

"When your brother approached me in the street, he claimed to have a connection to some nasty character. Maybe a gangster? Do you know anything about that?"

She sniffled. "Every time Lenny had a few drinks, he'd start hinting that we had a second or third cousin who was a hitman for the mob—the Russian mob, the Mafia, the Albanians, the story kept shifting. It seemed fantastical to me, but Sonny ate it up. Sonny and Lenny had a lot in common. Fantasies, mainly. Funny how people sometimes have so much in common they can't stand each other."

She was gazing at Gurney, but her mind seemed to be reviewing sad memories.

"A minute ago you said you weren't sure you believed what your father told you at the restaurant. Why was that?"

"The extortion scheme—it just wasn't like him."

"In what way?"

"It sounded too confrontational."

"That was out of character for him?"

"Very much so."

After a silent minute, he stood up from the table and thanked her for her time.

She raised her hand. "Before you go, I'd like to ask *you* a question. It's something that's been on my mind ever since . . . ever since they told me about finding my father's body. I couldn't bring myself to ask about it."

He waited.

She bit her lower lip. "Do you know . . . if he was alive . . . when his fingers were cut off?"

Gurney recalled Barstow's testimony that there was only slight bleeding at the finger stumps, indicating the absence of cardiac function.

"No, Adrienne. He was not alive at that point."

She sat back with a long exhalation as though a great tension had been relieved.

"Thank you. I couldn't bear thinking he was conscious for that."

AT THE MIDPOINT between Winston and Walnut Crossing, the precipitation began—first as an intermittent drizzle, then a lashing rain that obscured Gurney's vision. He pulled over onto a weedy shoulder by a cow pasture.

As he waited for the downpour to subside, he became increasingly conscious of an uncomfortable feeling that had begun during his confrontation with Sonny and grown over the course of his conversation with Adrienne. There was something out of joint in the emotional dynamics of the Lerman family—something connected to the "out of character" nature of Lenny's scheme. Before he could recall everything that had been said, he was interrupted by a call from Madeleine.

"Just wondering if you've spoken to Kyle yet."

The reminder felt like a jab in the gut. "Not yet."

"Thanksgiving is next week. It would be nice to invite him, don't you think?"

PART II

ZIKO SLADE

13

THEY SAT AT THE PINE TABLE NEXT TO THE FRENCH DOORS. It was just past noon. The frost on the patio had finally melted, darkening the bluestone slabs. The gray November sky rendered the low pasture colorless. They'd just finished a quiet lunch. Madeleine gazed at Gurney over the rim of a cup of spearmint tea.

"So," she said, "when are you going to tell me about it?"

"About what?"

She lowered her cup. "You spent yesterday talking to Marcus Thorne, then Adrienne Lerman. You came home frowning and hardly said a word all evening. Same thing this morning. It's obvious you're wrestling with something."

"I just have an unsettled feeling. Probably a product of the weather."

She nodded, her expression attentive but otherwise unreadable.

After a while, he cleared his throat. "Those inconsistencies you said I'm good at noticing? Some small ones have popped up."

"You can point them out to Emma."

"And then walk away?"

"Yes."

He nodded slowly, trying to find the right words for his next question. "Maddie, I keep getting this start-stop message—that I'm supposed to respond to Emma's request, but only give her about a tenth of what she wants from me. I understand she's your friend, or was your friend, but considering how dead set you are on my not actually doing anything, wouldn't it have been a lot smarter not to have opened the door in the first place?"

"David, for Christ sake, why are you making such a big deal out of this?"

"You think I'm good at spotting discrepancies? Well, I'm spotting one right now. Emma told you she wanted to talk to me about a murder case. *A murder case.* But instead of saying no, we had a recent experience here that makes that a bad idea, you said sure, come on over. And the fact that you were friendly at some point in the past doesn't come close to explaining that response. What is it you're not telling me?"

Madeleine stared in silence at her nearly empty plate for so long that he gave up hope of getting an answer. Then she began to speak in a halting voice.

"The reason I wanted you to . . . look into the case to begin with . . . was that I felt it was the right thing to do . . . because of what Emma had done . . . for us."

"For *us*?"

"It was when you were buried in that horrid incest murder case . . . years ago . . . the one that got you involved with Jack Hardwick. You were never home. Sometimes your body was, but your mind never was. The case went on and on and on. I was never so alone before in all my life. I felt completely abandoned with no reason to believe you'd ever be present again. I thought this couldn't be what a marriage was supposed to be. Even my work at the clinic felt empty. How could I help clients whose depression told them their lives were pointless, when that's exactly the way I felt about myself? I didn't feel connected to you or anyone else. I kept asking myself, what am I doing with my life? I thought maybe . . ." Her voice trailed off. She closed her eyes, her jaw muscles tightening. Seconds passed. When she opened them, her gaze was fixed on the middle of the table.

"I thought maybe if I started over, maybe that would be the way out of the pit. I couldn't see any other way. I had to start over. Leave. Go away. Start a completely new life. But I felt paralyzed."

Shocked by her revelation, Gurney tried to remember his own experience of the period, but the only details that came to mind were of the case.

She continued. "I wasn't all that close to Emma, but she sensed that I was in trouble and offered to listen if I wanted to talk. I have no idea how long I talked or even what I said. When I finished, she smiled. It was the warmest, most comforting smile I'd ever seen. And I remember what she said—not just the words, the way she said it. The power it had.

"She said you were a good man. She told me to have patience . . . to pay attention . . . to trust you . . . and our life together would be good."

"That's it?"

"That's it. But that smile . . . that voice . . . it was like she was speaking to a part of me that had never been spoken to before."

Gurney was at a loss for words.

"So," Madeleine went on, "based on what she'd done—pulling me out of the mental hell I was in, essentially saving our marriage—I felt that helping her, at least in some limited way, would only be right."

He remained silent, trying to absorb what he'd just heard—a bomb detonating in slow motion.

AN HOUR LATER, alone at his desk in the den, he remained locked in that dislocated state of mind. The sudden rearrangement of the narrative of his past wasn't exactly a house of cards collapsing, but the ground had definitely shifted. Madeleine had been on the verge of leaving him. The realization disturbed him. Equally disturbing was the fact that he'd been so insensitive to the depth of her distress that the possibility of her ending their marriage never occurred to him.

Gazing out the den window at the hillside, he caught sight of her in her fuchsia ski jacket, making her way along the mown swath that separated the overgrown pasture from the surrounding forest. She found solace in the outdoors, in pacifying her mind through physical movement, through immersing herself in the natural beauty of the countryside. He found peace and purpose in filling his mind with a puzzle, in turning it this way and that, until it surrendered its secret. Even now he sensed that some part of his brain was viewing his marriage and his own ignorance of its fragility as a puzzle to be solved. Uttering a sharp little laugh at the intractability of his thinking, he pushed himself up out of his chair. Maybe there was something worth considering in Madeleine's preference for getting out in the open air—

His phone interrupted his train of thought. The caller was, by one of those unnerving coincidences, Emma Martin.

"Emma. I'm glad you called. I was just thinking we need to talk."

"Because Madeleine wants you to drop the case?"

"Have you spoken to her?"

"No. It's just a position I could imagine her arriving at."

"There's a tangible reason for it. The Harrow Hill case ended up making both of us targets of a homicidal maniac—who came within seconds of adding us to his body count. It's had a powerful effect. The possibility that I might put us in that position again—"

"Is the last thing on earth Madeleine would want," Emma said. "It's also the last thing I want. This is not about you becoming a front-line combatant. It's about you taking a calm, safe look at the available facts and detecting the flaw in the prosecutor's narrative. I'm talking about the sort of intellectual challenge your brain was built for, not a gunfight."

Gurney said nothing.

Emma added, "If even that limited prospect would be disturbing to Madeleine, we can part company right now. Your call."

Again, Gurney said nothing.

"Let me make a suggestion," Emma said. "Talk to Ziko. He may hold the key to the truth and not even know it, because he hasn't been asked the right questions by the right person." Those last words were delivered in a way that conveyed an absolute conviction that Gurney was the right person.

"You're suggesting I visit him in Attica?"

"It will occupy one day in your life. I was planning on visiting him tomorrow, but you are welcome to take my place. I think you'll find it interesting."

GURNEY SET OUT at nine the following morning for what Google Maps told him would be a four-hour drive from Walnut Crossing to the maximum-security prison in the village of Attica.

For the first hour, his route took him through the frost-covered western Catskill foothills and on through a series of bucolic valleys, pockmarked by the occasional abandoned commercial enterprise. Small herds of cows stood motionless in muddy pastures or rummaged through hay piles on open hillsides. Farmhouses and outbuildings in need of repainting, ancient tractors, and tilting silos bore witness to the region's battered agricultural heritage. His route took him past some relatively prosperous places, suburbs of university towns, areas with well-kept homes and landscaped lawns, but mile after mile, the landscape revealed its two primary characteristics—natural beauty and economic pain.

To Gurney the saddest things were the abandoned farmsteads. As he slowly rounded a curve, he noticed on a row of fence posts several bluebird houses in the same state of dilapidation as the old house beyond the fence. These abandoned birdhouses, once the lively embellishments of a beautiful place, had become symbols of a lost world.

Whatever it passed through, the road always returned to a rolling panorama of fields and forests, placid lakes, and winding rivers. Every so often a small thicket of larches, whose amber needles were yet to fall, gave a burst of color to a wooded hillside.

———

GURNEY ARRIVED ON the outskirts of Attica twenty minutes early.

Just past an area of modest village homes was the region's gloomy center of gravity—a century-old penal fortress with concrete walls two feet thick and thirty feet tall, host to two thousand of the most dangerous convicts in the country, and location of one of the worst prison riots in modern American history.

The last time he had been here was on an equally dreary day shortly before his retirement from the NYPD. He'd come to interview a convict who claimed to have information on an open homicide case, the details of which were particularly grotesque.

Pushing those disturbingly vivid thoughts aside, Gurney locked his wallet and phone in the car and entered the medieval-looking tower that housed the prison's main entrance. He was led to a large, windowless space filled with small pedestal tables and flimsy chairs, about half of which were occupied. The acoustics muddied the mixture of unhappy voices, and an odor of sweat and pine-scented disinfectant permeated the room. Six corrections officers were spaced out around the perimeter walls.

Soon after Gurney was seated, he saw Ziko Slade in a standard green convict uniform being directed to his table. That strange combination of soft, pampered features and calm, intelligent eyes Gurney had first noted in the trial video made the man instantly recognizable.

He took the chair opposite Gurney. He made no effort to force a handshake. Leaning forward, he spoke softly. "Thank you for coming here, sir. Your kindness means a great deal to me."

"Emma believes in you."

"Her belief is a blessing. Especially since so many facts appear to incriminate me. Every night, before I fall sleep, I wonder if the case will ever be understood, or if the person who killed Mr. Lerman will ever be found. But I must let go of these questions and focus on what's good in my life." He paused. "Thank you for making the long drive. I hope it wasn't bad."

"Not bad at all."

Slade smiled. "The land is beautiful."

"Yes."

"It's hard sometimes to see we're surrounded by beauty. We do too much thinking. When I believe my ideas are real, what is real becomes invisible."

Gurney wondered if Slade's philosophizing was the product of serenity, psychosis, or manipulation. "How are you dealing with the reality of being here?"

"Often I wish I were somewhere else. Some people see this place as hell. I try to see it as purgatory.

"Meaning?"

"The fire of purgatory is purifying. The pain of clarity. The fire of hell is nothing but remorse. I agree with whoever said that hell is the truth seen too late. I've been blessed to have seen the truth while there was still time to live by it."

"Even here in prison?"

"Wherever you are, you can live an honest life. But you know this already. I suspect you've always been an honest man." He smiled, showing perfect teeth. "For me honesty is a relatively new concept."

"How do you like it so far?"

Slade laughed as if Gurney had made a clever joke. "Honesty is astonishing. A key to another world."

"A world Emma Martin introduced you to?"

"At the precise moment I was ready for it. Do you know I was stabbed and near death?"

"Emma told me."

"Something happened while I was in the intensive care unit. I had a sudden vision of my life as a selfish, cruel, useless progression. A life of lies. I felt a desperate desire for my life to be the opposite of everything it was. That's when I was brought to Emma. A magical connection."

Gurney was skeptical of dramatic conversions, and particularly of their staying power. "So, that was the end of the old life? No thoughts of going back?"

The perfect smile reappeared. "Why would I go back to being the old me? That man was an idiot. I was drowning in money and buying one useless piece of junk after another. I had a fifty-thousand-dollar gold watch. Why? Because my East Hampton neighbor had a thirty-thousand-dollar gold watch. I was also fucking his very expensive wife. In fact, I fucked her in my laundry room the night of my own wife's birthday party. I fucked her twice on her husband's yacht. And I fucked their daughter for three days straight in a hotel room on a ten-grand crack buy. This was not unusual. This is what I did."

"There are people who might envy that old life of yours."

"People who don't know what it really is. People who've never seen themselves as the scum of the earth, desperate to stay high because the crashes are devastating, and the crashes only get worse, and you get crazier and more terrified and more desperate. The dark is full of devils, and the light is unbearable. You want to die, but you're terrified of dying—the claustrophobia, the paralysis, the suffocation—and the only way to escape the grave is to grab for another woman, another hit, another delusion of power. Then the next crash drives you back to the grave, and you can't breathe and your mind is going to explode."

Gurney had listened to a lot of addicts over the years, and Slade's description of the low-bottom life rang true. Of course, where he came from was never in dispute. The more interesting questions centered around his post-conversion life—if that's what it really was—and how that life related to the murder of Lenny Lerman.

"Are you still married to the woman who stabbed you?"

"No. She was too addicted to the insanity. When I got out of the hospital and backed away from the old life, she convinced herself I was either a total phony or a religious bore. She was done with me."

"Why did she stab you?"

"We were arguing, she picked up an ice pick, and . . . it happened."

"And since then you've been leading a straight life?"

"Yes."

"A life that means a great deal to you?"

"It means everything to me." His steady gaze met Gurney's. "So, if someone threatened my new life with proof of an old crime, I would have a powerful motive for killing him. Is that what you're thinking?"

"I think that's what Cam Stryker wanted the jury to think."

"It sounds reasonable. But it actually makes no sense."

"Why not?"

"If I killed Mr. Lerman, I would have been trying to preserve the appearance of my new life at the cost of destroying the reality of it. That would be insane, wouldn't it?"

14

THAT WOULD BE INSANE, WOULDN'T IT?

Even though his meeting with Slade continued for another twenty-five minutes, that was the comment most vivid in Gurney's mind during his drive home. Viewed one way, it could be seen as the straightforward observation of an innocent man. Viewed another way, it might be the smirking humor of a psychopath.

He felt a similar uncertainty about Slade's post-stabbing life of virtue. Perhaps it was all true, a legitimate road-to-Damascus awakening. Or it could be a long-term con job, aimed at some yet-to-be-revealed payoff.

Gurney went back over the final questions he had asked Slade.

Did he receive the threatening phone calls from Lerman that Stryker had referred to?

No, he hadn't.

How did he explain the three calls made from Lerman's number to his, and Lerman's description of them in his diary?

He couldn't explain them because they never happened.

If he was in the lodge the evening of the murder as he claimed, how could Lerman have been knocked unconscious a few feet from the front porch, dragged to a grave in the woods, beheaded, and buried without his noticing anything at all?

He'd been making preparations for the following day's Thanksgiving dinner. The kitchen was in a rear corner of the building, and he had a Mahler symphony on the stereo, parts of which could have drowned out a machine gun.

How did his DNA get on the camos Lerman was found wearing?

It must have been stolen from a closet in the lodge. He never bothered to lock the upstairs windows. Getting in would have been a cinch when he wasn't there, which was most days.

Slade's answers sounded reasonable, but if true, it would mean that Cam Stryker's persuasive courtroom narrative was a total fiction.

That thought produced a small frisson—and a new realization, not so much about Slade as about himself. He recalled his inclination after the Harrow Hill horrors to avoid active involvement in future criminal investigations—an easy enough boundary to maintain in the absence of temptation—but now he could feel the familiar pull of a closed case that just possibly should not have ended the way it did.

Under the influence of that magnetic pull, he might talk himself into something best avoided. He decided to share his thoughts with Jack Hardwick, the former New York State Police detective with whom he had an often contentious but ultimately productive working relationship.

Hardwick was vulgar and combative, but he was also smart and fearless. He and Gurney shared a special connection, formed as the result of a macabre coincidence. When Gurney was still with the NYPD and Hardwick with the NYSP, they were both involved in the investigation of the infamous Peter Piggert murder case. On the same day, in jurisdictions a hundred miles apart, they each found half of Mrs. Piggert's body.

Gurney pulled into a roadside gas station and convenience store. He parked next to a battered pickup truck and placed the call. After four rings, it was answered by a female voice with a Puerto Rican accent.

"Dave?"

"Esti?" Esti Moreno was Hardwick's live-in girlfriend. She was also a New York State Trooper in what was still very much a man's world, which said a lot about her toughness and determination.

"Who else?" she said in a tone of teasing reprimand. "I saw your name on Jack's phone screen, so I picked it up. He's outside. We have groundhogs. Jack hates groundhogs. You want to talk to him?"

"I wanted to ask him if he knows anything about a murder case involving Ziko Slade."

"The tennis player?"

"Years ago, yes."

"I had such a crush on him!"

"On *Ziko Slade*?"

"I was such a tennis fanatic back then, and he was incredible. So graceful. He made it look so easy. Like he was born for it. Such a beautiful boy. The girls, the women, the gay men at the court where I played—we were all in love with him."

"He's not a boy anymore."

"Sad but true. There were stories about crazy things—wait, hold on, Jack just came in."

He heard the phone switching hands, then Hardwick's rough voice.

"I'm blowing up goddamn groundhog burrows. Little bastards are undermining the house. The fuck do you want, Gurney?"

"Whatever you know or can find out about Ziko Slade and Leonard Lerman."

He uttered a snorting little laugh. "According to my TV, Lerman is dead and headless, and Slade's doing thirty-to-life in an upstate shitcan."

"I've been asked to look into the situation. I just met with Slade, but I'm not sure who the hell is living in his body."

"I had the impression the case was a slam-dunk."

"You know who the prosecutor was?"

"Not a clue."

"Cam Stryker. The murder took place in Rexton Township,

other end of the same county as Harrow Hill, so the same district attorney."

"Does she know you're screwing around with her case?"

"Not unless she's keeping tabs on the visitor log at Attica."

"This poking around you're up to—what's the endgame?"

"The person who asked me to look into it is sure the case was flawed and that the verdict should be reversed."

"Suppose you come up with something that turns Stryker's golden victory to shit. Result number one is you turn Stryker into a lifelong enemy. Where's the fucking advantage in that?"

"I haven't given much thought to the personal implications. All I want to know at this point is whether the case against Slade was as solid as it looks. Facts—that's all I want. Especially ones that didn't make it into the trial record. I figured with your upstate law-enforcement contacts you might be able to unearth something."

"You getting paid for this?"

"No payment has been mentioned."

"Davey-boy, you must be out of your goddamn mind. Besides, I can't focus on this in the middle of my groundhog situation. One fucking battle at a time. I'll be in touch."

As usual, Hardwick disconnected first.

Gurney gave little thought to Cam Stryker's potential reaction to his investigation. There was another matter of greater interest on his mind: Exactly how strong was the supposedly unassailable physical evidence? Marcus Thorne took a few potshots at it during the trial, but wasn't willing to subject it to rigorous questioning—perhaps because he knew that the answers would make the defense position even weaker. In Gurney's mind, however, the actual strength of the physical evidence remained an issue worth looking at more closely. The question was how.

Gurney purchased an overpriced bottle of water from the convenience store, then set out again for home—with the evidence issue very much on his mind.

His thoughts on the subject, however, were interrupted from time to time by glimpses in his rearview mirror of a dark nondescript car on the otherwise traffic-free country road. He first noticed it shortly before his stop. When the car reappeared, trailing him at the same distance, mile after mile, he paid closer attention.

His rational mind told him there was nothing to be concerned about. The car behind him now might not be the same car from before—and even if it was, there could be any number of innocent explanations. But an uneasy feeling persisted, and when he was about twenty miles from Walnut Crossing, he pulled off the road into a gravelly turnaround area used by the county snowplows in the winter.

Less than half a minute later, a dark blue sedan sped past. In the early dusk, all he could see of the driver, who was staring straight ahead, was a shaved head and a thick neck. On the door he noted the circular gold insignia of the New York State Department of Corrections. The car was out of sight before he could get a clear view of the plate number.

15

DUSK HAD DARKENED INTO MOONLESS NIGHT BY THE time Gurney reached the top of the hillside road that ended at his barn. From there, a grassy lane led up to the house through the lower of two unused pastures.

As he passed the barn, he saw a light shining through the window of the back room where he kept his tools. His initial inclination was to continue driving up to the house and come down the next morning to turn off the light. But he hadn't used that room for several days, and Madeleine never used it—making the light a bit of a mystery.

He backed the car up, got out with a flashlight, and made his way to the door on the far side of the building, shivering in the frigid air. The door was unlocked, which surprised him. He stepped inside, sweeping the flashlight beam around the barn's large open area, then proceeded to the door of the back room.

Pushing it open, he saw nothing unusual, beyond the light being on. His tools were in their normal places, the dust on the workbench was undisturbed, the paint cans and brushes were as he'd left them. He was about to leave when he noticed the window wasn't completely closed. He couldn't remember whether it was open or shut the last time he'd used the room. He shut the window, switched off the light, and secured the barn's outer door, then got back in his car.

As he parked by the asparagus bed, it occurred to him that the barn light probably wouldn't have bothered him if he hadn't noticed it right after his experience with the Corrections Department car. He chalked it up as another example of the fact that the mind is basically a connection machine, with a special affinity for connecting oddities.

Before making his way to the house, he checked on the chickens, making sure they had enough food and water, and closed the little door between the coop and the run. When he finally entered the house, he sensed that peculiar atmosphere of emptiness when Madeleine was out. Her absence was confirmed by a note on the refrigerator door:

In case you forgot, I'm at Liz's house for our poetry discussion group. Have you called Kyle yet about Thanksgiving?

He resolved to get in touch with Kyle later and made himself an omelet. While he ate, his mind kept returning to the increasingly strange Ziko Slade affair. As soon as he finished eating, he took his dishes to the sink, went into the den, and called Emma Martin.

"Hello, David." Her tone revealed no hint of surprise at hearing from him.

"There are a few things I'd like to resolve, and I was wondering if I could get hold of the evidentiary material Cam Stryker provided to Marcus Thorne during the pretrial discovery process."

"I'll call Thorne and tell him to rush you whatever he has."

"It's not all that super-urgent."

"I disagree. If there's a chance of getting Ziko out of prison, timing could make all the difference. I'm sure his fellow inmates view
him as a privileged brat who killed a poor man to protect his wealth.
One of them may try to even the score."

After finishing with Emma, Gurney made himself a cup of coffee
and called Kyle.

It went to voicemail, and he left a message: "Hi, Kyle. It's Dad.
Long time since we've seen you, or even talked on the phone. Maddie
and I were wondering if you might be free for Thanksgiving. Be great
if you could join us. Let me know. Hope all is well. Love you."

He took his coffee to the table by the French doors and tried to relax, letting his mind drift through the events of his day. Out of the jumble of conversations and perceptions, the item that rose to the surface
was the conundrum of Lerman's severed head and fingers. Not only
the question of why they'd been removed, but what had been done with
them. Had they been discreetly discarded? Or retained by the killer?
He couldn't help picturing them in the freezer in some madman's base-
ment. And two hours later, when he was too tired to think clearly and
finally went to bed, that was the image that troubled his sleep.

16

HE AWOKE THE NEXT MORNING FEELING GROGGY AND
unrested. Ten minutes in the shower brought some improvement. By
the time he shaved, dressed, and made his way out to the kitchen, he
felt almost normal.

Madeleine was at the table by the French doors, eating cold cereal with blueberries and reading a book about seashells. He made a
cereal and berry mixture for himself and joined her.

She looked up from her book. "Are you okay?"

"Sure. Why?"

"You were thrashing around all night, mumbling. What were
you dreaming about?"

"I don't know."

"Do you know someone by the name of Sonny?"

"What did I say?"

"Mostly gibberish and half sentences."

"Do you remember any of it?"

She laid her cereal spoon down. "You mentioned a grave."

"What did I say about it?"

"You said something about fingers."

"And I mentioned the name Sonny?"

She nodded. "Angrily, like you were accusing him of something. And a woman's name, too."

"Adrienne?"

"I'm not sure. I was half asleep." She went back to reading her book.

He finished his cereal, went to the coffee machine, and made himself a double espresso. He brought it to the table and angled his chair toward the glass doors.

The morning sun was a pale disk in the overcast sky. White frost coated the brittle stalks of the black-eyed Susans and milkweed pods in the low pasture. A thin sheet of ice outlined the perimeter of the pond. Two vultures, dark shapes against the gray sky, circled slowly over the eastern ridge.

He couldn't recall anything from his restless dreams, but he did remember what Adrienne said about the insurance company lawyer, Howard Manx, and his follow-the-money view of the case. It was conceivable that Sonny wanted that money badly enough to kill his father to get it, but engineering the murder to incriminate Ziko Slade was another matter entirely. It seemed impossible, but Manx might have other ideas about the case that were worth listening to.

Gurney brought his phone into the den and called Adrienne Lerman.

She answered immediately, sounded pleased to hear from him, and gave him Manx's office address and phone number with surprisingly little curiosity about his need for it.

Figuring right then was as good time as any to reach out to the man, he made the call.

It was answered by a brusque voice.

"Manx."

"Mr. Manx, my name is Gurney. I'm a retired New York City homicide detective, and I've been asked to look into the Leonard Lerman murder case with a view to appealing the verdict. I'd appreciate an opportunity to discuss it with you."

There was a perceptible pause. "What did you say your name was?"

"David Gurney."

"Phone?"

Gurney gave him the number.

"I'll get back to you," Manx said and disconnected.

His return call came thirty-five minutes later.

"You want to discuss the case, we can do it here in my office. You know where it is?"

"I have the address."

"One o'clock today. Suite 201. Don't be late, Supercop."

Manx had obviously done a quick check on him, and the old *New York Magazine* article had surfaced. Its gushing over his record number of NYPD homicide arrests was a continuing embarrassment to the publicity-shy Gurney, but he had to admit that it opened doors.

SUITE 201 WAS located in a modern low-rise building in a corporate office park in a suburb of Albany. The landscaping around it was suggestively Asian, all raked gravel and large gray stones. The signage over the entrance read NorthGuard Insurance Company.

After checking in with a frowning receptionist sporting a coral crew cut, Gurney proceeded up a polished metal staircase. He knocked on the door to 201.

"Come in!" The abrupt tone matched the voice on the phone.

The chaotic state of the office was a surprise after the austere geometry of the lobby.

File folders and loose papers covered most surfaces. The man peering at Gurney from behind the cluttered desk radiated a twitchy energy. He flicked a finger toward the only chair in the room that didn't have something on it.

"Sit."

Gurney remained standing. "Look, Mr. Manx, if you'd rather do this another time . . ."

The man riffled rapidly through a pile of papers in his open desk drawer. "There is no other time."

Gurney sat and looked around the room. He noted a group of enlarged, framed mugshots covering half the wall nearest him. Manx slammed his desk drawer shut and followed Gurney's gaze to the wall.

"Trophies," he said. "I hunt down thieving bastards and mount their heads on my wall."

"Perpetrators of insurance fraud?"

"More of them every year. Geometric progression. They don't even think it's a crime. Assholes. Zero moral compass! You know what that says? It says this country is falling apart. Insurance theft is the canary in the coal mine—leading indicator of societal decay. Larcenous termites! They not only steal but tell themselves they have a right to steal."

He tapped the desk, looking at Gurney as if expecting a reaction. When he didn't get any, he sat back in his chair and switched subjects. "So, tell me, Detective—what do you know about this goddamn Lerman case that I don't know?"

"I suspect you know a lot more about it than I do. All I have are questions."

"Like what?"

"Do you believe Ziko Slade killed Lenny Lerman?"

Manx's eyes narrowed. "Beliefs aren't worth a damn."

"But if you were forced to put your money on one side or the other."

Manx looked pained. "I'm of two minds on the subject. My position in the insurance arbitration case was the same as Stryker's in the trial. Namely, that Lerman was killed in his effort to blackmail Slade—a fact I hoped might trigger clause thirteen, absolving the company from payment in the event that death occurs in the commission of a felony. But the arbitrator found in favor of the beneficiaries."

"Why?"

"Her rationale was that the prior expression of a seemingly felonious intent was insufficient to prove that an extortion demand was actually made during the fatal encounter."

"You said you were of two minds on the subject of Slade's guilt. Does that mean, your insurance argument aside, that you personally suspect someone else?"

Manx leaned forward, baring his teeth. "I'm a follow-the-money guy. It's a reliable principle. And it points me at Psycho Sonny Lerman. He had a powerful financial motive, and he hated his father."

"How do you know that?"

"His sister's got no filter. Ask her anything, she'll lay it all out. Family secrets, dirty laundry, whatever. She's either got a pure heart or a mental disorder."

Gurney said nothing.

"End of the day, whoever did whatever they did for whatever reason, there's one bottom line. NorthGuard Insurance was fucked out of a million bucks, and I take that personally."

Again, Gurney said nothing.

The rapid drumbeat of Manx's fingers on the desk grew louder. "Okay, Detective, that's it. I've told you everything I know. Bared my soul. So, tell me where you are in this mess. No bullshit."

"I appreciate your candor, Mr. Manx, but I'm afraid I don't have much to tell you. I'm looking into the case as a favor to someone who believes that Slade was wrongly convicted. But frankly, if I was just a little more comfortable, I'd be happy to sign off on the official version."

"What's your discomfort about?"

"The missing body parts."

Manx stared at him. "Because hacking off a blackmailer's head with an axe seems a little over the edge?"

"That's one way of putting it."

"Ever occur to you that Slade might be crazy? That maybe this is what he does to people who threaten him? He wouldn't be the first nutcase to have a few heads in his freezer."

17

GURNEY CONSIDERED THE MURDER SCENE EVIDENCE. THE bits and pieces were strung together by a plausible but not necessarily accurate narrative. To imagine an alternative narrative, he needed firsthand knowledge of the site. Crime scenarios had often shifted in his mind as he stood in the spot where killer and victim collided.

From his Outback, he called Emma Martin.

"What can I do for you, David?"

"I'm trying to clarify a few issues, and it would help if I could visit Slade's lodge."

"It's currently being watched over by a young man in our addiction recovery group. When do you want to go there?"

"I'm near Albany right now. I could take a detour up into the Adirondacks."

"If Ian isn't there now, he will be later today. I'll let him know you're coming."

"Ian?"

"Ian Valdez. One our success stories and a great fan of Ziko."

Gurney entered the lodge address into his GPS and pulled out of the NorthGuard parking lot. As he left the Albany metro area, the urban traffic thinned out, and by the time he was heading due north into the Adirondack foothills on a winding two-lane road, there were no other vehicles in sight.

The vistas around Walnut Crossing were essentially bucolic.

Hillside meadows and thickets of deciduous maple, beech, and cherry trees alternated with old farms, barns, and silos. In contrast to the Catskills, the Adirondack vistas appeared less cultivated. This was a land of log cabins rather than farmhouses. Instead of meandering through broad valleys, the streams tumbled through boulder-strewn gullies. The forests seemed vaster, the silence deeper, the air colder. This was not a place of planting and harvesting but of hunting and trapping.

The farther north he drove, the stronger these impressions grew—along with a feeling of apprehension. A thin fog reduced visibility of the road ahead. The giant pines and hemlocks encroaching on the pavement darkened in the haze.

An edgy sense of again being followed crept up on Gurney, justified only by a momentary glimpse of a vehicle far behind him. Twice he slowed and once pulled over to test his suspicion, but no vehicle appeared. Still, the uneasy feeling persisted.

By the time his GPS told him he'd arrived at his destination, the temperature had dropped below freezing, and the fog was depositing films of ice on the trees. The announced "destination" was actually the point at which Slade's private road—essentially, a very long driveway—met the public road. Gurney turned onto Slade's property and followed the narrow lane through the forest to a clearing dominated by an imposing two-story log structure. There were no lights on, nor any other vehicle in sight.

He stopped at the edge of the clearing, got out, zipped his light windbreaker up to his neck, and stuffed his hands in the pockets. The fog, the dead stillness, and the motionless evergreens with their drooping branches gave the place an eerie look. All that was needed now, thought Gurney, was the screech of an owl to send shivers down his spine.

Based on what Emma had said, Ian, the house minder, would be arriving at any moment, but Gurney saw no reason to wait for him before proceeding. Soon, the November dusk would fade into darkness.

He approached the front porch of the lodge and stopped a few feet from the broad wooden steps—the spot where the prosecution claimed Lerman had been knocked unconscious. Gurney didn't expect to find any remaining traces of the event. It was the place itself that interested him.

He began by making his way around the building. It was constructed of giant logs on a laid-stone foundation, in the style of the opulent Adirondack "camps" of the early 1900s. As he walked, he calculated the depth of the main structure to be about fifty feet. A square addition appended to the rear corner added another twenty or so feet. The windows in that section were larger. Gurney identified that part of the building as the kitchen.

He conceded that someone preparing a meal in there would probably not have been able to hear something occurring out by the front porch. That by itself didn't argue for Slade's innocence, but at least it explained how he *could* have been ignorant of someone else's attack on Lerman.

Continuing around the back of the building, he saw a padlocked shed at the edge of the woods, perhaps the shed where the investigation team found the axe bearing the traces of blood with Lerman's DNA. A generator hummed from behind the shed. A couple of the upstairs windows did not appear to be tightly shut, perhaps due to some warping or swelling of the sashes—another fact that proved nothing but was consistent with Slade's explanation of how someone could have gotten into the lodge to take one of his camo suits as part of a framing scheme.

Gurney completed a full circuit of the lodge, then headed out of the clearing and into the woods in the direction the unconscious Lerman was said to have been dragged. Counting his paces to approximate the distance mentioned in the trial, he arrived at a spot bearing no noticeable characteristics identifying it as the location of Lenny Lerman's shallow grave.

Because the deepening gloom under the trees was making it difficult to see clearly, he activated his phone flashlight app, sweeping the beam from side to side. Then he returned to his starting point in front of the lodge, changed the angle of his exploration, and repeated the process half a dozen times without success.

He was about to give up the effort when his phone light illuminated an area next to a huge pine where the ground was slightly hollowed out. The layer of pine needles over the sunken area was thinner here than on the surrounding ground and the earth was a little softer. His recollection of the crime scene photos confirmed that this was the spot where Lerman had been beheaded the previous November.

A slight tremor ran through him as he pictured the unconscious man being dragged facedown and dumped in the shallow waiting grave . . . the axe swinging down through the back of his neck . . . the blood spurting from the severed carotid arteries and seeping slowly into the dark earth . . . the fingers being clipped off one by one . . . loose soil being shoveled over the body . . . and finally the—

Gurney's mental reconstruction of the murder was cut short by a scream.

18

THE SCREAM WAS A SOUND OF PURE TERROR—MADE EVEN more hair-raising because its distance and direction was obscured by a creeping fog. The uncertainty stymied Gurney's police instinct to run toward a sound of distress.

"Who's there?" he shouted. "Where are you?"

He waited a few seconds, listening, then shouted both questions again.

The silence was absolute.

He retreated from the grave site, using his phone to illuminate the way back through the woods and to his car. He unlocked the glove box and took out his 9mm Beretta.

He was imagining possible scenarios for the scream and deciding on his next move when a glint of light caught the corner of his eye.

And then it was gone.

He peered into the woods, searching for it, but saw nothing in the murky dusk but the black ghosts of trees.

The light appeared again.

It seemed to be moving.

And there was a second light moving with it.

Then there was the sound of a vehicle coming from the same direction.

Intermittently, through the trees, a pair of headlights turned onto Slade's long driveway. A minute later, a white pickup truck entered the clearing and came to a stop behind the Outback.

A short male figure in ski pants, ski jacket, and a wool watch cap got out of the truck. Backlit by the headlights, he approached Gurney.

"Sorry I'm late. Fog, ice on the road. I am Ian Valdez."

Gurney couldn't place his mixed accent.

They shook hands as the beam of the pickup's headlights went out.

Valdez started leading the way to the porch.

"Hold on a second," said Gurney. "There's a problem. I heard a scream in the woods a minute ago."

"Yes. Common thing."

"Excuse me?"

"Rabbit."

"Sorry?"

"When caught by a fox, the rabbit screams. Like a small child. Always in the dusk or the night. You get used to it. Like many terrible things. Come."

He opened the front door, flipped a switch on the inside wall, and the front room was flooded with amber light. They stepped inside, Valdez removed his hat and jacket, and Gurney got his first clear view of him. He was taken aback to see how much younger he looked than the tone of his comment suggested—perhaps in his late teens or early twenties. He had the broad face and prominent cheekbones of some Eastern Europeans, but the brown eyes and warmer skin color of a Southern European.

"I can make tea or coffee."

"Coffee would be fine."

"You like it strong?"

"Yes. Thank you."

"First, I must tell you. Ziko is very happy you are here."

"You spoke to him?"

"Today, yes. I am returning now from seeing him."

"How is he?"

"The same as always. He says worry is a waste of time. Maybe one day I will be so calm." He gestured toward a seating area in front of a ceiling-high stone fireplace. "Please be comfortable while I make the coffee."

Instead of sitting, Gurney walked around the large room. The decor suggested an upscale hunting lodge—polished pine paneling, exposed beams, wide-board flooring, oversized leather armchairs, rustic table lamps, colorful framed prints of upland game birds.

A long line of tennis trophies sat on the fireplace mantel. Lined up chronologically, they commemorated a series of victories in local, national, and international tournaments. From the trophy dates, Gurney calculated that Slade won them between the ages of fifteen and nineteen.

"Such a brilliant start." Valdez returned with two mugs and handed one to Gurney. "So much success. So much love. Many people are killed by this. Almost Ziko, too. But God wants Ziko to live." He pointed at two armchairs by the hearth. "Come, sit, tell me why you are here."

They settled into their chairs.

"To see the actual murder scene." Gurney sipped his coffee. It was very hot, very strong. "To visualize what happened here. Maybe to understand Ziko better."

"He is the most amazing person."

"What do you like best about him?"

"Best, I think, is the truth. When you speak, he listens, helps you see what is true, what is not true. He brings peace with him. This is why I have made him my father."

"Your father?"

"My guide. This is what a father should be, yes?"

The question brought to mind memories of Gurney's uncommunicative father and his meager childhood relationship with the man.

"Is he really that perfect?"

"He says he sometimes feels anger, fear, but this can be good— because what upsets us tells us what motivates us, and what motivates us tells us who we are."

"This way of thinking made him a father figure for you?"

"No." There was hard insistence in Valdez's voice. "I have made him my father. Not *father figure*. Real. Not bullshit."

Gurney paused, wondering if this sensitive issue should be pursued. He decided to take a chance. "Sometimes I wish I could have replaced my father with someone who talked to me, did more things with me, taught me things. But that's not the kind of man he was. He never shared much of his life. Not with me, not with my mother."

Valdez watched him intently.

Gurney took another sip of coffee. "Was your father like that?"

A long moment passed before Valdez answered in a tone that sounded purposely flat. "I never speak about him. He is dead."

In another room, a device beeped.

Valdez set his coffee mug on a side table and stood up. "I set a timer for reminding me to leave to get propane tanks refilled before the hardware center closes tonight. They stay closed for all deer hunting season. Employees are all hunters. Please remain here as long as you wish. You are free to go through the lodge, inside, outside."

"Thank you, Ian."

He gave Gurney a long, questioning look. "Something I think is troubling you?"

"I'm wondering . . . if Ziko is innocent, why do you think there's so much evidence against him?"

"It's not a mystery, Mr. Gurney. It's the power of evil."

ONCE VALDEZ LOADED several portable propane tanks in the back of his truck and departed, Gurney examined the other rooms of the lodge. He didn't know what he was looking for, but that was often the case when he explored the location of a crime.

An hour later, he entered the last of the lodge's five bedrooms and saw something that got his attention—a pair of framed photographs on the wall facing the foot of the room's single bed.

The photo on the left appeared to have been taken at a boozy party. Ziko Slade sat on a couch, shirt open, hair tousled. He had one arm around a barely clad young woman on his left, while exchanging an intense kiss with a similar young woman on his right. A third was kneeling on the floor in front of him with her head in his lap. It was the kind of louche disco scene the tabloids loved.

The photo on the right was riveting in a different way. It was an enlarged mugshot. This version of him was strikingly ugly. The features of the former Greek god radiated a dull menace that Gurney had seen in the eyes of hitmen. Together the images told a story a moralist might have titled "The Price of Sin."

Gurney wondered if that was the point Slade was trying to make. Was the display a reminder to himself of where his egomania had led him, or was it the phony confession of an unrepentant con man?

He completed his examination of the house without making any more discoveries. Concluding that his visit had served its main purpose of acquainting him with the lodge and its immediate environs, and feeling no need to wait for Valdez's return, he decided to set out for home. The weather would make it slow going, at least until he was out of the Adirondacks. He switched off the lights in the house, zipped up his jacket, and stepped out onto the porch.

There was a scent of pine in the cold air. The darkness was as deep as the mountain silence. He took out his phone and activated the flashlight app. In the plummeting temperature, the fog condensed into tiny ice crystals. He felt their pinpricks on his face as he made his way to the Outback, his steps crackling through the glaze that covered the ground.

He opened the car door and was starting to get in when he was stopped by the sight of something on the front seat. His first impression was some sort of fur hat, or muff, or . . .

As he looked closer, a grimace tightened his lips.

He was looking at the body of a rabbit.

A rabbit whose head was missing.

19

AFTER RETREATING INTO THE LODGE, GURNEY CALLED the Rexton Police Department and described the situation. The duty sergeant considered it no more than someone's prank and suggested calling back in the morning.

Gurney explained that it could be connected to the Lerman murder case and suggested getting Scott Derlick out to the Slade lodge ASAP.

The sergeant's voice went up a notch. "You want me to disturb Lieutenant Derlick at home? So he can drive all the way out there in this weather? To look at a dead rabbit?"

"That's right."

"Who the hell are you?"

"My name is David Gurney, retired detective first grade, NYPD Homicide." He hated identifying himself this way, but it occasionally served a purpose.

There was a noticeable pause. "So, how come you're at the Slade place?"

"I'll explain that to Derlick when he gets here."

FORTY-FIVE MINUTES LATER, a large black SUV entered the clearing and came to a stop with its headlights on Gurney's vehicle. The man who emerged wore a hooded parka and carried a steel-cased flashlight of the type that can do double duty as a truncheon.

The man approached the Outback and peered inside. He bent over with his head inches from the glass, aiming his flashlight at the front seat. He scrutinized the registration certificate at the base of the windshield, then swept his flashlight up to the porch and let it rest on Gurney.

"This your vehicle, sir?"

"Yes, it is."

"And you are . . . ?"

"David Gurney."

"NYPD?"

"Retired."

"I assume you have appropriate identification?"

"I do."

"Are you carrying a firearm?"

"I am."

"If I asked, could you produce your carry permit?"

"I could."

"Please come over to your vehicle." The tone had no "please" in it.

Gurney stepped down from the porch and walked into the area illuminated by the SUV's headlights. He recognized Scott Derlick from the trial video—although in person the man's eyes were smaller, his nose more porcine.

He was studying Gurney as though he were a suspect in a break-in.

"This is not your residence, is it, sir?" He gestured vaguely toward the lodge.

"No."

"So, what brings you here?"

"Curiosity."

"You have permission to be here?"

"I do."

"If I were to check, that would be confirmed, would it?"

Gurney smiled. "Lieutenant, I'm here because I've been asked to look into the Lerman murder case to determine if Ziko Slade's conviction was a mistake. Until this evening, I was skeptical of that possibility. Now, I'm not so sure. The placement of that little cadaver in my car feels like an effort to scare me off, and I'd appreciate your reaction to that possibility."

"You'd appreciate my reaction?"

"I would."

Derlick stared at him in mock amazement. "You came here to determine if Slade's conviction was a *mistake*? Did I hear you right?"

"You heard me right."

"Well, that does make me wonder."

Gurney said nothing.

"Do you know what it makes me wonder?"

"No, sir, I don't."

"It makes me wonder what kind of ex-officer would sell his services to a piece of crap like Ziko Slade. Fancy-ass society boy, slime-bag drug dealer, cold-blooded murderer. Even for a downstate cop, that's a mighty deep dive into the sewer."

"It's understandable why you might see it that way."

"Don't you goddamn tell me what's *understandable*! Let me make something clear to you. Slade is guilty as sin. Period. Thirty-to-life was too lenient for that piece of shit. I don't know what you're up to, but you're on the wrong track. You understand what I'm saying?"

"I do."

"Good. Now, listen up. I don't want to see you or hear from you again. I don't care who the hell you are, or who the hell you used to be down in that rat's nest of a city. You make trouble up here, you try to pull some slippery crap to subvert the conviction of Ziko Slade, you'll walk into a buzzsaw a hell of a lot more serious than a goddamn dead rabbit. Am I getting through to you?"

"You are."

Derlick gave Gurney a hard stare and returned to his big SUV. Gurney watched its taillights recede down the long driveway and disappear onto the county road.

He considered the meeting a success in every way. The question of whether to expect simple noncooperation or active obstruction from Derlick was now answered. From the intensity of the man's anger, Gurney also concluded that Derlick wasn't at all sure of Slade's guilt. Derlick's lack of interest in the headless rabbit and his failure to take possession of it for forensic examination meant Gurney could bring in someone he trusted for the job.

He returned to the lodge and retrieved a large plastic container and some oversized tongs. He used the tongs to lift the rabbit carcass into the container. Then he left a voicemail for Kyra Barstow and headed home.

20

INTERMITTENT SLEET AND FREEZING RAIN SLOWED THE drive from Slade's lodge to Walnut Crossing. Gurney didn't arrive home until midnight. His mental review of the day's meetings—with Howard Manx, Ian Valdez, and Scott Derlick—kept him awake into the wee hours.

The phone on his bedside table roused him from a claustrophobic dream at 9:05 a.m.

He cleared his throat. "Gurney here."

"I got your message about wanting to bring me a headless rabbit you found in your car. Thing is, I don't perform animal autopsies, so I'm not sure what you want me to do."

"Good morning, Kyra. Thanks for getting back to me. No autopsy required. What I'm hoping is that the person who chopped off its head may have left some trace evidence on it."

"That's a long shot."

"I know."

"Is the body in decent condition?"

"No obvious decomposition."

"I suppose I can take a look. But don't get your hopes up."

"There's something you should know. This rabbit incident occurred while I was at Ziko Slade's lodge—and after I reported it, I had a run-in with Scott Derlick."

"No surprise. That man is touchy."

"I just don't want you to get blindsided by a hostile reaction from the Rexton PD or the DA's office if they find out you're looking into this for me after being part of the prosecution's case at Slade's trial."

"I don't report to them. I gathered the forensic evidence and presented my conclusions on the stand. That's it. Facts are facts. I'm not on anybody's side. If you want to know whether there's foreign residue on the rabbit, and what it might be, I'll tell you what I can. Drop the carcass off today, if you can. Be nice to see you again."

The call left Gurney fully awake and energized. When he went out to the kitchen for his first coffee of the day, he found a note on the refrigerator from Madeleine, saying she'd left for an early shift at the Crisis Center and should be home by 3:00 p.m.

After a quick breakfast, he set out for the Russell College Department of Forensic Sciences in the wealthy enclave of Larchfield. The drive took a little over an hour and passed through the grim neighboring town of Bastenburg. Their juxtaposition was a stark example of the growing gap between the fortunate and the unfortunate—the gap that had become a fertile ground for conspiracy theories, lies, and political chaos. Topographically, all that separated Bastenburg from Larchfield was a gentle ridge, but to pass from one side to the other was to move between worlds increasingly at war with each other. As Gurney descended the Larchfield side of the rise, intense memories of the horrific drama six months earlier that had left fifteen people dead and nearly cost him and Madeleine their lives accosted him. He chose a roundabout route that avoided Harrow Hill entirely.

Gurney parked outside the forensic sciences building. He removed the plastic container with the remains of the rabbit and started toward the starkly modern structure.

Halfway there, his phone rang. "Kyra?"

"I can see you from my office. Stay there. I'll come out. It'll be quicker than getting you through building security."

He returned to the Outback. A minute later Barstow strode across the parking area with the same easy grace she displayed at the site of the first Harrow Hill murder. Despite the tension and ugliness of that scene, her comportment struck him as a sign of self-possession, a no-drama quality he respected.

"David! Good to see you!"

"You, too, Kyra."

They shook hands. Her grip was firm. She eyed the container on the hood. A dark shape was visible through the translucent plastic.

"That's our subject?"

"That's it."

"The head is the only missing part?"

"As far as I know."

Her gaze moved to Gurney. "You see it as a warning to back off?"

He nodded. "And I'd love to know who issued the warning."

She picked up the container. "Maybe this will give us a clue."

"You're sure it won't put you in a difficult position?"

"Difficulty is the spice of life. Besides," she added with a wink, "you're the one who needs to be careful. The dead bunny was in your car, not mine."

They parted ways. Barstow returned to the big glass-cube home of the Forensic Sciences Department, and Gurney checked his phone for messages. He found a new one from Hardwick.

"You want the dirt I dug up on Slade, buy me lunch. Dick and Della's Diner in Thumburg at one o'clock."

Gurney returned the call. "You lost your fondness for Abelard's?" he asked when Hardwick picked up.

"Abelard's doesn't fucking exist anymore. The glorious Marika sold it to some asshole from Soho who renamed it the Galloping Goose and doubled the prices."

"Okay. Dick and Della's at one."

"I'm hungry. Don't be fucking late."

21

UNLIKE DINERS DESIGNED WITH RETRO FIXTURES TO CRE-ate a feeling of nostalgia for a bygone era, Dick and Della's was authentically old and shabby.

The murky vinyl-tile floor might once have been brown and green. In addition to the frayed red-vinyl pedestal seats at the counter, there were half a dozen Formica-topped tables by the front windows. The few patrons lingering over their lunches looked like part of the decor.

It was just twelve forty-five, and Gurney was the first to arrive. He chose a table by one of the windows. A smiling waitress brought him a menu, asked if he wanted coffee, and departed.

He opened his menu. It appeared that a previous patron who'd ordered "Della's Homemade Pot Roast with Dick's Smothered Onions" had left remnants of both on the menu. When the waitress returned with his coffee, he ordered pancakes and sausages.

The coffee tasted burnt, but he drank it anyway. An avocado-green refrigerator behind the counter brought back a sudden memory of his father—the man finishing off a pint of whiskey, then searching through that green refrigerator for a six-pack that Gurney's mother had thrown out with the garbage.

What the hell did she do with it, Davey?

With what?

My beer, what else?

I don't know.

You don't, or you're just saying you don't?

So the dance went. All he had wanted in those childhood years was to be grown-up and gone.

He was distracted from these thoughts by the familiar growl of the big V-8 in Hardwick's classic GTO, pulling into a parking space just outside the window. The old muscle car looked better than Gurney expected. The last time he had seen it, the front end had been smashed in, the result of the head-on collision that stopped the escape attempt of the Harrow Hill murderer. A major restoration had finally been completed, including a fire-engine-red paint job. He was still admiring it when Hardwick arrived at his table.

"Slick, eh, Davey?"

"Looked ready for the junk heap last time I saw it."

"An Esti ultimatum—make it nice or make it go away."

He took a seat across from Gurney. His hard, muscular frame was evident even under a loose black sweatshirt, and the ice-blue eyes of an Alaskan sled dog were as unsettling as ever.

He signaled for the waitress.

"BLT on toasted white, bacon should be crisp, plenty of mayo. Sides of baked beans and coleslaw. Coffee and cherry pie."

She wrote it all down on a little pad with green-tinted pages. "All at once?"

"Except the cherry pie."

She retreated in the direction of the kitchen, and he turned to Gurney.

"Sweet kid. No Marika, but there aren't a hell of a lot of those around. So, anyway, I did a little research on the slippery scumbag you want to turn loose on society."

Gurney said nothing. Provocation was a natural part of any conversation with Hardwick.

"Digging up shit on this creep was easy. There's plenty of it, but he always managed to skip out of serious legal consequences—until this Lerman thing nailed him to the fucking wall."

Hardwick launched into a vivid tale of Slade's history, most of which Gurney already knew. Hardwick's narrative painted a clear picture of Slade's dissolute past but fell short of providing any new insights into the man.

"Did you find out anything about his background, prior to all the notoriety?"

"Not a lot. His father was a champion fencer and a lifelong womanizer who eventually died of a coke-induced heart attack. Ziko was too busy fucking a Grammy-nominated teenager to attend the funeral."

Like father like son, thought Gurney.

The waitress arrived with his pancakes, sausages, and a bottle of maple syrup. She told Hardwick that his BLT "and other stuff" would be ready soon and headed back to the kitchen.

"Did you find out anything about the period of Slade's life after his wife stabbed him?"

"He disappeared into some weird rehab, grew a halo, pretended to be a saint—until the blackmail threat brought the old Ziko back to life and he chopped off Lenny Lerman's head." He paused, eyeing Gurney with obvious skepticism. "You don't actually think this shitbag's conversion was for real, do you?"

Gurney cut his sausages neatly into quarters and ate a piece. "I met Slade, and I'm not honestly sure about him one way or the other. Also, some details of the murder don't make sense. And now someone is trying to scare me off the case."

Gurney told him about the rabbit.

Hardwick's face screwed up in disbelief. "You think a dead rabbit in your car makes Slade innocent?"

Gurney shrugged. "It does put some weight on that side of the scale."

"Not a hell of a lot, in my opinion. What details of the murder are bothering you?"

"Mainly the missing head and fingers. Plus, Slade's property is more than a hundred acres. Why would he bury the body so close to the lodge? And why wouldn't he get rid of the axe—and the clipper that cut off the fingers? Keeping them seems incredibly stupid."

Hardwick shook his head dismissively. "Crazy shit happens in murders. Distraction. Panic. If killers thought things through, we wouldn't catch so many of them."

"I get that, but Slade struck me as not only intelligent but super-calm."

"Okay, let's say that the former scumbag is now a Zen master who wouldn't hurt a fly. What's your hypothesis for the crime? You must have an idea or two. This is the kind of shit you live for."

The waitress arrived with Hardwick's order. Gurney waited until she was gone.

"Here's the first thought that came to mind. Someone who was aware of Lerman's plan to blackmail Slade saw it as an opportunity to kill Lerman and let Slade take the blame."

"Like who? With what motive?"

"Possibly Lerman's son. He despised his father and knew about his life insurance policy."

"You're saying Lerman's son could have gotten into Slade's lodge on a day when he wasn't there, swiped the camo outfit, got the axe and pruning clipper out of the shed, then followed Lenny the night he went to see Slade, chopped off his head, and buried him there without Slade knowing?"

"Something like that."

"So, how come Slade's attorney didn't dangle this evil son in front of the jury?"

"He did, in a way, in his closing argument; but he couldn't do more with it, because there was no physical evidence to put him at the site, and he supposedly had a solid alibi."

"Any other options?"

"Suppose someone who hated Slade gave Lerman sensitive information about Slade and suggested the extortion plan. Maybe the idea was for Lerman to do the work, and they'd split the money. But then he decides to kill Lerman on Slade's property rather than going through with the blackmail plan. Maybe the idea of framing Slade for murder appealed to him more than extorting money from him."

Hardwick stared skeptically at his coleslaw. "Any idea who this criminal mastermind might be?"

"None. And there's a problem with this scenario. It doesn't track with the excerpts from Lerman's diary that were presented at the trial."

"So, basically, you have no fucking idea what's going on."

Gurney poured syrup on his pancakes. "I'd like to know what damaging information Lerman had on Slade. The only mention of it in Lerman's diary was something that went down between Ziko and someone by the name of Sally Bones. That mean anything to you?"

Hardwick took a large bite of his BLT. He shook his head.

"I did a search on it," said Gurney, "but it led nowhere."

Hardwick swallowed, then sucked at his teeth. "That wouldn't by any chance be another of your subtle requests?"

Gurney shrugged. "Sally Bones. Interesting name. Could belong to a low-level mobster who never got enough media attention to pop up on the internet. But he may have come to the attention of law enforcement at some point in his career. If you get an itch to check it out with your old state police contacts, there's another name you might want to mention. Ian Valdez."

"Who the hell is Ian Valdez?"

"Good question."

22

GURNEY'S DRIVE HOME FROM THUMBURG WAS NOT A happy one. The information Hardwick had dug up on Slade, apart

from a few unpleasant facts about the man's fencing-champion father, added nothing of substance to what he already knew.

By the time he parked in his usual spot by the asparagus bed,
it was a little after four. The sky was already darkening and an icy
breeze was blowing. On evenings like this, Madeleine enjoyed having
a fire blazing on the big fieldstone hearth.

He zipped up his jacket, went to the woodpile behind the chicken
coop, and brought an armload of split cherry logs into the house.
The aroma of baking bread greeted him. As he carried the logs to
the fireplace, he could hear the strains of a baroque cello piece coming from Madeleine's music room upstairs. He took off his jacket
and set about arranging the wood in the firebox. It was a task he
enjoyed—getting the geometry and spacing of the logs just right to
ensure that the fire would start easily and burn steadily without further attention.

The stove timer chimed, the cello music stopped, and a minute
later Madeleine entered the kitchen. She removed the bread from the
oven and placed it on a cooling rack.

"Oh, good," she said, seeing him at the fireplace. "I was about to
do that myself. I can't seem to get warm. Did you see your package?"
She pointed to a flat box on the table by the French doors. "It arrived
by FedEx, right after I got home."

He made a final adjustment to the top log before going over to
the package.

He recognized Marcus Thorne's return address. He ripped open
the package and slid a pile of documents onto the table. The sheet
on top was headlined, "Evidence and Witness Files Provided by the
Prosecution to the Defense."

Gurney scanned through the list of enclosures—transcripts of
interviews, the ME's on-site notes, the autopsy report, crime scene
photos, and some phone call records. Thorne hadn't labeled any of
the documents as contradictory or exculpatory, which suggested they
were consistent with what Stryker presented at the trial.

"Have you run into any new oddities in the case?" Madeleine

was peeling a carrot at the sink island, her tone of voice determinedly nonchalant.

"Maybe one or two. Hard to say." The rabbit "oddity" was surely more significant than his reply suggested, but he didn't want to mention it to her, at least not now.

She paused to regard him skeptically, then continued peeling the carrot. He gathered up the pile of documents from the table, carried them into the den, and spread them out on his desk.

It was getting dark. Looking out the north window, he could barely see the outline of the pine ridge above the high pasture. He switched on the desk lamp and read through the list of documents again, starting with a transcript of the interview with Bruno Lanka, the hunter who found Lerman's body. The document included the interviewer's name—Detective Lieutenant Scott Derlick.

> *S. Derlick: Please state your full name and address.*
> *B. Lanka: Bruno Lanka, 39 Carrack Avenue, Garville, New York.*
> *S. Derlick: What brought you to this area?*
> *B. Lanka: Deer season. I'm a hunter.*
> *S. Derlick: Did you have permission to hunt on this property?*
> *B. Lanka: I thought it was state land.*
> *S. Derlick: Where did you enter the woods?*
> *B. Lanka: Mile or so down the road.*
> *S. Derlick: What time was that?*
> *B. Lanka: A little before six this morning. Dawn's good for deer. Dawn and dusk.*
> *S. Derlick: Did you remain in one spot, or did you move around?*
> *B. Lanka: I like to move around.*
> *S. Derlick: Did you see any property boundary markers?*
> *B. Lanka: No.*
> *S. Derlick: Any reason you came in this direction from the parking area?*

*B. Lanka: This way was uphill. When I start out, I like to
head uphill. So when I'm tired, or dragging out a carcass,
it's downhill to the car.*

S. Derlick: What drew your attention to the buried body?

*B. Lanka: The back of the foot, the heel. It was sticking up out
of the dirt.*

S. Derlick: What did you do when you saw the heel?

*B. Lanka: I went over to look closer. I'm thinking it was just
the back of a boot. Then I'm thinking why the fuck would
somebody bury a boot? I kick away some of the dirt. I see
there's a foot in the boot. I kick away more dirt, the foot's
attached to a leg. Then there's the stink. Could make you
sick, that stink. That's when I think holy shit, what the fuck
is this? And I call 911.*

*S. Derlick: Apart from kicking dirt away from the victim's
foot, did you disturb the scene in any other way?'*

B. Lanka: No, nothing like that.

S. Derlick: Did you see anyone else in the area?

B. Lanka: No.

*S. Derlick: Is there anything else you can tell us? Anything that
seemed odd. Anything else that got your attention.*

B. Lanka: Nothing else.

*S. Derlick: Thank you, Mr. Lanka. An officer will drive you
back to your car.*

Gurney thought of at least one additional question he would
have asked: *Of all the deer hunting locations in upstate New York,
Mr. Lanka, what was it that brought you to that particular spot?*

He returned to the list and found the two items involving the
medical examiner, Dr. Kermit Loeffler. He began with the transcript
of Loeffler's recorded observations of the body in situ.

*K. Loeffler: We're looking at the headless cadaver of a
male of average height and weight. The head appears*

to have been severed from the torso at the level of the third or fourth cervical vertebra by a sharp instrument, likely a heavy cleaver or similar long-bladed tool. Substantial blood residue in the surrounding earth suggests this severing was the cause of death. All ten fingers are missing and appear to have been removed postmortem by a sharp compression instrument at the proximal interphalangeal joint. Preliminary estimate places the time of death between two and three days ago.

A second transcript described the autopsy findings.

Loeffler placed the likely age of the victim in his mid-forties to mid-fifties and shrank the time window of death to between 3:00 p.m. and 9:00 p.m. on the Wednesday prior to the Saturday discovery of the body. During the trial that window was further narrowed to two hours—based on Lenny having left a message on Adrienne's voicemail at 7:00 p.m.

What Gurney found most interesting was the difference between Loeffler's on-site description of the likely weapon and his description of it in this autopsy report.

In place of his in situ opinion that the weapon was likely a long-bladed, cleaver-like tool, he now concluded that it was a short-bladed axe. He explained that though the evenness of the cut originally suggested a single stroke, subsequent analysis of the neck tissues under magnification indicated that the severing was achieved not with one stroke of a long blade but with two end-to-end strokes of a short blade. "A level of precision demanding considerable expertise on the part of the axe wielder," Loeffler noted.

GURNEY WAS PONDERING Loeffler's comment later that evening while he and Madeleine ate dinner. Short of working as a lumberjack, how might someone acquire that sort of proficiency?

Madeleine had stopped eating and was gazing across the table at him.

"You haven't said a word since we sat down."

He shrugged and shifted his focus to the braised chicken with rice and apricots on his plate. He was hesitant to discuss the case because he didn't want to admit his growing involvement to Madeleine.

"The chicken's good," he said.

There was another silence, broken by Madeleine.

"Kyle called this afternoon. He said he got your phone message and yes, he'd love to come up for Thanksgiving."

"Good."

"You should get in touch with him more often."

"I know."

They finished their dinner without further conversation. Madeleine cleared the table, brewed some chamomile tea, and headed upstairs to practice her cello pieces. Gurney made himself an espresso and retreated to the den and the case materials.

Instead of reviewing documents, he placed a call to Bruno Lanka. He got Lanka's voicemail.

"This call is for Bruno Lanka. My name is David Gurney. I'm reinvestigating the Leonard Lerman murder, and I need to speak to you regarding the statement you made last November to the detective at the scene. You can reach me tomorrow morning between nine and noon." He'd long ago discovered that providing a time window for a response made it more likely to get one. He included his cell number and ended the call.

23

GURNEY'S PHONE RANG AT 9:01 THE NEXT MORNING WHILE he was washing his breakfast dishes. He expected the caller to be Lanka, but the name on the screen was Hardwick.

"Yes, Jack?"

"Those names you gave me—Sally Bones and Ian Valdez? I found three people called Ian Valdez, but I doubt any of them would interest you. One's a retired dentist in Chicago. Another's a Jesuit in Boston. And the third's a middle-aged choreographer in Los Angeles."

"No one younger?"

"If your Valdez is young, either he's using a phony name or he just hatched out of a fucking egg. Better luck with Sally Bones. I found a reference to a Salvatore Bono who died in odd circumstances about six years ago. A short news item mentioned he was known to his friends as Sally Bones. No one was listed as surviving him, no wake, no funeral notice."

"What were the odd circumstances?"

"Body was found in a dumpster behind a fast-food joint in Albany, not far from where he lived. But get this—he was crushed to death."

"Crushed . . . how?"

"News item quoted someone in the medical examiner's office, saying it was like something had been wrapped around him and tightened until it cut off his circulation and respiration, literally squeezed the life out of him."

"Interesting murder weapon. Who investigated it?"

"Albany city police."

"Were you able to check it out?"

"A little. I know a guy over there from my NYSP days. He told me the investigation went nowhere. Victim was unmarried, no kids, no known employment. Turns out the 'friends' mentioned in the news item were a couple of acquaintances in a local bar, plus a stripper who lived with him but claimed to know nothing about him. She didn't even know his real name. She said he called himself Sally Bones, and that was good enough for her. Same with the 'friends' in the bar. Case was technically open for a couple of years, then got dropped into the inactive file. Basically, nobody gave a shit. It happens."

"Any motive theories at the time?"

"Maybe gambling debts. Maybe he got on the wrong side of

some psycho. The guy was a loner. Goddamn loners are the hardest murders to solve."

"No hint of any connection to Ziko Slade?"

"None."

"And the weird method of execution didn't lead anywhere?"

"Nowhere useful. Shit, I don't even like to think about that. Having the breath crushed out of him. I'll be having goddamn suffocation dreams. Any other sickening favors I can do for you, Sherlock?"

"Funny you should ask. There's another name I'm curious about. Bruno Lanka."

GURNEY GAZED OUT the French doors. The ground was covered in snow. In contrast with the stark white of the pasture, the leafless trees looked black. It was frustrating how little progress he'd made on the question of Slade's guilt or innocence.

It was time for another call to Emma Martin.

"Good morning, David. What can I do for you?"

"What can you tell me about Ian Valdez?"

"That depends on what aspect of his life you're asking about."

"Let's start with his name. Is it legitimate or an alias?"

"I can't say. People who come to me can remain as anonymous as they wish. I'm not interested in names, only in who they really are. Why do you ask? Has something happened?"

"While I was at the lodge, someone put a decapitated rabbit in my car. I discovered it shortly after Ian left on some sort of errand."

"And you're thinking Ian put it there?"

"It's possible."

"That's not the person I know him to be."

"And who, exactly, is that?"

"A person, like Ziko, who has learned the value of integrity."

Gurney sighed impatiently but said nothing.

"I understand your skepticism. Perhaps you should visit Ziko again."

"Why?"

"The better you know Ziko, the surer you'll be of his innocence, and the better you'll understand Ian."

He suppressed an itch to argue. Instead, he thanked Emma and ended the call. There might, in fact, be some value in meeting with Slade again.

After phoning Attica to arrange a visit later that day, he refilled the watering device in the chicken coop, left a note for Madeleine, and set out on the long drive.

THE VISITING ROOM was busier than on his previous visit. The conversational murmur was louder, and the odors of sweat and disinfectant more pronounced.

Slade entered the room, found his way to the table, and sat across from Gurney. He looked just as untroubled by his circumstances as before.

"Good to see you, Mr. Gurney."

"How are you doing?"

"The food has room for improvement." His tone suggested indifference to this fact.

"I drove up to your lodge the other day."

The tilt of Slade's head indicated interest. "To view the scene of the crime?"

"Yes."

"Did you meet Ian?"

"He arrived a little after I did." Gurney paused. "Interesting young man. How much do you know about him?"

Slade smiled. "Ian is one of Emma's miracles."

"Where did he come from?"

"Hell."

"Did he share any details with you?"

"Some, but there were things he wouldn't talk about."

"Can you tell me what he did talk about?"

"One of Emma's rules is that anything divulged in her home is confidential. But I can tell you that I felt horror at what he told me and sorrow over what it did to him."

"Ian told me he'd adopted you as his new father."

"True."

"What do you make of that?"

"I suspect it has little to do with me. It is about something in him. 'Desperation' may be the best word for it. Whatever it is, making me his 'father' has had a calming effect on him. Perhaps it helped him to deal with some of his hideous memories of the father who raised him."

"He needed that kind of help?"

"Very much so. When Ian first came to Emma, he was . . . insane."

"Do you know if 'Ian Valdez' is his birth name?"

He shook his head. "Emma discourages that kind of curiosity."

"Do you trust him?"

"I believe he's been truthful with me, to the extent that he knows what the truth is."

Gurney sat back in his chair and waited for the officer patrolling that part of the room with unusual persistence to pass out of earshot. The man's shaved head and thick neck brought to mind the driver of the Corrections Department vehicle he spotted tailing him after his last visit.

"Have you given much thought to why you're here?"

Slade shrugged. "The evidence convinced the jury I was guilty."

"But if you're innocent, that evidence must have been planted by someone else. The questions are by whom and why. Any ideas?"

Slade shook his head. "I don't even know whether I was the target or the scapegoat. Was the objective to kill Lerman and, as matter of convenience, deflect the blame on me? Or was killing Lerman simply a way to frame me for murder?"

Gurney had arrived at that same fork in the road. That Slade shared his thinking was a point in his favor.

"How about a list of your enemies—do you think you could put one together?"

"For the two or three years leading up to my wife stabbing me, I was out of my mind." He paused, a smile revealing his movie-star teeth. "You should talk to my ex-wife. She was high all the time, but she didn't have memory blackouts like I did. If you want to know about the enemies I made, she's the one to ask. Tell her you're working on my case and you want some insights into my character. She'll be delighted to tell you the worst."

"Did she do any prison time for stabbing you?"

"She claimed self-defense, and I declined to testify against her. It was the least I could do to make up for my behavior. I'll give you her contact information. She's living in my Dutchess County house—the result of a divorce provision. You have something to write on?"

"I have a good memory."

Slade spelled out his ex-wife's name—Simone Delorean—along with her phone number. Gurney closed his eyes and pictured the number, repeating it to himself. When he opened them, the bull-necked guard was once again walking slowly past their table.

24

ON THE HOMEWARD DRIVE, GURNEY DIVIDED HIS ATTEN-tion between his rearview mirror and puzzling out a case hypothesis that would combine Lerman's extortion plan, his murder at Slade's lodge, and a murderer other than Slade himself. The few possibilities that occurred to him all contained significant logical obstacles.

He stopped for coffee and gas at the same convenience store where he had gotten a bottle of water on his previous trip. After re-filling the tank, he placed a call to Adrienne Lerman.

"Mr. Gurney?" Her earnest, obliging tone reminded him of her desire to find homes for the kittens she was fostering. Kittens that were meowing in the background. "What can I do for you?"

"I'd like to share some thoughts I have regarding your father's death."

She didn't reply.

"Do you have time now, or would you prefer that I call back later?"

"Now is probably best. There's a hospice client I need to see at dinnertime. Have you discovered something?"

"It's not so much a discovery as a feeling."

"A feeling about his death?"

"About the way his death has been explained."

Gurney got the impression that she'd stopped breathing.

He continued. "Based on what your father said about his plan, and where his body was later discovered, the natural assumption was that Ziko Slade killed him. That made perfect sense. But—"

Adrienne cut him off. "You put that in the past tense."

"Excuse me?"

"You said the assumption that Slade killed him *made* perfect sense. But it doesn't now?"

"I'm saying the case against Slade may not be as strong as it seemed."

"But the trial . . . the evidence . . . how could he be innocent?"

"Sometimes when investigators pinpoint someone as the obvious perpetrator, their minds close, and they ignore facts that don't support their conclusion. They see everything through the lens of what they've already decided is true."

"Is that what you think happened?"

The meowing in the background grew louder.

"I think it's possible. But I need your help. I'd like you to consider the possibility that someone else killed your father, and that—"

"What about the DNA, the axe . . . ?"

"Put that aside for the moment. What I want you to focus on right now is your father—on his behavior in the days and weeks leading up to his death—everything you can remember, even the smallest details. Can you do that?"

Gurney waited, relying on that deep vein of helpfulness that seemed to define her.

"I can try," she said. "But you're asking about things that happened a year ago."

One of the cats sounded a lot closer. He pictured it standing in front of her, demanding attention.

"There's no rush. Over the next few days, when you have time, try to picture the interactions you had with your father. Whatever comes to mind. Things he said. Things he did."

He heard her taking a deep breath.

"I can try," she said again.

"One last thing. Before the trial, had you ever heard the name Sally Bones?"

"Not that I remember. I think I'd remember a weird name like that."

"No problem. Call me anytime with any thoughts, recollections, questions, anything at all. I really appreciate your help."

After ending the call, he finished his coffee, crumpled up the container, and tossed it into the makeshift garbage bag hanging under his glove compartment.

He was tired, hungry, and eager to get home, but he decided to try reaching Simone Delorean first. Her number rang three times before switching to a recording that sounded both intoxicated and provocative.

"I'm busy right now. Very busy. So, at the tone, beep-beep, tell me what you want. Okay? Just spell it out. Be explicit. Bye-bye."

Gurney began leaving a message, but at the mention of Ziko's name he was cut off by a live voice, a sharper version of the one on the message. "Who the fuck is this?"

Gurney identified himself and explained that he was looking for insights into Ziko's character.

"*Insights?* You want *insights* into that son of a bitch?"

"We're trying to get a sense of his character before we commit to the appeal process. We were hoping that you might be able to—"

"*Appeal?* He's *appealing* his conviction? You mean, like, trying to get it *reversed*?"

"That would be the objective."

"But he's guilty."

"That's what we're taking a second look at."

"You some kind of a lawyer?"

"An investigator. His attorney is Marcus Thorne."

"I know who his fucking attorney is. You actually think you have a chance of getting that prick off?" She sounded both incredulous and furious.

"That depends. We're trying to get a picture of his character."

There was a silence during which Gurney guessed she was assessing the angles. "Where are you?" she asked.

Gurney started to describe his location when she interrupted him again.

"Actually, I don't give a fuck where you are. You have my address?"

"No."

"You know where Dutchess County is?"

"Yes."

"You know Rhinebeck?"

"Yes."

"Good. Forty-two Heron Pond Road. Can you get here by eight tonight?"

Gurney did a quick calculation. "Yes."

"And you want the truth about Ziko? The whole truth?"

"We want to know as much as possible about him. He appears to be a charming man, but the evidence at the trial—"

"The evidence at the trial proved he was a *fucking axe murderer*! But that, sweetheart, is just the tip of the Ziko iceberg. Be here by eight."

25

BEFORE SETTING OUT FOR RHINEBECK, he left a brief voicemail message for Madeleine, saying only that he'd be home later than expected. He had no appetite for explaining why.

By the time he crossed the Hudson River on the Kingston bridge three hours later, the wind had risen, and the glow of a full moon was shimmering on the water.

His GPS took him through the prosperous village of Rhinebeck and into the rolling countryside beyond it. The final GPS instruction directed him onto Slade's estate via a private lane. Unlike many of the county's painstakingly restored eighteenth- and nineteenth-century homes, the two-story structure at the end of the lane was modern, glassy, and angular. Lamplight shone from an upstairs window. The rest of the house, the gravel parking area in front of it, and the spherically trimmed boxwoods around it were bathed in moonlight.

He got out of the car. On the far side of a multi-acre lawn, he saw a line of stables, reminding him that Marcus Thorne referred to the place as Slade's horse farm. Beyond the stables sat a glass structure he assumed was a greenhouse.

He climbed the broad concrete steps to the front door—a glossy black slab with a nearly invisible camera lens at eye level—and knocked. Then knocked again, louder. Just as he was taking out his phone to call Simone Delorean, the door swung open to reveal a shirtless, muscular teenager with disheveled hair and wild eyes. There was a sheen of sweat on his face and chest and a trace of white powder on one nostril.

"Fuck are you, man?"

"David Gurney. Here to see Simone Delorean."

"Yeah?" He stared at Gurney, as if trying to comprehend a difficult concept.

"Maybe you should tell her I'm here."

"Who the fuck are you?"

"I told you, David Gurney."

After another prolonged stare, he slammed the door.

The meeting was turning out to be more complicated than anticipated. As a precaution, Gurney returned to the Outback and strapped on his Beretta ankle holster. He returned to the door just as it opened.

The woman standing in the soft light of the entrance hall wore nothing but a white tee shirt that reached halfway to her knees. Her long dark hair was wet from a shower she'd evidently just stepped out of.

Her pale gray eyes neither welcomed nor engaged. Like a predator, they assessed. She was equally beautiful and unsettling, and he suspected that upon meeting a man, the first thing she assessed was the impact she had on him. The second would be what possible use he might be to her. He imagined how the appraisal might have played out for the young fellow with the coke-powdered nose.

"He's over eighteen," she said, as if reading his mind. "Not that it's any of your business."

An engine started up somewhere behind the house with a loud burst, followed by the whine of a high-revving trail bike receding into the distance.

"You want to come in?" Her tone was a parody of coyness.

He followed her through a dim-lit hallway into a large room with three black couches around an open granite hearth. A conical chimney of black metal was suspended above it. Rather than creating the warm ambience of a traditional fireplace, it had a chilling effect on the room.

The way she settled herself at the end of one of the couches made it increasingly obvious that the long tee shirt was all she was wearing. Gurney sat at the far end, determinedly focusing on her face. A cool hint of a smile suggested that she found this amusing.

"So," she said, "you want to know about Ziko?"

"I do."

"Because he's appealing his conviction?"

"Yes."

"Even though he's a totally guilty piece of shit?"

"On the phone, you called the Lerman murder the tip of the Ziko iceberg. What did you mean by that?"

She shifted a bit in her seat, making the sight of her thighs more distracting.

"Some people do nasty things, but underneath they're not so bad. Their crazy shit makes you kinda like them. But with Ziko, it was the opposite. He's a sweet talker, lots of charm, does favors with a smile. But underneath all that grinning he's a piece of shit. He lies the way other people breathe. People think what a charming guy. How nice. How open. Doesn't seem to have a secret in the world. And that's exactly what he gets off on. Ziko's got nothing but secrets. The man's a walking, talking, smiling lie."

"You don't buy the truth of his new life?"

"Give me a fucking break!"

"You don't believe he's changed?'

"He's changed, alright. The lies are bigger now. He's not just lying about who he's fucking, he's lying about being a fucking saint!" She leaned forward, as if she were about to spring off the couch. "You don't goddamn get it, do you? You're dealing with the most poisonous, deceptive scumbag on the face of the earth!"

Simone's display of rage felt authentic. But Gurney wasn't sure if it was rage against an evil hypocrite or against a former partner who moved on to a better life—a life that excluded her.

"Why did you stab him?"

She shrugged. "We weren't getting along. We argued about everything."

"And in the middle of one of those arguments you decided to stab him?"

She yawned, as if she suddenly found the subject tiresome. "I discovered he'd been fucking my mother, which I found . . . inappropriate."

It was far from the first revelation of intergenerational infidelity that Gurney had encountered, but it was definitely the most nonchalant. It made him wonder whether she was as corrupt as her tone suggested, or coke-addled, or lying.

She yawned again.

He decided to move on. "As you know, the trial narrative was based on the premise that Ziko was the target of a blackmail attempt.

Do you know of any particular event in his past that could be the basis for that?"

"Ziko was capable of anything. He did things all the time that could come back and blow that fucking halo off his head."

"Anything he'd be absolutely desperate to keep to himself?"

"Could be a hundred things. When he was high, nobody in the fucking world was crazier than Ziko." She moistened her lips with the tip of her tongue. "Maybe there's another headless body out there. You ever think of that?"

He had, but he preferred asking questions to answering them.

"Does the case of a victim being crushed to death ring any bells?"

She recoiled. "Fuck, no!"

"Where did Ziko's money come from?"

"What do you mean?"

"A big estate in a pricey area like this can't have been cheap. Did the money come from his drug dealing?"

She uttered a dismissive laugh. "Most of that went up his nose. Along with thousand-dollar bottles of wine. Ziko liked to drink Lafite Rothschild with takeout pizza."

Gurney detected a nostalgic note. The good old days with crazy Ziko, before he put an end to it all by fucking her mother. Or was it by finding religion with Emma Martin?

"So where did it come from—the money for this place, the money he still has?"

"Some from the sale of his sportswear company. But mostly it was handed to him by his father. Nasty prick who wanted nothing to do with his son. Threw money at Ziko to keep him away." She yawned again. "How much more of this shit you want to wade through? The family crap is totally boring."

"Ever hear the name Sally Bones?"

"Yeah, at Ziko's trial."

"That was the only time you heard it?"

"Yeah."

"How about the name Jingo?'

"Same. The trial."

"Okay, Simone. That's it. Unless there's anything else you want to tell me."

She sat quietly in her corner of the couch for a long minute, with those cold eyes fixed on him. When she spoke, there was ice in her voice.

"He's guilty. Burn that into your fucking brain. He deserves to be where he is. I hope he dies there."

26

"You want to talk about it?"

Madeleine was gazing at him across the table by the French doors, where they were having a mostly silent breakfast of scrambled eggs, toast, and coffee.

"Not really, but it might help." He put his fork down on the edge of his plate and took a moment to collect his thoughts.

"I was hoping that Slade's ex-wife would provide some new insight into the case. Or into Slade. The fact is, she only added to the fog. She insists his reformation is a con job, and she hates him with a venom that's hard to overstate."

"A woman scorned?"

"Scorned and having an affair with a kid who looks about sixteen."

"How old is she?"

"At least twice the age of her houseboy."

"Attractive?"

"And repellent."

"What were you expecting?"

"That she might reveal something useful. Possibly the event that was the basis for Lenny Lerman's blackmail plot. Maybe a few objective facts about Slade's background that would sharpen my picture of the man. She did say with particular conviction that he's a superb liar."

He poked at a remaining bit of egg, then put his fork down again. Beyond the glass doors, everything was white or gray or black, except for the muted red of the barn across from the now-frozen pond.

"It's snowing again," he said.

She finished her coffee. "So, where do you stand with the case?"

"Nowhere. I have major problems with every hypothesis."

"Including the 'Slade is guilty' hypothesis?"

He nodded. Truth be told, the main source of his doubt regarding Slade's guilt was the decapitated rabbit. But he wasn't about to mention anything that threatening to Madeleine. "The evidence is inconsistent with Slade's temperament. The man I visited in Attica is nothing if not cool under pressure. I don't see him making so many incriminating mistakes—leaving that axe and pruning clipper where they could be discovered, putting one of his own camo suits on Lerman, burying the body so close to the house, dropping a cigarette butt with his DNA on it by the gravesite."

"You're saying he was framed?"

"It's one way of explaining the evidence. But it raises a difficult question. Was framing Slade a way for the killer to escape responsibility for killing Lerman? Or was killing Lerman a way to set up the framing of Slade?"

Madeleine eyed him warily. "That's the sort of question that obsesses you."

"The answer could be crucial. If the primary goal was to kill Lerman, then that's where we'll find the key to this whole affair. The insurance investigator insists it was all about the insurance money. Meaning the suspects would be the victim's beneficiaries, Sonny and Adrienne. But I just don't see them as perps. Adrienne is a hospice worker, and she fosters homeless kittens. Sonny may be explosive enough to kill someone, but framing Slade would have required planning, not explosiveness."

Madeleine continued watching him without comment.

"The other possibility—killing Lerman to frame Slade—has its own problems. It would require knowledge of Lerman's blackmail plan, knowledge of when Slade would be at the lodge, and knowledge of exactly when Lerman planned to confront him. It seems like a hell of a coincidence that one of the few people to whom Lerman confided his plan would just happen to hate Ziko Slade enough to want to destroy his life and be willing to murder Lerman to do it."

"You've obviously given this a lot of thought."

"But all I can see are three possibilities. One, Slade is guilty as charged. Two, someone else killed Lerman and framed Slade to get away with it. Three, someone wanted to frame Slade and killed Lerman to do it. But there are major flaws in all three."

"I think this would be an ideal time to put your final thoughts on paper—the pluses and minuses of the three possibilities—pass them along to Emma and let her take it from there. You've done enough."

Gurney nodded vaguely.

27

YOU'VE DONE ENOUGH.

Madeleine's comment was echoing in his mind later that morning as he sat in the den, going through the files he'd received from Marcus Thorne. He realized she had a valid point; he just wished he could pass along a possibility that had more pluses and fewer minuses. But if he were to come up with a new Lerman murder hypothesis, he needed either new facts or a new way of interpreting the ones he had. He decided to begin with the GPS map of Lerman's trip, which showed the route Lerman had followed from his apartment in Calliope Springs to Slade's lodge in the wilderness above Rexton.

The duration of the trip—two hours and twenty-one minutes—seemed a bit on the long side. But Lerman's sixteen-minute gas-station stop could explain it.

That did, however, seem like a long time to spend at a gas station. Perhaps Lerman spent some time in the station's convenience store or restroom. Or a neighboring store. Gurney opened his laptop and entered the gas station's address in Google Maps Street View.

The facility that appeared on the screen was small and scruffy. There were only two pumps, and the tiny store behind them looked more in need of demolishing than updating. He rotated the viewing angle 180 degrees. Directly across the road from the station was a shabby strip mall housing a discount cigarette outlet, a martial arts dojo, a liquor store, an auto supply shop, and a vacant storefront.

He imagined Lerman stopping for gas, noticing the liquor store, and going over to buy something to settle his nerves before going on to his meeting with Slade. But the fact that he could imagine that scenario didn't mean much.

Kyra Barstow might have more information than she'd presented at the trial. Gurney retrieved his phone from the breakfast table and called her.

"If you're calling about the rabbit, David, I'm not finished with it yet."

"No, another request, if you have a moment."

"Barely."

"In addition to examining the physical evidence at the Lerman murder site, did you do any other forensic work on the case?"

"Anything in particular you have in mind?"

"A possible security camera video at the gas station where Lerman stopped on his way to Slade's lodge."

"There wasn't any. The station owner claimed his system was broken."

"How about the strip mall across the road?"

"Nothing operational there either."

"How about Lerman's credit card statements?"

"Covering that same day?"

"Yes."

"Hold on. I need to check our files."

Five minutes later she was back. "We have his Visa statement for last November. Stryker had no interest in it."

"How about his phone records for the same month?"

"Stryker used those as evidence of Lerman's calls to Slade's number."

"Any chance I could get copies of them, along with the Visa statement?"

"I assume, if questioned, you'd have no idea how they came into your possession?"

"I've forgotten already."

"By the way, regarding the rabbit? I was waiting until I had a final answer to call you, but as long as we're speaking, I'll tell you what I have so far. There's considerable foreign DNA on the rabbit's fur—from various sources, none human. Some from other rabbits. Some from other living organisms, species yet to be identified. I'm cross checking non-human databases. I hope to have a species match soon, assuming it's not something totally weird."

"Great, Kyra. Your help is beyond anything I could hope for."

"Do I detect another request buried in that sweet talk?"

He laughed. "Now that you mention it, could you look at Lerman's Visa statement for the day of his trip to the lodge and tell me what purchases he made and where he made them?"

She paused. "Two purchases that day. One at that gas station for fourteen dollars and fifty-seven cents. And one at Cory's Auto Supply for sixteen dollars and nineteen cents. Is that helpful?"

"Could be," he said, recalling that Cory's was the name of the auto supply store across from the gas station. "At the very least, it's interesting."

And baffling, he thought, after ending the call with Barstow. What automotive need could a man have had on his way to such a monumental encounter—perhaps the most important of his life? The price of the purchase seemed too high for an urgent quart of oil. So, what could the need have been? Emergency windshield wipers? A gas can? The possibility reminded him that Lerman's car had been torched, but the torching occurred after Lerman was killed—a situation that raised more questions than it answered. So, would a windshield-wiper purchase make more sense?

Gurney went to an archival weather site and entered the name of the county and the date of Lerman's murder. He discovered it had been partly sunny that day with zero precipitation—making wipers an unlikely purchase. Additional speculation would have to wait for additional facts. With a sigh, he turned his attention back to the trial materials.

He reviewed the medical examiner's initial comments on the body and the autopsy report. The cause of death was the severing of the victim's head with two successive blows of a sharp axe-like implement. The mechanism of death was cardiorespiratory arrest, subsequent to catastrophic neural interruption and rapid blood loss.

As always, he was struck by the disparity between the cool medical description of a murder and the gruesome visual impact of the body. It made him wonder about the emotional state of the killer. Had he been as dispassionate as the pathologist or was he driven by a hatred as ugly as the deed itself?

Gazing at the autopsy photos of the headless torso and fingerless hands, Gurney again asked himself what motivated the amputations. The explanations put forward so far—preventing or delaying the identification of the corpse—seemed to make no sense. And precisely because of that, he suspected those mutilations might be the key to the case.

He felt a new urgency to discover new facts, new dots to connect. Glancing through the titles of the remaining folders on his desk, he stopped at one labeled *Photographs of victim's incinerated car.* He opened it and pulled out a handful of color prints. He counted sixteen of them—twelve of the car, four of the location.

The latter showed an abandoned granite quarry in the process of slipping back into the wilderness. Saplings had taken root in the larger crevices, and weeds filled the narrower ones. The excavated area, no more than a couple of acres, was surrounded by a dense hemlock forest. There seemed to be just one access road entering the clearing from the woods. In the corner of one photo, he saw a discarded red plastic gasoline can, probably the same one used to transport the fire accelerant to the scene.

Next he studied the vehicle photos—reminders that few things on earth looked more derelict than the skeleton of a burnt-out car. The windows had shattered and collapsed in the flames. The tires had been consumed. The interior photos showed even more extensive damage, since that was where most of the plastic components—controls, gauges, screens, panels, upholstery, padding, carpeting—were located. Virtually everything except the metal framework had been reduced to crusts and ashes. Gurney knew from his experience with homicides involving arson that a gasoline fire could reach temperatures close to two thousand degrees. Virtually no non-metallic part of a vehicle could survive that heat.

Neither could a human body—which raised an interesting question. Why did the killer go to the trouble of burying Lerman's body, when it could have been disposed of more efficiently in the car fire? At two thousand degrees, there would have been only charred skeletal remains, and that heat would have destroyed the DNA molecules in the bones—a far more effective way of preventing identification than removing the man's head and fingers. Perhaps the murder had been misunderstood from the beginning.

The thought energized him. He spread the other case files out on his desk and chose one at random. It was a transcript of Detective Lieutenant Scott Derlick's interview with Thomas Cazo—Lerman's boss at the Beer Monster.

Although Gurney had a clear recollection of Cazo's testimony at the trial—testimony shaped by Stryker's choice of questions—it was possible that the full interview might contain other facts of interest.

As he sat back in his chair to read the transcript, his phone rang. It was Madeleine.

"I have a favor to ask. Actually, two favors. Could you bring my cello to the clinic? Any time before three thirty? I'm supposed to join our string group for a concert at Highfield Assisted Living right after work. I'd forgotten about it."

"Sure. No problem."

"Thank you. And the second favor. The snow in the chicken run. Could you shovel it off to the side? They love being out there, but they won't come down the ramp if the grass is covered with snow."

After they ended the call, he picked up the transcript, then put it back down. He decided to get the chicken errand out of the way first. Large snowflakes descended in slow motion through the windless air. Soft pillows of snow collected on the seats of the Adirondack chairs on the patio, on the top of the little cafe table, on the bird-house by the old apple tree, on the roof of the coop.

Being outside on a snowy day like this instantly immersed him in another world, one colored by fragments of memories. Sitting on a sled pulled by his father. The sled gliding silently between high drifts. He wondered if his lifelong love of snow dated back to that moment—he and his father alone in that silent, untroubled place.

The restless squawking of the hens in the coop brought him back to the present. He went to the shed he and Madeleine had built the previous spring. Currently, it was used for garden tools, hoses, fertilizer; but there was a possibility that it might someday house a pair of alpacas—animals Madeleine was especially fond of.

He retrieved a snow shovel and began clearing a broad area at the base of the ramp. As soon as he scraped away enough snow to expose a patch of grass, the five hens came strutting down the ramp in single file—the fearless Rhode Island Red in the lead—and began scratching at the ground. He headed back into the house.

His phone was ringing as he entered the mudroom. He pulled off his snowy boots and hurried through the kitchen into the den. The caller's number had been blocked.

"Gurney here."

"David Gurney?"

"Right."

"I have information for you." The voice was male, soft, insinuating.

"Who is this?"

"I know who killed Lenny Lerman."

Gurney said nothing.

"Are you still there?"

"I'm here."

"Would that information be useful to you?"

"That depends on who you are and how verifiable it is."

"Perfectly verifiable, and very valuable to your friend Ziko Slade. It will free him from prison. Prisons are dangerous places. I suggest a simple transaction. I provide the truth about the hit on Lenny Lerman, and Mr. Slade pays for value received."

"Does this truth come with proof?"

"Of course."

"Let me make sure I understand. You have concrete proof—not just hearsay—that someone other than Ziko Slade killed Lenny Lerman. And you're willing to turn that proof over for an appropriate payment. Is that right?"

"Exactly."

"How would this exchange occur?"

"I will give you part of the information—enough for you and Slade to understand what happened to Mr. Lerman. Along with that, I will give you a price. I will retain the final proof until we have a firm agreement."

"The partial information—what does it consist of?"

"Some names, dates, photographs."

"How soon can you give me these things?"

"I have business this afternoon in Harbane and tomorrow in Scarpton. You know those towns?"

"More or less."

"Good. Pick a spot, pick a time."

Gurney thought about it, hesitated, then made his choice. "This afternoon, two o'clock, in front of the Harbane town hall."

"I look forward to seeing you, Mr. Gurney. At two o'clock."

The man's voice was as placid as the purring of a cat.

28

IT DIDN'T TAKE LONG FOR GURNEY TO START FEELING UN-comfortable about the meeting in Harbane. It wasn't the physical situation that made him uneasy. The town hall was next to the police station, cops would be coming and going all day, he'd be armed himself, and he'd faced hundreds of situations riskier than this down in the city. It was the silky confidence of the voice on the phone.

He decided to call Jack Hardwick.

The man answered the way he often did. "The fuck you want now?"

"Any chance you might be free this afternoon?"

"I'm on standby."

"Standby?"

"I provide occasional security for a major asshole. He may call today."

"This major asshole needs armed protection?"

"*Wants* it more than he *needs* it. He's got a conspiracy theory website—a shitload of lunatic nonsense. But he wants people to think his life is in danger because of all the truth he's exposing. Like the fact that the big California tech companies are run by a secret society of satanic dwarfs. He likes having a visible bodyguard at his public appearances. He thinks creating the impression that he might be shot makes him newsworthy. He plans to run for Congress. Probably win by a landslide. Big appetite out there for bullshit. So, why do you want to know if I'm free?"

"I'm meeting someone in Harbane at two o'clock in front of

the town hall—a guy who claims to have inside information on the Lerman murder. The Lerman 'hit' is what he called it."

"You know anything about this guy?"

"Nothing."

"You have a concern about his intentions?"

"I have a concern about his lack of concern. Sounded too relaxed."

Hardwick cleared his throat in his disgusting style. "I should get a call by noon to let me know if he needs me. If not, I'll head for Harbane. By the way, I checked out that guy you asked me about."

"Bruno Lanka?"

"Owns a specialty-foods market in a seedy suburb of Albany. No rap sheet. You want me to go see him, ask a few questions?"

"Not at the moment. Hope to see you this afternoon."

Gurney's gaze returned to the snow that was falling in slow motion on the high pasture, but he hardly saw it. His mind was on Harbane. A bleak place. The buildings along the main street, more than a century old, exhibited the decrepitude of age without the charm of antiquity. Among the shabby storefronts on that street there was, inexplicably, an excellent Vietnamese restaurant that he and Madeleine had visited three times in the past year.

Thinking about their first meal there, he remembered they chose that restaurant because it was near a town where they were attending a chamber music concert. All he recalled of the concert itself were the dramatic gyrations of the young Asian cellist—an image that suddenly reminded him to bring Madeleine her cello. It would be most efficient to go first to Harbane and then to the clinic. Doing it that way would also give him more time with the case files before setting out.

With everything squared away, he returned to the transcript of Scott Derlick's interview with Lerman's old boss at the Beer Monster.

He was still on the first page of the six-page document when a *Bing!* announced the arrival of an email from Kyra Barstow. He put down the transcript and clicked on the email.

There was no covering note, just two attachments. The first was a copy of Lenny Lerman's Visa statement for the previous November.

He glanced through it. Other than the transactions at the gas station and the auto supply store that Barstow mentioned, he saw nothing of interest.

The second attachment was a printout of Lerman's phone calls for the months of October and November. He counted twelve outgoing and ten incoming calls. Barstow had put a check mark next to six of the incoming calls, all from the same number. At the bottom of the printout she had written, "That number was assigned to an anonymous prepaid phone that was used exclusively for the six calls to Lerman. The first call occurred on October 23 and the final call occurred on November 23, the day of Lerman's death."

The fact that someone acquired an anonymous phone for the sole purpose of communicating with Lerman—and solely during the weeks when he was developing his blackmail scheme—suggested that he and the caller might have been partners in the affair.

Gurney sorted through the case files on his desk until he found the photocopy of Lerman's brief diary—his handwritten record of key moments in that five-week period. Checking the dates of the diary entries against the dates of Lerman's communications with the owner of the anonymous phone, he noted several correlations.

The first call Lerman received—on October 23—was followed by an October 24 diary entry: *Ran into Jingo at the Monster yesterday. Can't get what he told me out of my head. Question one—is it true? I'm thinking sure why not? Z and Sally Bones. I can see how that would happen. Question two. What's it worth? A hundred K? An even Mil?*

On the morning of November 2, Lerman received his second call. That night he made the diary entry describing the dinner he had with Adrienne and Sonny: *Took A and S to the Lakeshore. Said hello to Pauly Bats at the bar. Big Pauly! Nobody fucks with Pauly Bats!! Explained the plan to A and S. Adie worries like always. What if? What if? What if? Like her mother. Sonny doesn't talk. But Sonny likes money. Now we'll have money. Serious money!*

He received a third call the evening of November 4, and on

November 5 he made this diary entry: *Got Z's number and made the call. The asshole picked up. I asked him how much it was worth for me to forget everything I knew about Sally Bones. I told him to think about it. I made the scumbag worry.*

On November 6 Lerman quit his job at the Beer Monster and recorded the event in the diary.

On the evening of November 12, he received a fourth call, and on November 13 he made this diary entry: *Called Z again. Told him I figured an even Mil was the right number to save his evil fucking ass. In used twenties. Whining son of a bitch said that was like two suitcases. I told him so what, you worthless prick. What the fuck do I care about suitcases? You got ten days I told him.*

Early on the morning of November 23, Lerman received the fifth call. That same evening, the evening of his fatal trip to Ziko Slade's lodge, he made his final diary entry: *Called Z, told him his time was up, he better have the fucking Mil. He said he did. I told him to have it ready tonight, make sure he's alone. I walk with the Mil, or the whole fucking world hears about Sally Bones.*

Lerman's diary contained no mention of the six calls he received from the owner of the prepaid phone. Why had Lerman kept that element out of a written record that was in its other respects such a detailed admission of criminal intent?

Gurney wondered if the omission might be as important to the case as the decapitation.

29

GURNEY SECURED MADELEINE'S CELLO IN THE REAR SEAT of the Outback and set out at twelve thirty for his two o'clock appointment. Harbane was less than fifty miles away, but the route was hilly, snow was falling, and there was a chance of getting caught behind one of the road plows.

The broad valley that stretched in a westerly direction from

Walnut Crossing was bereft of human activity. There was no traffic. The sporadic herds of cows he'd noted on his trips to Attica were out of sight, sheltering in their ramshackle barns. The snow-covered landscape seemed as lifeless as whitewashed stone. Near the end of the valley, he turned onto the road that led up over Blackmore Mountain into the next county.

He spent most of the drive wrestling with the implications of a second person being involved in the blackmail plot and with the perplexing fact that Lerman's phone contacts with that person began the day before "Jingo" provided the information that made the plot possible. It was hard to see how that sequence made sense.

Unless . . . the scheme to blackmail Slade had been devised by someone other than Lerman. Say, by the owner of the anonymous phone. Perhaps that person and Jingo were using Lerman as a front man to minimize their own exposure.

He wondered if Kyra Barstow had given any thought to these issues. He pulled onto the shoulder and made the call.

"Hi, David. Are you calling about your rabbit?"

"Something a bit more complicated."

"I love complication."

"I've been looking at the record of the phone contacts between Lerman and Mr. Anonymous."

"Or Ms. Anonymous."

"Good point. Anyway, you mentioned in your note on the printout that the anonymous phone was used only for communications with Lerman. Odd in itself, but what do you make of the fact that the calls were limited to the period leading up to Lerman's trip to Slade's lodge?"

"Maybe Lerman had an accomplice, at least in devising the extortion plan."

"Did you also notice an interesting time correspondence between some of those calls and the events Lerman later noted in his diary?"

"I did."

"Did you bring this to Cam Stryker's attention?"

"I did."

"Did she discuss it with you?"

"That's not the way she uses me or my department. She's frequently made it clear that we're here to answer her questions, not to generate unasked-for hypotheses. I think she regarded the notion of Lerman having a partner in crime as something that could muddy the prosecution narrative. She was fond of pointing out that it was Slade who was on trial, not Lerman. I don't know whether you noticed it during the Harrow Hill case, but the lady is a control freak. She is the boss. The rest of us are the hired help." Barstow paused, then changed the subject. "Regarding your rabbit, I should have some news for you in a day or so."

After ending the call, Gurney remained parked for a few minutes at the side of the road—his eyes on the snowflakes landing on his windshield, his mind on the questions raised by Lerman's phone records and by Stryker's stranglehold on the case against Slade. Hopefully his meeting in Harbane would shed light on the situation.

As the road ascended Blackmore Mountain in a series of S curves, the wind picked up and eddies of snow swirled across the tarmac. After another mile or so the road began to level off. The top of Blackmore was more like a rolling plateau than a peak. A sign indicating the county line was the only sure way of knowing that one had reached the road's highest point.

Gusts at this elevation were at their strongest, and visibility was reduced by the horizontally driven snow. Due to the howling of the wind and Gurney's close attention to the road ahead, he failed to notice the big tow truck coming up behind him until it started moving out into the other lane, as if preparing to pass him. The truck was moving much too fast for the weather conditions—perhaps, thought Gurney, in response to some emergency. He moved a bit to the right to let it pass with less risk of encountering a vehicle in the oncoming lane.

The truck pulled up next to Gurney, reduced its speed slightly, and remained abreast of him for a few seconds . . . before swerving sharply toward him, slamming into the Outback and sending it skidding sideways off the pavement. Gurney struggled to regain control, but the icy gravel of the shoulder provided no traction. The vehicle wildly slewed away from the road. He glimpsed a tree stump ahead but had no ability to avoid the brutal collision.

The airbag's violent deployment against his face and chest threw him against the seat back, stunned. In his semiconscious condition, he was dimly aware of his door flying open, followed by a flood of cold air and the pinpricks of blown snow against his cheek.

The final sensation to become fixed in his memory was of a sudden blow to the left side of his head. The impact shot like an electrical charge from his scalp to the soles of his feet.

30

HE WAS RUNNING AND SLIDING IN THE MIDDLE OF THE FROZEN pond as the grown-up skaters circled around and around in a single-file line just inside the perimeter. Swoosh-swoosh, swoosh-swoosh, swoosh-swoosh went the rhythm of their skates. His father called to him. Time to go home. Time for dinner. He ran faster now, faster, toward the edge of the ice, through the procession of skaters, building up speed for a final slide. Out of control. Too fast to stop. Hitting the edge of the frozen ground, falling forward, his forehead smacking against something hard. His father's handkerchief dabbing at the tender spot on his head, peering at it. "Just a scratch. You may get a bit of a bump. That's all."

At home, his mother glaring at his father.

"What happened to him?"

"Bit of a fall on the ice. Just a scratch."

"He's bleeding, for God sake! Weren't you paying any attention?"

"It's nothing. A bit of a bump."

"You make little of everything! You pay no attention!"

A bell was ringing.

Louder.

Ringing inside his head.

Pulsating.

"Sir?"

A strange voice.

"Can you hear me, sir?"

The bell was a siren. He opened his eyes.

"Sir?"

"Where am I?"

"You've been in an accident. You're on your way to the hospital."

"For a bit of a bump?"

The voice didn't answer.

HE WOKE UP in what he recognized as an ICU unit. He saw dimly that he was connected by wires to monitor screens above his bed. His head felt huge and heavy.

"David?"

A thin nurse in green scrubs stood next to the bed. She held a computer tablet.

"Where am I?" he asked. His voice didn't sound like his own. He tried clearing his throat, but the effort sent jabs of pain through the side of his head.

"Parker Hospital intensive care unit. Do you know where that is?"

"Harbane. What time is it?"

"About three o'clock." She checked her tablet. "Five minutes past."

"In the afternoon?"

"In the afternoon. How are you feeling?"

"I'm not sure. Do you have my phone?"

"The police have all your personal items."

"I need to call my wife."

"I have to ask you some questions first. Can you handle that?"

"Depends on the questions." His voice sounded to him like it was coming from the other side of the room.

A small grin softened the bony contours of her face. "I'll start with the easy ones. What's your name?"

"David Gurney."

"What month is this?"

"November."

"What's the capital of the state you live in?"

"Albany."

"Can you name a major holiday this month?"

"Thanksgiving."

"Next month?"

"Christmas."

"I'm going to give you a list of numbers, and I want you to repeat them back to me in the same order. Four . . . seven . . . nine . . . three . . . two . . . ten."

"Four, seven, nine, three, two, ten."

"Can you tell me what year JFK was assassinated?"

"Nineteen-sixty-three."

"How about the square root of your zip code?"

He started to laugh, but that made both his head and chest hurt.

"Close your eyes," she said and tapped his left foot. "Do you feel anything?"

"Yes. You. Tapping my foot."

"How'd you know it was me?"

"I'm psychic."

"Keep your eyes closed." A moment later, he felt a light tap on the back of his right hand. "Feel anything?"

"You again. Back of my hand."

"You pass," she said, her fingers rapidly entering some information into her tablet. "The doctor will be in to talk to you soon." She turned and opened the sliding glass door to leave.

"Just a second," he said. "Why can't I move my head?"

"Neck brace. Part of EMS protocol. Precaution in the event of cervical injury. X-rays were taken as soon as they brought you in. Nothing fractured or broken, as far as I know. You're very lucky. Doctor can tell you more." She smiled and was gone.

Feeling a strain from the bright light in the room, he closed his eyes. His mind meandered back through softly falling snow to the skaters on the pond. Around and around. *Swoosh-swoosh, swoosh-swoosh, swoosh*—

"Mr. Gurney?"

The skaters disappeared. He opened his eyes and saw a short, sour-looking man in neatly fitted scrubs standing at the foot of the bed.

"I'm Dr. Dietz. Can you hear me?"

"Yes. Would it be possible to get hold of a phone? I need to make some calls."

"We'll get to that. Do you know why you're here?"

"Someone ran me off the road into a tree stump."

His eyes narrowed. "Then what happened?"

"Airbag went off. Not sure after that. Impact to the head. Sirens, I think. Woke up here. How soon can I leave?"

Dietz smiled in a way that was less friendly than no smile at all. He raised three fingers on his right hand. "How many fingers do you see?"

"Three."

He raised the forefinger and middle finger on his left hand, while moving them moving them back and forth as if bidding goodbye. "How many now?"

"Two. I'd like to have my phone. There are people who need to know where I am."

Without replying, Dietz came around to the side of the bed and pointed a small flashlight into each of Gurney's eyes. "You've had a moderate-to-severe concussion. Although your symptoms appear minimal at the moment, within the next seven days they may grow more pronounced."

"Symptoms such as . . . ?"

"TBI post-concussive manifestations—headaches, blurred vision, dizziness, loss of memory, fatigue, insomnia, nausea, irritability."

"Traumatic brain injury?"

Dietz responded with the slightest nod, eyeing Gurney coldly. "A police officer needs to take a statement from you regarding the events surrounding your injury. Are you willing to provide a statement at this time?"

"No problem. However, I would like my phone."

Dietz headed out of the room. He didn't look back.

Gurney's eyelids grew heavy. After a few moments, they drifted shut.

The skaters returned. Their circling became dizzying. He tried to turn away from them but found that he couldn't. The swooshing of their skates grew sharper, like knives on sandpaper.

He blinked and was back in the ICU. A man in a blue shirt was pushing a portable table from the corner of the room toward the bed. The man had a sandy-brown crew cut, a pale face, and a dark blue tie. He positioned the table a short distance from the bed and swiped a finger several times across a device Gurney couldn't see. The man smiled in a way that could be confused with a facial twitch.

"Mr. Gurney?"

"Yes?"

"Dale Magnussen, New York State Police Bureau of Criminal Investigation. I'm documenting the incident you were involved in earlier today on the Blackmore Mountain road."

"Glad to hear it."

Magnussen stared at him for a moment with the expressionless look that was as much a part of some cops as their fraternal solidarity.

"For your information, Mr. Gurney, I'm recording this interview.

We'll also be requiring a written statement as soon as you're able to provide one. Understood?"

"Yes."

"Let's start at the beginning. At the time of the incident, where were you coming from and where were you going?"

"Coming from my home in Walnut Crossing, going to Harbane."

"Was anyone else in your vehicle?"

"No."

"What was the purpose of your trip?"

After briefly considering how much it would be wise to reveal, he decided to hold back nothing. What happened to him on the mountain was clearly intentional and surely linked to his planned meeting. "I received an anonymous phone call this morning from someone offering me information on the Lenny Lerman murder case. We agreed to meet at two o'clock in the Harbane town square."

"What kind of information?"

"I was told it would exonerate Ziko Slade."

Magnussen directed his no-reaction stare first at Gurney, then down at his device on the tabletop, his jaw muscles tightening. When he resumed his line of questioning, it was with an element of distraction in his voice.

"Alright, let's . . . let's focus for now on the specifics of what happened up on Blackmore. Describe your encounter with the other driver. Step by step."

"There was no encounter with the driver, just the vehicle—a red tow truck. There was a lot of wind noise on the mountain, gusts of snow across the road. I didn't notice it until it was coming up fast behind me, very close, swinging out into the other lane, as if to pass me. That's what I assumed was happening. But then it swerved into the side of my Outback and pushed me off the road."

"Was it your impression that this was done on purpose?"

"My impression was that the truck was under control."

"Okay, so you were pushed off the road. What then?"

"I hit a tree stump at the edge of the woods."

"Then what?"

"Airbag blast."

"And then?"

"My sense of time may have been thrown off, but I'm thinking there was a gap between the shock of the airbag detonation and a slam to the side of my head."

"A gap?"

"Like there were two separate impacts. It doesn't make much sense, but that's the way I'm remembering it."

"After that second impact, what did you do then?"

"I passed out."

"Are you saying you had no contact with the other driver?"

"None."

"You never saw him?"

"No."

"Never spoke to him?"

"No. I didn't even know it was a *him*. But you obviously do. Does that mean you have him in custody?"

"We'll come back to that." Magnussen peered down at his device for a long moment before continuing. "You have a currently valid concealed-carry permit, is that correct?"

"That's correct."

"And you possess a registered Beretta pistol, is that correct?"

"That's correct."

"Do you have any other handguns—registered or unregistered?"

"No."

"Have you ever had any other handguns—registered or unregistered?"

"A Glock 9, when I was in NYPD Homicide."

"No other handguns at all?"

"None."

"Have you discharged any firearm recently for any reason?"

"No. Any chance you might want to tell me what these questions have to do with my being run off the road?"

Looking more determined than ever to communicate nothing, Magnussen picked up his device and left the room.

31

"MADDIE! FINALLY! SORRY IT TOOK ME SO LONG TO reach you. I had some difficulty getting hold of my phone. And sorry I couldn't deliver your cello."

"The concert was canceled. What happened? Where are you?"

"Up in Harbane. At Parker Hospital, actually. I'm okay, but the car isn't. Another vehicle rammed into the side of it. I got a knock on the head, and they brought me here for some tests." He wanted to present the least alarming version of events that he could. The disturbing details could be held for a later conversation.

"My God, are you alright?"

"A little sore from the impact of the airbag, but that's about it. They had me in a neck brace earlier, but that's off now. They want to keep me overnight—no doubt to cover themselves legally. But at least I'm in a regular room now, getting restless. Where are you right now?"

"Halfway home from the clinic, with Gerry. You want me to do something?"

"Maybe Gerry could make a little detour and drop you off at the car rental place? The Outback may be out of commission for a while."

After a brief exchange between the two women, Madeleine said, "Any particular kind of car you want me to get?"

"Doesn't matter, so long as it has all-wheel drive."

"Can I bring you anything tonight?"

"No point in that. But I'd like to get out of here tomorrow morning. Could you manage to come and get me without screwing up your work schedule?"

"I can be there by ten. Will that be okay with the hospital?"

"I don't much care what's okay with the hospital."

"You're positive you're feeling well enough to come home?"

"I'm fine."

"You don't sound fine."

"I'm still annoyed at the attitude of the BCI investigator. And it took too damn long to get my phone back. I'll tell you more about it in the morning."

There was a brief but fraught silence. "Okay."

"Love you."

"Love you."

He checked the time—5:01 p.m. A nurse hurried past the door of his room, pushing a wheeled stand of the sort used to suspend bags of intravenous fluids.

Swiping through his phone messages, he found the one he was sure would be there. It was left by Jack Hardwick at 2:27 p.m. He played it back.

"Hey, Sherlock, you said to meet you at two o'clock in the town square. It's now half past. I'm standing here in a goddamn sleet storm. Where the fuck are you?"

Gurney returned the call, got Hardwick's voicemail, and left him a quick summary of what happened. Swiping through his phone messages again, he could find none from the potential informant regarding his failure to appear.

He eased himself off the bed and made his way to the bathroom. A few minutes later, he gingerly lowered himself into one of the two chairs in his room. The seat back felt cold through the open back of his hospital gown. He tried turning his head from side to side and discovered that this was an exercise that would be better postponed. He shifted his chair so he could see through the room's single window without moving his head.

Dusk had descended into darkness, and the parking lot floodlights had come on. Big snowflakes were floating past the window. He listened to the murmur of voices out at the nursing station, the bell-like *dings* of patient monitors, the muffled comings and goings of various contraptions in the hallway, a groan, an odd burst of laughter. His eyes drifted shut.

The ringing of his phone roused him from a dream that evaporated without a trace as he opened his eyes. The phone was on the edge of the bed. He just managed to reach it from his chair, his neck muscles rebelling at the effort. A glance at the screen told him it was Hardwick.

"Hello, Jack. Sorry about the Harbane inconvenience."

"Damn near froze my balls off. But even if you came, it wouldn't have mattered. Whoever you were supposed to meet never showed up. You found out yet who rammed you?"

"No. And the BCI guy who interviewed me was being weirdly cagey about it."

"Who'd they put on it?"

It took Gurney a moment to recall the name. "Dale Magnussen. Do you know him?"

"Not personally, but I know the guy he reports to—one of the few people in that organization I got along with. What do you mean by 'weirdly cagey'?"

"Like he knew something I didn't, and he wanted to keep it that way."

"Could just be an attitude. Lot of them fuckers have attitudes."

Gurney almost laughed out loud. It was Hardwick's authority-be-damned attitude that had ended his state police career.

"I got the impression he thought I knew who the other driver was. And he wanted to know how many guns I owned. Makes me wonder what the hell's going on."

"You suggesting in your subtle way that I should do your snooping for you?"

"Only if the peculiarity of the situation interests you."

"Peculiarity is not a major motivator in my life. But if you—"

Gurney's attention was distracted by a nurse's voice in the hallway.

"This is his room. You can go right in."

He looked over and saw Madeleine in the doorway.

"Jack, I have a visitor. I'll get back to you."

As Madeleine came closer to him, the concern in her eyes increased. "You look . . . awful."

"I thought you were coming tomorrow morning."

"There's no way I could sleep tonight without seeing you first."

"Sorry if I alarmed you that much on the phone."

"What alarmed me was how hard you were trying not to. You had that minimizing strain in your voice. It's a sound I've gotten very familiar with. You always make little of the bad things that—"

He interrupted her. "I'm basically alright. Bit of a knock on the head, that's all."

"That's exactly what I mean. Your face is pale, your eyes are glassy, I saw you wince with pain when you turned your head toward the door. So, you're not 'alright' at all."

"Look, I've had a mild concussion, I didn't want to make a big deal out of it."

"When you pretend that everything's fine, I get the impression that you just want to keep doing what you're doing and you'd rather not think about the costs."

"Or maybe I'm just trying to save you from unnecessary worry."

"By lying to me?"

"Oh, Christ, it's not lying, it's a simple matter of perspective." An arrow of pain shot through his head, causing a split-second grimace.

Madeleine's expression switched from anger to fear. She took a quick step closer to his chair. "Should I call a nurse?"

"No need. I get these little jabs, but they pass as quickly as they come. Part of the territory with this sort of injury."

Madeleine stood gazing down at him. The anger and fear had morphed into something softer. "Is there anything I can get for you?"

"I just want to go home."

There was a brief silence, broken by Madeleine. "Have the police caught the driver who sideswiped you?"

"They haven't told me a damn thing."

"I hope they get him and put him in prison for a good long time."

"Fine with me."

"Your eyelids are drooping."

"All of a sudden . . . I'm sleepy."

HE WAS AWAKENED by a rapping on his open door.

A sharp-featured woman in a fashionable leather jacket and pricey-looking jeans stepped into the room. Having seen her before only in conservative business attire, it took him a few seconds to recognize District Attorney Cam Stryker. She gave him a chilly once-over.

"I've been told you're in good enough condition to talk. Do you agree?"

"I do."

"Good."

She moved an empty chair to a position facing Gurney's, settled into it, and took out her phone. She tapped it several times and placed it on a small rolling table near her chair. "Everything said from now on will be recorded. Understood?"

"Understood."

She smiled with all the warmth of a predatory fish. "So, David, I'd like to hear the full story of what happened on Blackmore Mountain."

"Apart from someone running me off the road?"

"Let's start with the reason you were there."

"As I already told Investigator Magnussen, I was on my way to meet someone who claimed to have information that would exonerate Ziko Slade."

"And who might this individual be?"

"I don't know."

"You thought it worth driving over a mountain in a snowstorm to meet someone who wouldn't give you their name?"

"Yes."

"Why?"

"Because I have doubts about Slade's guilt."

She let out a harsh one-syllable laugh. "Because of that business with the rabbit?"

"Scott Derlick told you about that?"

"He told me that you were at the lodge with Slade's creepy pal, and that you tried to turn a dead rabbit into a major crisis."

"Not just dead. Decapitated. Placed in the front seat of my car, as I was looking into the decapitation death of Lenny Lerman. You'd have to be willfully blind not to see a connection."

Stryker's anger at the accusation was evident in the tightening of her jaw muscles.

"The placement of that mutilated animal in my vehicle should have been viewed as a threat. The failure of the Rexton police to investigate it, and the failure—"

"Stop right there! I'm not interested in your opinion of the Rexton police. I want to know exactly what happened this afternoon on Blackmore Mountain."

"What happened on Blackmore Mountain is a direct escalation of the rabbit incident—a second warning to me to back away from the Lerman case. Whoever ran me off that road was sending a clear message—if not actually trying to kill me. Now, please answer a simple question. Do you have the driver in custody?"

"*Do we have him in custody?* That's what you want to know?" She stared at him, anger mixed with disbelief. "Tell me the last thing you remember happening on that mountain."

He repeated what he'd told the BCI investigator.

"That's it?" said Stryker, leaning forward. "Hit the stump, knock on the head, lights out? No further recollection?"

"What am I supposed to be recollecting? And why the hell was Magnussen asking me how many guns I own?"

"The other driver is dead. Shot in the head. The evidence indicates you were the shooter."

"*What?!*"

"No memory of that?"

"It's absurd!"

"So, you're claiming to have zero recollection of the shooting?"

"I didn't shoot anyone. I have nothing to recollect."

"The gun found in your hand says you did."

"What gun?"

"A .38 special with the serial number filed off."

"Christ, Cam, this reeks of a setup."

"Our gunshot-residue test says you fired it."

He spoke as calmly as he could with adrenaline flooding his brain. "Don't you see it's an obvious frame job? Someone doesn't want me looking into the Lerman case. The rabbit warning didn't stop me, so now I'm being framed for a homicide—just like Slade was. Think about that."

She leaned forward again in her chair.

"A smooth defense attorney might be able to spin your notion of a setup—for which there is zero evidence—into enough 'reasonable doubt' to get you a hung jury and a lifetime of retrials. But I wouldn't bet on it if I were you."

"What's your point?"

She lowered her voice. "I'm going to be under tremendous pressure to arrest and charge you. Because of your police background, I'd like to postpone that decision as long as I can. Of course, the media would accuse me of giving a former cop special consideration." She paused with a pained expression.

Gurney said nothing, intrigued by where this was leading.

"Should I charge you immediately in this apparent road-rage homicide? Or can I justify leaving that option open, pending further investigation?" Her expression suggested that the dilemma was giving her stomach cramps. "I'm an elected official. Some people with political ambitions would love to use this situation to damage me." She paused, as if to let the magnitude of the political risk sink in.

She inched her chair closer to his, her earnest tone undermined by the coldness in her eyes. "I can't fight battles on two fronts at the same time. If you make the Slade conviction a matter of public controversy, then my focus will be split between defending that verdict and defending a decision to let you remain free. Of course, the simplest course of action would be to arrest you immediately—an option the evidence supports, but which, out of respect for your NYPD career, I would prefer to delay. I may be able to defend that delay—but only if that's the *only* media battle I have to contend with. Do you understand my position?"

"I do."

"It's essential that you have zero contact with the media. It that understood?"

"Understood."

"Crucially, you are to make no public comments regarding the Slade case."

"Understood."

"The final condition is that you must remain in Walnut Crossing for the duration of the Blackmore investigation. If you violate any of these restrictions, I'll have no option other than to arrest and charge you, based on the current evidence. Is that clear?"

"It is."

She sat back in her chair, evidently pleased with his apparent acquiescence.

"I'm glad we understand each other. Any questions?"

"Were you able to ID the driver you're claiming I shot?"

"Yes."

"Did he have a record?"

"Yes."

"For what?"

"Assault, among other things."

"Can you tell me his name?"

She eyed him with an odd combination of skepticism and curiosity.

"Leonard Lerman Jr.," she said finally. "Also known as Sonny Lerman."

PART III

CONSPIRACY

32

WEATHER IN THE CATSKILLS WAS ALWAYS UNPREDICTABLE
and especially so in the late fall, when a morning's blue sky could
disappear behind an afternoon's sleet storm. That seemed to be the
direction of things now—at 11:05 a.m.—as Madeleine drove him
home from Parker Hospital.

He decided earlier that morning that full disclosure, problem-
atic as that might be, was the only reasonable way forward with
Madeleine, and so he spent most of their drive filling her in on everything he could remember about the "incident"—plus his own position as prime suspect in the shooting death of Sonny Lerman.

After expressing outrage that Cam Stryker could suggest such a
thing, she'd fallen silent and remained that way until they were close
to Walnut Crossing. Then, gazing straight ahead, she began to speak.

"I know I encouraged you to take a look at the Slade case as a
favor to Emma. I imagined you'd review the evidence, discover the
flaws, and write a report. Like a radiologist would study X-rays and
provide an opinion without coming into contact with the patient.
Stupid of me to think you could keep it at arm's length. Even now,
with all that's happened, you don't want to drop it, do you?"

"Stryker sure as hell wants me to." He paused while a high-
pitched ringing in his ears grew louder and then subsided like the
passing of siren, fading into a low-level tinnitus. "She's holding a

murder charge over my head to make me stop looking into it. She's scared to death I'll discover something that'll kick the political ladder out from under her."

"You didn't answer my question."

"About dropping the case? If no one cared whether I did or not, I might be willing to."

"But someone trying to kill you on Blackmore Mountain, then ending up with a bullet in his own head, and the DA threatening to arrest you for murder if you don't back away . . . that adds up to an irresistible attraction?"

He didn't reply. His tinnitus was creeping back up in volume. His eyelids were growing heavy, and soon all he could see were the skaters circling on the frozen pond.

AN ABRUPT CHANGE in momentum awakened him. Blinking to clear his vision, he saw that the car had come to a stop between the asparagus patch and the side door of the house. Snow was falling. Madeleine was looking at him with evident concern.

"Are you alright?"

He winced as he turned to unfasten his seat belt. "Just a sore neck."

He tried rotating his shoulders and discovered that wasn't a good idea either.

"Shall I give you a hand?"

"I'm fine." As if to prove his point, he got out of the car a bit too energetically and nearly fell before regaining his balance and making his way into the house.

She was close behind him. When they reached the kitchen, she asked if she could get him anything.

He shook his head. "I need to make some phone calls. I'm fine, really. My problem is maybe a three out of ten."

Her lips tightened. "I don't think that's true. Not physically, not emotionally, certainly not legally. The idea that Stryker might prosecute you for murder is terrifying. On a scale of one to ten, that's an eleven!"

He put his hand on the sink island to steady himself. "I don't know how serious she is about that. All I'm sure of is that she wants me off the Slade case."

Madeleine's distress seemed to deepen. "Just like Sonny Lerman running you off that mountain road."

"Probably. But that wouldn't explain his getting shot. That's where I get lost. It's obvious that somebody other than Sonny is pulling the strings. Someone who talked him into doing what he did. Someone who either followed him to the spot where he rammed me or was waiting there. That's the only way what happened makes any sense to me."

Madeleine looked like she had questions she was afraid to ask. After a fraught silence, she changed the subject.

"Do you want some lunch?"

He was about to say no, not until he made a phone call—to discuss the latest developments with Jack Hardwick—but then he thought better of it. This was not the moment to abandon Madeleine to her fears.

"Sure," he said. "Good idea."

33

MADELEINE ASSEMBLED A SALAD WITH THE CONCENTRA-tion of a person struggling to keep other thoughts at bay. After bringing it to the table, she focused on arranging the plates, silverware, and napkins just so before taking her seat.

"You first," she said with a tight smile, nudging the bowl toward Gurney.

He served himself some lettuce and a chunk of avocado, but he wasn't hungry. His hospital breakfast of watery scrambled eggs, a dry muffin, and a slice of unripe melon had killed his appetite.

"We need to think about getting the shed ready," she said, gazing out through the glass doors. "For the alpacas."

That took him by surprise, not just because it seemed such a far leap from the current crisis but because the possible acquisition of a pair of alpacas hadn't been mentioned for the past six months, not since the conclusion of the Harrow Hill case.

Nothing more was said as they nibbled at the edges of their salads for another ten minutes or so. After they'd put down their forks, Madeleine cleared the table and Gurney retreated to the den, closing the door behind him. He needed to be able to speak frankly with Hardwick without Madeleine overhearing.

He settled down at his desk in a position that minimized the dull ache in his back and placed the call.

"The fuck is it now?"

"The driver of the other vehicle was Sonny Lerman."

"Son of Lenny?"

"Yep."

"Holy shit. What's his explanation for ramming you?"

"No explanation. He's dead. With a bullet in his head. After he ran me off the road, somebody shot him."

"Who told you this?"

"Stryker, last night in the hospital. She claims the gun that killed him was found in my hand, along with traces of gunshot residue."

"How'd the GSR get on you?"

"After I hit the tree stump, a blow to the side of my head put me out cold. I figure that's when the shooter hit Sonny, then held the gun in my hand and fired it a second time to deposit the residue."

Hardwick uttered a thoughtful grunt. "So, the proposed meeting in Harbane was just a way of getting you on that deserted road at that particular time."

"So it seems."

"But you're still a free man. How come?"

"Stryker told me she's proceeding slowly out of respect for my NYPD background."

"Bullshit!"

"I realize that. So, I'm thinking there might be some evidence at the scene that doesn't add up. I'd like to know whatever she knows about the vehicle that hit me. Also, did Magnussen's crew find any evidence consistent with the presence of a third party?"

"You suggesting I should just use my instant X-ray vision to look inside Stryker's head and the BCI case file?"

"Sounds good to me. Also, Magnussen had my phone for a while—which means he made a record of my calls, including the one from the guy offering to meet me in Harbane. I assume he was using an anonymous phone, but the phone company would have the originating cell tower location. If Magnussen tracked that down, I'd like to know what he found out."

"Okay," said Hardwick finally, making the word sound more threatening than compliant. "I'll risk destroying my last positive BCI relationship to apply the kind of pressure this'll take. But holy fuck-ing shit, Gurney, you are gonna owe me!"

Gurney sat for a while gazing out the den window. A snow squall had engulfed the high pasture. He could hear the faint melody of one of Madeleine's favorite string pieces coming from her upstairs prac-tice room. She must've been using her backup cello, the one she kept as a spare after acquiring a better one from a retiring member of the Glimmerglass orchestra. He explained that her newer one couldn't be retrieved from his wrecked Outback as long as BCI was treating the vehicle as part of a crime scene.

The day was barely half gone, and he was already feeling ex-hausted. Determined not to let his concussion symptoms control him, he forced himself to sit up straight, went through the Slade files on his desk, and picked out the transcript he'd been about to read the previous day before he headed for Blackmore Mountain.

The transcript was headlined "Interview with Thomas Cazo, Lerman's Supervisor at the Beer Monster." As he made his way through it, an exchange between Derlick and Cazo piqued his curiosity.

*S. Derlick: How would you describe Lenny Lerman's attitude in
the period leading up to his resignation?*

*T. Cazo: Kind of out of it for a month or so. Real quiet. Moody.
Then, all of a sudden, he's excited about his big plan. He tells me he
don't need the job no more. It's like fuck you, I'm outta here.*

It might not mean much, but that reference to Lerman being "kind
of out of it for a month or so" prior to quitting his job felt like information worth looking into. The question was who to ask about it.
Adrienne would be dealing with the shock of Sonny's death and, depending on what the police told her, perhaps a belief that Gurney had
been involved in it—making an objective conversation impossible.

So that left Cazo. As Gurney considered how to approach the
man, his gaze drifted back to the window and the swirling snowstorm. A dark bird flew wildly past the window. Hearing the den door
behind him, he turned and saw Madeleine, eyeing him anxiously.

"How are you feeling?"

"Not bad," he answered, not quite truthfully. "I heard you playing. Is the old cello okay?"

"The tone isn't great."

"We can probably retrieve your good one in another couple of
days."

"What about our car?"

"Depends on the verdict of the insurance company. I suspect
they'll total it and give us the money. We should discuss what we
want to replace it with."

She was looking through the window at the snow devils whirling
across the hillside. "I hope the hens are in their coop."

He didn't reply.

She turned to him. "Any pain?"

"Bit stiff." It was more than that, but he found it difficult to
admit being in pain. He equated pain with weakness, and that was
something he couldn't acknowledge.

She looked at his desk, covered with the case folders. "Are you
getting any closer to giving Emma your opinion of all this?"

"It's hard to tell. I'm intrigued by the odd connection between what happened at Slade's lodge last November and what happened on Blackmore Mountain yesterday."

"You mean, the murder victims being father and son?"

"Not only that, but the fact that I was set up to take the blame for the son's murder—just as Slade may have been set up to take the blame for the father's. The blackmail demand gave Slade a motive to kill Lenny, just like being rammed off the road gave me a motive to kill Sonny. But the killer's priority eludes me. Was the ultimate goal to kill both of the Lermans—or were they just collateral damage in an effort to incriminate Slade and then me?"

"The more important question is how involved you should be in any of this. It seems that people on both sides of the law want you out of it. I certainly do, the sooner the better."

Ignoring her attempt to recast the issue, he went on. "I'm convinced there's a piece missing from the puzzle, the piece that will make sense of the murders, the frame jobs, everything."

"That's magic for you, isn't it? That missing piece that promises to explain everything, regardless of the danger. And danger is part of the attraction, isn't it?"

He didn't reply. He suspected that what she said was true. He'd faced armed killers many times. The fear he felt in those moments had been matched by a sharpening of his focus, a speeding up of his reflexes. He never felt more alive than when his life was threatened.

"I think I'll scrape the snow out of the chicken run," said Madeleine in one of those abrupt changes of subject that he'd never quite gotten used to. "Before it gets too deep."

"I'll help," he insisted, rising from his chair. "The air will clear my mind."

He was halfway out of the den when his phone rang. Seeing Barstow's name on the screen, he stopped and took the call.

"I have news," she said. "About your rabbit."

"I'm listening."

"The foreign DNA on its fur was degraded. It's reliable only to the biological class level, so we can't take it down to genus or species. However, the class is somewhat surprising. *Reptilia.*"

"Reptiles?"

"Lizards and snakes—including roughly eight thousand species."

"You're saying the rabbit came in contact with that sort of . . . creature?"

"Or in contact with something that a lizard or snake had been in contact with."

"Is that something that could happen naturally in a wilderness area?"

"Theoretically yes, but unlikely. The quantity of DNA deposited on the rabbit's feet and stomach would suggest a prolonged exposure, probably in a confined space."

"What's the likely scenario?"

"It's possible that the rabbit spent some time in a herpetarium."

"That's not a word I hear every day."

"A reptile enclosure. Could be the size of a large fish tank. Or the size of the reptile house at a zoo. Or anything in between. There would be enough reptile DNA in that kind of environment to account for its presence on the rabbit."

"Okay . . . but what's the context for that situation?"

"You mean, why was the rabbit there to begin with? I would assume as food for a fairly large lizard or snake."

"Those things are fed live animals in captivity?"

"Not as a rule."

"Then why . . . ?"

"Perhaps," she said, "the owner enjoys watching."

34

STANDING THERE IN THE MIDDLE OF THE DEN, HE'D BEEN so absorbed in what Barstow was telling him that he didn't notice Madeleine watching him with growing alarm.

"What was that all about?" she asked as soon as he ended the call.

He opted for the truth—softening it only to the extent of referring to the thing merely as a dead rabbit rather than a beheaded one. He then explained the forensic work Barstow was doing and her unsettling conclusions.

"Why didn't you tell me before about the rabbit?"

"I didn't want to worry you."

"Like you didn't want to worry me when you called me from the hospital and failed to mention that the accident on Blackmore Mountain nearly killed you?"

"There are a lot of ways of describe a situation. I generally prefer the least dramatic."

"Why?"

Such a simple question, yet he had no ready answer.

"Think about it," she said on her way out of the room.

THERE WERE A number of things he was more comfortable thinking about, and the Lerman murders sat at the top of that list. He wondered if the elusive motive for those killings was one of those that accounted for virtually all premeditated murders—power, greed, lust, envy, revenge—or if it was something else, something festering in the mind of a psychopath. If the killer was indeed deranged, the ingenious setups of both murders suggested that whatever that derangement might be, it was accompanied by a cool intelligence.

The transcript of Scott Derlick's interview with Thomas Cazo— with its reference to Lenny Lerman being "out of it" for a month prior to his resignation—indicated preoccupation or depression. But Cazo's description of Lerman's attitude on the day he resigned sounded lively, feisty, optimistic. It was frustrating that Derlick had failed to probe the details of these mood changes.

Gurney found Cazo's number on the master list of trial witnesses and placed a call. He told himself that this was such a minor violation of the strictures placed on him by Stryker that he could easily find a way of explaining it in the unlikely event that it came to her attention.

The phone rang more than a dozen times before it was answered by a harried voice.

"Beer Monster."

"Thomas Cazo, please."

"He's not here."

"When will he be in?"

"Night shift."

"What time does that start?"

"What?"

"What time will Mr. Cazo be in?"

"Four, five, around there."

"Is that the time he gets in every day?"

"Except Mondays and Tuesdays he's off. You want to talk to someone else?"

"No, he's the one I need. Thank you. I appreciate your time. You sound busy."

"We're short-handed, and our only forklift's down. They should have a couple of back-ups."

"Heavy work, right?'

"Wouldn't be so bad, you know, if everybody did their share. Some people think others should do it all."

"A free ride," said Gurney sympathetically.

"But it ain't free. Somebody drops their end, somebody gets screwed with the load. So, yeah, free—on somebody else's sweat. It's bullshit, is what it is. Entitlement." He drew the word out in slow, contempt-laden syllables.

"I hear you, brother."

"What'd you say your name was?"

"Dave."

"Okay, Dave, you take care, I gotta go."

"Before you go, tell me something. Do you remember a guy who used to work there—Lenny Lerman?"

"You want to know about Lenny, talk to Cazo. I gotta go."

The line went dead.

He'd handled the transition to Lerman too abruptly, and probably shouldn't have tried it at all. Patience was a virtue Gurney needed to work on. He'd start by suppressing the urge to drive to the Beer Monster. Speed was important, but it wasn't everything. Putting off questioning Cazo for twenty-four hours would give him time to come up with the right approach and give his headache time to abate.

In the meantime, he pulled up a satellite photo of an area encompassing Walnut Crossing, Blackmore Mountain, Harbane, and the neighboring town of Scarpton on his laptop. The image was dated the previous July.

Apart from the two villages, most of the area was forested. The remainder consisted of small pastures, many of which had been abandoned to the gradual encroachment of shrubs and saplings. More than the topography itself, however, he was interested in the roads connecting Walnut Crossing with Harbane and with Scarpton. The only direct route from his home to either of those towns passed directly over Blackmore Mountain. An alternative route would have doubled his driving time. The caller had let him choose between Harbane and Scarpton to give him the illusion of being in control. Bottom line, both Harbane and Scarpton required taking the same mountain road, which solidified his belief that no actual meeting was ever intended.

Gurney manipulated the satellite photo to zoom in on the mountain and locate the spot where he'd been forced off the road. He then centered that spot on the screen and adjusted the photo coverage to include an area of one mile in every direction from that point.

His initial impression was of uninterrupted woodland on both sides of the road. Closer inspection revealed two small clearings— one about a quarter mile in from the left side of the road, the other—a little farther in the direction of Harbane—half a mile into the woods on the right side.

Zooming in first on the left-side clearing, he was able to make out a log cabin, a shed, a woodpile partly covered by a tarp, and two raised planting beds. A dirt lane through the woods connected the clearing with the road.

Shifting to the right side of the road, he zoomed in on the other clearing. It contained a larger cabin and half a dozen tent platforms with a picnic table and fire pit adjacent to each. It appeared to be a small campground. Given the current weather, it probably wasn't in use, but both sites were worth exploring.

"David, there's a van down by the barn, and someone with a camera."

Madeleine was at the den door, and her tone was an unmistakable call to action.

He closed his laptop and followed her out through the kitchen to the French doors. She pointed down past the low pasture to the area between the barn and the pond. He saw what he hadn't expected to see for at least another day or two—a van with a satellite dish on the roof and a RAM News logo on the side. Two figures in hooded parkas were standing in front of it.

The one with the camera raised it to eye level and began a slow pan around the property. The other figure lowered her parka hood, revealing a mass of blond hair. The camera operator completed the panning shot and aimed the camera at her. She made a sweeping movement of her arm up toward the house. She appeared to be speaking to the camera.

Madeleine's lips tightened. "Are you going to tell them to get off our property, or shall I do it?" She sounded eager to accept the second option.

"Not a good idea."

"Why not?"

"Because they'd like that."

"Like being told to get lost?"

"They'd be happy to engage with either one of us on video. Ideally, they'd like me to answer questions about Blackmore Mountain, but they'd settle for a shouting match over their right to be here, the people's right to know, et cetera—any contentious dispute they could

play back on their so-called news program. These people don't deliver information, they deliver conflict. That's what they sell to their
brain-dead audience. Battles boost ratings. A trip that doesn't generate a fight is a zero for them. So that what we'll give them—zero."

It was obvious from Madeleine's body language that zero conflict
in this situation was not appealing.

Gurney added, "Their next move will be to come up to the
house to badger us into responding. I'll lock the doors and we'll go
upstairs."

He watched as the blond reporter and her cameraman began to
make their way awkwardly up through the snow-covered pasture.

"That's it?" said Madeleine. "We let them have the run of our
property, pound on our doors, do whatever?"

Gurney let out a small sigh. "However frustrating it may be for
us, it'll be more frustrating for them. Trust me."

Madeleine waited while he secured the doors. After a final glare
at the intruders approaching the house, she followed him upstairs.

Soon the door-knocking began, growing more insistent as
the pair moved from the side door to the French doors and on to
the door at the rear of the house. As she progressed from door to
door, the reporter's shouted challenges increased in insinuation and
hostility.

"Mr. Gurney, we're from RAM News. Please come to the door."

"We have important questions for you. It would be in your interest to answer them."

"Come to the door. This is of vital importance."

"This is about your role in the Blackmore shooting."

"It's your chance to tell your side of the story."

"What were you doing on that mountain road?"

"How long did you know the victim?"

"Did you shoot him? Now's your chance to set the record
straight."

"Is it true you had a grudge against Sonny Lerman?"

"Are you being paid by Ziko Slade?"

"Are you the missing link between the two Lerman murders?"

"Why are you getting special treatment?"

During the onslaught, Madeleine decided to give the RAM invaders her own aggressively nonchalant response. She discreetly opened one of the second floor windows and began playing a lively Bach cello piece.

The effect of the baroque melody was both powerful and comical—the music of beauty, precision, and light, floating above the discordant merchants of conflict. There was a fierce satisfaction in Madeleine's smile as she wielded her bow like a sword.

When Gurney watched the frustrated RAM pair finally heading down to their van through the slippery pasture, he had a pleasant feeling of victory. But the victory, he suspected, was fleeting.

35

A THROBBING HEADACHE DROVE HIM TO BED SHORTLY after dinner, and he had a restless night—the headache rising and receding in waves. Several times he was on the verge of abandoning sleep altogether, but simple inertia kept him in bed. Once, as he was drifting into unconsciousness, the image of a huge green snake with red eyes jerked him awake.

Sleep finally overtook him at dawn. The longed-for oblivion was shattered by the ringing of his phone, which turned out to be either a wrong number or bad joke. An anxious voice asked if the veterinarian had anything to kill lice on a parrot.

As he was putting the phone back on the nightstand, hoping for another hour or two of sleep, it rang again. This time it was Emma Martin, her voice full of anxiety.

"Are you alright, David?"

"More or less."

"Thank God! What happened?"

"How much do you already know?"

"Just what I heard a minute ago on the Albany news station—that there was a collision and shooting on Blackmore Mountain. I wasn't paying much attention, then I heard your name mentioned, along with Sonny Lerman's. What on earth happened?"

"Good question. All I know for sure is that I was rammed off the road and whacked on the head. While I was unconscious, someone apparently shot Lerman and arranged the scene to put me in the frame for his murder."

"Dear God! I'm so sorry, David! How badly were you injured?"

"Concussion, some strained muscles. Physically, no big deal."

"Legally, it sounds like a very big deal. You should have an attorney, a good one. Whatever it costs, I'll take care of it."

"Thanks for the offer, but I'd rather deal with this myself."

"You think this is related to your investigation of the Slade case?"

"Yes."

"Then drop it. I didn't intend for you to be in any danger."

"I appreciate that. But I don't walk away from things like this. Besides, a violent effort to stop me tells me I'm making progress."

He could hear a sigh of resignation. "Please be careful. And let me know the minute you need anything."

Sure now that getting back to sleep would be impossible, he rose cautiously from the bed, noting with relief that his headache was gone. He showered, shaved, dressed, and went out to the kitchen, where he found a note from Madeleine taped to the coffee machine.

Early shift at the Crisis Center. Gerry Mirkle picked me up. Home by 3-ish. Stay in bed! Get some REST!

Rest was the last thing he wanted. After a quick breakfast of oatmeal and coffee he checked the supply of feed and water in the coop, let the hens into the fenced run, and set out in the rental car for Blackmore Mountain.

The squalls of the previous two days had passed, leaving alternating swaths of windblown snow on the farm fields—pure white under a shockingly blue sky. When he reached the mountain road, flashes of morning sun through the trees added to the brilliance of the world around him. The light made everything look so different, he was almost past the site of the "incident" before he recognized it.

He stopped for a closer look. A stump about twenty feet from the pavement with crushed wood fibers and shredded bark at bumper height assured him that this was indeed the place. Trying to align his memories, shrouded in swirling snow, with this sun-streaked scene was disorienting.

He drove on until he spotted the point on the left side of the road where the satellite photo showed a dirt lane leading into a pine thicket. As he slowed before making the turn, he heard the harsh revving of an engine from somewhere farther up the lane. He came to a stop, and a few seconds later a car came racing down the toward the road.

Gurney caught a glimpse of the driver—a gaunt young man, his face contorted in what might have been fury, as he braked the car into a swerving skid, whacking the trunk of a giant hemlock, caroming sideways out onto the pavement, and skimming the corner of Gurney's front bumper. With its rear tires squealing and exhaust pipe scraping the pavement in a shower of sparks, it hurtled away in the direction of Harbane.

Gurney made a mental note of the plate number and turned into the lane. As he reached a point that offered a partial view of the clearing ahead, a heavyset woman in a shapeless brown blouse and slacks came half running, half stumbling toward him. He stopped the car and got out.

"Did he hit you?" she cried in a panicky voice, trying to push her glasses, which were falling off, back in place. "Is he alright? Are you alright?"

"I'm fine, just got a tiny kiss on the bumper. You are . . . ?"

"What?"

"May I have your name?"

"Nora. I'm his mother. I heard a crash. Is he alright?" Her glasses were thick, magnifying her watery eyes.

"If you mean the driver of the car that went speeding out of here, I don't know anything about his condition. He hit a tree sideways, skidded out of the lane, and drove off. May I have your full name?"

"Rumsten. Nora Rumsten. Do you think he's alright?"

"I don't know, ma'am. What's your son's name?"

"Colson. It was such a loud crash. But you're alright? What about your car? Was there any damage?"

Gurney checked his bumper. There was only a slight scrape. "No big problem. Perhaps we could go up to your house?"

Pushing her glasses higher on the bridge of her nose, she looked back toward the clearing, as if to confirm the location of her house. "Yes, I guess, yes, okay."

When she didn't show any sign of moving, he pointed up the lane. "You lead the way. I'll follow."

He drove slowly behind her. When they entered the clearing, he got a ground-level view of what he'd seen the day before from the satellite's perspective. The cabin and the shed were both larger than the impression he'd gotten from the out-of-date aerial photo. A covered front porch had been appended to the cabin, and the raised planting beds with drifted snow against their sides now had the bare look of most Catskill gardens at that time of the year.

The woodpile, thirty or forty feet from the opening of the clearing, was covered with patches of windblown snow. A second woodpile, smaller and in a state of disarray, was in the process of being disassembled by a balding, gray-bearded man in rubber boots, muddy jeans, and what looked like an old Carhartt work jacket. His abrupt movements, grabbing and scattering the logs, conveyed more agitation than planning. Gurney got out of his car and joined the woman, who was pointing at the log hurler.

"Just look at him!" she cried. "That's what sent Colson flying out of here. I don't blame him, not when his father gets like this, which is too often. I mean, I'm sorry if he gave you a start, racing by you like that, but it's not all his fault, not really, not when—" She shook her head, as though the situation were beyond explaining.

She called angrily to the man assaulting the woodpile, "I hope you intend to restack that mess you're making!"

"The mess *I'm* making?" He turned toward her, holding a split log like a weapon. "The problem's the mess he made. Damn waste of my time!"

"Fact is, Bert, Colson's had another accident—thanks to you and your foul mouth!"

"The hell are you talking about?"

"You're so deaf you didn't hear the crash?"

Still holding the log, he walked toward her. "What crash?"

"He ran into a tree and grazed this gentleman's car. Colson could've been killed!"

He eyed Gurney warily. "Ran into a tree? How? Where?"

Gurney answered calmly. "End of the lane. He was driving too fast, skidded, ricocheted off the big hemlock down there, nicked my front bumper, and kept going."

Bert nodded slowly. "So . . . we're not talking about a lot of damage. Tree's no matter." He took a few steps toward Gurney's car and peered at the bumper. "Little smudge is all I see. Little polish ought to—"

His wife cut him off. "That's not the point, Bert! Temper of yours sends the boy out of here like he's been shot from a cannon. Not the first time, is it?"

He uttered a dismissive grunt. "Nothing to do with me. Not a damn thing! Running fast as he can from real life, is what it is. Boy's allergic to the right way of doing things. A contrary nature from the day he was born. Say the ocean's blue, he'll say it's black. Agree it's black, he'll say it's purple. Tell him the right way of anything, guaranteed he'll do it wrong. Screw it up on purpose."

"Did it never occur to you there might be a better way of providing guidance than calling your son a fucking idiot?"

Bert bared his discolored teeth. "Lucky that's all I called him, after the goddamn trouble he's brought us, the money he's cost us!"

She stared at him, a warning glare in her big myopic eyes.

He shook his head and wiped his mouth with a dirty red hand. Blinking and clearing his throat, he turned to Gurney with a cagey look. "So, that little affair down the road—way I see it, that's between you and Colson. Got nothing to do with us."

Gurney shrugged. "If you say so."

"He needs to take his consequences. He scratched your car, you make him pay for it. Reckless driving. Sue him. Tell him you need a new bumper. Maybe a headlight, too. Thousand dollars, minimum. Dose of reality. Pay the piper."

"Actually, that's not why I'm here."

Husband and wife both gave him blank looks.

"I'm investigating the incident that occurred down on the road the day before yesterday."

There was a flash of interest in Nora's eyes.

Her husband shook his head emphatically. "We don't know anything about that."

"But you know what I'm talking about, right?"

"The fact of it, is all. There was mention of it on the Harbane radio yesterday, something about a collision—maybe a road-rage thing? We weren't hardly listening. Nothing we can tell you. If that's what you come for, you're wasting your time."

The man's position arose either from the all-too-common fear of anything that might involve the police, or from something else. Regardless, pursuing the matter with him right then would be a mistake.

"Does your son live here?"

"He does not." Bert's denial carried an edge.

"He has his own apartment in Harbane," offered Nora with a defiant hint of pride, as though his apartment represented a significant achievement. "I can give you the address, if that would be helpful. You come to the house, and I'll make a note of it for you."

Her husband scowled at her, then turned and strode back to the wreckage of the woodpile.

Bert and Nora appeared to be one of those couples with a taste for litigating their disputes in the presence of strangers, as if points could be amassed toward some Pyrrhic victory in the ongoing battle of their marriage. Gurney suspected that offering him their son's address was Nora's way of drawing him aside to bolster her viewpoint in private. He followed her to the cabin.

She seemed disappointed that he chose to wait on the porch while she went inside. She came back out a minute later with a piece of paper with something written on it. A thin halo of frizzy hair surrounded the loosely gathered bun on the back of her head.

"Sir, I do want to apologize for Bert's behavior. Shame you had to be exposed to that. But maybe it gives you some idea of what Colson's been battered by his whole life. Bert believes there's only two ways of doing anything, his way and the wrong way. The man's got no sense of his own human frailty, you understand what I'm saying?"

"I think so."

"Colson's got potential. Talents. Smarts. But a boy needs the right kind of guidance, not getting cut down all the time by his own father." Her voice dropped to a near-whisper. "Specially now that he's come off the drugs. Any kind of stress right now . . . it could send him right back."

She paused, looking down at the paper in her hand. "Which is why I put my phone number on here alongside Colson's address. Whatever it costs to take care of that scratched bumper, I'd appreciate you letting me take care of it . . ." Her voice trailed off and she handed the paper to Gurney.

He slipped it in his pocket. "When I mentioned the incident I'm investigating—and your husband said neither of you knew anything about it—I got the impression you didn't agree with that. Am I right?"

"I just know what I heard. Bert's half deaf. But the problem's not just his ears, it's his pride. If he didn't hear something, then it plain didn't happen. Plenty of times Colson would tell him something, and Bert'd insist he never did. Call his own son a damn liar right to his face."

"Regarding that incident on the road, Nora, what was it you heard?"

"Big *smashbang* collision kind of sound. I was out here digging a storage pit for the potatoes. I said to Bert, my God, what do you suppose that was? He claimed he didn't hear a thing. I thought, if he could miss that, he'd miss the trumpets of Armageddon."

"Did you hear anything else?"

"The gunshots. On the farm back in Harbane my brothers had every kind of firearm, shooting the damn things morning, noon, and night. You get to know the sounds. What I heard was a pistol, big one, no twenty-two plinker."

Gurney gave her an admiring smile. "Sounds like you have a very good ear."

"Maybe God gave me that, knowing Bert'd have no ear at all."

"Did it sound like both shots came from the same gun?"

"Most likely. Same caliber, anyway."

"How about the timing between the shots?"

She paused, her lips pursed in concentration. "A minute. Two at the most."

"How long after the crash did you hear the first shot?"

"I'd say that was about a minute also."

"So, the first sound was the crash. A minute later, the first shot. And a minute or two after that, the second shot. Do I have that right?"

"Except the first sound wasn't the crash. The first sound was the motorbike."

"Motorbike?"

"The one that came up to the road through the woods."

"You saw it?"

"I heard it."

"When you say it came up to the road through the woods—"

"I know the sound. When one of those things is on the pavement, it's a steady whine. But in the woods, it keeps changing—loud, not loud, loud again—because the rider keeps changing the gears."

"Your brothers had motorbikes?"

She shook her head. "The kid down at the campground used to have one. Raced around all day like a lunatic. I think there was something the matter with him."

"You're talking about the campground on the downhill side of the road?"

She nodded.

"But the kid doesn't have one anymore?"

"He was the owner's kid, and he hasn't been there for a while now. Not since the owner left and brought that new woman in to manage the place. Sometimes the campers bring motorbikes with them."

"So, you heard a motorbike come up through the woods to the road before the crash. How long before?"

She shrugged. "Maybe fifteen, twenty minutes."

"And there was no sound of it leaving, until . . . when?"

"Right after the second gunshot."

"Did you consider calling the police?"

"Bert said people who stick their noses in other people's business get their noses cut off."

"Was he threatening you?"

She let out a dismissive snort. "'Course not. Bert's just a lot of noise. But I couldn't have called anyway. No landline and we don't get cell service up here. They keep saying it's coming, but it never does. I would've had to drive down to Harbane, which I couldn't do, cause Bert had the truck jacked up in the shed to change the oil, and there was the snowstorm going on. I guess I could've drove down when he was done with the oil, but . . . I didn't feel like getting into another set-to with him."

She fell silent. Tears began to well up in her magnified eyes. "He's not a bad man, you know? It's just that he's always trying to be in charge of things he's not in charge of. He's scared, really, is what it is. He's got fear of everything he can't control, and, come right down to it, Bert can't control very much."

She glanced back at the man waging his hectic war on the wood-pile. "It's sad, is what it is. I've seen men like him drink themselves to death. Leastways, Bert doesn't drink hard liquor. That's something, right?"

36

AT THE FOOT OF THE LANE, JUST PAST THE HEMLOCK whose bark had been ripped open in Colson Rumsten's flight from his father, Gurney made a left onto the road and began watching for the turnoff to the campground.

He found it almost immediately. The words BLACKMORE PINES CAMPSITES were painted in rustic letters on a sign affixed to a roadside tree. Rutted and icy, the lane leading down into the forest looked more challenging than the one to Bert and Nora Rumsten's property. Rather than taking a chance on skidding or getting his rental car stuck on the slope, he decided to park by the sign and proceed on foot.

He stepped carefully around patches of ice. His concussion had made him wary of falling. It felt like a decade had been added to his age. The lane eventually brought him down to a clearing that was more deeply shaded than the Rumstens'. The evergreens surrounding it were taller and denser. There were no planting beds here, no sun, no grass, just frozen earth and pine needles. On the left side of the clearing there was a single-story log house with a wide porch. On the right were the six tent platforms and adjoining fire pits and picnic tables that he'd seen in the aerial photo.

A blue pickup truck was parked next to the house. Somewhere out of sight a generator was humming. At the top of a tall spruce, a raucous crow was voicing what Gurney imagined to be displeasure at his presence.

As if in response to the loud caws, the door of the log house opened and a woman holding a long wooden spoon stepped onto the porch. She wore a red flannel shirt and khaki cargo pants with mud stains on the knees. Her expression, framed by a casual mop of blond hair, was quizzical but not unfriendly.

He introduced himself and explained that he was investigating the incident involving a car and a tow truck that occurred two days earlier up on Blackmore Mountain Road.

"Sorry, but there's not much I can tell you about that."

He smiled understandingly. "Anything at all would be helpful. You're obviously busy. I apologize for intruding like this, but if you could spare a moment for a few quick questions . . ."

After sizing him up, she shrugged. "I'm in the middle of concocting a sweet potato soup. If you want to come in, you can ask your questions while I stir the pot."

He followed her into the house and found himself in a multipurpose room with a stove, sink, refrigerator, and work table at the near end, a large pine dining table in the middle, and at the far end a sitting area with a leather couch and a pair of armchairs. A fire was burning in a stone fireplace behind the dining table.

As she headed for the stove, she pointed to a chair at the end of the table. "I'm Tess Larson. Have a seat. What happened to your head?"

"Something collided with it."

She began stirring the contents of a black pot on the stove. "Considering the size of the bruise, I'm surprised you're walking around."

"When things need to be done, they need to be done."

"Profound. So, what needs to be done?" She continued stirring the pot.

"We're trying to find out as much as we can about that incident up on the road—by talking to people in the area while any memories are still fresh." He knew his use of the word "we" was deceptive, since it implied that his inquiries were part of the official investigation, but it seemed justified by the fact that he intended to turn over whatever he discovered to BCI.

She turned down the gas under the pot. "I don't know how I can help you. The thing is, I wasn't actually here when it happened."

"Not *actually* here?"

She grinned. "What I mean is, I'd gone down to Harbane on a little errand of mercy, and on my way back I discovered the police had closed off this part of the road. I asked a trooper what the problem was. He said there'd been a serious traffic incident and there could be a long wait before I could get through, but when I explained that I had a visitor who might be seriously ill, he let me pass. That's all I know."

"You haven't heard any more about it since then? No news reports, nothing at all?"

She shook her head. "I have no radio, no TV, as little outside contact as possible. That's the point of my being here. Peace. Meditation. Reevaluation." She paused. "Would you like something to drink? Coffee? Tea?"

Seeing little chance of getting any useful information, he was about to refuse her offer, then on an impulse accepted it. "Coffee would be great. No milk, no sugar."

She popped a pod into a machine on the counter next to the stove, inserted a mug, and waited until, with much hissing and gurgling, the mug was filled. She brought it to Gurney and took a seat across the table from him, eyeing him with interest.

He broke the silence. "You were saying that the point of your being here is—"

"To take some time out. Escape from the hamster wheel of life. Reevaluate."

"Reevaluate what?" He hoped his tone hadn't revealed his reflexive contempt for New Age navel-gazing.

"The purpose of my life. My career. I've been a social worker for the past ten years. I have that gene—that deep-seated itch to make everyone okay, especially the ones who have the least chance of being okay. It can wear you down. At some point, if you have any sanity left, you have to back away. I saw an ad for a wilderness camp caretaker. I met with the owner, was offered the job, and took it. So here I am. In the middle of nowhere, battling the gene, which is still alive and well. In fact, it's why I wasn't here when that accident happened."

"How so?" He sipped his coffee, looking forward to the effect of the caffeine.

"I was gone because of the guy who was here that day. He arrived that morning in a big black pickup truck with a motorcycle in the back—one of those off-road things with high fenders." She shook her head. "I never cease to be amazed at how grown men can be so fond of noise and speed. Anyway, he paid fifty dollars cash for one of the campsites, then spent the rest of the morning sitting in his truck."

"Do you remember his name?"

"Jim Brown."

"You said he was the reason you weren't here?"

"About one o'clock that afternoon he knocked on my door and asked if I could go down to the drug store to pick up his angina prescription. He said he felt an attack coming on, but he'd forgotten to bring his pills with him, and he'd just called his doctor's office to have them phone in a prescription to the CVS in Harbane. He said the way he was feeling made him afraid to drive there himself. I offered to drive him—either to the drugstore or the ER—but he said someone was coming here to see him, and he had to be here when he arrived. He looked terribly anxious, which put that fixer gene of mine in high gear. I told him to lie down on the couch while I went for his medicine."

Gurney nodded, noting the leather couch at the far end of the room. "Let me guess what happened next. When you got to the CVS in Harbane, they told you they hadn't received a prescription order for anyone named Brown, and when you got back here he was gone."

She stared at Gurney, her mouth open. "How on earth . . . ?"

"Did I leave anything out?"

"Just that he left another fifty dollars on the table for my trouble, along with a note apologizing for the confusion and explaining that he'd just discovered that his doctor wasn't able to phone the prescription in, that the friend he was supposed to meet couldn't make it, and he had to leave. But . . . how did you know?"

"Long story. Do you still have that note he left for you?"

She thought about it for a moment. "I tossed it in the fireplace."

"Do you remember where his truck was parked when you set out for Harbane?"

"I can show you." She went to a row of pegs by the door, where some outdoor clothes were hanging, and slipped on a puffy blue ski jacket.

He zipped up his own jacket and followed her out across the chilly clearing to one of the tent platforms, shaded by the towering evergreens. The crow on the top of the tallest one watched in silence.

She pointed to the rutted, frosty ground next to the tent platform. "If you're looking for his tire tracks, you're in luck. He was here during that snow and sleet storm, but the temperature was barely below freezing, and the ground was still soft from the last rain. I know, because I almost got stuck on my way up to the road—on my pointless drugstore trip."

Gurney studied the ground around the platform. The cold snap had hardened the earth and preserved the tread impressions of two vehicles—one with four wheels and one with two. The motorcycle she'd seen in the visitor's truck bed had evidently been unloaded and ridden while she was in Harbane. Ridden where was the question.

Gurney guessed it was to the site of the ramming—which would square with the sequence of engine and gunshot sounds heard by Nora Rumsten. If so, it would suggest that the rider was involved in the shooting, either as triggerman or in some backup capacity. One possible scenario was that whoever shot Sonny arrived in the truck with him, and the motorcyclist's job was to get the shooter away from the scene as quickly as possible. He could also have been responsible for the blow to the head Gurney received in the moments after his collision with the stump.

Tess Larson watched as Gurney walked in a widening circle around the tent platform, intent on the tire tracks. It appeared that the motorcycle had been offloaded from the truck and ridden into an adjoining area of the forest that was free of underbrush. If the intended destination had been the ramming site, the rider had decided not to take the easy route up the lane and along the road, possibly to avoid being seen by a passing driver.

Before following the motorcycle tracks into the woods, Gurney turned to Tess. "I need you to do one more thing. Go back in the house, get a sheet of paper, relax, and take yourself back to the day before yesterday, to your meeting with Jim Brown. Take your time and write down everything you can remember about him. Physical details, mannerisms, voice, accent—anything at all, no matter how trivial it seems. Can you do that?"

"Only if you tell me what this is all about."

"What happened up the road while you were in Harbane wasn't an accident. Two vehicles collided, the occupant of one of them was shot, and I think your visitor was involved."

Her eyes widened. "You mean, that guy sent me to Harbane to get me out of the way?"

"That would be my guess."

The fear in her eyes increased. "What if I'd refused to go?"

"Not worth thinking about."

"Good lord. Alright, I'll see how much I can remember about him." She turned and went into the house.

As Gurney followed the motorcycle tracks into the woods, he wondered how long he could avoid revealing his own position in the affair. He'd led Tess Larson to believe he was part of the official police team. He wasn't comfortable with the deception, but there were moments in any investigation when expediency trumped openness.

The clear tread impressions made the route easy to follow. It extended from the campground nearly all the way up to the site of the ramming. Since the destination was far out of sight from the starting point, he concluded that the rider must have been following a route programmed into an off-road GPS. Interesting, but no big surprise. It was already obvious that everything about the attack had been carefully planned. The tread marks stopped short of the roadside, at a point in the woods where the motorcycle would have escaped the notice of any motorist who happened to be passing.

From the few remnants of yellow crime scene tape, Gurney got a sense of the area that had been cordoned off by the police. It consisted of a rough circle with a radius of forty or fifty feet, centered on the point of the collision. He noted it failed to extend far enough into the woods to encompass any evidence of the motorcycle's presence—an omission that would create a major blind spot in the BCI investigation.

He took out his phone and photographed the tire marks, adding wide-angle shots to locate them within the overall scene. He walked back down through the woods to the campground and completed his photo inventory with shots of the tire tracks left by the truck.

He had a responsibility to make the photos available to the state police or at least to inform them of the presence of the tire tracks, along with Tess Larson's story of what had transpired with her elusive visitor, but he was reluctant to do so before initiating an inquiry of his own, with the help of Kyra Barstow.

He was composing a text to accompany the photos he planned to send to her when Tess Larson emerged from the house and handed him three pencil sketches. One was of a man's face, one of a pickup truck, one of a motorcycle. She shrugged apologetically. "I'm lousy at describing things in words. I'm better at drawing."

"These are great," he said. "Is there anything you remember about this 'Jim Brown' character that wouldn't show up in your drawing?"

She frowned in concentration. "One thing, maybe. Most men tend to minimize their physical problems, especially pain, especially in the presence of a woman. In fact, I get the feeling that's what you're doing right now, probably without even thinking about it. The cautious way you move tells me you're probably a lot more uncomfortable than you're letting on. But with him, I think it was the opposite—like he wanted to appear to be in pain. I didn't think about it at the time, but now, when I picture that strained look on his face, that's what comes to mind."

"You think he was manipulating you?"

"Yes. And it makes me feel like an idiot."

37

WHEN HE GOT BACK UP TO HIS CAR, GURNEY SENT PHO-tos of the sketches Tess had given him and the tire treads to Kyra Barstow. Since the investigation of Sonny's murder fell within the jurisdiction of the NYSP and their own forensic department, Barstow had no official connection to it. He was relying on her natural curiosity, just as he had with the beheaded rabbit.

In this case, he was asking her to access a comprehensive tread database, ID the tires, link them to the various vehicles on which they would have been installed as original equipment, and see if Tess's truck and motorcycle sketches matched any of the possibilities. As for the sketch of the man who called himself Jim Brown, Gurney didn't expect anything concrete from Barstow. But since the face in the sketch likely belonged to the shooter or to an accomplice, it added an element of interest.

His next stop was the Beer Monster in Calliope Springs to talk to Thomas Cazo, Lenny Lerman's former employer. He found it mentally jarring to change focus from the son's murder to the father's. But it also felt appropriate, since he was increasingly certain the two murders were connected.

Because he had to pass through Walnut Crossing en route to Calliope Springs, he decided to stop at the house and pick up the transcript of Scott Derlick's interview with Cazo. Having the transcript of a BCI interview in hand would convey an official connection. Deceiving Cazo that way troubled him less than deceiving Tess Larson.

Halfway between Blackmore Mountain and Walnut Crossing, the crazy Catskill weather shifted. The cobalt sky disappeared behind a gray cloud mass, and by the time he parked by the asparagus patch there were snowflakes in the air. The chickens were standing perfectly still in the run, as if attentive to the altered atmosphere. Gurney hurried into the house, ferreted out the Cazo transcript from the files on his desk, got back in the car, and resumed his drive to Calliope Springs.

By the time he pulled into the parking lot in front of the aggressively plain Beer Monster building, the ever-changing sky had darkened, the breezes had become gusts, and the snowflakes were more numerous. The windowless concrete-block structure looked more like an industrial warehouse than a retail store. It wouldn't be the first business, thought Gurney, to rely on rock-bottom aesthetics to suggest rock-bottom prices.

Its strip-mall environment was hardly any cheerier. The adjoining enterprise was a lawn-and-garden nursery, closed for the season. Empty metal racks and stacked wooden pallets were surrounded by a chain-link fence, giving the place the look of an abandoned detention center.

With the transcript in his jacket pocket, Gurney got out of the car and headed for the Beer Monster's plain metal entry door. It reminded him of the doors on adult video shops.

The inside of the place reflected the same no-frills philosophy as the outside. Workers pushed hand-trucks, piled with cases of beer, through aisles that ran between tall steel shelving. Customers pushed oversized supermarket wagons, loaded with six-packs and twelve-packs. The dusty-smelling air had a sour edge. Cold, shadowless light emanated from banks of fluorescent fixtures hanging from the steelwork that supported the high ceiling. There was a steady low rumble coming from vibrations in the heating system.

It struck Gurney as a hellish place to work. If Lenny Lerman had come upon a means of escaping from this to an imagined life of ease and wealth, however perilous the route, the temptation might well have been irresistible.

As a hand-truck worker was passing by, Gurney asked him where he could find Cazo. Without stopping, the man pointed to a glassed-in office at the rear of the center aisle. When Gurney reached it, he recognized Cazo's stony features and thick-set body from the trial video. He silenced his phone and knocked on the door.

After regarding him for a long moment through the glass, Cazo pushed a button on the side of his desk. The door's lock clicked open. Gurney entered the office, which reeked of cigar smoke, and introduced himself as an investigator following up on some loose ends related to the Slade murder trial. Apart from a slight tightening of his lips, the man showed little reaction. The hostility in his small dark eyes had a chronic look.

Gurney took the transcript out of his pocket. "According to this record of your interview with Detective Scott Derlick, when he questioned you regarding Lenny Lerman's state of mind, you stated that his attitude and behavior had changed a month or so prior to his resignation."

Cazo shrugged. "So?"

"Could you describe that in more detail? How exactly did Lerman change?"

"I don't get the point. Trial's over. Slade's in the can. End of story, right?"

"Slade may be appealing the conviction. So we're double-checking everything—especially what Lerman knew about Slade and how it affected him. Those changes you saw in him could be important. Can you describe them?"

Cazo picked up a paper clip and began examining it. "He got quiet."

"Quiet?"

"Lerman liked to talk. Liked to make people think he had some juice, always saying he knew this guy, knew that guy. You'd see in the news that the feds pulled some major sting, all of a sudden Lerman knows the guy, could even be a relative. Uncle Vinnie, Uncle Joey, whatever. You listen to him, you'd think every wiseguy was his fuckin uncle."

"Then he stopped doing that?"

"Like somebody turned off his switch. Not a fuckin word for like four, five weeks. Then, all of a sudden, he comes back to life, like he'd been storing up all his bullshit, talking for the next week or two like he was connected to some guy so big he can't even say how big the guy is. Tells me he's got this hot-shit idea to shake some celebrity down for who the fuck knows how much, enough that he don't have to bust his balls here no more. So I can take the job and shove it up my ass." Cazo paused, shaking his head in amusement at such foolishness. "Big idea got the little fucker iced, right?"

"Were you surprised that it turned out that way?"

Cazo let out a whispery laugh. "Only a fuckin moron woulda been surprised."

The dead-cold look in his eyes brought to mind Marcus Thorne's interjection of the man's nickname into Slade's trial—Tommy Hooks—and its ugly meaning.

38

IN HIS CAR, GURNEY SWITCHED ON THE WIPERS TO BRUSH away the snow that had accumulated during his meeting with Cazo. He was thinking about the changes in Lenny Lerman, and the timing of those changes in relation to the dated entries in Lerman's diary. Three dates seemed significant. October 24 was the date of the diary's first entry, and it referred to the conversation between Lerman and someone named Jingo, during which he learned of an event in Slade's past that struck him as an opportunity for a blackmail scheme. The November 2 entry referred to the dinner with Sonny and Adrienne at which Lenny described the plan he intended to implement. The November 6 entry described his resignation from the Beer Monster.

That two-week stretch—beginning with his October 24 discovery of Slade's secret and ending with his November 6 resignation—aligned closely with Cazo's description of the period in which Lerman came "back to life."

However, it was the three or four weeks prior to Lerman's discovery of Slade's secret—the period during which Lerman, according to Cazo, had been uncharacteristically quiet—that now interested Gurney. Since there were no diary entries for those weeks, discovering the reason for Lerman's odd behavior at that time would require additional digging.

Remembering that he'd silenced his phone for his meeting with Cazo, he turned it back on and found two new messages. The first was from an unfamiliar name, Samantha Smollett.

The fake friendliness in her voice was like frosting on a knife. "Hello, Mr. Gurney. I hope you get this message in time. I'm Sam Smollett, producer on the top-rated RAM-TV show, *Controversial Perspectives*. Our lead segment tonight will be an examination of the Blackmore Mountain shooting, and we want our audience to hear your side of the story. This could be your best chance to confront the troubling speculations swirling around your involvement. I need to hear from you by 7:00 p.m. today at the latest. It may be the most important call you ever make. We want to hear from you. America wants to hear from you."

She ended her message with her personal phone number, repeating it three times. He didn't bother making a note of it.

The second message was from Madeleine, her tone more upbeat than it had been for a long while.

"I'll be leaving the clinic in a few minutes. Gerry Mirkle is going to drop me off at the Winklers'. They have a pair of alpacas that have just been weaned. They're six months old—the perfect age for us to adopt them. Of course, I won't do anything until we talk about it, but it sounds perfect, doesn't it? We just need to put a door on the shed and install some fencing. Dennis Winkler said we only need to enclose half an acre, maybe an acre at the most if we wanted to get a couple more after the first two. The low pasture would be perfect. There are some fence posts in the barn from when we were planning to put in a big vegetable garden. You could check and see how many we have. If you get home before I do—Deirdre Winkler said she'd drive me—take the scallops out of the freezer and get the rice cooker going. See you later."

Early in his law-enforcement career he'd become familiar with the gap between his work life and home life. Now, with the Lerman murders on one side and Madeleine's pastoral plans on the other, the gap seemed more like a canyon.

IT WAS NEARLY six when he reached the point where the town road ended and their property began. The dim light of the November dusk had faded into darkness. He parked beside the black mass of the barn, got out, and switched on his phone's flashlight app.

A spare key to the barn door was located under one of the flat rocks placed there to keep the weeds down. Inside, he was greeted by the familiar barn smell—a combination of sawn wood and faint remnants of the gasoline he had spilled the previous week, getting the snowblower ready for winter.

As he turned his phone light toward the stack of lumber where he dimly recalled storing the fence posts, another light caught his eye—a thin line of it at the base of the closed door to his tool room— the same room where a few days earlier he had found the light on and one of the windows ajar. He remembered turning the light off the last time he was in there. There was no reason for Madeleine to have been in there since, and even if she had been, she was religious about turning off lights.

He opened the door and took a good look around the room. Seeing nothing unusual or out of place, he switched off the light, locked up the barn, and returned to the car. Instead of driving immediately up to the house, he sat there for a while, pondering the peculiarity of the light. Three possible explanations occurred to him. The first was a loose wire in the fixture or in the switch. He made a mental note to check that out. The second was someone getting in through one of the barn windows, not all of which were lockable, and turning on the light as part of a nasty game aimed at disconcerting him. The third, equally troubling, was that his memory of having turned the light off the last time he was in the barn was a false memory.

He could learn to live with certain physical limitations, even episodes of pain, but mental limitations were a different matter. If he couldn't trust his perceptions and recollections . . . the very thought of that sent a shiver through him.

39

AFTER PUTTING THE RICE ON AND TAKING THE SCALLOPS out of the freezer, Gurney was at his laptop in the den. He heard the side door out by the mudroom opening and shutting.

A minute later, Madeleine came into the den, smiling.

"Thanks for getting the rice going. I'll run some water over the scallops to hurry the defrosting along. But first, I have to tell you about the alpacas. Actually, when they're young, they're called crias. They're amazing. You should see their—" She stopped, noting the expression on his face. "What's wrong?"

"Have you been in the barn recently?"

"No. Why?"

"The light in the back room was on again."

"Again?"

"A few days ago, I noticed it was on. I went in and turned it off. Then, this evening when I got home, it was on again."

"Are you saying that someone is sneaking into our barn and using the back room for something?"

"Or just turning the light on and leaving it that way."

"What on earth for?"

"Maybe to create exactly this sort of confusion."

"What sort of lunatic . . . ?" Her voice trailed off, her eyes registering the possibilities. "You think it's connected to your investigation?"

"It's possible."

She took a slow breath, her lips tightening. "I want a gun."

"There's a shotgun in the upstairs hall closet."

"I'd like to have another one for downstairs."

"I thought you hated guns."

"Not as much as I hate feeling threatened. I've had to move out of this house before, for fear of some homicidal madman you were playing cat-and-mouse with, but I'm not being driven out again. You understand?"

DINNER WAS A silent affair. Long after Madeleine cleared the dishes, Gurney remained at the table, trying to decide how to tell Cam Stryker what he'd learned from Nora Rumsten and Tess Larson without revealing the extent to which he had ignored her warning to stay away from the case.

His thoughts were interrupted by a call from Hardwick.

"Hello, Jack. You have news for me?"

"I do. If you want to know what it is, you can buy me breakfast tomorrow."

"You want to give me a hint?"

"The phrase would be 'toxic clusterfuck.' Everyone working on the Sonny Lerman case has their own personal objectives, and your best interests are not on anyone's top ten list. You want to know more, be at Dick and Della's Diner at 8:00 a.m. By the way, I saw a promo for that bullshit RAM-TV show, *Controversial Perspectives*. It's streaming live on their website at eight o'clock tonight. Those fuckers are taking a big interest in your connections to the dead Lermans. You might want to give it a look. Sweet dreams, Sherlock."

When he looked up from his phone, he saw Madeleine watching him from the sink island.

"Hardwick?" she said.

He nodded.

"And?"

"He's managed to extract some information about the Blackmore investigation. He wants to discuss it at breakfast. In the meantime, he suggested I watch a RAM-TV show tonight at eight o'clock."

Madeleine pointed at the antique Regulator clock on the kitchen wall. It was 7:45 p.m.

Fifteen minutes later, they were sitting in the den in front of Gurney's open laptop. On the screen the red and blue RAM logo exploded, the spinning shards of color flying back together to form the words CONTROVERSIAL PERSPECTIVES. Underscored by a driving drumbeat, a subtitle marched across the screen: TOUGH QUESTIONS—SHOCKING ANSWERS. Those words in turn flew off the screen, revealing the stage set of a typical TV news program. Two desks were set at a forty-five degree angle to each other, allowing the co-anchors to turn easily from the camera to each other.

A name plaque in front of the anchor on the left identified her as Tarla Hackett. A carefully constructed coif, makeup-enhanced facial contours, and predatory eyes a bit too small for her other features created the impression of a beauty-contest winner morphing into a weasel. The name plaque in front of the anchor on the right identified him as Jordan Lake. With an up-to-the-minute haircut and eyes gleaming with a shallow intensity, he reminded Gurney of a bachelor contestant on a reality show.

As the camera moved in on both anchors, he was the first to speak. "Good evening! I'm Jordan Lake."

"And I'm Tarla Hackett. Tonight on *Controversial Perspectives* we'll be taking a look at some disturbing events. What are we leading off with, Jordan?"

"At the top of my list, Tarla, is the Blackmore Mountain mystery." He turned to the camera. "At first, it looked like just another road-rage tragedy—flaring tempers leading to a collision between two vehicles, followed by a fatal shooting."

"It barely made the local news," interjected Hackett. "But now I gather there may be more to it."

"A lot more. It turns out that the two drivers weren't your typical road-rage strangers. We discovered that earlier in the week they had an argument on a street in Winston, an argument that included serious threats."

"Wow—that definitely gives it another dimension."

"The man who was murdered on Blackmore Mountain was Sonny Lerman. His father, Lenny Lerman, was murdered one year earlier, almost to the day. And get this—the driver involved in the incident with Sonny is retired NYPD detective David Gurney, who's been looking into the year-old murder of Sonny's father. Our sources tell us he's been trying to get Ziko Slade, the celebrity drug dealer convicted of killing Lenny Lerman, out of prison."

Tarla Hackett's expression tightened with disapproval. "Sounds like too many coincidences involving this retired detective."

Jordan Lake nodded. "Too many coincidences, and too many unanswered questions. Starting with, why hasn't Gurney been arrested and charged? When only two people are present and one of them is shot dead, it doesn't take a genius to figure out who the shooter was. Besides, we've been told that the murder weapon has Gurney's prints on it."

"But they haven't brought him in. So, what the heck is going on?"

"That's what we keep asking, Tarla. The state police keep referring us to the DA's office, and the DA's office keeps giving us their standard 'ongoing investigation' brush-off."

"Meanwhile Gurney is free as a bird. Any idea what his secret power is?"

"A smart detective can accumulate a lot of dirt on a lot of people. And a lot of dirt can provide a lot of leverage."

"Enough leverage to avoid a murder charge?"

"Who knows, Tarla? But that's a real possibility."

"Sounds like this could be shaping up to be the political scandal of the year. We'll be back in just a minute with some wise words from RAM's legal analyst, Maldon Albright. But first, these important announcements."

Madeleine sat glaring at the screen, her arms folded.

After a commercial touting investment opportunities that required immediate action, Lake and Hackett were back on the screen, reprising their furrowed-brow expressions of indignation at cover-ups in high places.

Hackett spoke first. "In just a moment we'll be moving along to tonight's other high-octane story, scalp cancer—the secret killer. Why is the medical establishment refusing to talk about it? But now, a final comment on the Blackmore shooting from our renowned legal and political analyst, Maldon Albright."

The video cut to a split-screen view of Hackett on one side and a fleshy-faced man who struck Gurney as an aging Ivy League frat boy on the other.

Hackett was sporting the envious smile of a climber gazing up the corporate ladder. "We appreciate your joining us, Maldon. Any insights into this baffling affair?"

Albright spoke with aristocratic disdain. "The stench of a cover-up is overwhelming. This Gurney character appears to be the missing link between the two Lerman murders, but his exact role is yet to be determined. We can safely predict that the mainstream media will prove worse than blind, and it will be up to RAM-TV to ferret out the facts and present them to America, without fear or favor. It promises to be an exciting ride."

Albright disappeared, and the video cut back Hackett and Lake at their angled desks.

"*Please*," cried Madeleine, "turn those idiots off!"

40

AT EIGHT O'CLOCK THE NEXT MORNING, GURNEY PULLED into the parking area in front of Dick and Della's Diner. He parked between Hardwick's gleaming muscle car and a pickup with a faded bumper sticker proclaiming SOCIALISTS SUCK. Hardwick sat at one of the front tables, peering at the window with tight-lipped hostility.

The old-fashioned diner was populated with an old-fashioned clientele. Hardwick—with his black leather jacket, hard-edged features, and disconcerting malamute eyes—seemed out of place in what looked like a convention of retired farmers and their flannel-shirted wives. As Gurney took a seat at the table, Hardwick was still turned toward the window, his baleful gaze fixed on a pair of flies crawling on the window glass.

He spoke without turning. "I hate those fucking things."

"My mother insisted they carried diseases. What's your problem with them?"

Hardwick's voice was stone-cold. "I don't like what they do to dead bodies. They lay their eggs in the eyes. Then the eggs hatch into fucking maggots."

Gurney said nothing.

After a while, Hardwick looked away from the window and cleared his throat in a way that sounded like a dog growling. "My father was a violent drunk. He terrorized the family. When I was sixteen, I broke his jaw. We didn't have much contact after that. A year later, my mother divorced him. After I joined the state police, I got a call from his landlord. He'd been dead on his bathroom floor for four days. Summertime. The maggots were . . . active." He shook his head in a violent motion as if to dislodge the memory, then waved to a young waitress who was delivering waffles to a nearby table.

She came over with a rosy-cheeked farm-girl smile. "What can I get for you gentlemen on this beautiful morning?"

"A flyswatter," said Hardwick.

"Excuse me?"

He pointed to the flies on the window.

"I don't think we have any swatters, but they won't bother you. They're just trying to get out." She was grimacing, clearly disturbed by the subject.

Hardwick eyed her curiously. "You have some special feeling about flies?"

"You'll think my family is weird."

"Try me."

She bent over the table and lowered her voice. "My brother kept them as pets. It drove my father nuts."

Hardwick responded with an expressionless stare.

"Miss!" A customer's voice from a few tables away hurried her off without another word.

"Fathers and sons," muttered Gurney. "It's becoming a repetitive theme. Every time I start to ignore it, it gets pushed back in my face."

"The hell are you talking about?"

"I've been thinking about Lenny and Sonny Lerman. And Ziko Slade and a young acolyte of his who considers him his father—and who hates his real father so much he won't even talk about him. Yesterday I went to interview some people up on Blackmore Mountain, and I happened to arrive at their property at the end of a father-son blow-up."

Gurney fell silent, his mind following a well-traveled groove to his own failings as a father, including the death of his four-year-old son, Danny, which he'd been reliving painfully for over twenty years.

Hardwick stared at him. "Fathers and sons? That's a *theme*?"

"It keeps coming up."

Hardwick shook his head. "Any fucking thing can remind you of any other fucking thing, if you want it to. Facts are facts. *Themes are bullshit.*"

Gurney was aware of the danger of adopting an overall belief about a case, then cherry-picking facts to support the belief. That trick of the mind was, after all, the basis of every lunatic conspiracy theory. It was time to change the subject.

"On the phone last night you called BCI's Blackmore Mountain investigation a toxic clusterfuck. Tell me more."

"It's a clusterfuck with knives out and colliding agendas."

"Can't wait to hear the details."

Before Hardwick could begin, the rosy-cheeked waitress reappeared. "Sorry, I got pulled away. What would you gentlemen like for breakfast?"

After a quick look at the menu, Hardwick ordered four fried eggs, a double portion of sausages, hash browns, and coffee. Gurney chose a western omelet, toast, and coffee. When the waitress hurried off toward the kitchen, Hardwick began.

"The source of this intel is my contact at BCI, and who the hell knows how objective he is. So bear that in mind. Best to start with Dale Magnussen, CIO on the Blackmore case. He wrote up the incident report—in which he interpreted the circumstances as a road-rage confrontation. Like most incident report writers, he's more committed to his initial impressions than he ought to be. And your big-deal NYPD reputation rubbed him the wrong way. Bottom line, he's dug in on his road-rage theory, making you the shooter."

Gurney had gotten a hostile vibe from Magnussen, so this didn't surprise him.

Hardwick continued. "Lucky for you, not everyone is on Magnussen's wavelength. The BCI evidence tech found gunpowder residue on the side of the truck that she says is consistent with the gun being fired from about six feet away, while the truck was standing still, and probably from a position higher than that of a driver seated in another car. So it seems that for you to be the shooter, you would have to have gotten out of your car after it hit the stump, walked over to the truck, shot the victim, returned to your car, and passed out in the driver's seat. An unlikely scenario."

"Its unlikelihood didn't change Magnussen's mind?"

"Assholes do not have changeable minds. But it wasn't just the tech who had doubts about the road-rage idea. Based on the angle of the bullet's path through Lerman's head, the ME agreed with the evidence tech's opinion that the shooter was probably standing next to the truck. And finally, the doctor who examined you in the hospital claimed that the location of your head injury seemed inconsistent with a frontal collision. He didn't say someone must have sandbagged you from the side after you hit the stump, but that would seem to follow from what he did say."

Gurney was absorbing this with a cautious sense of relief. "That's consistent with what I learned from two women who live near the scene." He went on to relate what Nora Rumsten told him about the motorcycle and gunshot sounds and what Tess Larson told him about the visitor who left motorcycle tracks up to the shooting site after sending her off on a phony errand.

"So," he concluded, "it seems that Stryker's case against me isn't all that strong."

"Not in a logical sense, but that doesn't mean shit, Sherlock. According to my BCI guy, Stryker's a wild card—with enough brains and ambition to be dangerous. She'll view any development in the Blackmore case that could raise questions about the Slade case an existential threat to her career. That conviction was a rare big-time success in a county where crime mostly consists of drunks pissing in public. If she sees you as any threat at all to her hot-shit new rep, she'll be looking for ways to cut your dick off."

Gurney's sense of relief was fading.

Hardwick went on. "Before I forget, I did get answers to a couple of things you asked about. The tow truck that smashed into you was reported stolen that same day. It's registered to an LLC called Top Star Auto Salvage, owned by a Charlene Vesco. And the call you got to set up the meeting in Harbane came from a prepaid phone—from which no other calls were made, before or since. Plus, there's an interesting little geographical echo. The salvage company's address and the phone call's origination cell tower are both within a mile of a specialty food store owned by Bruno Lanka. And they're all located in the grimy little town of Garville, just this side of Albany." He paused. "You don't look surprised."

"I'm not."

"Because these details fit into a giant blueprint in your head?"

"More like each little piece is starting to form a picture."

"Yeah, well, watch out how you arrange those little pieces. Or the big picture could be totally fucked up."

Gurney said nothing. He was used to Hardwick's cynicism. Besides, the man had a point. In the ensuing silence the rosy-cheeked waitress brought them their breakfast orders. She transferred the items quickly from her serving tray to the table and left.

Halfway through his omelet, Gurney's appetite waned. He laid his fork down on his plate and pushed the plate an inch away.

Hardwick eyed him curiously. "What aren't you telling me?"

"Madeleine wants me to drop the case."

"Could be a sign that it's time to bail."

Hardwick wasn't often on the same page as Madeleine, and Gurney's surprise showed.

"You serious?"

"What the hell are you chasing after, anyway? The real murderer of Lenny Lerman? The real murderer of Sonny Lerman? Vindication for that slimebag Ziko Slade? Suppose you get Slade out of the can—and it turns out he chopped off Lerman's head after all?"

"What's your point, Jack?"

"My point is that you're charging full speed ahead without a clue as to where the fuck you're going or who you're chasing. And you're stirring up some poisonous shit along the way. The headless rabbit, a bash on the head, a crude effort to frame you for murder, an unhappy wife, a pissed-off DA, and fuck only knows what's next."

"So?"

"So, maybe the smart move would be to drop the whole fucking thing and walk away."

41

THE SKY WAS THAT PIERCING BLUE THAT SOMETIMES AC-companies a frigid autumn day, and the morning sun glistened on the dew in the farm fields, but Gurney hardly noticed. After leaving

Dick and Della's, he could focus on little beyond Hardwick's final comment.

Even though he'd unearthed some facts that appeared significant, he wasn't much closer to understanding the Lerman murders. Someone was trying to stop his inquiries, but the reason was less clear. He'd been assuming it was to keep him from discovering something that would exonerate Ziko Slade, but what if he was wrong about that?

His thoughts were interrupted by his phone. The name on the screen was A. Lerman. He pulled onto the shoulder and answered.

"Gurney here."

"What the hell is going on?" There was a sharp quaver in her voice, the sound of someone crying angry tears.

"Adrienne?"

"Did you . . . kill my brother?"

"No, Adrienne, I didn't kill your brother."

"Tell me what happened! Tell me the truth!"

"I'll tell you everything I know, but I'd rather do it face-to-face."

"Why can't you tell me now?"

He spoke as calmly as he could. "Someone attacked me on Blackmore Mountain. Probably the same person who killed Sonny. Your own life may be in danger right now. We need to talk, but I don't think the phone is a good way to do it. Are you at work?"

"No. I couldn't work. I couldn't . . ." Her voice trailed off.

"Are you at home?"

"Yes." The word was barely audible.

He glanced at the time on his dashboard—9:20 a.m.

"I can be there by a quarter past ten."

COMING INTO THE main street of Winston, he noted an antique shop he'd missed on his previous trip—the Flying Turtle—another genuflection to the god of rural cuteness.

Three minutes later, as he was climbing the steps of the rhododendron-shaded porch of the big Victorian on Moray Court, he received a call from Kyle. He let it go to voicemail and silenced his phone. He pressed the bell for apartment B, and a few seconds later the door buzzed open. The now-familiar litter box odor greeted him. It grew stronger as he climbed to the second floor.

Adrienne met him at the landing and led him into the kitchen with the cat-motif wallpaper where they'd spoken on his previous visit. Her battered but determined optimism seemed to have suffered a fatal blow. There was a new hopelessness in the downturned corners of her mouth. After they'd taken their seats, she wiped tears from her eyes.

"Tell me," she said in a strained voice. "Tell me what happened."

"What have the police already told you?"

She shook her head. "All they did was ask questions. About Sonny. About you. They asked, did you and Sonny argue? What about? How long did you know each other? Did he plan to meet you the day he was killed? How well did I know you? On and on like that, and they wouldn't tell me a single thing about my brother's death. It was like they were interviewing a stranger. They told me nothing, except he'd been shot and found dead in a tow truck on Blackmore Mountain, and that you were involved. It made no sense. All they wanted to talk about was you! Then, last night, that RAM program! Saying you were there, on the mountain. There was a gun. Fingerprints. A big cover-up. What are they talking about? For God's sake, *I want to know what happened to my brother!*"

"So do I, Adrienne."

"Were you really there?"

"I was there, but I was unconscious. I was on my way to Harbane to meet someone who'd promised to give me information about your father's murder. As I was driving over the mountain, a tow truck ran me off the road—into a tree stump. I was knocked unconscious. I didn't know Sonny had been shot until a detective told me later in the hospital."

"Was Sonny driving the truck?"

"He was found in the driver's seat, but that may have been a setup. I believe at least one other person was at the scene. I'm trying to find out who that was."

He turned on his phone, brought up Tess Larson's sketch of her visitor, and showed it to Adrienne. "Does that face look familiar to you?"

She peered at it with a desperate intentness that faded to disappointment. She shook her head and wiped her eyes again. "You don't seem to know any more about Sonny's death than I do."

"I'm trying to get to the truth of it. And you can help me."

She shook her head again. "I never knew anything about Sonny's comings and goings, who he hung around with, nothing. We weren't close."

Her reaction reminded Gurney that the pain of losing a relationship that hadn't lived up to one's hopes could be worse than losing a satisfying one. Regret over what might have been was probably the most painful of all emotions.

"Actually," he said gently, "it's not Sonny I want to ask you about. I'm sure what happened on Blackmore Mountain is connected to your father's murder. If I can get to the bottom of what happened to your father at Ziko Slade's lodge, I think what happened to your brother will be clearer."

Seeing a hint of curiosity in her sad eyes, he continued. "The prosecutor's understanding of why your father was at the lodge came mainly from comments he'd made to you and Sonny, along with entries he made in a diary. But the diary only covers the period from his learning about something in Slade's past to his setting out for the lodge. Had he ever kept a diary before?"

Adrienne shook her head. "I don't think I ever saw him writing anything except lists of things he wanted me to get at the store."

"But you're sure that was his handwriting on the diary pages you saw at the trial?"

She nodded. "That was his messy little scrawl, alright. His

writing was like a little kid's." Her voice had become shaky. She took a paper napkin from a holder on the table and dabbed at her eyes.

"When we met before, you told me that your father admired gangsters and sometimes hinted at having a connection to a big one."

She nodded.

"When your brother was trying to scare me off the first time I came here, he claimed to have that same sort of connection. Do you have any idea who that mob figure might be?"

"Not really. I used to wonder if it was all made up. Dad mainly talked about it when he had too much to drink. And Sonny would say it to threaten people."

"Did either of them ever mention a name?"

She shook her head. "If you want, I could ask some of my cousins. If this person was related to our family, they might know about it."

"That could be very helpful. Now, there's one more thing. When we spoke on the phone a few days ago, I asked if you could remember anything unusual about your father's behavior in the weeks leading up to his trip to the lodge. Has anything come to mind?"

"Not really. He didn't do anything unusual, nothing I was aware of. But for a while, he did seem depressed. He could be moody, so I didn't think much of it at the time."

"But it was noticeable enough that you can still recall it a year later. Why is that?"

"It may have been a little different from his other down moods. I think maybe it lasted longer and ended more abruptly than the others."

She paused, as if straining to see into a foggy past. "Now that you're making me think about it, it was like he was hit with some big problem, then a month or so later the idea of getting a load of money from Ziko Slade seemed to solve it. Do you think that's important?"

"I think it might be."

Adrienne looked suddenly exhausted, the red blotches on her face more pronounced.

"When will they release Sonny's body? I have to make arrangements for his funeral."

"You should hear from them soon. Maybe today or tomorrow."

She nodded vaguely. "I'm used to people dying. That's what hospice nursing is all about. Dying is natural. But being killed . . . that's horrible."

"Yes," said Gurney gently, "I know."

"It makes it worse when the police won't tell you anything. As if everything about my brother belongs to them, and I have no right to know anything."

He could see in the movement of her eyes her mind going from frustration to frustration, feelings of fury and sadness contending with each other. His own mind kept returning to her father's abrupt depression and its later reversal. What sort of problem did Lenny Lerman have that he hoped to solve by blackmailing Ziko Slade?

Gurney had a frisson-producing suspicion that the solution to both Lerman murders would lie in the answer to that question.

42

HE WAS DRIVING THROUGH FROST-COVERED CORNFIELDS a few miles out of Winston when he remembered Kyle's call. He pulled over into the grassy edge of a pasture.

Checking his phone, he saw that he'd also gotten a call from Kyra Barstow. He chose Barstow first, which said something about his priorities that made him uncomfortable, but not uncomfortable enough to switch the order.

Her message was brief but promising. "I have answers to your questions. Call me."

Kyle's message was more substantive. "Hey, Dad. Got a question for you. Kim Corazon is here in the city, visiting her mom. She called me this morning about getting together. I was wondering, would it be okay for me to bring her up to your place on Thanksgiving? If that would stir up ugly memories of the Good Shepherd case, and you'd rather I didn't bring her, I'd understand completely. If you have any qualms, just say so, and I'll come alone. Totally up to you. Love you. See you soon."

Gurney didn't think much of Kim Corazon or her insatiable quest for journalistic stardom. Kyle had been involved in an on-and-off relationship with her for a couple of years—"on" when it was convenient for her and "off" when a shiny career opportunity pulled her in another direction.

He called Kyle, got his voicemail, and said, with a conspicuous lack of enthusiasm, that bringing Kim on Thanksgiving would be fine.

Then he called Barstow, who picked up right away, her lilting West Indian accent more pronounced than it had been in her terse message.

"Some good news, David. Regarding the truck and motorcycle tread photos you sent me, the database ID'd the tires, along with several vehicles on which they were factory-installed. Then the truck and the motorcycle sketches you sent me narrowed the possibilities to one truck and one motorcycle—a Ford-150 pickup manufactured between 2014 and 2019, and a Moto Guzzi trail bike manufactured between 2002 and 2012."

As she spoke, Gurney entered the information in a notebook app on his phone.

"I also made progress with the reptile DNA on your rabbit. I pushed the analysis a little further and narrowed the possibilities down to several snake families, all quite dangerous, each in their own way."

"When you say, 'each in their own way' . . . ?"

"Each of these snake groups has a distinctive aggressive weapon. They fall into two broad categories—venom and constriction."

"Constriction, as in boa constrictor?"

"Boa constrictors, anacondas, pythons, to name a few."

"And the venom category would include rattlesnakes, copperheads, et cetera?"

"Exactly. The *et cetera*, by the way, would include some species far more dangerous than rattlesnakes or copperheads."

HALFWAY FROM WINSTON to Walnut Crossing, Gurney passed a billboard with a circle of red, white, and blue stars surrounding these words:

FREEDOMLAND

GUNS AND AMMO

NEXT RIGHT

With Madeleine's demand for a gun in the back of his mind, along with his own feeling that it might be a good idea to have a second shotgun in the house, he made the indicated right onto a dirt road that brought him through a patch of evergreen woods to a single-story building in a small clearing. Its wood facade, wide porch, and flat roof reminded him of a western-movie saloon. A smaller version of the roadside billboard stood on the roof, with the words "ERSKINE STOPPARD PROPRIETOR" in place of "NEXT RIGHT."

Gurney pulled up in front of the porch. There was only one other vehicle in sight, a tan military-style Humvee with a LIVE FREE OR DIE bumper sticker.

When Gurney entered the store, the first things he noted, after the mixed odor of old wood and insecticide, were the security cameras—half a dozen of them, positioned to cover every inch of the place.

Free-standing shelf units displaying camping gear, first-aid kits, water purifying devices, flashlights, and beef jerky occupied the center of the space. Beyond them, a glass-topped counter ran across the width of the store. Signs along the wall behind the counter segmented it into areas of interest: HUNTING, TARGET SHOOTING, PERSONAL SECURITY, and HOME DEFENSE.

In the Home Defense area, a short, dark-bearded customer was conferring with a tall, white-haired clerk behind the counter.

"I hear what you're saying, Hedley," the clerk said. "I know it can seem like a tough decision, what with the different advantages. The AR-10's going to give you more down-range knock-down power. The AR-15 can't quite match that, but I personally find it to be a sweeter-handling weapon—lighter, smaller, more manageable all around. Higher fire rate, too, and less recoil."

The customer nodded. "I kinda like that down-range capability with the AR-10."

"Lot of folks do, Hedley. More power, flatter trajectory, bigger impact. Those are fine qualities. I have a suggestion for you, what a lot of smart folks 'round here have done. Get yourself one of each."

The customer uttered a thoughtful grunt.

"You give that some serious thought, Hedley, while I see to this other gentleman." The clerk moved along the counter to the Hunting end where Gurney was standing.

"Yes, sir, how can I help you?" He had a smiling mouth and assessing eyes.

"I'm looking for a simple, short-barrel, pump-action shotgun."

"No surprise. Folks are snapping them up fast as I can get them. I've got some Mossbergs and Remingtons on backorder, but if you're in a hurry, I've got some darn nice used ones." He reached under the counter for a printed sheet and handed it to Gurney. "That's our pre-owned inventory. Lot of them like brand new. Take a minute now, see if there's something there that interests you. I'll finish with this other gentleman and be right back."

As Gurney looked over the list, the clerk resumed his sales pitch at the other end of the counter. "You see the sense of what I'm saying, Hedley? You get them both, you got all your situations covered, a hundred percent. That's peace of mind. And I just happen to have one of each in stock right now. Wouldn't be surprised if they're both gone by tomorrow—what with the news coverage of that business up on Blackmore."

"You talking about the road-rage shooting?"

"What I'm talking about is how once again the pansy-ass gun

haters will all be shouting about how we need more laws and less guns—and the thing is, whenever they start that crap about taking away our rifles and handguns, our sales go through the roof. Right through the goddamn roof, Hedley. Smart thing for you right now would be to pick up this pair of ARs while you can."

Hedley cast a nervous glance in Gurney's direction, looked around the store, and lowered his voice. "What kind of background check you got to do?"

The clerk smiled the smile of a successful salesman. "I wouldn't worry too much about that, Hedley. See, that system only applies to official sales through this licensed establishment here. If the official system isn't right for you, we can work out a transaction as private individuals. I've always considered background checks an invasion of privacy, and I hate conducting them. Forces me to act as an unpaid agent of the state. It's socialism, is what it is. Now you just wait here a minute while I see to this other fellow."

He approached Gurney. "Some real nice firearms on that list. You'd hardly know they were ever used. Which ones would you like to see?"

"Hard to decide right now. I need to give the matter more thought."

The man's smile faded, and Gurney departed.

There were, in fact, a couple of shotguns on the list that might have addressed the need, but he was less than eager to deal with anyone at that establishment.

When he returned to his car, he took out his phone to check for gun stores within a twenty-five-mile radius of Walnut Crossing. He found half a dozen and was about to get in touch with the nearest when the phone rang. The screen said the call was from C. Stryker. Rather than taking the call, he waited for her to leave a message.

Her voice was icily formal. "David Gurney, this is District Attorney Stryker. Your attendance is required in my office tomorrow at 10:00 a.m. to determine your status in the matter of the Blackmore

Mountain homicide. If you choose to be accompanied by counsel, please arrive by 9:45 a.m."

Listening to her message a second time, he was struck by two things. One, it had no legal force, and two, by her tone and choice of words, she was trying to make it sound like it did. His conclusion was that she'd seen RAM's *Controversial Perspectives* program, and it had left her anxious and angry. Still, skipping the meeting would be a pointless provocation, so he needed to prepare for it. That meant gathering as much information as he could as quickly as he could. He called Jack Hardwick.

"The fuck do you want now, Sherlock?"

"I'm meeting with Stryker in the morning, and the more I can find out before then, the better. I'm thinking Garville might be a good starting point. It's where the tow truck came from, it's where the call that set me up for the Blackmore attack came from, and it's where Bruno Lanka's store is located—which makes it the place that links the two Lerman murders."

"How the hell does it do that?"

"The bullshit phone call I got promised me information about Lenny's murder. Then the route to get the information put me in the frame for Sonny's murder."

"Shit, Gurney, that way of putting it sounds like a major connection, but it doesn't tell us fuck-all about what actually connects the two murders. And how does Bruno Lanka fit into it, besides being the guy who found Lenny's body?"

Gurney sighed. "I'm not sure, but Lanka's role has gnawed at me from the beginning. Why didn't he testify at Slade's trial? In murder trials, the prosecutor generally puts the person who found the body on the stand to describe the discovery. It's a natural first step in the narrative and juries love it. But Stryker skipped it and had the CIO describe the scene instead. How come?"

"Maybe Lanka looks shady?"

"Or maybe he *is* shady. I mean, she was willing to put 'Tommy

Hooks' Cazo on the stand, which makes me wonder what made Lanka too big a risk."

"You think if we pay him a visit he's going to confess his sins?"

"No, but it might be interesting to rattle his cage."

"Cage rattling is fun, so long as you don't get kicked in the balls while you're doing it."

"I'd also like to drop in on whoever runs Top Star Auto Salvage, see if we can get a sense of their moral principles."

Hardwick uttered a contemptuous grunt. "You're saying we should take a two-hour drive to some shithole town near Albany and annoy some potentially dangerous scumbags?"

"Something like that."

"So, instead of taking my heartfelt advice that this might be the ideal time for you to walk away from this goddamn mess, you've decided to double down?"

"I just want to turn over a few more rocks. See what's there."

"And the worst that could happen is one of the annoyed scumbags shoots us. Sounds fucking irresistible. Mind if I bring my Glock?"

"I was going to suggest it."

43

GURNEY AND HARDWICK MET IN THE PARKING LOT OF A Home Depot adjacent to the interstate and proceeded from there in Gurney's rental car to Top Star Auto Salvage on the scruffy outskirts of Garville.

The sprawling automotive junkyard was surrounded by a razor wire–topped fence. An industrial gate stood open to the street. Wind gusts raised eddies of dust from the bare ground between the gate and a large travel trailer—the only office-like structure in a landscape of derelict vehicles.

Hardwick got out of the car first, stretched his thickly muscled neck from side to side, and spat on the street. Despite the icy gusts, which he seemed not to notice, he wore only a light windbreaker over his shoulder-holstered Glock.

A demented-looking pit bull made a straining, snarling appearance at the end of a rusty chain attached to the corner of the trailer. Staying outside the radius of the chain's arc, they approached the trailer. The door opened abruptly, and a large, heavy-jawed woman in a pink track suit filled the doorframe. She eyed them with bored hostility.

Gurney spoke first.

"Charlene Vesco?"

"What do you want?" She had the hoarseness of a lifelong smoker and the yellow skin that went with it.

He answered loudly enough to be heard over the barking of the pit bull. "We're following up on a statement you made to Detective Magnussen regarding the theft of your tow truck."

"When do we get it back?"

"That's up to Magnussen. Right now we need to ask you about your security system."

"It's all in my statement."

"We double-check everything. Tell me what you told him."

She looked like she was about to refuse, then thought better of it. "There was a short-circuit in the system is what my electrician said, so the cameras didn't pick up anything. That's it."

"How about the key for the truck? Where was that?"

"Right here in the office, where it always is. When I came in that day, the truck was gone, but the key was still here. There's other ways to start a vehicle. Look, the point is, we need the truck back. My lawyer says you got no right to keep it."

"Did you know Sonny Lerman?"

"The guy that got shot?"

"Right."

She shook her head.

"How about his name? Did you ever hear it anywhere other than on the news?"

"No."

"How about Lenny Lerman?"

"Who?"

"Lenny Lerman. Father of Sonny Lerman. Also murdered. One year ago."

"Never heard of him."

"Never?"

"Look, if you don't mind, I got things to do."

"Where was the truck parked when it was taken?"

She pointed. "Right there on the street, in front of the gate."

"You don't keep it in here at night?"

"Not always."

Gurney turned to Hardwick. "Any questions for Ms. Vesco?"

Jack pointed at the pit bull. "Where was that fucking dog the night the truck was taken?"

Something shifted in her eyes. "In the doghouse."

"Where's that?"

She pointed to the end of the trailer where the chain was attached. "Around that side."

"And he didn't go batshit crazy when some stranger was stealing your truck?"

"I don't know what he did. I'm not here at night."

"Too bad. You might have been able to save your truck."

She didn't reply.

Gurney smiled. "Thank you for your time, Ms. Vesco."

He led the way back to the car as the door of the trailer closed firmly behind them.

Hardwick sucked at his teeth. "She's a lying sack of shit."

"No surprise. How about we pay a visit to Lanka's Specialty Foods?"

THE BUSINESS DISTRICT of Garville had a morose look about it, due in part to the soot-darkened brick facades of the buildings.

Lanka's Specialty Foods was located on a side street off the main avenue. Gurney pulled into the "Customers Only" parking lot next to the single-story building.

"If Lanka's here," said Gurney, "I'll use a following-up-on-the-Slade-trial approach and see where it takes us. You should come in a few minutes after me and keep an eye on what's happening between me and Lanka, assuming he's here."

"You mean I should save your sorry ass if the situation goes south?"

Gurney got out of the car and walked around to the front of the building. The first thing he noted was the sign on the door indicating the limited hours the store was open—from noon to four, weekdays only. When he pushed the door open, a bell rang in the rear of the store.

The ornamental tin ceiling, incandescent lighting fixtures, and wooden shelving belonged to a past era. There didn't seem to be any customers in the place, no clerk at the checkout counter, no visible employees anywhere.

The shelves were filled with canned specialty items, mostly imported. No prices were shown. There was a fine coating of dust over everything. The walls above the shelves were covered with large sepia prints depicting the store's history.

The only contemporary intrusions were security cameras mounted high on the walls at the ends of the aisles. At the rear of the store there was an old-fashioned butcher case of white enameled steel and heavy glass panels. It was empty. On the wall above it was a print showing two burly men in butcher aprons, one with gray hair, one with black hair. The resemblance between them and their age difference suggested a father and son.

A door opened in the wall beneath the photograph, and a lean, dark-haired man in a black silk shirt stepped out into the space behind the butcher case.

"You want something?"

"Just admiring that picture up there."

The man said nothing.

"Would that be Bruno Lanka and his father?"

"Who are you?"

"David Gurney."

"You want something?"

"I'd like to speak to Bruno."

"He's not here." The man's voice was as expressionless as his eyes.

"Do you know when he will be?"

"Maybe later, maybe tomorrow. Why?"

"I'd like to speak to him."

"About what?"

"A private matter."

"What should I tell him?"

"Tell him the Lenny Lerman murder case is being reinvestigated."

The man said nothing.

"Tell him it's being reinvestigated in connection with the Sonny Lerman case."

The man remained perfectly motionless, as if on the verge of a sudden tactical decision. His attention shifted to the far end of the aisle.

Gurney glanced back and saw Hardwick standing there, his fingers just inside the open front of his windbreaker, a dangerous glint in those ice-blue eyes.

NEITHER GURNEY NOR Hardwick said anything until they left the parking lot and turned onto the road that led out of Garville in the direction of Walnut Crossing.

"That place is obviously a fucking front for something," said Hardwick.

Gurney nodded. "Meaning Lanka's political connections are strong enough that he doesn't have to worry about how obvious it is. And the guy behind the butcher case was not your average grocery store employee. The second I saw him I recognized him."

"You know that little creep?"

"He's the guy in the sketch Tess Larson gave me. Or his twin brother."

44

AFTER DROPPING HARDWICK OFF AT THE HOME DEPOT parking lot, Gurney drove home.

He stopped at the barn before going up to the house. Wielding a sharp-tined rake as a potential weapon, he checked the interior. Satisfied that there was nothing amiss and the lights were off, he continued up to the house.

Madeleine was by the coop, carrying an armful of loose straw from an open bale into the attached shed. As he headed over to her, he noticed their shotgun leaning against the side of the coop a few feet from the straw bale.

Emerging from the shed, she followed his gaze to the gun.

"I wanted it within reach," she said.

"You sure you know how to use it?"

"You went through all that with me years ago. And I got a refresher course this morning. Amazing what you can find on YouTube. So, yes, I know how to use it. And I will, if I have to."

She gathered another armful of straw and strode back into the shed.

He followed her as far as the doorway. "What's the objective here?"

"Coziness."

"For the alpacas?"

"Who else?

"Can I help?"

She looked surprised. "If you want, you can carry the straw in, and I'll smooth it out."

"Okay. I just have to go into the house for a minute, and I'll be right back."

She nodded, her surprise fading.

After using the bathroom, he decided to take a quick look at his email.

The one that grabbed his attention was from Cam Stryker. It seemed to be a word-for-word reiteration of the message he'd gotten from her earlier. He read it again, convinced that it was driven by fear and anger, powerlessness masquerading as power. But being in a legally dubious position didn't mean she couldn't create serious trouble for him.

He'd need to marshal every available fact for his meeting with her. He sat down at his desk and began putting his discoveries in order, starting with the recollections of Nora Rumsten.

IT WASN'T UNTIL he and Madeleine were in bed that night that he remembered his promise to help with the straw. She hadn't mentioned his forgetfulness—not even at dinner, when problems and irritations were often aired. But her silence was troubling.

For their first couple of years in Walnut Crossing, their conflicting expectations of what life there would be like had led to an undercurrent of tension, centering on his involvement in murder investigations. She'd been hoping for a clean break from the fraught experience of being the wife of a homicide cop. Instead, she'd watched him being drawn into a series of cases as dangerous as any in his city career.

What followed was a kind of quiet accommodation—which felt like a welcome development. But now, lying awake in the middle of a moonless night, a bleaker interpretation crept into his mind— the specter of his parents' marriage. There were no pitched battles between them. In fact, there was hardly anything at all between them. Perhaps the lack of explosive disagreements between him and Madeleine was a warning sign that his marriage was moving in that same empty direction.

He was reminded of a question a therapist had asked him decades earlier, at the brink of his divorce from his first wife: "What do you think is the key ingredient of a good marriage?"

He'd responded with a list of possibilities: love, patience, tolerance, kindness, generosity, forgiveness. The therapist agreed that those were desirable attributes, but the essential one was missing, one without which a marriage would always be flawed: partnership. He went on to say that most people weren't really looking for a partner. They were looking for an assistant, or a parent, or a possession.

As Gurney lay there in the darkness, uneasily pondering the nature of partnership, coyotes began howling in the woods above the high pasture.

45

GURNEY PULLED INTO THE PARKING LOT OF THE COUNTY office building at 9:55 the following morning.

The structure was a product of 1960s institutional architecture—relentlessly rectangular, joyless, and cheap. The Office of the District Attorney occupied a prime corner of the main floor. At 9:59 he opened the frosted-glass door and stepped into a reception area whose gray carpet, beige walls, and overly bright lighting echoed the building's aggressive plainness.

Along the left wall there was a row of uncomfortable-looking Danish-modern chairs. Along the right wall there were two partially enclosed cubicles. In the rear wall there were three frosted-glass doors. On the center one were the words DISTRICT ATTORNEY. There was a desk next to it, occupied by a woman with the etched frown of a gatekeeper vigilant for the arrival of trouble.

"Can I help you?"

"David Gurney for Cam Stryker."

She gestured toward the chairs against the wall. "Wait there."

Several minutes later, her phone rang. She picked it up, listened for a moment, and looked over at Gurney. "The district attorney will see you now."

Stryker's office was no more welcoming than the reception room. The perfunctory smile on her face was equally chilly.

"Have a seat." It was more a command than an invitation.

He settled into one of the two chairs facing her nearly bare desk.

"So," she said, steepling her fingers in front of her chin, "what did you think of RAM's treatment of the Blackmore affair?"

He shrugged. "Irresponsible and unsurprising. What did you think of it?"

"I thought it was devastating to you personally. The pressure on me to have you arrested is growing by the minute. Albright's reference to 'the stench of a cover-up' is being quoted in all the upstate news sites. It's political poison!"

Gurney was tempted to point out that arresting the wrong person could be even more poisonous, but he said nothing.

"As bad as the cover-up claim is, even worse was his suggestion that the two Lerman murders are connected. That's something RAM will be pursuing with a vengeance. And they'll be pressuring you to help them create that connection."

"Don't worry about my cooperating with RAM. That's not going to happen. But you do need to look into the relationship between those murders. They're definitely linked."

"Goddamnit, David! There's no evidence for that! None! Lenny Lerman tried to blackmail Slade, and Slade killed him. End of story. As for Sonny Lerman, he was killed in a totally unrelated confrontation, for which you are the prime suspect—a fact you seem to be ignoring."

Gurney sighed. "Cam, you know damn well there's evidence that points away from me in the direction of a third party." He went on to add what he'd learned during his trip to Blackmore Mountain—beginning with Nora Rumsten's recollection of hearing a motorcycle before and after two shots being fired.

"The first shot was the one that killed Sonny. The second was fired into the air with someone holding the gun in my hand to get my prints on it and the powder residue on my skin."

Stryker waved her hand. "That's wild conjecture, based on easily misinterpreted sounds some woman in the woods claims she heard."

"Except that a second woman had a visitor that day with a motorcycle, and its tire tracks show that it was ridden from her campground to the crime scene."

Stryker frowned, leafing through a file folder on her desk until she found the page she was looking for. "This campground woman you're talking about—would that be Tess Larson?"

"Yes."

"The trooper's report I have here says that he questioned her at a roadblock regarding what she might have seen or heard in connection with the incident that occurred half an hour earlier on Blackmore Mountain Road. He ended the interview when he determined that she had no knowledge of the incident, being down in Harbane at the time it occurred."

Stryker closed the folder and gave Gurney a questioning look.

"The fact is, she has more knowledge of the situation than she realized at the time. If the trooper had mentioned there'd been a shooting, she might have put two and two together."

"What the hell are you talking about?"

After explaining the circumstances surrounding Tess Larson's trip to the Harbane CVS and her visitor's absence when she returned, Gurney described his discovery of the truck and motorcycle tire tracks. "I have photos of those tracks, as well as sketches Larson made of the man and his vehicles. I can give them to you right now."

Her voice was as unrevealing as her expression. "It would be appropriate for you to turn over all relevant material in your possession."

He took out his phone, selected the photo files, and sent them to her cell number. Moments later a muted chime announced the arrival of the files on her phone. She swiped slowly through the photos, making an obvious effort to appear unimpressed.

"All this proves is that you've ignored the terms of our agreement."

"What agreement?"

"That I would endeavor, out of respect for your background, not to rush to judgment regarding your role in the Lerman shooting; and that you, in turn, would refrain from any disruptive investigations into the Lerman cases. You've been violating the letter and the spirit of that understanding."

"Self-preservation is a powerful motivator."

"Your behavior calls for your arrest. You call that *self-preservation*?"

"Someone's been playing an intimidating game with the light in my barn—letting me know how vulnerable I am. And how vulnerable my wife is."

"Sounds unpleasant," said Stryker without a speck of concern. "But I don't see the connection to what we're discussing."

"I already told you about a headless rabbit being placed in my car, and—"

Stryker cut him off. "Another irrelevant event. Is that it?"

"Hardly. The Blackmore Mountain setup was an obvious effort to stop my investigation of Lenny Lerman's murder by framing me for the murder of his son. You'd have to be blind not to see a pattern in those events."

Stryker's rigid gaze was fixed on her desktop. "Apparently it hasn't occurred to you that the events that you believe were designed to make you back away from the case may have a different purpose altogether."

"Such as?"

"Every one of these supposed 'warnings' has had the *actual* effect of making you pursue your inquiries with increasing determination. If those events have any relevance at all, you may be looking at them backward. Their real purpose may be to motivate you."

"That's quite a creative interpretation."

"Call it whatever you want. But it's possible you're being played for a fool by someone who wants you to stir up confusion about Slade's conviction."

Gurney smiled. "If the case against him is solid as you say, why on earth would someone want me to stir up confusion?"

"Obviously, to create controversy. You're not just anyone, David. Your reputation gives you weight. I can see headlines like 'Top NYPD Detective Challenges Outcome of Slade Trial.'"

Gurney shook his head. "But what would the endgame be? If there's ultimately no fire under the smoke—"

Stryker's anger broke through the forced calmness in her voice. "The endgame would be to embarrass me politically! People focus on controversy, not on its legitimacy. Next year, when I'm up for reelection, they'll be thinking, 'Oh, yeah, Stryker, she's the one behind that questionable conviction.' That kind of thing ends political careers."

"You're actually suggesting that someone put a decapitated rabbit in my car as part of some complicated plot to obstruct your reelection?"

She fixed Gurney with an unblinking stare. "Politics is a blood sport, David. Don't underestimate what some people might be willing to do."

He said nothing.

She seemed pleased by his silence. She relaxed, just a little. "So we understand each other, let me make this perfectly clear. As a condition of your freedom during the investigation of the Blackmore homicide, you are to remain in Walnut Crossing, unless I specifically request your presence in this office. You are to have no contact with anyone connected to the Slade case or the Blackmore case. Break this agreement, and you'll regret it for the rest of your life."

46

GURNEY SAT FOR A WHILE IN THE COUNTY OFFICE BUILD-ing parking lot, reviewing his meeting with Stryker, trying to sift the truth from the nonsense. He saw no way that the crime scene evidence, in light of the information provided by Nora Rumsten and

Tess Larson, could be used to justify his arrest. The sense of relief that provided, however, was diluted by the discovery that Stryker's sharp mind was warped by paranoia. One of her comments was particularly unsettling: *Don't underestimate what some people might be willing to do.* It was clear that *some people* included her.

He had intended to tell her about the peculiar atmosphere of Bruno Lanka's store and his impression that the store's sole visible employee was the same man who sent Tess Larson on a fabricated mission to Harbane. But her burst of irrationality stopped him cold.

He was sure now that there were aspects of the investigation better kept to himself. That thought reminded him that his Beretta was still being held by BCI, presumably as evidence connected to a crime scene. Retrieving it should eventually be a simple matter, but he had no faith it would be quick. He needed to get a replacement ASAP.

He reentered the county office building, located the county pistol clerk, and went through the process of securing an approval card for the purchase of a new sidearm. At the end of the brief bureaucratic transaction, the clerk smiled and said, "Have a nice Thanksgiving."

The reminder that the holiday was upon them, plus concerns that had been intensified by Stryker, made it seem like a good idea to get in touch with Kyle immediately and suggest postponing his visit.

As soon as he was back in his car, he called Kyle. Expecting it to go to voicemail, he was surprised to hear a live voice.

"Hey, Dad, what's up?"

"I'm having some second thoughts about your coming up this week for Thanksgiving."

"How come?"

"It's kind of a dangerous time, because of a case I'm involved in."

"You still have to eat dinner, right?"

"True. But the situation here has become risky. It's not something I want you to be exposed to."

"Are you and Maddie leaving town?"

"As far as I know, we'll be staying put. On high alert, though, eyes wide open."

"If it's safe enough for you and Maddie, then it's safe enough for me."

"But what about Kim? It wouldn't be right to put her—"

"Into a risky situation? She's a crime reporter. She's in danger all the time."

Gurney took a different tack. "I thought you guys broke up."

"We did. Four times, five times. But we keep reconnecting. We're not living together, no commitments, just seeing each other."

"Sounds like the definition of insanity—doing the same thing over and over and expecting different results."

"I'm not claiming it makes sense. It's a magnetic thing, this incredible energy she has. She's off-the-charts ambitious, which ends up pushing us apart, but then I get pulled back in. I know she's pretty selfish, that she wants what she wants and she doesn't care how she gets it. I know all that. But her energy, it's like something wild inside her."

"That's what keeps pulling you back in?"

"Exactly. Maybe I have a secret fantasy of taming her. Somehow maintaining all that energy but getting rid of the selfish part."

Gurney was tempted to point out that such a fantasy would lead to endless frustration. But all he offered was a mildly sarcastic "Good luck with that."

"Yeah . . . well, anyway . . . about Thanksgiving. If I told Kim you didn't want us to come because there was an element of risk, she'd burst out laughing. And then she'd be pissed. Besides, if I have to wait until there's no danger in your life to see you, I'll never see you at all. It's been too long as it is. Hey, sorry, one of my law professors is calling. She's almost impossible to get hold of, and I really have to talk to her. Love you, Dad! See you Thursday!"

Gurney said nothing. He realized he'd been outmaneuvered. And Thanksgiving dinner was shaping up to be . . . interesting.

THERE WAS A sporting goods store in a mall less than a mile from the county office building. Gurney stopped to purchase a gun. Less than twenty minutes after he entered the store, he left with his new sidearm—a Glock 19; his preferred Beretta could be ordered, but the clerk couldn't promise a delivery date—a shoulder holster, and two boxes of 9mm ammo.

Before setting out again for Walnut Crossing, he called Madeleine to see if she wanted anything from the supermarket on his way home. She didn't. She'd already gone shopping and had gotten, in addition to the basic necessities, all the ingredients for their Thanksgiving dinner.

"By the way," she added, "I invited Gerry Mirkle to join us."

He suspected that she'd invited Gerry as a kind of distraction from the presence of Kim, whom she'd never liked.

"Is that a problem?" she asked.

"No problem at all. The more the merrier."

After ending the call, he sat gazing at the comings and goings in the sporting goods store parking lot, his mind on the potential personality conflicts at the upcoming dinner, on Kyle's somewhat unsettling portrait of Kim Corazon, on the Gerry Mirkle wild card, and on the unquantifiable possibility of danger—which brought him back to the two Lerman murders.

That in turn reminded him of a conversation he'd been meaning to have. He scrolled through his contact list until he found Rebecca Holdenfield, the high-profile forensic psychologist with whom he'd worked on several murder cases.

Her left a message.

"Becca, this is Dave Gurney, with a request. I'd love to have your opinion of a recent trial—*NY State v. Z. Slade*. You can see the video in the *Murder on Trial* section of the RAM website. I'm hoping you'll be able to find the time to take a look and tell me what you think of the evidence, attorneys, witnesses, and Slade himself."

He avoided any promises of being forever in her debt—knowing they would only irritate her. She was one of those individuals who valued both honesty and brevity.

———

HE WAS PARKING in his usual spot by the mudroom door when Madeleine emerged with their shotgun in one hand and retractable measuring tape in the other.

"I want to measure the opening in the shed, so we can start making the door," she explained as he was getting out of the car.

He nodded, shifting his mind from his Lerman-Slade-Stryker problems to the simplicities of carpentry. "I'll give you a hand in a minute. I just need to take care of something."

He gathered his purchases from the front seat and brought them into the house and on into the bedroom. He opened the pistol and ammunition boxes and loaded the Glock magazine with the legal maximum of eight rounds. He took off his jacket, strapped on his new shoulder holster, slipped the gun in place, and put his jacket back on. The Glock, he decided, would remain on his person or within easy reach until there was no longer any cause for concern.

On his way through the kitchen, he picked up a pad and pencil to take down the doorway measurements. He found Madeleine out at the shed on her toes, trying to hold the metal tape steady across the top of the door opening. The shotgun was resting on a nearby straw bale.

He made some suggestions for successive placements of the tape, then jotted down the numbers Madeleine called out.

"Okay," she said after the final measurement, "time to make the door."

He hadn't planned to spend the afternoon that way but, craving some balance between his two worlds, he agreed. With a satisfied smile she picked up the shotgun, and they walked together down to the barn.

Gurney performed a careful inspection, first of the perimeter, then the interior, with particular attention to the partitioned room that housed the woodworking equipment they'd be using—equipment that came with the property but which he'd rarely taken advantage of—a table saw, chop saw, planer, power sander, jointer, and router.

From one of the equipment cabinets he retrieved a drill, screws, clamps, exterior wood glue, outdoor paint, and brushes. From the lumber stacked along the barn's sidewall he chose the best two-by-fours and a sheet of furniture-grade plywood.

Four hours later, they were able to step back and admire the product of their labor—a solid door with perfect ninety-degree corners, painted bright yellow and equipped with a black iron latch and matching hinges.

They carried it up through the pasture to the shed, positioning it in the opening to check for fit. Satisfied that it was ready to be installed, they decided to delay that tricky step until the following morning. It was getting dark, and it wasn't the sort of job to be done with flashlights.

Their joint achievement cast a pleasant glow over dinner and the rest of the evening, including an earlier-than-usual retreat to their bedroom.

Later, as Gurney was drifting off to sleep, his phone rang. He picked it up from the night table, where he'd placed it next to his new Glock. The name on the screen was Rebecca Holdenfield. He assumed with a pang of disappointment that her rapid response meant that she was calling to let him know she wouldn't have time to review the video. He took the call in the den to avoid disturbing Madeleine.

As usual, Holdenfield got to the point immediately. "You're in luck. The outfit I'm consulting with is closed for Thanksgiving week. I was able to spend the afternoon and evening viewing the trial. So, what do you want to know?"

He settled into his desk chair. "For starters, what was your impression of the evidence?"

"Vivid facts, nicely strung together. Nothing a jury would find difficult to swallow."

"How about the prosecutor?"

"Smart, controlled, brittle."

"Brittle?"

"Could crack under pressure. Or explode."

"And Marcus Thorne?"

"Clever, careless, self-important. Coasting on the glory of past victories."

"How about the witnesses?"

"Nothing unusual in the ones I saw. No signs of prevarication."

"*The ones you saw*? Meaning what?"

"A likely witness was missing."

"Bruno Lanka?"

"Having him describe his experience of finding the body would have been a natural way to engage the jury. I felt like I was looking at a group photo with a face cropped out."

"How about Ziko Slade?"

"Ah, yes, Ziko. The interesting one. Like a Buddhist who'd achieved satori. Startling disconnect with the monster the prosecutor was describing."

"Which Ziko would you say is the real one?"

"Difficult question. What I saw *in* him was the opposite of what was said *about* him."

"Do you think he killed Lenny Lerman?"

Holdenfield paused before answering, a rarity with her. "My impression was that he was baffled by the evidence that seemed to prove he did."

"So, the guilty verdict was . . . ?"

"A reasonable response to the prosecution narrative . . . but possibly a mistake."

47

HOLDENFIELD'S COMMENTS KEPT GURNEY AWAKE INTO the wee hours of the following morning, not because they surprised him, but because they reinforced what he was already inclined to believe. He decided to make a return trip to Garville later that day for a closer look at Bruno Lanka's store and the man in Tess Larson's sketch.

He finally fell asleep in the gray light of dawn, only to wake up an hour later with a dull headache and a stiff neck. He eased himself out of bed, swallowed a couple of ibuprofens, and took a long, soothing shower. By the time he'd shaved, dressed, and made his way out to the kitchen, the headache had faded. Madeleine, waiting for the coffee machine to warm up, appeared to be her energetic morning self.

"I don't start at the clinic until ten," she announced cheerily, "so we'll have plenty of time to install the shed door."

With his focus on the Garville excursion, he'd forgotten about the door, but he chose not to mention either of those facts.

After breakfast, while Madeleine dealt with the dishes, he strapped on his Glock and went down to the barn for the mounting screws, the power driver, and the shims and clamps that would hold the door in place while the hinge flanges were attached to the opening. He brought the necessary materials up to the shed, where Madeleine was waiting, her work gloves on.

Half an hour later, the job was completed. The door's position in the opening required no hinge-shimming or other adjustments, confirming that the abutting surfaces were plumb and level. It gave him a simple sense of closure that the murkier work of homicide investigations rarely did.

Gerry Mirkle picked Madeleine up at nine thirty, and Gurney departed for his two-hour drive to Garville at nine forty-five, aiming to arrive just before Lanka's store opened. Most of the trip was on the interstate where, despite the speed limit being sixty-five, it seemed that everyone had set their cruise control at seventy.

The passing landscape was made up of rolling hills, farm fields, and patches of evergreen woods on slopes too steep for cultivation. This pastoral expanse gave way to a flatter, more populated area as he entered the suburbs of Albany. One sight jarred him briefly out of his contemplation of Bruno Lanka—a dead deer on the shoulder of the highway, legs extending stiffly out from the body in rigor mortis. Vultures circled overhead.

From time to time, a sight like this—a deer, a dog, a possum— along the edge of a road touched something in him that he'd learned to suppress at the sight of a human victim. But stifled emotions have a way of coming to the surface, and a dead creature lying alone in a cold, hard place could sometimes bring him close to tears.

His route to Lanka's Specialty Foods took him through the grungy outskirts of Garville and past Top Star Auto Salvage. He slowed down, noting that the red tow truck had been returned by BCI. It was parked inside the fenced compound next to the trailer- office. He could see the scrapes on the truck's side, incurred during its collision with his Outback.

He drove into the center of town, turned onto the side street where Lanka's store was located, and chose a parking spot half a block past it from which he could observe the store's front door and the entrance to its parking lot in his rearview mirrors.

He had no specific expectations nor any firm plan. He knew from experience that stakeouts were open-ended exercises in patience and improvisation. He tilted his seat back into a semi-reclining position and adjusted his inside and outside mirrors. The dashboard clock said it was 11:49 a.m.

Twelve noon came and went without anyone arriving to open the store. During the next half hour, a Garville police cruiser drove by three times—particularly noticeable, since there was so little traffic on that street. When the cruiser appeared a fourth time, it came to a stop behind him.

After two or three minutes, during which he assumed that his plate number was being being run through the system for outstanding tickets or warrants, a uniformed cop emerged from the cruiser and approached Gurney's window. He had the shoulders and neck of a bodybuilder. His mouth was set in an approximation of a polite smile. The plastic ID tag on his jacket said his name was Gavin Horst.

"Good afternoon, sir. May I see your license and registration?"

Rather than questioning the reason for the inquiry, he handed over his license and the auto rental agreement, and the cop returned to the cruiser. In his mirror Gurney could see that he was making a phone call rather than checking the license on the in-car computer. After ending the phone call, the cop returned with Gurney's documents. The smile was gone. "So, where are you coming from today, sir?"

"Walnut Crossing."

"And where are you heading?"

"Just here, then back to Walnut Crossing."

"You drove all that way just to park on this street?"

"I'm waiting for Lanka's Specialty Foods to open. Any idea when that might happen?"

"You came all the way from Walnut Crossing to buy something in that store?"

"Right."

"That's a long drive."

"Interesting store. Unusual merchandise."

The cop nodded slowly, sucked at his teeth, and handed Gurney his documents. "Store's not open today. You're wasting your time."

"Shame. I was hoping to meet Mr. Lanka."

"Why is that?"

"A private matter. Do you know him?"

The cop's artificial smile reappeared. "Like I said, you're wasting your time. Be a good idea to move on. You have a nice day." He returned to his cruiser and sat there, watching, as Gurney pulled out of his parking space.

At the end of the block, where Gurney was about to make a turn that would take him back to the main avenue, a black Cadillac SUV drove by in the oncoming lane. He caught only a brief glimpse of the driver, but he recognized him as the unpleasant character he encountered in his last visit and the subject of Tess Larson's sketch. In his side mirror, he could see the receding license plate, as the SUV turned into the store's parking lot. He made a note of it on his phone.

Once he was out of Garville and back on the interstate, he pulled into the first rest area and placed a call to Hardwick.

"Yeah?"

"The Garville situation just got more interesting. I had an odd little dance with a cop there, Gavin Horst, who's probably on Lanka's payroll."

"The fuck were you doing there anyway?"

"Watching Lanka's place of business. I was curious to see who might show up. And guess what. A black Escalade turned into the street as I was being chased away—driven by the same character we saw yesterday in the store."

"Piece of dirt, in my humble opinion."

"I agree. So, I'll give you the Escalade's plate number, and maybe your guy at BCI could run it though the system. Be nice to know who owns it—along with any other vehicles linked to the same name."

"Any particular reason my guy would want to do that?"

Gurney gave that some thought before answering, as a convoy of ten-wheelers roared past the rest area.

"If one of those other vehicles turns out to be a Moto Guzzi trail bike, he could get credit for solving the Blackmore Mountain murder case. Plus, he might get to embarrass someone on the case he doesn't like, maybe someone who zeroed in on the wrong suspect. Or he might just have a natural hunger for the truth."

"Only natural hunger that fucker has is for women half his age. But the idea of sticking it to a fellow officer might appeal to him."

"If he's willing to check out the Escalade owner for other registered vehicles, maybe he could be encouraged to run a similar check on the tow truck owner, Charlene Vesco. Be nice to know how she might fit into the big picture."

Hardwick let out a harsh one-syllable laugh. "The big picture being some yet-to-be-concocted grand theory that ties Sonny's murder to Lenny's murder to Bruno Lanka to the Escalade driver to Charlene Vesco to a shady Garville cop to Cam Stryker to the abominable fucking snowman?"

"Something like that."

"So, everybody's a suspect? Everybody except Ziko Slimebag Slade?"

OVER THE COURSE of several homicide investigations, Gurney had come to appreciate the unique nature of Hardwick's contributions. In discussions, the man invariably raised aggressive objections to just about any proposed hypothesis, but when action was required, he was all in. Therefore, despite his ridiculing any theory that might explain the Lerman murders, Gurney knew that Hardwick would extract every fact he could from his contact at BCI, and if a dangerous confrontation should arise in the future, he would be there without reservation.

At the moment, Gurney's own potential for action was limited. Short of returning to Garville to stir the pot again, there was little he could do. Any significant next step would depend on whatever information Hardwick could get hold of.

This enforced hiatus allowed Gurney's mind to move from case-related speculations to concerns about Thanksgiving. As he pulled out from the rest area, those concerns centered on ensuring that the planned dinner would take place without fear of a hostile invasion.

The possibility of installing electronic monitoring devices came to mind, but he'd never put much stock in them. When he and Madeleine lived in the city, protection against intruders consisted of a lobby attendant in their building, a substantial deadbolt on their apartment door, and his NYPD sidearm. After they moved to the old farmhouse, the deadbolt and lobby attendant had been replaced by a shotgun, and by letting it be known that the place was occupied by a former detective.

Now, however, with three guests coming for dinner in the wake of the unsettling RAM coverage of the Blackmore shooting, he was looking at the situation from their perspective. He came to the conclusion that a visible array of surveillance cameras might help, not only to discourage an intrusion, but to foster peace of mind.

His route home would take him past the Oneonta mall's Epic Innovations, a vast cavern of a store that carried cutting-edge electronics gear. Surely they'd have a well-stocked home-security department.

48

THANKSGIVING DAY BROUGHT A STUNNING WEATHER REversal. A major warm front moved into upstate New York during the night, bringing Indian summer to Walnut Crossing.

Gurney had spent the previous evening and most of that morning installing the system he purchased at Epic Innovations. The fast-talking techie salesman had made the process seem a lot simpler than it turned out to be, with the bizarrely translated manual providing more confusion than assistance.

After charging the batteries in the six cameras, whose mounting plates he positioned on the corners of the barn and on the side of the house that faced the woods, the final step was downloading the operational app to his phone and making sure that the promised capabilities of the system were actually functioning.

At two o'clock that afternoon the system got, and passed, its first real test. Gurney was gazing out through the French doors at the old apple tree, where a few red McIntoshes were still clinging to the branches above the height where the deer could reach them, when he received a beeping security notice on his phone that a vehicle was passing one of the cameras mounted on the barn. Moments later, as he watched, a Subaru Outback began making its way up through the low pasture toward the house. The vehicle looked like his own, or at least like his own had looked before its smash-up on Blackmore Mountain.

When it came to a stop next to his rental car and the handsome young couple emerged, he experienced the slight shock that results from the changed appearances of people you haven't seen for a while. He hadn't seen Kyle for over a year, Kim for more than two.

He opened the French doors and headed across the patio to greet them.

"Welcome!" he said as they strode toward him, Kyle leading the way.

"Hey, Dad! Wow! Great to see you! You look great!"

"So do you, son, so do you!"

Kyle's face was fuller than Gurney remembered, his hair shorter and neater, his grin broader. The differences in Kim were deeper. There was something harder in her eyes, less open in her expression.

Gurney gave Kyle a hug, then, a bit awkwardly, repeated the gesture with Kim.

"The place looks great," said Kyle, his happy gaze traveling around the fields and back to the area around the house. "That shed on the side of the coop—that's new since I was last here, right? And the patio looks different. It used to be . . . a little rounder?"

"You have a good memory."

Kyle eyed the rental car. "No more Outback?" There was disappointment in his voice.

"I'll be getting a new one, as soon as we get a check from the insurance company."

"The old one got totaled in that Blackmore Mountain thing?"

"That's my assumption. I'm waiting for a call from the adjuster. Then I'll be able to replace it."

"That must have been quite a crash," said Kim. "The coverage on RAM was, like, crazy."

Although it sounded like a simple statement, Gurney heard in it a reporter's hunger for more information. Not inclined to offer any, he simply nodded in agreement.

Kyle broke the brief silence, pointing at the shed. "You built that yourself?"

"A joint project with Maddie."

"I love the iron hardware on the door." He added in an aside to Kim, "My dad can do anything. He just figures out whatever it is and does it."

She turned to Gurney. "What's it for?"

"Well, it seems that one of these days we may be getting—"

"Alpacas!" The enthusiastic contribution came from Madeleine, who'd just emerged from the side door. "A pair. Twins. The cutest things."

Kim frowned. "You want them for the wool?"

"The wool is nice, but it's not the main thing. They're just wonderful little creatures."

"Aren't they a lot of work?"

"Depends on what you mean by work."

As Kim glanced meaningfully at the hay bales stacked against the shed wall, the sound of a vehicle coming up through the low pasture ended the exchange.

It was a buttercup-yellow VW Beetle.

After jouncing up the rutted lane at a speed too enthusiastic for the terrain, it came to a stop behind Kyle's Outback. Gerry Mirkle emerged from the driver's seat with a bright smile and a pot of multicolored mums.

"Happy Thanksgiving!" she cried, approaching the group, surprisingly light on her feet for a plump woman. "What a glorious day, spring in November!"

She handed the mums to Madeleine, who thanked her effusively and, after introducing her to Kim and Kyle, carried the pot to the sunniest corner of the patio.

"So," said Gerry, addressing Gurney with sudden seriousness, "you look better than I expected, considering what you've been through. How do you feel?"

"There's just enough discomfort to remind me that I've had a concussion, but it's nothing that keeps me from doing what I need to do."

She flashed a quick grin. "Is that a roasting turkey I smell? Possibly with a sage-and-thyme bread stuffing?"

"Plus chestnuts and sausage," replied Madeleine happily. "Shall we go into the house? Everything will be ready soon."

The cherrywood fire that Gurney had started an hour earlier was blazing in the stone fireplace. Cheeses, olives, and glasses of cider were laid out on the coffee table in front of the hearth. Madeleine headed for the kitchen end of the big open room to check the stove, while the others took seats around the coffee table. Kim pointed to a crystal vase of beige hydrangeas on the mantel.

"Are they real?"

Madeleine answered from the kitchen. "Real, but dried out. When I cut them from the bushes by the pond, they were pink. When they dry out they lose their color, but the petals last for months."

"Lovely," said Kim with fading interest.

Kyle was gazing up at the mantel. Next to the hydrangeas, there was a photograph of the house in the state of neglect when Dave and Madeleine purchased it.

"You look deep in thought," said Gurney.

"The photo up there just reminded me—I brought something for you. It's in the car. I'll be right back." He went out through the French doors, which had been left open to let in the soft Indian summer air.

Gerry Mirkle, whose expression suggested an attitude of mild amusement, leaned over the table and cut herself a small wedge of Irish cheddar.

Kim was leaning back in her chair, holding her cider glass in front of her chin with both hands. She was studying Gurney's face. "You haven't changed. Not even a little."

But you have, he thought, without replying.

"Murder cases must be your fountain of youth."

Again, he said nothing.

"Considering what happened on Blackmore Mountain and the awful way the media are treating it, I expected you to be radiating

anger, tension, *something*. But I don't see anything at all." Her quiz-
zical tone turned her comment into a request for an explanation.
Even if he had one ready, he wouldn't have been moved to provide it.
He responded only with a shrug and a vague smile.

The awkward silence that followed was interrupted by Kyle's return. Smiling, he handed Gurney a flat gift-wrapped box.

"For you."

Gurney was surprised and mildly baffled. "Thank you."

"Before Mom moved to her new condo, she was clearing out
some old stuff, and she told me to take whatever I wanted. I found
two old photos that I really liked, especially side by side."

Undoing the wrapping paper, Gurney found a double picture
frame, the two sides hinged together. The photo on the left was of
his own father, shockingly young, smiling, with a toddler, also smiling, on his shoulders. It took Gurney a couple of seconds to realize
the toddler was himself.

"I think your mother gave that to Mom ages ago," said Kyle,
"when you and Mom were still married."

Gurney's attention moved to the photo on the right. It was of
himself in his mid-twenties, and there was a little boy on his shoulders. The little boy was Kyle.

"It's a long time since I've seen these pictures." He felt the pressure of a nameless emotion in his chest. "I think maybe . . . maybe
we can put this right up here." He got out of his chair and placed the
hinged frame on the mantel, angling the sides carefully to avoid glare
from the nearby window.

"Thank you," he said again, at a loss for what else to say. An
open expression of feelings, especially strong ones, never came naturally to him.

"Turkey time!"

Madeleine's cheery announcement from the kitchen end of the
room dissipated the odd mood created by the photographs, and everyone headed enthusiastically for the dinner table.

49

"I WANT TO KNOW MORE ABOUT THE ALPACAS," SAID Gerry Mirkle, as Madeleine was passing her a dish of cranberry sauce.

"The most important thing about them is the hardest to describe. It's the expression in their eyes. It's like they're sizing you up, but in a friendly way. I can't wait for them to arrive."

"Do you have names for them?"

"I want to wait until they're here, so I can match the names to their personalities."

Gerry glanced over at Kim. "How about you—any favorite pets?"

Kim wrinkled up her nose, as though she'd been asked if she was fond of any unpleasant odors. "Only a least favorite. When I was little, my father had an iguana. Horrible thing." She punctuated the statement with a little shudder.

"No furry friends in your life?"

"Investigative reporting doesn't leave a lot of time for dog-walking."

"Sounds like the kind of work that could take over your life."

"Only if you love it."

"And you do?"

"Absolutely."

"What's the best thing about it?"

"Ripping the mask off a creep who's pretending to be what he's not."

Kyle spoke up for the first time at the table. "Exposing the bad guys—that's what you do, Dad, just from a different angle, right?"

Gurney was cutting a piece of turkey on his plate, which he continued doing as he replied. "And from a different starting point. Investigative reporting—correct me if I'm wrong, Kim—generally begins with a whiff of smoke, then tries to locate the fire, if there is one, with the goal of exposing it in the media. A homicide investigation, instead of a whiff of smoke, starts with a dead victim, and the goal is to gather enough evidence to arrest the person responsible."

Smiling, Kim laid her fork down. "Aren't we both pursuing the truth?"

"Yes, but for very different reasons."

"I think what matters is the truth. Why we pursue it seems like a secondary issue."

Gurney realized that further debate could only dampen the Thanksgiving spirit and would be best abandoned. "Good point, Kim. Could you reach that salt shaker for me?"

"Speaking of investigations," said Kyle, leaning toward Gurney, "the way those RAM idiots were talking about you was frigging awful. They were pushing right up against the edge of slander. I wish they'd step over the line, so we could sue." He looked over at Gerry Mirkle. "Did you see that *Controversial Perspectives* segment about the shooting?"

"Madeleine told me about it, and I watched it on the RAM website."

"What did you think of it?"

"Apart from it being a trash can of poisonous nonsense?"

Kyle flashed a grim smile. "And what about that guy at the end, that Maldon Albright character?"

She shrugged. "I got the impression he was trying to give a sophisticated-sounding gloss to RAM's garbage. Dave, can you pass the gravy?"

The conversation turned to the dinner—the moistness of the turkey, the sweetness of the yams. Everyone seemed happy to retreat into these pleasant observations except Kim, who was toying with her food, seemingly eager to find a way back to a more serious subject. She finally just laid down her fork and turned to Gurney.

"I have to ask. Do you have your own theory of what the Blackmore shooting was all about?"

Everyone stopped eating. Madeleine gave Kim a cold stare. Kyle's eyes widened. Gerry Mirkle's expression revealed nothing. Gurney felt annoyed, not so much by the question as by the coolly probing tone in which it was asked.

"It's not really a theory—just a suspicion that a toxic relationship between a father and son is responsible for everything that's happened."

"You mean, a problem between Lenny and Sonny?"

"It sounds like you've been doing some research on the original Lerman murder case."

"That's my job."

It was suddenly clear to Gurney that Kim wasn't present at dinner because Kyle invited her. Kyle had no doubt mentioned his planned visit, and she'd invited herself. Which meant there was a possibility that whatever he said would appear, sooner or later, in the media.

He chose his words carefully. "I believe there was something poisonous in the relationship between Lenny and Sonny Lerman that ended up causing both their deaths."

Her eyes widened. "So, you don't believe Ziko Slade killed Lenny because Lenny tried to blackmail him?"

"It sounded good in court, but it doesn't account for the peculiarity of the murder."

"You mean, the . . . decapitation?" She articulated the word with something like awe.

Madeleine broke in with the shy little smile she often used to lighten the tone of a serious request. "While we're having our turkey, maybe we could talk about something other than severed body parts?"

"Good idea," Gurney said.

Kyle launched into a change of subject so complete Gurney nearly burst out laughing.

"Madeleine, I love the way you made the yams."

She blinked in surprise. "The yams? They're just mashed up with some butter and salt and a dash of cinnamon."

Gerry Mirkle said, "Yams were a point of dispute in the house I grew up in. My mother served one of her yam concoctions at every holiday dinner. My father hated yams. 'I've never made them this way before, you should try them,' she'd say. He'd reply, 'This way, that way, makes no damn difference. They're godawful, no matter how you make them!' Then she'd start talking to the cat, telling it how nice yams are and how some people couldn't appreciate good things. At that point my father would slam down his fork and stomp out of the room. They say opposites attract, but attraction can turn into a collision. And the collision either blows the relationship apart, or freezes it in a state of perpetual frustration, with each partner wishing the other would change."

"What sort of man was your father?" asked Kim.

"He was a college professor. An authority on macroeconomics. I doubt he ever thought of himself as a husband or a father." Gerry paused. "He liked to swim and went off every Saturday in the summer to a nearby beach. One Saturday, he took me along. I'm sure it wasn't his idea, just something my mother pressured him into doing. He forgot I was with him, and he drove home without me."

Around the table there were sounds of dismay.

"Over the years, my mother told that story with increasingly bitter humor. It was her way of letting everyone know that the professor was a self-absorbed idiot. I ended up feeling sorry for him—even though I once heard him say he wished I was a boy."

"Patriarchy!" said Kim with disgust. "If you were a boy, he wouldn't have forgotten you at the beach."

"His relationship with a boy might have been worse."

"How? Why?"

"Fathers often have expectations for sons that they don't have for daughters. They see the son as an extension of themselves, and if they have serious control issues to begin with, the results can be explosive."

"Last year," said Kyle, leaning in, "Kim reported on a case where the father and son were serial killers, working as a team." He turned to her. "You want to tell the story?"

Her eyes lit up in a way that reminded Gurney of the sensation-loving "personalities" on RAM-TV.

"Noah and Tanner Babcock, the father and son from hell," she began—only to be interrupted by the beeping of the security alert on Gurney's phone.

Unexpected visitors were rare enough that he and Madeleine exchanged questioning looks for a moment before he got up from the table. He went to the kitchen window and watched as a white van rounded the barn and drove up on the pasture lane to the house. A uniformed driver got out, carried a large, square shipping carton to the side door, and returned to the van.

Gurney made his way out through mudroom and opened the door in time to see the driver getting back into the van. It had a blue logo on the side that said NORTHEAST EXPEDITED DELIVERY. The van departed as quickly as it came.

Gurney looked down at the carton on the step. He picked it up, discovered it weighed at least thirty pounds, brought it into the house, and laid it on the kitchen sideboard. The label listed the sender's name as C. Hadley.

"It's from Christine," he said.

"Christine?" Madeleine made the name sound like a problem.

"That's what the label says."

"My rich sister in Ridgewood," she said, by way of explanation to the others at the table.

Gurney cleared his throat. "Do you want to open it?"

"You're there. You open it."

Gurney sliced through the packing, pulled the top flaps open, and looked inside. "It's a holiday gift basket. Jams, relishes, fancy mustards."

"Fine," said Madeleine, with a dismissive wave of her hand. "We'll figure out what to do with it later."

Gerry Mirkle broke the ensuing silence. "I believe Kim was about to tell us a father-and-son serial murder story."

Kim glanced around, making sure she had everyone's attention. "Noah Babcock lived with his son, Tanner, on an isolated dairy farm. When his son was six, he beat the boy's mother to death in front of him—with a shovel—stripped the body, and dumped it into a tank full of liquified manure. Over the next fifteen years, he dumped eleven more women into the same tank, and the son, who had become an emotionless zombie, assisted with the heavy lifting. The murders were accidentally discovered when a state inspector was doing routine checks of slurry tanks. When he opened the tank, he found a partially decomposed ear floating on the surface. The father received twelve consecutive life sentences in a maximum-security prison. The son was remanded to a facility for the criminally insane."

Kyle added, "Kim wrote a prize-winning article, based on her interviews with the son."

Madeleine's gaze was fixed on Kim. "How did you manage to get those interviews?"

"Tanner was allowed one visitor a week. So, I visited."

"I'm surprised he was willing to speak to you."

Kim produced a self-satisfied smile. "It took some effort."

"What did you promise him?"

"'Promise' is too strong a word. I suggested that telling his version of the story would help people understand what had happened."

"Any idea what his IQ was?"

Kim's expression tightened, but before she could respond, Gerry Mirkle interjected. "The Fertilizer Murders. I recall that's what the case was called by RAM News. They do have a way of characterizing events."

Kim said nothing.

Gerry continued. "As a professional journalist, you no doubt have an opinion of RAM's approach to the news?"

"Their approach?"

"The way they turn complex, tragic events into vulgar, simplistic headlines."

Kim's smile failed to conceal the hostility in her eyes. "It's easy to criticize the style of the product, but it wouldn't exist if it wasn't what the audience wanted."

Gerry picked up her fork, studied the tines for a moment, then put it down. "Trouble is, so many of the things people want end up poisoning them."

The tenor of that idea, if not the exact words, reminded Gurney of Emma Martin. He asked Gerry if she was familiar with Emma or with her therapeutic approach.

Gerry's eyes lit up. "Oh, yes, indeed. But more by reputation than direct contact. Emma was always a bit of an outsider when it came to the clinical community. I recall an incident at a conference in Aspen. A famous psychiatrist had just presented the details of a study he claimed established the relative impacts of nature and nurture on human behavior. You could have heard a pin drop—until Emma burst out laughing and proceeded to demolish the underlying structure of the research. Academic pretension was one thing she could never stomach."

That brought on a silence that lasted while the dishes were cleared away. Madeleine got coffee going and brought a pumpkin pie to the table.

"While we're waiting for the coffee," she said, "I'm going to make a quick call to Christine to thank her for the jam basket, before I forget." She started to leave the room, then stopped. "If anyone is fond of jams, jellies, et cetera, please go over and take whatever you want. Don't be shy. My phone's in the den—be back in a sec."

"Shyness has never been my problem," said Gerry, standing up and heading for the open carton on the sideboard. Kim followed her, and they began tentatively removing a jar at a time and studying the fancy labels with polite admiration. They took their time, as if instinctively relating speed to greed. Proceeding this way, it took them a good three or four minutes to remove, admire, and comment on half a dozen items.

"Well," said Gerry with a grin, "those goodies only filled the top section of the carton. Must be a lot more under this divider."

She reached into the carton and tugged for several seconds at the cardboard insert. Glancing around the top of the sideboard, she picked up a spare serving fork and pushed it down under the edge of the insert—just as Madeleine was returning from the den, looking puzzled.

"I spoke to Christine. She said she had no idea what I was talking about. She didn't send us anything."

Suddenly the insert flew up out of the carton, followed by a flash of something bright green. The serving fork was knocked from Gerry's hand and clattered to the floor as she staggered back, uttering a sharp cry.

Kim stood frozen in place, mouth agape.

Madeleine approached tentatively and looked into the carton. Her eyes widened and she screamed, tripping backward. Her body collided with the kitchen wall, and she slid to the floor.

"What the hell is it?" cried Gurney, leaping to his feet, knocking his chair over, stumbling toward Madeleine. "Are you alright? What the hell . . . ?"

She pointed. "Look! For God's sake, look!"

A coiled green snake with curved needle-sharp fangs and malevolent eyes the color of red-hot coals was rising from the carton, its triangular head rocking ever so slightly from side to side.

PART IV

OBSESSION

50

"ARE YOU STILL AWAKE?" GURNEY ASKED SOFTLY.

He was pretty sure that she was. He could tell by the way she was breathing, lying next to him in the moonlight from the bedroom window, but she didn't answer. In fact, she'd hardly said a word in the many hours that had passed since the sight of the hideous thing in the jam basket sent her reeling against the kitchen wall.

When the state police came, it was he who answered all their questions. And when Gerry, Kyle, and Kim were leaving, it was he who assured them that he and Madeleine would be okay; no, there was nothing they could do; yes, he would definitely keep them abreast of developments.

Once he and Madeleine had the house to themselves, she'd begun cleaning with a tight-lipped obsessiveness, beginning with the kitchen sideboard where the "gift" carton had been opened and then proceeding to scrub the kitchen floor and the hallway floor between the kitchen and the mudroom with a sponge mop. Finally, with a pail of soapy water and a brush—down on her knees—she scoured the outside step where the delivery person had left the carton. She did all this with a fierceness that closed the door to any offer of assistance. He'd watched with apprehension, hoping that her exertion would diminish the lingering shock of what she'd seen.

When the cleaning fit passed—and there was nothing left to scrub—she'd gone to the sitting area at the far end of the room, wrapped herself in an afghan that had been lying unused for months on one of the armchairs, and settled down, staring into the fireplace. The afternoon's blaze had long since died out and only cold ashes remained. He asked several times if there was anything he could do, but she showed no signs of having heard him. Eventually, she'd gotten up from the chair and gone to bed.

Now, as they lay there next to each other, Gurney was feeling the first stabs of panic.

"Are you awake?" he asked again.

She said nothing.

"You're frightening me."

Still nothing.

He felt a desperate need to do something. But what? Bring her to the nearest emergency room? Would that help? Or would the dislocation drive her deeper into whatever she was experiencing? Or would she just refuse to go?

All at once, coyotes in the high pasture began to howl in eerie unison. Then, as abruptly as they began, they stopped.

Madeleine's head shifted slightly on her pillow.

"They know where my sister lives."

Her voice, barely above a whisper, was so unexpected it gave Gurney a little start.

"The people who sent us that hideous thing."

He had no answer.

"What will it take to make you stop? Will one of us have to end up dead?"

"That's exactly what I'm trying to prevent."

"Are you?" It was less a question than a weary comment.

The silence was broken only by the rustling of the breeze through the frozen lilac bush outside the bedroom window.

51

MADELEINE EVENTUALLY FELL ASLEEP. GURNEY DIDN'T.

At the first gray hint of dawn, he got up, showered, dressed, picked up his Glock and shoulder holster from the night table, went out to the kitchen, and switched on the coffee machine. While it warmed up, he strapped on the Glock, got his jacket from the mud-room, and stepped outside.

Overnight, the temperature had plummeted again. Frost covered the drooping asparagus ferns, and the briefest Indian summer in memory had come to an end. He took a series of long, slow breaths in the hope that the bracing air might restore some linear logic to his thoughts.

After a while, he began to shiver. The frigid air and deep breath-ing were only sharpening his headache. He retreated into the house, took off his jacket, and put a pod of dark roast into the coffee ma-chine. When his mug was filled, he took it into the den, opened his laptop, and searched for Northeast Expedited Delivery—the name on the truck that had delivered the snake.

He wasn't surprised to discover there was no such company—a fact further strengthening his conviction that the enemy was a careful planner with significant resources. He thought for a mo-ment of passing along his discovery to BCI, then decided not to for two good reasons. They surely would make the same discovery on their own, and they wouldn't appreciate his conducting a parallel investigation.

Instead, he turned his attention to the Lerman-Slade case files. Glancing from one folder to another, he stopped at the one contain-ing the printout Kyra Barstow had sent that showed Lenny's route from Calliope Springs to Slade's lodge with GPS time notations. This was the raw material Stryker simplified in graphic form for the trial.

In the same folder he found the printout of the two credit card charges Lenny had incurred—the gas-station one for $14.57 and the one at the auto supply store for $16.19. He checked the time notation next to each and saw that the auto supply transaction occurred six minutes before the one at the gas station.

Recalling the Google Street View image of the station, $14.57 seemed like too much to have been spent on anything in the tiny, seedy-looking store behind the pumps. But it seemed on the low side for a gas purchase. Gurney went to a fuel price website and checked the average upstate gas prices for the previous November. Regular grade, which was what Lerman's Corolla would have used, was $3.19 a gallon at the pump. At that price, he would have gotten only about four and a half gallons—an oddly small amount for a car, but just about right for a five-gallon gas can.

He went back to the time-coded printout of Lerman's trip. It seemed entirely consistent with the map Stryker had shown the jury. Then something caught his eye—a stop Lerman made just a mile before he reached Slade's private road. It was a very brief stop, just one minute, and Stryker hadn't bothered to highlight it on her map. It was one more oddity in a case increasingly defined by its peculiarities.

He sat back in his chair, gazing out the den window at the high pasture. The dawn light seemed to impart an added chill to the frost on the beige grasses. There was a dead stillness about it all that was adding to his leaden mood. With sudden determination, he decided to *do* something. Anything would be better than trying to imagine the significance of minor events that had taken place a year ago and a hundred and fifty miles away. He couldn't do anything about the time that had passed, but he could visit the places where these things occurred. And he had learned long ago that action was the surest path out of a mental cul-de-sac. He checked the Glock in his shoulder holster and put on his jacket.

He was leaving a note for Madeleine when he heard the bedroom door opening. A few seconds later, she came into the kitchen, holding her bathrobe tightly around her, hair uncombed. She frowned at his jacket.

"Where are you going?"

He crumpled up the half-written note and explained that a couple of things about Lenny Lerman's trip to Slade's lodge were bothering him and he wanted to check them out. He added, "I know you hate the idea of my pursuing anything connected with the case, but Jesus, Maddie, I don't know what else to do. I don't trust Cam Stryker or BCI or the Rexton PD to get to the bottom of this. I just don't believe—"

She interrupted him, her voice rising. "So, you have to keep digging. And digging. And digging. Regardless of the consequences. Is that it?"

"I don't see an alternative."

"The alternative is to stop. Just *stop*!"

"Turning my back on the case now would be the most dangerous thing I could do."

She nodded in slow motion, a gesture that conveyed more anger than agreement, then returned abruptly to the bedroom.

AT 9:55 THAT morning, Gurney pulled into the parking area in front of Cory's Auto Supply.

Since the $16.19 store charge on Lerman's Visa bill would have included an 8 percent sales tax, he did a quick calculation to determine what the tag price would be on whatever Lerman had purchased. The number he arrived at was $14.99.

He got out of the car, steadying himself against the door as a sudden pain ran from the base of his skull into his shoulder—an unsubtle reminder that he should be wearing a neck brace. Once the sharp edge of the pain dulled, he entered the store. Passing among the racks of motor oil, antifreeze, windshield wipers, floor mats, tool kits, gas additives, car waxes, and cleaning solutions, he arrived at the sales counter, behind which a large gray-haired man was eyeing him with the fixed smile of a minister greeting a new congregant.

"What can I help you with on this fine day?"

"Do you stock gasoline containers?"

The man pointed. "There, against the far wall."

Gurney found two kinds on display—old-fashioned round metal ones and the currently more popular red plastic ones, both in five-gallon sizes. He picked up a plastic one, checked the sticker, and with the distinct little rush of an expectation satisfied, saw a price of $14.99.

He took it to the man at the counter and asked how long he'd been selling that particular item.

"Years."

"At this same price?"

"Same price as the big auto supply chains. Don't make any profit on it, but it's the only way we can stay in business. Somewhere along the line, this country of ours made a wrong turn. We don't even know who the hell is calling the shots. The Chinese? Who the hell knows?"

Gurney paid for the gas container, took it out to his car, and placed a call to Kyra Barstow.

"David?"

Knowing her as well as he did, he wasn't surprised to find her at work the day after Thanksgiving. "Quick question. Do you have the digital files from which Stryker printed out the crime scene photos she used at the Slade trial?"

"Not in front of me, but I can access them. Why?"

"Among the photo printouts that Thorne sent me there were some of the quarry where Lerman's Corolla was incinerated. A red plastic gas container was visible in the corner of one of them. I assume that you or one of your people brought it in for forensic examination?"

"Of course. But there were no prints on it, and Stryker lost interest in it."

"Do you remember if you retained it, or passed it on to Rexton PD?"

"I'll have to check. Where are we going with this?"

"I'm wondering, if you still have it, could you take a few quick photos from various angles and send them to my phone?"

She laughed. "I assume you mean now?"

"Now would be good."

"You haven't told me why."

"I'm pretty sure the purchase Lerman made at the auto supply store was a five-gallon gas container. The price is consistent with the charge on his Visa statement, and his gas purchase a few minutes later is consistent with the size of the container. I know that neither of those facts prove anything, but if it turns out that the container you found in the quarry matches the one sold at that store—"

Barstow interrupted him, her tone incredulous. "You're suggesting that Lerman bought the gas used to incinerate his own car? Why on earth would he do that?"

"I have no idea. This case just keeps getting stranger and stranger."

"I'll get back to you as soon as I can," she said and ended the call.

Gurney detected a sense of urgency, perhaps even excitement, in her voice.

There was one more thing he wanted to check on before leaving the area. He got out of the car and walked across the street to the dingy store behind the gas pumps. Entering it, he discovered that it wasn't really a store in any normal sense of the word. It was just a dusty room with a row of vending machines lined up against three of the walls, offering candy bars, chips, and canned sodas. A tattooed teenage attendant with green hair sat in a corner of the room, holding a phone in both hands.

Gurney went back across the road to his car, feeling doubly sure now that Lerman's Visa charge at the station was indeed for gas, there being nothing else in that place that he could have spent $14.57 on. Encouraged by a feeling that progress was being made, he decided to continue on to the site of Lerman's peculiar one-minute roadside stop.

He checked the printout of Lerman's route, noted the coordinates of that stop, entered them as a destination point in his GPS, pulled out of the parking lot, and headed north into the Adirondacks.

Over the next hour and quarter, as the elevation rose, the

temperature fell. The readout on his dashboard was down to 18°F by the time his GPS told him he had arrived at his destination—a cleared area off the right side of the road, just large enough for a plow truck or salt spreader to turn around. He pulled over and got out of the car, zipping his jacket up to his chin.

He studied his surroundings—a typical Adirondack forest of giant evergreens. The ground beneath them covered with a thick blanket of brown needles. Patches of ice here and there. Piney smell in the air. Dead silence. His hope that the location might reveal Lerman's reason for stopping there was rapidly fading. He was about to give it up when something caught his eye. He hadn't noticed it at first because of the pine needles covering everything, but there appeared to be a narrow lane leading from the edge of the clearing into the woods. Moving closer, he saw that it was just wide enough for the passage of a car. He wasn't about to take a chance on getting his rental vehicle stuck in the woods, but he was curious enough to proceed on foot.

He soon discovered a much larger clearing, consisting mainly of a granite quarry. A brief exploration revealed that it was the same one where Lerman's Corolla had been reduced to a burnt-out hulk. He made his way to the point where the site photos showed the remains of the car. A blackened area on the gray stone confirmed the location. He spent another twenty minutes going over the site before returning to his car.

He started the engine, got the heater going, and tried to make sense of the situation. Surely it wasn't just a coincidence that Lerman stopped by a lane that led to the place where his car would later be burned. But why?

As he struggled to come up with even one slightly plausible explanation, his phone announced the arrival of a text. It was from Kyra Barstow, and it was accompanied by four close-up photos of a red plastic gas container.

The container Gurney purchased was on the seat next to him. He turned it carefully to match each of the angles in Barstow's photos.

The comparisons convinced him that the item stocked by Cory's Auto Supply was identical to the one found at the scene of the car fire. It produced that familiar little surge of satisfaction he felt whenever a pair of puzzle pieces snapped together.

But it didn't last. The satisfaction was replaced by bafflement. Why would Lenny Lerman, on the verge of attempting to extort a small fortune from Ziko Slade, bring a container of gasoline with him? Had he intended to kill Slade and torch the lodge, once he'd gotten the money? And, then, when the plan went awry, was the gasoline conveniently used by Lenny's killer to destroy the Corolla? That scenario was conceivable, but it seemed unlikely. Nothing Gurney had learned about Lenny supported the idea that his naive blackmail scheme would include premeditated murder and arson. Greedy and foolish he might well have been, but icy and ruthless didn't seem to fit.

As the interior of his car began to warm up, Gurney unzipped his jacket, leaned back, and pondered what to do next. He considered driving on to the lodge—it was only a mile or so away. If Ian Valdez was there, he could have another talk with him. After giving it more thought, however, he opted to wait until he was better prepared for the interview. In the event that Ian's role in what happened was deeper than it first appeared, gathering more information about the man was essential.

With a darkening sky promising snow, and nothing else to accomplish in the Adirondacks, he decided to head back to Walnut Crossing. He tossed the gas container into the back seat, put the car in drive, and his phone rang again. His first guess was Cam Stryker, and he was right. The fact that it was the day after Thanksgiving, when most elected officials would be enjoying the long weekend, would mean nothing to an obsessed workaholic like Stryker.

"David, where are you?"

Something in her tone told him that she knew he wasn't at home. Might she have sent a trooper or one of her own investigators to follow him? The truth seemed the wisest response.

"At the quarry where Lerman's car was burned."

"You're *where*?"

"It appears that Lerman himself bought the gas that was used in the fire—which Rexton PD could have discovered if they'd paid attention to his GPS route readout and Visa bills."

"What the hell are you talking about?"

"I'm talking about an extremely complicated crime that was addressed by a half-assed investigation and cherry-picked evidence in pursuit of an easy conviction!"

The tone of Stryker's response was artificially calm. It reminded Gurney of the way someone might speak while defusing a bomb. "It sounds like you may have made some substantive discoveries. We need to talk about them—in person. Based on your current location, you should be able to get to my office by two this afternoon. Can I depend on your being here by two o'clock?"

"Definitely," he said with what he hoped sounded like determination.

He didn't trust Stryker's sudden pose of open-mindedness. He suspected that the proposed meeting might be a convenient way for her to take him into custody after discovering exactly how much he'd found out and how damaging it might be to her.

Ever since the Blackmore shooting, she'd made it clear that detaining him was an option. His fingerprints on the gun and the powder residue on his hands would give her enough probable cause, as well as a shield against a civil case for false arrest. He figured that her calculus was based on a simple risk analysis. As soon as his investigation posed a greater risk than arresting him, she'd have him arrested and later absorb whatever embarrassment might result from having to release him.

He suspected that his own comments moments earlier might have pushed her to that point. If so, he had no regrets. Their colliding objectives made it inevitable. Only the timing had been undecided.

If she was already seeking a warrant for his arrest, it would be prudent to take certain precautions immediately. He had no intention of being taken into custody, but leaving the upstate area wasn't an option either. He had to be present to pursue his investigation—present, but not findable.

Stryker might be arranging for real-time surveillance of his position via the GPS locator on his phone. That function was easy enough to disable in the phone's location settings, so he did so. It was also possible, if she suspected that he might skip the meeting and go straight home from the Adirondacks, that she'd have the approach road to his house watched. He brought up an area map on his phone screen and chose a route into Walnut Crossing that would bring him to an old farm lane a mile or so from the back end of his property, with only a forested stretch of state land intervening. He'd find an inconspicuous place to park and make his way to his home on foot. He entered the new route in the car's GPS and set out with a reasonable sense of security.

About an hour into the trip, he passed an outdoor mall. A logo on the front of one of the stores caught his eye. The store's name, Camper's Paradise, set off a train of thought that prompted him, a few miles down the road, to turn around and go back.

He emerged from the store half an hour later—carrying a small tent, a propane tent heater, and a sleeping bag—and continued on his journey to Walnut Crossing.

THE BACK ROAD bordering the forest behind Gurney's property provided access to several old logging trails. He chose the least overgrown one and drove in far enough that the car would no longer be visible from the road.

From there, he followed the trail on foot up a steep rise, lugging his purchases. Fallen trees repeatedly obstructed the way, forcing him to make detours over moss-covered rocks, slippery as if they'd been greased. It occurred to him that if Madeleine were with him, she'd be enthusing over the variety of the mosses and their palette of greens. His focus was on not getting another concussion.

Long after the trail had petered out, he reached the summit of a broad ridge-like hill. Through openings in the drooping branches of the hemlocks, he could see his house, most of the low pasture, and part of the barn. He checked his phone for the time. It was exactly 2:00 p.m. As he searched for a flat spot to erect his tent, he wondered how much longer Stryker would wait before calling him again.

The answer turned out to be nine minutes. He let her call go to voicemail.

"David, I need to speak to you. Urgently. You agreed to be in my office by two o'clock. Please call me the moment you get this message."

He was in no rush to talk to her. He wanted to give his new status as someone outside the law, in spirit if not technically, some more thought.

He soon located a relatively level patch of ground, sheltered by dense evergreens on all sides, to set up his secret campsite. He didn't know if he'd actually be spending time here, but given the volatility of the situation, having an emergency retreat seemed wise.

As he finished pitching the tent, he heard a vehicle approach from the direction of the town road. He moved to a spot that provided a better view. Soon a dark sedan appeared, driving quickly past the barn. Simultaneously, his phone produced its distinctive beeping notification that the security camera on the front of the barn had been activated.

The sedan continued up the pasture lane and came to a stop a short distance from the house. A murky midnight blue, it had the nondescript appearance of an unmarked police vehicle. Two occupants emerged—crew-cut men in dark windbreakers and dark pants. One remained by the car, phone to his ear, while the other approached the house. Because of Gurney's angle of vision, he almost immediately lost sight of the man. A moment later, he heard loud knocking at the side door. Then silence. Then more knocking, accompanied by a raised voice, but he couldn't make out the words.

After a quiet couple of minutes, during which Gurney pictured the man making his way around the house, he came back into sight, walked over to the car, and engaged in a short conversation with the phone holder—whose attention then returned to his phone, most likely to receive further instructions.

After the phone call ended, the pair got back in the car. They turned around and headed down through the pasture, but instead of continuing out onto the town road, they stopped at the side of the barn. Gurney noted the quick little taillight flash that occurs when a transmission passes through Reverse into Park—a sign they might be settling in for a while.

Since they appeared to be focused on his potential arrival by way of the road, he figured it would now be safe for him to return to the house via the back field and one of the bedroom windows. He put the propane heater and the sleeping bag inside the tent, zipped up the entry flap, and made his way down the hill.

52

STANDING AT THE SINK ISLAND, DEFROSTING HIS ACHING hands under a stream of lukewarm water, Gurney glanced at the clock on the kitchen wall. It was just a few minutes past three, although the wintry gray light at the windows made it feel later. Snowflakes drifted down through still, cold air. An afternoon like this cried out for a fire, but the chance that the watchers by the barn might notice smoke coming from the chimney made that unwise. A similar concern stood in the way of turning on any lights. The big room was so depressingly dim he'd almost missed the terse note from Madeleine on the refrigerator door, reminding him that she was sharing a shift with Gerry at the Crisis Center.

As his hands began to feel normal, he became more aware of the dull headache that never completely disappeared. He dried his hands and turned his attention to preparing for his next encounter with Cam Stryker. His best defense, his only defense, depended on solid information. Maybe Hardwick had discovered something new since their last conversation. He took his phone into the den and made the call.

It was answered by Esti Moreno, her light Puerto Rican accent sounding less charming than usual. "Jack is busy. He'll call you back, okay?"

"I won't take much of his time, just a couple of quick—"

"He's in the middle of weatherstripping."

"Sorry?"

"On a day like this, we get a cold wind through the house. I'm telling him again and again, the bedroom is not a refrigerator. In the bed I should not be freezing my butt off. Old houses are terrible. Like being outside."

"So, Jack is putting weatherstripping tape—"

"Everywhere. He has to insulate around the windows, the doors, everywhere. I don't want to stop him. Not now."

When Gurney was about to give up, he heard Hardwick's voice in the background. It was followed by Esti's, sounding as though she were muffling the phone. "It's Gurney. You can finish what you're doing and call him back later."

Hardwick's voice, coming closer: "I'll talk to him now."

Gurney heard the phone being laid down, none too gently, then Esti's voice, petulant, receding into the distance. "Whatever I want, something you want comes first."

Then Hardwick's rough voice. "Yeah?"

"Bad time, Jack?"

"What do you want?"

"Were you able to get answers to my last batch of questions?"

"You still riding that horse?"

"No way to get off. Not with what happened yesterday." Gurney went on to relate the snake episode, adding, "This is not something I can walk away from."

"You're hoping it'll make Stryker think twice about Slade?"

"It ought to. Stands to reason he didn't send me that thing from Attica."

That generated a guttural laugh. "*Stands to reason* is a nice concept, Davey-boy, but it won't mean shit to Stryker."

"Thanks for your optimism. Did your guy at BCI answer any of my questions?"

"Seems like my guy is no longer my guy. Got a message from him, telling me to fuck off. Won't return my calls."

"So, we're at a dead end, information-wise?"

Hardwick sighed. "God knows why the fuck I bothered, but I called an old contact at DMV headquarters in Albany. I did her a favor back in the day, so she owed me one."

"And?"

"First, she ran Bruno Lanka's and Charlene Vesco's names through the state DMV files to see if either of them owned a Ford 150 or a Moto Guzzi. Nothing. But she did find a Cadillac Escalade registered to Lanka, with the plate number you took down in Garville."

"Hardly a surprise."

"She also ran a vehicle search for all Ford 150s and Moto Guzzis registered in Albany County. Shitload of 150s. Only a handful of Guzzis—but the name of one of the Guzzi owners caught her eye. Vesco. *Dominick* Vesco. It didn't show up on her first search, because that was for vehicles owned by *Charlene* Vesco. So then she ran a targeted search on Dominick and discovered that he also owns a Ford 150."

"Did you get his address? Or a scan of his driver's license photo?"

"Yes to the address, no to the photo." He spelled out the Garville address.

After making a note of it on the cover of one of the file folders on his desk, Gurney thanked him. "This is huge, Jack. The pieces are starting to connect."

Hardwick made a sucking noise through his teeth that conveyed his normal skepticism and then some. "Huge? You mean, the fact that someone by the name of Vesco owns the tow truck and someone else by the name of Vesco owns a pickup and motorcycle like the ones that were on Blackmore Mountain that day?"

"That's a pretty significant fact."

"But what the hell does it mean? That the Vesco family had it in for Sonny Lerman? And they concocted a scheme to kill him and incriminate you? What the fuck for? And what's it got to do with Bruno Lanka—who you keep saying is part of all this?"

"It's an interesting coincidence that Lanka is a butcher, or used to be one, according to the photo over the meat counter in his store."

"Coincidence? The fuck are you talking about?"

"Something in the medical examiner's autopsy report. Describing Lenny Lerman's decapitation, he said that it had been performed with great precision—by someone who knew what he was doing. I can think of two possibilities—a surgeon or a butcher."

"Like if we find a guy with a nail through his head, a carpenter should be our prime suspect?"

The comment struck Gurney as a sign of Hardwick's growing hostility toward the investigation. He wished him luck with his weatherstripping project and ended the call.

He sat for some time staring bleakly out the den window, slowly rotating his shoulders, trying to alleviate a pain that was spreading from the back of his head down his back. With his growing estrangement from local law enforcement, with Hardwick in retreat from the case, and with Madeleine pressuring him to drop it, he was feeling very much alone.

The snow was falling more heavily now from a low, slaty sky. The white expanse of the high pasture was broken only by the gray-brown stalks of dead goldenrod. It was then that he became aware of a small voice within him, faint but insistent.

Do something. Do anything. Do it now.

He picked up his phone and placed a call to Cam Stryker.

She answered immediately.

"David?"

"Yes."

"Are you alright?"

"I'm calling to give you some information."

"We agreed to handle that face-to-face."

"Just listen to what I have to say. It's more important than—"

She cut him off. "This is not how this matter should be—"

Now he cut her off. "This is about Sonny Lerman's murder. You need to hear it now. At our last meeting, I passed along Tess Larson's account of the man who appeared at her campground the day of the shooting. I also gave you her sketches of him, his pickup truck, and his motorcycle, along with photos of both vehicles' tire tread impressions. As I'm sure you've learned by now, those tread impressions and sketches ID the pickup as a Ford 150 and the off-road motorcycle as a Moto Guzzi."

She remained silent, so he continued.

"What you may not have discovered yet is that there's just one person in Albany County who owns both that model pickup and that model motorcycle. Dominick Vesco. Same last name as the woman who owns the tow truck that ran me off the road. Interesting coincidence, isn't it?"

Stryker again remained silent.

"I suggest that you get Vesco's photo from the DMV and compare it to Tess Larson's sketch of her campground visitor. You'll see quite a resemblance. And a little further investigation on your part will reveal that Dominick Vesco is an employee of Bruno Lanka."

"How do you know that?"

"I saw a man in Lanka's store who looked exactly like the sketch. And I saw him again driving Lanka's Escalade."

"I see. Once again, you've violated our agreement."

He ignored the comment. "What really matters here is that the Vesco-Lanka connection ties the two Lerman murders together."

"It doesn't do any such thing. This supposed connection you've come up with is inferential, at best."

"You think there's no significance in the fact that a man who was present at Sonny Lerman's murder happens to work for the man who discovered Lenny Lerman's body?"

"What I think is that this father-and-son obsession of yours is pathological. And what I know for a fact is that your interference in the Blackmore investigation has reached the level of obstruction of justice."

Although Stryker's new legal charge was a big step down from road-rage homicide, it did nothing to allay Gurney's concern. The fact that it was a less serious offense was offset by it being easier to prove. It was still a felony, and conviction could mean prison—not a healthy environment for a retired detective.

He decided to change direction. "I'd like to know what priority you're giving to arresting and prosecuting the individual who sent that snake to my home."

"I'd be happy to discuss that with you—in my office."

53

FOR THE REMAINDER OF THEIR CONVERSATION, STRYKER single-mindedly hammered away at the possible legal consequence of Gurney's interference in the Sonny Lerman case. After a few minutes of that, he ended the call.

In windless silence the snow continued to fall on the high pasture, as the afternoon's gray light faded into a wintry dusk. As the den darkened, he was tempted to switch on his desk lamp. It seemed safe enough since the room's windows were on the side of the house that faced away from the watchers in the car down by the barn, but caution prevailed.

The most obvious point of connection between the Lerman cases was the father-and-son relationship.

The next link was Bruno Lanka, who was both the finder of Lenny's body and the employer of a man who, according to Tess's sketch, was on Blackmore Mountain the day of Sonny's murder.

There was also the phone call that set Gurney up for his encounter with the tow truck—a call that promised him the facts on Lenny's murder and then resulted in Sonny's.

And, of course, there was Adrienne Lerman, daughter of the first victim, sister of the second. She'd stated a willingness to find out as much as she could about her family's vague connection with an underworld figure. It was time to check in with her.

She answered immediately, sounding weary and apologetic. "I've been meaning to call you, but I've had so much to deal with. They finally released Sonny's body. I've been going around in circles with the arrangements. And one of my hospice patients just passed. But I'm glad you called. I spoke to some of my relatives, some I hadn't spoken to for years. When I asked if they knew anything about a mobster at the edge of the family, most of them had no idea what I was talking about. I got the impression that a few knew something, but they said they didn't. The only one who was willing to talk about it was my great-aunt Angelica, who's ninety-one but sharp as a tack."

"What did she tell you?"

"Crazy things. Crazy-scary. I'd rather not talk about this on the phone."

"Would you like me to come to your apartment?"

"There's a place I'd rather go. Do you know the Franciscan Sanctuary?"

"I don't think so."

"It's a sanctuary for abandoned pets. Our dad used to take Sonny and me there when we were little. It's just few miles north of my place here in Winston. I think that's why I wanted to live here."

A pet sanctuary struck Gurney as a peculiar place for their meeting, but given Adrienne's emotional state, he didn't object. "How soon can we do it?"

"Eleven o'clock tomorrow morning? I'm seeing one of my hospice patients at nine and helping another with her lunch at twelve thirty, but I'll be free in between."

"Eleven is fine."

No sooner had he ended the call than his phone began emitting a series of beeps—signaling the activation of a security camera on the barn. He hurried from the den out to the kitchen window.

The high-beam headlights of the unmarked vehicle were illuminating a small yellow car which had come to a stop. He recognized Gerry Mirkle's Volkswagen. As he watched, the plainclothes officers approached it. One went to the driver's side window, while the other went to the passenger side. The one at the driver's window appeared to go through the standard procedure of checking Gerry's license and registration. He then went to the trunk, opened it, and looked inside. Meanwhile, the officer on the far side of the car appeared to be questioning the passenger, no doubt Madeleine. Eventually, both officers returned to their car, and the Volkswagen proceeded up through the snow-covered pasture to the house.

Realizing that Madeleine would start turning on the house lights as soon as she came in, he stepped back from the kitchen window. Once he heard the side door opening and closing, he called out gently to avoid startling her, "I'm in here, Maddie."

She came into the kitchen and switched on the light over the sink island. She was frowning. "Those cops down by the barn are looking for you."

"I know."

"What's going on?"

He explained how the Visa records of Lenny Lerman's purchases led him to the conclusion that Lerman himself had bought the gas that was later used to incinerate his car. He also told her about his phone call with Stryker and his emergency campsite up in the woods.

Madeleine reacted with a deepening frown and an announcement that she intended to take a shower. As she was leaving the room, he asked her about the encounter by the barn.

She uttered an impatient sigh, as if to say that it was one more invasive disturbance caused by his refusal to drop the case. "They wanted to know where you were. One of them even checked Gerry's trunk."

As she turned again to leave, he asked, "Did they say anything else?"

"That you should get in touch with Stryker ASAP."

"You weren't going to mention that to me?"

Anger flared up in her eyes. "Are you claiming you didn't already know that she wants to see you, to persuade you to drop this damn Lerman business?"

"I was just wondering why you didn't tell me the one thing they asked you to tell me."

"*Because you already know it!* For Christ sake, David, didn't you just finish telling me how you came over the hill from the farm road and pitched a tent up in that freezing forest to avoid facing her? You know damn well she wants to talk to you! What planet are you living on? What planet do you think I'm living on?"

54

GURNEY AWOKE THE FOLLOWING DAY WITH A DULL HEADache. However, the sky was blue and the sun was sparkling on the ice-encased branches of the trees, so he didn't feel as bad as he would have on a grayer morning. He was looking forward to his meeting with Adrienne.

The clock on his nightstand read 8:10 a.m. He needed to get moving if he was going to get to the Franciscan Sanctuary by eleven, considering that it might take him an extra half hour to scramble over that snow-covered hill to get to his car. He noted that the shotgun, which Madeleine had been keeping propped up each night by her side of the bed, was gone.

He showered, shaved, dressed, and strapped on his shoulder-holstered Glock. He found Madeleine at the breakfast table with a bowl of oatmeal and one of her books. She didn't look up. The shotgun rested on a spare chair between her and the French doors. He went to the kitchen window to see if the unmarked car was still by the barn. It wasn't, but that didn't mean much. It might be on the other side of the barn or down on the town road. He made himself a cup of coffee, two fried eggs, and a slice of whole-wheat toast. When he brought these things to the table, Madeleine closed her book and carried her bowl to the sink island.

"I have a meeting this morning over near Winston," he said. "I should be back in the early afternoon."

Drying her hands on a dish towel, she responded only with a raised eyebrow.

"Are you working today?" he asked.

"Yes."

"With Gerry?"

"Yes."

"All day?"

"Yes."

She folded the dish towel neatly and left the room.

GURNEY'S HIKE OVER the slippery hill to his car took all of the half hour he allotted. Along the way he checked on the condition of his tent. It was secure and weathertight. He hated the idea of being on the run, but maintaining his freedom was an absolute necessity.

He managed to back the car out of its hiding place with only a few traction-losing moments on the icy ground. The remainder of the trip was uneventful. Frequent checking of his rearview mirror didn't reveal any followers.

When the car's GPS made its "destination on right" announcement, he found himself next to an open gate in a fieldstone wall. A bronze plaque on the wall bore the words FRANCISCAN SANCTUARY. A sign beneath it said VISITORS WELCOME 6:00 A.M. TO 6:00 P.M. The gateway led to a driveway in far better condition than the rural road outside it.

He followed the driveway through a woodland of beeches that were still clinging to their autumn-gold leaves. The driveway brought him to a brick manor house in the middle of a parklike clearing, part of which was devoted to a modest parking lot. He spotted Adrienne standing next to an aging Subaru Forester. He pulled into a spot next to her.

She was wearing shapeless jeans, a down jacket, and a woolly stretch hat pulled down over her ears. There were splotches of red on her face and her ungloved hands.

"I apologize," she said as he got out of his car, "I forgot how far this is from Walnut Crossing."

"No problem, Adrienne."

"You must be wondering why I chose this place."

"You said you came here as a child."

She nodded. "With my father and Sonny, when things were . . . less complicated. Do you mind walking while we talk?"

She led the way out of the parking area to one of several paths into the beech forest. The foliage above them was thin, and the path was bathed in late-morning sunlight. "We came here once a month. Lenny only had us the first Sunday of every month—that was the divorce arrangement. He brought us here to see the animals."

"The animals?"

"Abandoned pets. That's what this place is all about. A thousand acres with huge enclosures, not like a typical animal shelter with little cages. The big house by the parking lot—that's where some of the dogs and cats live, the ones that don't like being outside. And there are lots of volunteers to take care of them—feed them, walk them, talk to them."

Her voice was wistful. "When we came here, it was like we were a happy family."

"You lived the rest of the time with your mother?"

"And her endless series of abusive boyfriends. I hated them all."

She fell silent, lost in the past.

"What was Lenny like back then?" asked Gurney.

"As I think about it now, just a younger version of what he turned out to be in later years. There was always a gap, an emotional separation, between him and Sonny. Dad was always trying to impress

Sonny. A grown man, trying to get the approval of an eight-year-old. Isn't it supposed to be the other way around?"

It was a statement, not a question. Gurney waited for her to go on.

"But Dad was always just a kid himself, an insecure kid trying to be accepted, trying to find a place in the world. Or maybe not so much a place in the world as a place in other people's hearts." She sighed. "He just never figured out how to make it happen."

"You think the blackmail money he hoped to end up with was part of that?"

"It's the only way it makes sense. And I'm pretty sure that's what all his gangster talk was all about. Lenny confused impressing people with making them like him. He had it in his head that if he sounded important, if he had the cars, the money . . ." Her voice trailed off.

"Are you suggesting he made up that talk about having a mob connection?"

"Apparently that was true enough, according to Great-Aunt Angelica. She was close to Lenny's father, my grandfather. One night after he drank too much he told her about a distant cousin of theirs, someone she'd never heard of before, who killed people for money. Money he then 'invested' in high-ranking cops and politicians, so he was never arrested for anything, or even investigated."

"Did your grandfather tell your great-aunt his name?"

"Only that he used so many false names, no one knew the real one. My grandfather called him the Viper."

"Can you get in touch with your grandfather?"

She shook her head. "He passed away years ago."

"And you never heard Lenny or Sonny refer to him by any actual name?"

"No."

"So," said Gurney, summing up the situation. "An anonymous professional killer with corrupt enablers in high places. Known as the Viper."

Adrienne nodded nervously. "That's the part that gives me gooseflesh."

"That nickname?"

"The reason for it. It's the creepiest thing Great-Aunt Angelica remembers my grandfather telling her. The man collected dangerous snakes. And used them to kill people."

55

AFTER ADRIENNE DEPARTED IN HER FORESTER, GURNEY settled down on a bench on the sunny side of the big house to review what she'd told him.

Great-Aunt Angelica's report of a Lerman connection to a hit man with a snake fetish felt substantive. It struck Gurney as far more than a coincidence that he'd received two warnings involving snakes—the decapitated rabbit on which Barstow found snake DNA and the fanged surprise in the jam basket. If Angelica's story was to be believed, the individual who was trying to stop the reexamination of Lenny Lerman's murder was a professional killer with a blood link to the victim.

What still remained in darkness was what actually happened at Slade's lodge—specifically, who killed Lenny and what it had to do with Ziko Slade. Was it possible that the shadowy Lerman relative had enlisted Lenny as a cat's-paw in a blackmail scheme that went off the tracks?

The only thing Gurney knew for sure was that he needed to know more. More about Lenny, more about the hit man with the snake fetish, more about Ziko Slade, and more about what connected them all—and whether that connection led to the shooting death of Lenny's son on Blackmore Mountain.

He relaxed as best he could on the hard bench, closing his eyes and raising his face to the sun, on the off chance that emptying his mind would make room for a touch of inspiration.

"Nice spot, isn't it?"

Gurney opened his eyes and saw a tall, colorfully dressed woman standing on the lawn in front of the bench. She was holding a leash in each hand with a tall, shaggy dog at the end of each one, their curious eyes fixed on him.

"Very nice," he answered.

"First time? I haven't seen you here before."

"Yes. First time."

She gave him an appraising look. "Are you a dog person or a cat person?"

"I'm not sure I'm either." Then he added, he wasn't sure why, "My wife has an interest in alpacas."

"But you don't?"

"I'm usually too busy to take care of animals, or even think about them."

"So, what are you doing here?"

"It was a convenient place to meet someone," he said, not entirely honestly, and changed the subject. "The big house here, with all the surrounding property—how did it come to be an animal shelter?"

"*Sanctuary*," she said pointedly. "Shelters are prisons. This place is about freedom. A miracle, really."

"Oh?"

"A deathbed conversion. Well, close to that. Do you know about Halliman Brook?"

"Doesn't sound familiar."

"He was a horrible lumber baron. Responsible for deforestation, erosion, pollution. Treated his workers like dirt. Paid them starvation wages and fired them the minute they got injured. His personal life was just as ugly. He nearly beat his first wife to death."

"This is the man who had the conversion?"

"At the end of his life. He knew he was dying. He suddenly saw that he had to get rid of everything he'd accumulated in his mean, ruthless life. He was afraid that the weight of it would drag him down into hell. So he gave it all away, including this estate and a huge endowment to transform it into a sanctuary for homeless animals."

The story reminded Gurney of Ziko Slade—how seeing death could change one's life.

"We're looking for dog walkers," she said, suddenly cheerful. "And the paths are lovely. You should consider volunteering."

GURNEY STOPPED AT Leapin' Lizards Latte Lounge in Winston for a much-needed coffee. The shop embraced the local style of mercantile cuteness. He ordered a large coffee and a toasted bagel with cream cheese.

Back in the car, he took out his phone and entered "The Viper" as a search term. He found hundreds of entries but nothing that led in a promising direction. Despite the vividness of that underworld moniker, the man seemed to be as elusive as Great-Aunt Angelica's report suggested.

Finding out more about Lenny Lerman, however, might not be so difficult. His GPS location data and Visa records had provided interesting facts that Stryker had overlooked or chosen to ignore. Perhaps there was more information to be mined from those sources. Kyra Barstow was still, as far as he knew, a reliable ally. He called her number and left a message.

"Kyra, it's Dave, with yet another request. The Lerman data you sent me led to some weird discoveries, and I'd like to take another look at that resource—especially any GPS data you might have for the two or three months prior to Lerman's murder." He paused before adding, "FYI, my situation with Stryker has deteriorated, and she's more eager than ever to stop my inquiries. For your own protection, discretion is important."

As he was ending the call, another was coming in—from Adrienne Lerman.

"David here."

She spoke rapidly, her voice high with anxiety. "I just got a call from some woman—I think it was a woman—named Sam Smollett, a producer at RAM News. She said there's been a frightening new development in my father's murder case, and they want to do a remote interview with me tonight on that *Controversial Perspectives* show."

The frightening development, thought Gurney, would probably be the Thanksgiving delivery of the snake. "What did you tell her?"

"About the interview? That I didn't want to do it. When I asked her what development she was talking about, she just kept using the word 'frightening.' What on earth was she talking about?"

He knew he had to tread carefully to find a path that involved neither a flat-out lie nor the appalling truth. He chose deflection rather than deception.

"I haven't heard anything from her. In fact, I'm not in touch with anyone at RAM, and I hope it stays that way. I have no trust in anything they do or say. As for there being new developments in your father's case, anything significant would be under the control of the Rexton Police Department or the District Attorney. They're the ones who get to decide how much to reveal."

"Well, according to this Smollett woman, RAM will be revealing everything they know tonight on that awful program."

"More likely, they'll be revealing whatever they believe will boost their ratings, regardless of its accuracy."

Adrienne let out a shaky sigh. "This is so awful."

"I agree."

To Gurney's relief, the call ended without his having to directly deny any knowledge of what Smollett might be referring to. He wanted to maintain Adrienne's trust as long as possible, and a direct lie could destroy that trust.

What interested him now was how much the slimy "journalists" at RAM actually knew, how they came to know it, and what slant they planned to put on it. At RAM there was always a slant.

Knowing the RAM penchant for promotion, he figured this instance would be no exception. He used his phone to go to their website. And there it was, in pulsating red letters:

LERMAN MURDER BOMBSHELL!

TERRIFYING NEW DEVELOPMENT IN THE CASE OF

THE BEHEADED BLACKMAILER!

TONIGHT ON *CONTROVERSIAL PERSPECTIVES*!

After wasting the next couple of minutes speculating on how Tarla Hackett and Jordan Lake would handle the snake event—and from whom they'd gotten their information—his phone rang. It was Sam Smollett.

His first instinct was to let it go to voicemail, especially after what he'd just told Adrienne about his unwillingness to engage with RAM. But the temptation to make his position perfectly clear was too strong to resist.

"Dave Gurney here."

"This is Sam Smollett, executive producer of *Controversial Perspectives*."

"Yes?"

"As you may know, our program recently devoted a special segment to the Blackmore Mountain murder. We'll be revisiting that tonight from the perspective of the original Lerman murder, because there's no doubt now that the two are connected—and you're part of the connection."

"Is that so?"

"Considering the delivery you received on Thanksgiving Day, I'd say it's absolutely so."

Gurney said nothing. Smollett went on, a chilly smile in her voice.

"Because of your unique perspective, we'd like you to be part of tonight's discussion. You can do it from wherever you are—totally convenient. I'm sure you'll have a lot to say to our audience."

"What questions would I be asked?"

"That would be up to Tarla and Jordan. But I'm sure they'll want your reaction to the item that was delivered to your home. It was clearly a warning to stop stirring up doubts about Ziko Slade's conviction. So, an obvious question is, are you going to drop your investigation?"

Gurney paused. Sure that Smollett was recording the call with an eye to airing it, he carefully considered his response.

"Everything I've learned about Lenny Lerman's death points to the innocence of Ziko Slade. And everything that's been done to discourage my investigation has strengthened my resolve to see Slade exonerated, and the actual murderer exposed."

"Wow! Okay! Now, to prepare for your participation in our program this evening—"

Gurney cut her off. "There'll be no participation. I've stated my position. I have nothing further to say."

He ended the call and went to get a second coffee for the drive home.

56

THE CLOSER HE GOT TO WALNUT CROSSING, THE WHITER were the hills and the grayer the sky. It felt like he was passing from autumn into winter—an impression underscored by the icy approach to the hill behind his property.

After parking the car out of sight, he made his way up the slippery incline to his campsite. He gave the tent a once-over, then went to the spot where an opening in the hemlock branches provided a view of his house, the low pasture, and the barn.

The area had a cold, forlorn, forbidding look about it. He saw no intruders, official or otherwise, but that was no guarantee of safety. Shivering, he began his descent toward the rear of the house under cover of the hillside evergreens. When he reached the base of the slope, he broke into a run across the exposed field and climbed through the unlocked bedroom window.

Once the stress of making it to the house without incident passed, he became aware of a cold-induced ache in his gloveless hands and a throbbing in his head from the sprint across the field. He swallowed a couple of acetaminophens and held his hands over a burner on the stove until his fingers tingled with renewed circulation.

He turned off the gas and peered cautiously out each kitchen window, then went to the den and looked out those windows as well. The only sign of life was a doe making her way along the edge of the clearing. He settled down at his desk, rubbed the last bit of stiffness out of his fingers, and opened his laptop.

There was a new email from Kyra Barstow—with no introductory note, just a long row of attached documents. He counted thirteen, covering the thirteen weeks leading up to the day of Lenny Lerman's murder. He opened one at random and saw that it contained a phone-location record of Lerman's movements during that particular week.

Although the original warrant seeking Lerman's location records had evidently covered those thirteen weeks, Stryker had chosen to focus the jury's attention solely on the day of Lerman's fatal trip to Slade's lodge. Gurney hoped that the data for the preceding weeks might offer a clue to what happened on that final day.

He put the documents in chronological order and conducted an initial review to get an overall sense of Lerman's movements—the basic geography of his life. The impression this yielded was of a man who led a limited and repetitive existence. Hardly ever in that quarter of a year had he ventured more than a few miles from his apartment. He was at home or at the Beer Monster, with occasional trips to a gas station and a supermarket.

A close examination of the mapped data revealed only a few departures from this pattern. The last and longest was the trip to the lodge, with its peculiar stop for a gas can and the gas to fill it. Prior to that, there was a trip to and from a location in Gorse, a village adjacent to Calliope Springs; a series of three trips to and from a location in Ploverton, a suburb of Albany; and a trip to the Franciscan Sanctuary.

There was one anomaly. Three days after Lerman's visit to the sanctuary, there was a four-hour period during which the location-tracking function of his phone had been turned off. Anomalies sometimes provided clues, but this one only raised questions. Where did he go that day? And why did he want there to be no record of it?

Lerman's trips to Gorse and Ploverton could be further explored, however. Gurney began with the forty-eight-minute stop in Gorse. He took its coordinates from the document and entered them into Google Street View on his laptop. He saw a single-story brick building on a tree-lined street. A sign on the lawn identified the building as Clearview Office Suites and listed its tenants: two dental offices, an urgent care facility, a financial adviser, a land surveyor, and a law firm.

Next, he entered the coordinates for the location in Ploverton. A street-side sign identified the place as Capital District Office Park, a label that seemed extravagant for a pair of modest two-story buildings, separated by a parking area. The list of tenants included a criminal defense attorney, a radiological imaging center, a hematology-oncology practice, a sleep-disorder clinic, an architect, an engineering firm, a real estate management outfit, a corporate security company, and a stock broker.

Gurney spent the next two hours going back over the entire thirteen-week GPS record Barstow had provided. When he came to the end of the final week, it was dark outside and the only light in the den was emanating from his computer. His eyes burned from staring too long at the screen, but he was too keyed up to rest.

Wondering what to do next, two things occurred to him—to see if there was any relationship between the dates of Lerman's trips and his reported mood changes, and to make whatever preparations might be required for an emergency retreat to his campsite.

He decided to deal with the second task first because it was mainly physical, and mentally he was nearing exhaustion. He needed to focus on some simple activity, such as detaching the propane tank from the outdoor grill and bringing it up to the campsite for the tent heater. And it would also make sense to bring up an extra jacket, gloves, boots, and a woolen hat, in case he had to leave the house in only the clothes he was wearing. He looked out the den window and concluded that the moonlight would provide enough visibility for the job.

As it turned out, he was right about the visibility, but he'd underestimated the weight of the full propane tank and the awkwardness of trying to carry everything at once. In the end, the project took two trips and produced a shooting pain in the arm that lugged the propane.

He was making his way across the field to the house at the end of the second trip, when a security alert sounded on his phone. Rather than reversing course and heading for cover, he proceeded to the corner of the house, peered around it, and was relieved to see Gerry Mirkle's Volkswagen proceeding up the pasture lane.

57

MADELEINE SHOWED LITTLE INTEREST IN DISCUSSING her day or her dinner with Gerry Mirkle, and even less interest in Gurney's activities.

While he consumed a dinner hastily concocted from leftovers, she sat silently by the fireplace at the opposite end of the room, a book in her lap, her gaze fixed on the ashes in the firebox, her shotgun leaning against the fieldstone facing. When he finished eating, he asked if she'd like him to clean out the ashes and build a new fire. She shook her head. He went over to the wall by the French doors and switched on the outside lights. It was snowing again, lightly but steadily.

As he was watching the flakes drift down over the floodlit patio, a sharp little "click" attracted his attention to the Regulator clock over the sideboard—a sound it made on the hour. It was 8:00 p.m., time for *Controversial Perspectives*. He considered telling Madeleine about the call from Sam Smollett, then thought better of it and went into the den alone.

By the time he got connected to the livestream, Tarla Hackett and Jordan Lake were sitting at their desks, expressions charged with grim excitement.

Hackett was speaking. "Just when we were thinking the Lerman murder cases couldn't get any wilder, guess what? That wildness just went into overdrive! Forgive my blunt language, Jordan, but I've got to ask the obvious question: What the hell is going on?!"

"That's what we're all wondering, Tarla." Lake turned to the camera, adding a note of confidentiality to his grim tone. "Folks, we're in a tough spot here in the RAM News organization. Here's the situation. There's been a monstrous attack on the man in the middle of the two Lerman murders—the man who's been investigating the first and may be implicated in the second—retired NYPD detective David Gurney. According to our inside information, a package was delivered to his home on Thanksgiving Day—a package containing something so hair-raising, so terrifying, we can only conclude that it was meant to stop him in his tracks."

Hackett nodded her agreement. "You said a moment ago that this story put us in a tough spot, Jordan. Maybe you could explain that."

"Absolutely! As I just suggested, the dreadful object delivered to Gurney's home was obviously a life-threatening warning. That's a serious crime, and the DA has asked that we delay disclosure of the details while her investigation is ongoing. We're cooperating with her request—although we do intend to give you, our viewers, the whole story as soon as possible."

Hackett nodded solemnly. "Apart from the awful specifics of what was delivered to the Gurney home, I understand there's plenty we can share with our audience right now."

"Absolutely! The object delivered to the Gurney household was clearly intended as a huge stop sign in the path of his investigation.

So, the question is, did it work? RAM's own Sam Smollett put that question to Dave Gurney this afternoon." Hackett pointed to someone off-camera. "Run the audio!"

Smollett's recorded voice came through loud and clear.

"The package you received was surely a warning to stop stirring up doubts about Ziko Slade's conviction. Do you plan to drop your investigation?"

"Everything I've learned so far about Lenny Lerman's death points to the innocence of Ziko Slade. And everything that's been done to discourage my investigation has strengthened my resolve to see Ziko Slade exonerated, and the actual murderer exposed."

"So there you have it, folks!" said Lake. "Despite being warned off, Dave Gurney is determined as ever to turn Slade's conviction upside down."

Hackett narrowed her already small eyes. "I wonder, am I hearing the voice of determination or the voice of obsession?"

Lake pursed his lips. "Or worse—is it the voice of a man in a compromised position trying to sound like a hero?"

"Great question, Jordan. In my own effort to get to the truth of who Dave Gurney really is, this afternoon I interviewed an individual who knows him personally. In order to protect that person's identity, we've electronically altered their voice."

Hackett pointed to someone off-screen. "Run the audio."

The first voice on the recording was Hackett's. "These days a lot of people are wondering, who is the real Dave Gurney? I asked someone who's known him for several years to share their insights with us. So, let's get right to it. When I say 'Dave Gurney,' what's the first characteristic that comes to mind?"

"Icy calmness." The altered voice sounded vaguely female. "You never know what's really going on inside him."

"You're saying the man is a bit of a mystery?"

"Exactly. You always have the sense that whatever he knows, he's probably keeping most of it to himself."

"You mean his own feelings? His own past actions?"

"Especially those things. He can sound like he's speaking with real conviction, but you get the impression he's never really telling the whole truth."

"Very interesting," said Hackett. "Especially in relation to the big issue in the news at the moment—his alleged involvement in the Blackmore Mountain shooting of Sonny Lerman. Does he have anything to say about that?"

"Absolutely! He claims that Sonny Lerman's and Lenny Lerman's murders are connected—that it was a toxic element in their relationship that led to both of them being killed."

Gurney's jaw tightened at the realization that those were almost the exact words he'd used in response to one of Kim Corazon's questions on Thanksgiving—making her identity as RAM's informant painfully clear.

The altered voice continued. "Dave Gurney insists that the district attorney's misunderstanding of Lenny's murder has made it impossible for her to understand Sonny's."

"Fascinating! One final question. And this is the *big* one. Would you say that Dave Gurney is capable of murder?"

"I can't say that he's not."

The recording ended and Hackett turned to Jordan Lake. "I have to admit, that last answer gave me a chill."

Lake nodded his head in an approximation of troubled thoughtfulness. "Coming from someone who knows him personally, it's pretty damning—and the perfect way to conclude tonight's coverage of the Gurney mystery." Lake turned to the camera. "More shocking news coming up, folks. After these important announcements, we'll take a hard look at some of the craziest ideas educators are forcing on America's kids. Stay with us!"

"Bitch!"

Gurney was startled by the closeness and intensity of Madeleine's voice. He turned in his chair and saw her standing a few feet away, her face tight with anger. She'd obviously come to the same conclusion he had about the owner of the altered voice.

She went on. "That young woman is laser-focused on herself and her career, period. That's where she begins and ends. She's just a nasty little appendage of the nasty media. When she was here, all she wanted was information. Information she could turn around and sell to her friends at RAM. What a rotten little manipulator!"

The palpable fury of Madeleine's attack left him momentarily speechless.

She added, "I can't imagine why your son is involved with her."

There was a brief silence, broken by Gurney. "Actually, he was pretty open about that when we spoke on the phone."

"Oh?"

"He's infatuated with her energy, ambition, drive."

"And blind to her selfishness?"

"Not entirely. But in his mind the energy part outweighs everything else."

"He's got a lot to learn."

"I know. I certainly did."

"What are you talking about?"

"When he was telling me what he found attractive about her, I realized it was the same thing that had attracted me to his mother when I was twenty-one."

"Did you describe to him how badly that ended?"

He shook his head. "I couldn't figure out how to bring that up without it sounding like a direct criticism of his mother, which would create an emotional distraction. Besides, you can't argue someone out of a romantic attachment. He'll have to find out for himself. But it's painful to see him repeating my mistake."

"Maybe he'll wake up before the mistake turns into a marriage. I hope so. He's a nice young man." She paused, her voice hardening. "But that woman is never to set foot in this house again. Never."

58

AFTER A RESTLESS, INCREASINGLY PAINFUL NIGHT IN BED, Gurney struggled in the morning to get to his feet and maintain his balance. He felt as though all the emotional impacts of recent days had joined forces with the after-effects of his concussion to batter him into submission.

What he found most unnerving was the disjointed swirling of his thoughts—the hideous green snake rising out of the carton; Madeleine reeling back against the wall; Kim's weirdly altered voice on RAM, suggesting to millions of listeners that he was capable of murder; Stryker's threats; Lenny's gas can in the quarry. All in a jumble. He headed for the shower, eager for the mental and physical balm it often provided.

Standing for ten minutes in the warm spray did take the sharp edge off the shooting pains that ran from his left temple down into his shoulder, but it did little to calm his racing mind.

Later that morning, as he was sitting at the breakfast table, gazing cautiously down toward the watchers' car by the barn, Madeleine announced that she and Gerry would be joining the string group in the afternoon for a concert at the Oneonta nursing home.

"I thought you only did concerts there on Sundays," he said, as though he found her departure from custom problematical.

She raised an eyebrow. "Today *is* Sunday."

He responded only with a blink and a small grunt of recognition, but he was bothered by this evidence of his scattered state of mind more than he was willing to admit. Mental acuity, after all, wasn't just his claim to fame, it was his identity.

Hours later, after Madeleine left for the concert, Gurney felt his anxious exhaustion finally morphing into a gentle doziness. He was wary, however, of falling into a deep sleep alone in the house, lest the security system alert on his phone fail to wake him in the face of an approaching police raid. After weighing the options, he strapped on his Glock, slipped into his jacket, and headed for his campsite.

———

HE AWOKE IN the cold darkness of his tent to the yipping of coyotes. His phone told him it was 9:35 p.m. The pain in his head and shoulder came back to life as he crawled out of his sleeping bag and got to his feet. The pain faded to a dull aching as he made his way by moonlight down the hill and across the back field to the house.

All the lights were out, which told him that Madeleine was either in bed or hadn't come home yet. He knocked softly on the bedroom window, waited, and tried again. He heard movement inside. A flashlight was switched on. Coming closer, the beam was directed out at him, briefly blinding him. Then the flashlight was extinguished, the window sash was raised, and he climbed through the opening. By the time he was standing inside and had closed the window behind him, Madeleine was already back in bed.

She said nothing.

Neither did he.

He felt a new wave of exhaustion overtaking him. He removed his clothes, put his Glock and phone on the nightstand, got into bed, and fell immediately into a deep, restorative sleep.

THE FOLLOWING MORNING, Gurney awoke feeling a lot more like his normal self. Part of that normality was the presence of a plan.

The plan was to compare the dates of Lerman's non-routine trips not only to the dates of his mood changes, but to the dates of the events in his diary and the dates of the calls from the anonymous phone.

As soon as he got dressed, he went straight to his desk in the den. He recalled that Thomas Cazo claimed Lerman appeared depressed for a period of about a month, then regained his bragging personality a week or so before quitting his job. That time frame corresponded with Adrienne's recollection of the same period. Apparently Lerman descended into his bleak mood toward the end of September but was reenergized at the end of October.

Gurney created a list of the trips Lerman had made to places other than his habitual destinations. He also included on the list the four-hour blackout of Lerman's GPS locator, the calls Lerman received from the anonymous phone, and his diary entries.

As he was arranging everything in chronological order, he thought of an additional date that might be meaningful. He took out his phone and called Howard Manx of NorthGuard Insurance.

The man answered immediately and brusquely. "Manx."

"This is Dave Gurney, still working on the Lerman-Slade murder—"

Manx interrupted. "You found anything useful to me?"

"Nothing that you can use to claw back the insurance payout, if that's what you mean. But I'm convinced that the official version is wrong."

"Good. What do you want?"

"I'm trying to put some key events in order. Can you give me the date Lenny Lerman applied for his million-dollar policy?"

"Hold on."

Sound of keys tapping. Manx sniffling, coughing, clearing his throat. More keys tapping.

"October 20 application date. Effective date October 30. That tell you anything?"

"If it turns out to be significant, you'll be the first to know."

Gurney added the two dates to his list and printed out a hard copy.

Lerman's visit to Clearview Office Suites: September 07
First visit to the Capital District Office Park: September 12
Second visit to the Capital District Office Park: September 25
Third visit to the Capital District Office Park: September 27
Start of his depression: End of September
Trip to the Franciscan Sanctuary: October 10
Four-hour disconnection of his phone's GPS locator: October 19
Insurance application: October 20
First call from the anonymous phone: October 23

Lerman learns Slade's secret from "Jingo":   October 24

Lerman decides on $1MM extortion amount: October 27

Emergence from depression: End of October

Second call from the anonymous phone: November 02

Dinner with Adrienne and Sonny: November 02

Third call from the anonymous phone: November 05

Lerman's first call to Slade: November 05

Lerman quits Beer Monster job: November 06

Fourth call from the anonymous phone: November 12

Lerman gives Slade 10 days to get $1MM: November 13

Fifth call from the anonymous phone: November 22

Lerman's final call to Slade: November 23

Lerman's trip to Slade's lodge: November 23

Gurney made his way slowly through the list, weighing the possible meanings of the time relationships. He was well aware of the mind's tendency to leap from temporal association to causality in order to create coherence. It would be easy to assume that Lerman's visits to the Capital District Office Park had caused his depression, and that his plan to blackmail Slade had ended it. That might be true, but the devil was in the details, and the details were unknown.

Just as intriguing were those calls Lerman received from an anonymous phone and their proximity to certain events described in his diary. One explanation would be that Lerman was receiving instructions from a collaborator.

Perhaps the collaborator was the "Jingo" that Lerman named in his diary as the source of his information about Slade. But why was there no further mention of him? And why no mention at all of the anonymous phone calls?

Gurney wondered if Lerman's failure to mention those calls was related to another omission—the four-hour disconnection of his phone's GPS locator.

"Are you watching the time?"

Madeleine was standing in the den doorway, dressed for work, her voice more critical than curious.

"The time?"

"For your neurology appointment."

LANSON-CLAVIN NEUROLOGY ASSOCIATES was on the top floor of a colorless four-story building in Albany. The mostly glass structure was set on pillars above a parking lot.

Dr. Lyn Clavin was a pale, thin-boned woman with straight brown hair pulled back into a tight ponytail. A white lab coat added to her chilly image. She walked into the small examining room with a blue file folder in her hand and, without acknowledging Gurney, sat at a small metal desk with her back to him, opened the folder, and began scanning through it.

Finally, she swiveled around and faced him, flashing a perfunctory smile that left so little trace he wondered if he'd imagined it. She looked down at the folder in her lap.

"David Gurney?"

"Yes."

"Date of birth?"

He gave it to her, adopting her clipped tone.

"The purpose of your visit today?"

"A follow-up assessment related to a recent concussion. It was scheduled at the time of my discharge from Parker Hospital in Harbane."

She took a black pen from the pocket of her white coat and held it poised over the top page in the folder. "I will ask a series of questions. You can answer yes, no, or sometimes. Understood?"

"Yes."

"Since the injury, do you have headaches?"

"Sometimes."

"Their average intensity, on a scale of one to ten?"

"Six."

"Dizziness?"

"If I stand up too quickly."

"Ringing in your ears?"

"Yes, but at a volume low enough that I can generally ignore it."

"Fatigue?"

"I feel tired more frequently than I used to. A minor inconvenience."

"Double vision?"

"No."

"Blurred vision?"

"No."

"Depression?"

"No."

"Anxiety?"

"No more than usual."

She'd been making check marks on a sheet in her folder after his answers, but now she hesitated. "Anxiety is a frequent emotional state for you?"

"I'm in an anxiety-producing line of work."

"Namely?"

"Criminal investigation."

She frowned and made a short note on the sheet before going on.

"Any changes in your sense of taste or smell?'

"No."

"Anger?"

"Sorry?"

"Have you found yourself becoming angry, impatient, irritated more frequently since your injury?"

That was the first question he had to think about.

"More frustration than usual, but with considerable justification."

That seemed to produce a hint of amusement, or maybe it was just a tic at the corner of her mouth. She made another note on the sheet.

"Any increased sensitivity to light?"

"No."

"Increased sensitivity to loud noises?"

"No."

"Any injury-related pains, other than the headaches?"

"Yes, in my neck and upper back."

"On a scale of one to ten?"

"Between four and six."

"Any change in your sense of balance?"

He hesitated. She looked up from the sheet, pen poised.

"It's possible," he said. "But very slight."

She pursed her lips, conveying that a slight loss of balance might be serious. "Stand up."

He got to his feet.

"Stand on one leg."

He stood on his right leg.

"Now the left leg."

He tried it, staggered a bit to the side, caught his balance, staggered a bit to the other side, caught his balance, tottered, then remained upright but unsteady.

"Sit down."

He did. She made another note.

"Medications?"

"Acetaminophen, sometimes ibuprofen."

She gave him a suspicious look. "Nothing else?"

"Nothing else."

She rose from her chair, laid the folder on the desk, stepped over in front of him, and held her pen up vertically. "Follow it with your eyes without moving your head."

He did so, as she moved the pen slowly to the right and left, then up and down.

She laid the pen aside and held up two fingers off toward the edge of his peripheral vision. "Look straight ahead and tell me how many fingers you see."

She did this several times, holding up one, two, or three fingers in various positions to his right, left, up, and down. He told her what he saw. She showed no reaction to his answers. She turned her back to him.

"Cat mat bat sat hat," she said and asked him to repeat what he'd heard.

He did so.

She went to the desk, made a longish entry on one of the pages, and closed the folder with a note of finality.

"So," he said with a polite smile, "what's the verdict?"

She made a little sucking sound through her teeth. "You've suffered a traumatic brain injury. You have ongoing symptoms that indicate a need for rest and additional monitoring. I recommend an MRI in thirty days if the symptoms are not resolved, sooner if they become more pronounced. Any questions?"

"Is there anything you suggest I do or not do?"

"Rest. Avoid exertion. Avoid stressful situations."

As if to punctuate the end of their meeting, she produced a split-second smile.

If he'd blinked, he would have missed it.

59

DOWN IN THE PARKING LOT, HE SAT FOR A WHILE IN THE car, feeling disoriented. He knew *where* he was, he just wasn't sure *who* he was.

Seeing himself as a *patient*, limited by a condition that might not improve and for which the only palliative was to stop doing the things he needed to do—seeing himself as Dr. Lyn Clavin saw him—filled him with a jarring sense of vulnerability. The hardy detective had been transformed into the impaired middle-aged patient of a cold-eyed neurologist.

The ringing of his phone kept him from sinking any deeper into self-pity. The name on the screen was Emma Martin.

"Gurney here."

"David, something has happened. I need to speak to you as soon as possible."

"I'm listening."

"Not on the phone. In person. Are you at home?"

"I'm in a parking lot in Albany. Where are you?"

"About fifty miles west of Albany. We could meet in Roseland, which is halfway between us. There's a small Catholic church there that's always open and empty. Saint Peter's, on the edge of town. Would that be alright?"

"I can be there in half an hour."

"Thank you."

The half hour drive was uneventful but far from relaxed, as Gurney was continually checking his mirrors for any signs of followers. Dark, anonymous sedans drew his particular attention, but none stayed with him long enough to prompt evasive action.

On a list of all the misnamed towns in the world, Roseland would surely be in the top ten. Its central feature was a huge stone quarrying operation, complete with the mammoth machines that grind boulders into gravel. The cliffs surrounding the excavation bore the vertical scars of holes drilled for the dynamite charges used to blow the mountainside apart. Machinery, dump trucks, prefabricated office structures, vehicles, everything in sight was covered with gray stone dust. The air seemed to vibrate with the grinding roar of the rock-crushers.

The town that radiated out from this hellhole grew quieter as the distance from the machinery increased. St. Peter's was on one of the last residential streets before the modest homes gave way to farmland. The neighborhood was almost free of dust and almost quiet. The church was a white wooden structure with a modest bell tower. It had a lawn on one side, dominated by an ancient apple tree, and a parking area on the other side.

Gurney tried the front door of the church, found it unlocked, and went inside. The image of the quarry evaporated in an oasis of stillness and soft light. The sense of smell had an evocative power that he found nowhere more powerful than in a traditional Catholic church. The unique mixture of incense, flowers, burnt candle wax, leather-bound prayer books, and dry wood never failed to transport him to the church of his childhood.

He sat in the last pew and slipped into recollections of his altar-boy days—of lilies on a linen-draped altar, shining gold chalices, satin vestments, unsmiling priests, dark confessional booths full of whispered transgressions.

His reveries were interrupted by a movement at the edge of his vision. He looked up and saw Emma standing next to the pew. She was wearing the same loose, cape-like coat she'd worn the day she came to his house with the request that began his investigation. But now there was a deep sadness in her eyes.

"May I join you?"

He slid sideways in the pew to make room for her.

"This morning, Ziko was found dead in his cell."

Gurney stared at her. "Dead? Jesus! How?"

"They're calling it suicide. But I'm sure he was killed."

"In his cell?"

She nodded. "With a hanging rope made of torn bedsheets. Or at least that was the way it was made to look."

Gurney let out a despondent sigh. He was picturing the body of one of the incarcerated men whose bedsheet "suicides" he'd investigated over the years.

"You're sure it wasn't actually a suicide?"

Emma shook her head adamantly. "I spoke to him yesterday afternoon. The man I spoke to was not about to kill himself."

Neither, thought Gurney, was the man I visited hardly more than a week ago. That man was as calm and positive as a man could be in a place like that. "Do you have any idea who might have been responsible?"

"I assume another prisoner or a guard—acting on the orders of the person who framed him to begin with."

"I may be getting closer to discovering who that person is."

Emma shook her head. "A dangerous pursuit. Not worth it."

Gurney blinked in surprise. "Not worth it?"

"Not at this point."

"You don't think justice is worth pursuing? I thought you came to me because you wanted justice for Ziko."

"I wanted the truth. Because it would lead to his release. That possibility no longer exists."

"You're saying his death has made justice irrelevant?" Gurney's voice had risen noticeably in the silence of the little church.

"Justice for the dead is a wolf in sheep's clothing—a pompous name for revenge. It's an absurd goal to risk your life for."

"So, principles like justice mean nothing?"

"Most 'principles' are shiny wrapping for selfish motives. Love is the only true guidepost, and love is always for the living."

He made an effort to lower his voice. "You sound like you've joined the chorus telling me to walk away from the case."

For a long while they sat in silence.

Then Gurney's curiosity took over.

"Did Slade have a will?"

"Yes."

"And a substantial estate?"

"Approximately eighteen to twenty million dollars, depending on the valuation of assets."

"Do you know who the beneficiaries are?"

"Ian Valdez and my recovery center."

"Half to each of you?"

"Yes."

"You've known about this for some time?"

"Ever since Ziko had an attorney draft the will. I am the executor. I also have power of attorney for Ziko's affairs and have been named next of kin. When his body is released, I'll arrange for its cremation in accordance with his wishes." She related all this with no visible hesitations, her voice reflecting only the sadness in her eyes.

Gurney had more questions he wanted to ask, mainly about Valdez—who remained an enigma, now a very wealthy one—but something in Emma's grief made it impossible.

60

DURING MOST OF HIS HOMEWARD DRIVE FROM ROSELAND, Gurney's mind was filled with alternating visions of Slade hanging from a bedsheet rope in his cell and of Slade calmly sitting across from him in the visiting room.

As he crested the last forested hill and began the descent toward the reservoir side of Walnut Crossing, those thoughts were displaced by a glimpse of a state police cruiser in a roadside turnaround about five hundred yards ahead. That distance dropped to no more than three hundred yards by the time Gurney reached a point where the road shoulder was wide enough to permit a quick U-turn.

As he sped back up the hill, in his rearview mirror he saw the cruiser swinging out of the turnaround, lights flashing, starting up the hill after him. As soon as he passed the crest and was momentarily out of his pursuer's line of sight, he floored the accelerator to get past a sight-obstructing curve in the road. He knew the heavily wooded area was criss-crossed with old logging trails and began searching for one. He passed one that looked impassable, then, glancing in his mirror, took a chance on a second, which rose steeply up from the right side of the road.

He hoped that the teeth-rattling blows to the rental car's undercarriage wouldn't turn out to be fatal, as the front and rear end alternately became airborne over the rocky ground. As soon as he could no longer see the road behind him, he jammed on the brakes and switched off the ignition—just in time to hear the cruiser racing past, siren blaring. A moment later, it was followed by a second cruiser with a matching siren.

Immediately, he backed down the trail, swerved out onto the

road, and sped down toward the reservoir. At the first intersection, instead of taking the county road toward Walnut Crossing, he took it in the opposite direction, paralleling the river that carried the reservoir's outflow. A few miles later, he made a sharp right onto a back road and proceeded via a long, circuitous route to the rear side of the hill behind his property.

After easing the car into its hidden spot in the woods, he sat back and took several deep breaths to calm down. As the adrenaline rush dissipated, anger took its place—first at the fugitive position Stryker had put him in, and then a deeper anger at the death of Slade. He took out his phone and called Hardwick.

He was surprised and relieved when the man answered. "Yeah?"

"Ziko Slade is dead."

Hardwick sounded unsurprised. "Inmate confrontation?"

"I've been told it was murder, set up to look like suicide in his cell."

"Which your paranoid brain is telling you is another warning, aimed at you personally?"

"I think it means I'm getting close to some facts that would have set him free—and someone would rather have him dead than free."

"So, what do you want from me?"

"The case against Slade began with Bruno Lanka just happening to find Lenny Lerman's body. But Lanka is a dodgy enough character that Stryker couldn't put him on the stand. Lanka's driver was Dominick Vesco—who owns a Ford 150 pickup and a Moto Guzzi trail bike, both of which were present on Blackmore Mountain. It's obvious those two are into this mess up to their necks. It's also obvious that they're not the brains behind it. They're taking orders from somebody—the same somebody who ordered the hit on Slade."

Hardwick uttered a snorting little laugh.

"What the hell is funny?"

"You sound so goddamn pissed off. It's not your usual state of mind."

"Not a goddamn thing is usual these days. I'm running into threats and dead ends like never before in my life." He paused. "Look, I know I'm ranting. But I'm sure Lanka and his accomplice were on Blackmore Mountain that day, and one of them smashed me on the side of the head, shot Sonny, got gunpowder residue on my hand, and turned me into a fugitive with a headache that won't go away."

"What makes you so sure they were both there?"

"Because the plan was to kill Sonny and frame me. And that would be a hell of a lot easier for two guys to manage than just one. I'm thinking Lanka came with Sonny in the tow truck. And I know Vesco came up from the campground on his Moto Guzzi."

"Jesus, Gurney, you make it all *sound* reasonable. But that doesn't make it true."

"I'm positive these bastards were involved in Sonny's murder. I'd bet my pension they were involved in Lenny's. And I'm equally sure they're not the organizing brains behind it all. Most important of all, I know where to find them."

Hardwick let out an exasperated sigh. "So, what's your plan? Tie them up and threaten to cut their balls off if they don't ID the boss?"

"Something like that."

"And you want me to bring a sharp knife?"

"Something like that."

Hardwick let out an ugly little laugh.

"What's so funny?"

"I keep thinking about a cartoon I saw. Guy in his yard with a shovel. There's a little pointy thing sticking out of the ground. He's trying to dig it out. But the cartoon shows this deep underground view, below the guy's lawn, and we see that the little pointy thing is the top inch of a spike on the back of a live brontosaurus that's twice the size of the guy's house."

"Cute," said Gurney.

"But you're hell-bent on digging that fucker up, right?"

"Right."

"Even if Lanka and Vesco are just two spikes on the back of a monster?"

"Right."

"You have a specific time in mind for this lunatic excursion?"

"Where are you right now?"

"Right now I'm in Home Depot buying putty for the loose window panes I promised Esti I'd fix today. So, right now is not good."

"Tomorrow?"

"Possible."

"Good. Let's meet a little before noon in the parking lot next to Lanka's store. Last time I was on that street, I saw Vesco arriving in Lanka's Escalade around that time, and I'm thinking Lanka was probably with him. Opening time at the store is noon, so one or both of them is likely to be there."

Hardwick grunted. "And sometime between now and then you'll figure out what the fuck our approach is?"

"We can nail that down in the parking lot."

"Fine. But this is it, Sherlock. It's the last fucking time I want to go near this case. It gives me the fucking creeps."

THE SUN HAD set by the time Gurney made his way from the car's hiding place up the slippery trail to his hilltop campsite, leaving a blood-red glow in the western sky. Darkness was closing in, the temperature was dropping, and his face was numb from the cold.

As he was starting down toward the house, he heard the distant sound of tires crunching the gravel on the town road. He reversed course, climbing back up to the place in the hemlocks that gave him the best view of the property. As the security camera alert sounded on his phone, a pair of headlights appeared at the corner of the barn, accompanied a moment later by a second pair. The barn reflected enough light for him to recognize the two vehicles as state police cruisers, then dimly make out an individual approaching the side of one of the cruisers and leaning down toward the driver's window.

Gurney assumed this was one of the watchers, and that their car was now on the opposite side of the barn, where it couldn't be seen from the house. Whatever he might have told the troopers about there being no sightings of Gurney returning to the property didn't deter them. The two cruisers proceeded past the barn and up the pasture lane to the house.

A trooper emerged from each cruiser, flashlight in hand. They made their way in opposite directions around the house, rapping on doors, aiming their lights through the windows, setting off another phone alert when they passed the cameras on the far side of the house. They even looked into the chicken coop and the attached shed before conferring briefly and departing the way they came.

After listening to the sound of the cruisers receding on the town road, Gurney made his way down the hill, across the back field, and into the house through the unlocked bedroom window.

The lights in the house were off, and he left them that way. In the near-darkness, he assembled a makeshift dinner of bread, cheese, and leftover vegetable soup. When he brought these things into the den to eat in the minimal illumination provided by his laptop screen, he noticed the landline phone blinking.

He pushed the Play button and was surprised to hear Madeleine's voice.

"I won't be home tonight. I'm having dinner again with Gerry, then we're going to the Harbane theater for the Coriander Chamber Group. Since we're both on the early shift tomorrow, I'll be staying at her house. I'll be home after work tomorrow."

Gurney was troubled by the fact that she'd called the landline rather than his cellphone. She'd called the house phone at a time when she knew he'd be out of the house, which meant that she didn't want to talk to him. The move felt like more than a petty bit of evasiveness; it felt like a symptom of a deeper estrangement, and that was something he didn't want to think about.

Sitting there at his desk, eating his dinner in the dim light of his laptop, he forced his attention onto the task of coming up with a plan for the following day's confrontation at Lanka's Specialty Foods. So much would depend on the circumstances and chemistry of the moment he soon realized that devising a detailed plan was impractical. In fact, he began to wonder if the whole idea of pursuing information via confrontation made any sense at all.

Still, Lanka and Vesco were the only links he had between the Lerman murders and whoever orchestrated them. And he was acutely aware that his time was limited. Powerful forces on both sides of the legal line were eager to stop him; their efforts, already disconcerting, were bound to become more intense. His only hope was to uncover the truth before Stryker's cops caught up with him or he became the third victim. So, confrontation it would have to be. Realizing that any further thought on this subject would be a waste of time, he headed for bed.

He was awakened shortly after dawn by an urgent series of beeps on the security app on his phone. He stumbled out of bed and half ran to the kitchen. Peering out the window, he saw one of the watchers' unmarked sedans. After it came to a stop, he could see the exhaust still billowing up into the frigid air. They were settling in for another long stakeout and letting the engine run to keep the heater working.

He took a fast shower, got dressed, strapped on his Glock, and returned to the kitchen. Keeping an eye on the watchers' car, he made himself a generous breakfast—half a dozen slices of bacon, three eggs, two slices of toast, and a coffee.

After finishing it all, he went into the den, now brightened by the morning sunlight, opened his laptop, and found his list of the key events in the last thirteen weeks of Lenny's life. Then he placed a call to Adrienne.

As usual, she answered quickly, sounding anxious and curious.

He gave her the date of Lenny's visit to the Clearview Office Suites in Gorse and the dates his three subsequent visits to the Capital

District Office Park in Ploverton. "Do you know of any reason why your father would have made these trips on these dates?"

"None of those dates mean anything to me," she said, her anxiety and curiosity rising. "Do you know who he went to see?"

"I don't. The tenants are a pretty varied lot. The thing is, his depression began around the time of those visits, so they may be significant."

"What kind of tenants do those places have?"

Gurney checked his laptop. "Lawyers, doctors, engineers, a sleep-disorder clinic, financial adviser, stock broker, and some real estate people."

"A sleep-disorder clinic?"

"Yes."

"That might be it. He used to complain about waking up from nightmares. For most people sleep is a natural escape, among other good things. But not for him."

She made a little sound like a stifled sob.

"Are you alright, Adrienne?"

"It's just . . . sometimes I see the sadness of my father's life so vividly it makes me cry."

There was a long silence, broken by Gurney.

"Another trip your father made got my attention. One day in the middle of October he spent two hours at the Franciscan Sanctuary. Was that something he did from time to time?"

"If it was, I wasn't aware of it."

"Do you have any idea why he would have gone there?"

"Maybe for the same reason I go back there. To put myself in a happier place."

61

THE FACTUAL TAKEAWAY FROM HIS CONVERSATION WITH Adrienne hadn't amounted to much, but its emotional impact on him was another matter.

Throughout his career, he'd tried to stay focused on the mechanics of a case. The objective facts. Rarely did he succeed entirely. He was unaffected by hysterical displays of grief, but his defenses were often pierced by the welling of a tear, the catch in a voice, the sharing of a memory.

Rather than dwelling on Adrienne's pain, he searched his mind for the next right thing he could do, and the needs of the chickens occurred to him. He stood up quickly from his desk, winced at the sharp twinge in his back, and went to the mudroom for his jacket and gloves. Getting from the house to the coop without being seen by the watchers involved exiting through a bedroom window. Once he was outside, the coop and shed blocked the line of sight from the barn. He got a shovel from the shed and scraped the snow out of the fenced run. After replacing the shovel, he hauled a sack of feed into the coop and refilled the feeders. Then he used a broad-bladed spackling knife to scrape the week's accumulation of chicken droppings off the roosting rods. Finally, he opened the low door between the coop and the run, and the hens proceeded cautiously down the connecting ramp—the Rhode Island Red in the lead, squawking.

He had a moment of concern that Stryker's men might hear the sound and come up to investigate, then realized that with their windows closed, engine running, and heater whirring, they weren't likely to hear anything short of a gunshot. He returned the makeshift scraper to the shed and secured the big yellow door with its wrought-iron latch.

Back in the house, he was thinking about the experience of assembling and painting the shed door with Madeleine. Working on it together had created a feeling of closeness that was miles away from the way he felt now. He asked himself which feeling best represented the reality of their marriage. He had no answer.

THE FASTEST ROUTE to Garville was composed mainly of the interstate with a few miles of country roads at either end of the trip. The downside of the interstate was its need of repaving. The patched seams in the concrete produced a constant drumbeat. It was a road that Gurney normally avoided, but ensuring a timely arrival for his meeting with Hardwick felt important enough to put up with the irritation.

Now, forty minutes into the drive, with the road surface getting progressively worse, he was tempted to take the next exit and make his way along town and village roads, but a ten-wheeler came up on his right as the exit approached, cutting off the opportunity. He sighed and drove on, determined never to take the interstate again—a decision that was soon underscored, as the traffic began to slow, then creep, then come to a dead stop.

Nothing in the stretch ahead was moving. He checked the time. Eleven thirty. If it weren't for this jam-up, he'd be arriving in Lanka's parking lot at eleven forty. If Hardwick was coming from his home in Dillweed, he'd be taking back roads all the way and arriving in Garville on time. Being punctual was a Hardwick trait, an anomaly in such a rule-despising man.

Ten minutes later, there was still no movement ahead. Taking out his phone to let Hardwick know he'd be late, he discovered he was in a dead cell zone. The side of highway he was on was separated from the opposite side by a drainage gully. There were no exits as far ahead as he could see, nothing but embankments and woods. He was trapped.

At noon, the traffic began to move, inching forward for about a mile, before stopping again. Gurney rechecked his phone and found that he now had cell service. He placed a call to Hardwick, but it went to voicemail. He left a message, describing the problem and saying that if he wasn't there by twelve thirty, Hardwick should abandon the mission and they'd reschedule it, perhaps for the following day. During the next hour and a half of immobility, he tried Hardwick's number three more times and left two more messages.

When the cause of the stoppage had finally been cleared—an overturned tanker truck—Gurney got off at the next exit and made his way back to Walnut Crossing via the country roads he should have used that morning.

After leaving the car in the woods, he climbed to the top of the campsite hill and surveyed the property. There was no sign of the watchers, but there was a small red car next to the house—in fact, in the spot by the asparagus bed where he'd always parked the Outback.

He was more curious than concerned. The chance of law-enforcement personnel arriving in a small red car was zero. He made his way down the hill and across the back field to the rear of the house. He could hear voices coming from inside. He edged around to a spot where he could see into the long ground-floor room. Catching a glimpse of Madeleine at the sink island, he realized the voices were coming from the radio.

He continued around the house to the side door, taking a close look at the red car on the way—a Subaru Crosstrek. Before going into the house, he knocked loudly at the door, then opened it and called in, "It's me," to avoid any reaction that might involve the shotgun.

When he reached the kitchen, Madeleine was still at the sink island, rinsing some sort of leafy vegetable in a colander. She glanced at him but said nothing.

"You rented that car?" he asked.

"I don't like feeling trapped. And with you hiding the other one in the woods somewhere, I didn't want to keep imposing on Gerry."

After an awkward pause, he asked, "Did you get a call from Jack Hardwick?"

"Why would he call me?"

"I meant, did he call the house?"

"Is there a problem?"

"I was trying to get in touch with him and haven't heard back, that's all."

It suddenly occurred to him that perhaps Hardwick hadn't made it to Garville either—that he might have gotten into a snarl with Esti, decided to stay home, and was in no rush to explain the situation.

Gurney's phone rang. He took it out, hoping to see J. Hardwick on the screen. Instead, he saw K. Barstow.

"Kyra?"

"Hi, David. I'm glad you picked up! I was just listening to the news on an Albany station, and I heard the name Bruno Lanka mentioned. Isn't that the name of the hunter who discovered Lenny Lerman's body?"

"Mentioned in what context?"

"According to the news report, there was a wild shoot-out in Garville today. Lanka was one of the victims."

"*One* of the victims?"

"There were two others, but I didn't recognize the names."

"Do you recall what they were?"

"Vasco, maybe Vesco. And Horwick, maybe Hartack, something like that."

Gurney felt the blood draining from his face.

"When you say 'victims' . . . ?"

"The report said that Lanka was killed, I'm not sure about the other two."

Gurney thanked her, ended the call, and went to his laptop. The lead item in the station's local news section read:

ONE DEAD, TWO CRITICALLY WOUNDED
IN GARVILLE GUN BATTLE

Gunfire broke out at noon today on a quiet side street in Garville. Police Chief Lloyd Clugger issued the following statement:

"We are currently investigating a violent incident that occurred earlier today next to Lanka's Specialty Foods on Fourth Street. Gunshots were exchanged between a man identified as Jack Hardwick and Bruno Lanka, the store owner, and Dominick Vesco, the store manager. Mr. Lanka was pronounced dead at the scene. Mr. Hardwick and Mr. Vesco were transported to Albany General Hospital. Both suffered life-threatening wounds, and both remain in critical condition. The cause of the confrontation is yet to be determined."

Jack Hardwick was formerly an investigator in the New York State Police Bureau of Criminal Investigation. Official sources have not speculated on whether his background might have a bearing on today's explosive encounter.

Sources within the hospital have confirmed that Hardwick underwent a two-hour operation by a trauma surgeon and remains in critical condition in the intensive care unit.

No additional information was available on Dominick Vesco. This developing story will be updated as more facts becomes available.

Gurney felt a nauseating chill pass through his body. He sat staring at the computer screen—willing it to tell him that Hardwick had turned the corner, that his condition had stabilized, that he was out of danger. He clicked on the page's Refresh icon once, twice, three times, but no new details appeared.

On his fourth try, the page was dominated by a flashing BREAKING NEWS banner above an article that Gurney was almost afraid to read.

STUDENT FILMMAKERS RECORD DEADLY GARVILLE SHOOT-OUT

Peter Flake and Yoko Klein, film majors at Marlon College, were in the right place at the right time to record the violent confrontation that took place in a Garville parking lot earlier today.

"We were driving around town, getting local footage for our term project, a video documentary on upstate towns in decline," Klein explained, "when we

spotted this amazing red GTO from the 1960s. Right
after we slowed down to film it from another angle, a
huge black SUV came along and pulled in behind it.
The driver of the SUV and the driver of the GTO got
into this super-bad thing, total insanity, everybody
getting shot, and we got the whole thing on camera."

The article went on to report that Flake and Klein had given
WSKZ access to their recorded audio and video footage of the
confrontation—which could be viewed via a link at the end of the
article. A warning was appended below it.

CONTAINS IMAGES OF EXTREME VIOLENCE

Gurney's hand was shaking as he clicked on the link icon.

The high-resolution video opened with a shot of a gleaming red
1967 Pontiac GTO parked just inside the parking area for Lanka's
Specialty Foods. Slouched in the driver's seat was Jack Hardwick. A
few seconds later, a black Escalade pulled in and stopped behind the
GTO. Gurney recognized the driver—Dominick Vesco.

He stepped out of the Escalade, approached the GTO, and rapped
on the side window. The audio was faint but sufficiently clear.

Hardwick lowered the window. "Yeah?"

"You're on private property."

"I thought this lot was for store customers."

"You already been to the store. I don't forget a face. Now get the
fuck out of here."

"Suppose I want to buy some of Lanka's specialty foods."

"Suppose I blow your fucking head off."

Hardwick sighed. "You're creating a problem."

"That so?"

As Vesco reached into the pocket of his gray windbreaker,
Hardwick suddenly thrust the heavy front door of the GTO open,
smashing it into Vesco and sending him staggering toward the Escalade. He leapt out after him, delivering a flurry of punches to his

head. As the man slumped against the vehicle's passenger door, the
window slid down, a pistol emerged, and a shot was fired, thrusting
Hardwick backward. A second shot propelled his body in a half rota-
tion, and he half fell, half dove to the ground, pulling himself toward
the front of the vehicle, out of the shooter's line of fire.

As Vesco struggled to his feet, Bruno Lanka emerged from the
Escalade. With weapons extended they moved toward Hardwick's
prone form. There was a rapid exchange of gunfire, seemingly from
all three combatants at once, then silence.

The silence was broken by a shaky voice—surely one of the student videographers.

"Holy shit!"

The video ended with a slow zoom in on three motionless bodies
on the ground beside the Escalade, a pistol in the right hand of each
one, blood seeping through their clothes onto the tarmac.

Gurney's fists were clenched, the knuckles white. He was rigid
with fury—a fury mingled with a terrible feeling of guilt.

As SOON AS a modicum of rationality returned, Gurney went to
the Albany General Hospital's website, got the patient-information
phone number, and called it. He asked about Hardwick's condition,
was told only that he was in ICU, that HIPAA regulations prohibited
the sharing of other information, and that no visitors beyond immediate family could be admitted.

He wondered if word had gotten to Esti. He knew there was
no landline, and he had no cell number for her. Should he drive to
Dillweed, in the event that she didn't already know? Or was it more
likely that someone who knew her cell number had already called
her? Surely, one or more of her state police contacts would do so.
Chances were she was already at the hospital.

He called the hospital again, and this time asked for the ICU.

When someone at the nursing station picked up, he said, "I need
to reach Esti Moreno, who I believe is visiting Jack Hardwick."

A harried female voice replied, "She stepped out for a moment. Try later."

Now he knew that she knew, and he knew where she was, but he wasn't sure what to do next. Wait a few minutes and call again? Call back now and leave his number, so she could reach him? Or forget about calling and just drive to the hospital?

It was the last option that seemed right. The point wasn't just to get information or express his concern. He should go there. Be there.

He slipped his phone back in his pocket and went to the kitchen.

Madeleine was stirring a pot of something on the stove.

"I have to go out," he said. "Albany. The hospital. Jack's been injured."

She looked at him. "How?"

"He was shot."

"*Shot?*"

"In a parking lot. Near Albany. I need to go. I'll call you."

HE ARRIVED IN the main parking lot of the hospital at 6:28 p.m. in a nervous daze. On the radio, the local Albany station was reporting on the fatal Garville clash.

"Today's violent confrontation has now claimed a second life," the reporter said. "Dominick Vesco suffered cardiac arrest following a surgical procedure and was declared dead at five forty-five this evening. We've been informed that Jack Hardwick, the other participant in the confrontation, has emerged from surgery and is being maintained in an induced coma to increase his chance of survival."

Gurney turned off the radio. He tried to organize his thoughts but found that his brain wasn't operating in linear fashion. The simple dictum that so often put him back on track—just do the next right thing— wasn't working. He had no idea what the next right thing might be.

With Hardwick in a coma, there was no point in trying to visit the ICU. Besides, either Garville PD or the NYSP would have personnel on site, since it now appeared that Hardwick was involved in two homicides. And it was possible that Cam Stryker, aware of Gurney's relationship with the man, had sent her own people to the hospital to be on the lookout for him. He sank down a little lower in his seat and gave the parking lot a careful once-over. As his gaze returned to the front of the hospital, a woman was coming out through the main revolving door. Despite the freezing temperature, she was wearing just jeans and a sweater. She had a cigarette in one hand and a lighter in the other. When she turned halfway toward the door to shield the flame from the wind, he recognized her profile.

It was no surprise that Esti Moreno would be there, but the actual sight of her gave his nerves a jab. He felt some resistance to the idea of approaching her, but he knew it had to be done. Figuring any cops assigned to the situation would be in the building, he got out of the car, turned up the collar of his jacket against the wind, and walked quickly across the parking lot.

She was in the middle of a long drag on her cigarette.

"Esti?"

She stared at him, slowly blowing out the smoke, her expression hardening.

"What are you doing here?" Her voice was hoarse, angry.

He blinked, taken aback by her tone. "I heard . . . on the radio . . . about the shooting."

"Go away! Just leave! Now!"

Gurney took a small step backward. "I don't understand."

"He may not make it. He may die. You hear what I'm saying?"

"My God, Esti, I—"

She cut him off. "You dragged him into this fucking case! You did this, you fucking son of a bitch! Get away from me! *Now!*"

62

GURNEY RETREATED TO HIS CAR. WHERE HE JUST SAT, battered by the growing impact of Esti's outburst.

A man he'd naively come to believe was indestructible was just as destructible as any other human being. And it was his own cajoling, his importuning, that had put him in the literal line of fire. If Hardwick should die . . .

He had no idea how long he'd been sitting there, his head bowed, when he looked up and for the second time that evening saw a familiar-looking woman emerging from the hospital's revolving door. As she made her way through the parking lot to a car a few spaces from his own, he recognized the grim face of the tow truck owner, Charlene Vesco. In the light from her open car door, he could see the tight set of her jaw, her lips pressed together in a thin, straight line. The emotion behind that expression wasn't clear, but it looked like there was more fear in it than grief. She pulled abruptly out of her space and headed for the exit. He decided to follow her. He had no objective in mind, other than a feeling that any action was better than none.

The evening traffic made it possible to keep another car or two between them as she made her way through the outskirts of Albany in the direction of Garville. When it became clear that she was heading for her auto salvage yard, Gurney dropped farther back. He switched off his headlights, parked at the far end of the block, and watched.

Charlene opened the tall steel gate and walked toward the trailer-office. The pit bull chained to a corner of the office barked, then stopped. A minute later she led the dog, on a short leash, to the car and let him into the back seat. Then she locked the gate and got back in her car.

He tailed her with his headlights off until they reached a busy avenue, where he switched them on and resumed a position two cars behind her. He followed her to the other side of Garville, to a tree-lined suburban-looking street. Halfway along it, she pulled into a driveway next to a modest ranch-style house. As he drove past, he caught a glimpse of her entering it through a side door, the dog following her.

Continuing along the street, he noticed one parked vehicle that seemed out of place. It was hard to imagine anyone in that blue-collar neighborhood driving that hundred-thousand-dollar Range Rover, its pearl-gray finish glistening in the dim glow of a distant streetlamp. Tinted glass kept him from seeing any more than a hint of someone behind the wheel.

Until he was well out of Garville, Gurney kept checking his rearview mirror, but never saw any evidence of being followed. The unsettled feeling produced by that looming gray vehicle, however, remained with him an hour and a half later when he pulled into the quarry trail on the back side of the campsite hill.

Why had Charlene Vesco gone out of her way to bring the pit bull home with her instead of leaving it to what he presumed was its normal job of guarding the salvage yard? Was it because she didn't intend to be at the yard the next day to feed it? Or because she thought she might need protection at home?

Protection from whom? And why?

THE SHOCKS OF the day left him without any appetite for dinner—nor, as the night wore on, any ability to fall asleep. At 2:00 a.m., he got up, slipped on a pair of jeans and a tee shirt, and retreated to the den.

He got the list of Lenny Lerman's activities in the weeks preceding his death. He focused on the visits Lerman made to the two office complexes—one to Clearview Offices Suites, followed by three to Capital District Office Park. Examining the directories of tenants in those complexes, he put together some plausible through-lines for Lerman's four trips.

His first scenario was based on the hypothesis that the trips were related to a medical problem. In that version, Lerman's trip to Clearview Office Suites would have been to the urgent care facility. His next trip—to the Capital District Office Park five days later—could have been for an appointment with the hematology-oncology practice. His next trip might have been to the radiological imaging group, perhaps for an MRI. And his final trip could have been back to the hematology-oncology practice to discuss the imaging results.

Gurney's second scenario hypothesized a legal problem. In that version, Lerman's trip to Clearview Office Suites would have been to the law firm. And that could have been followed by three consecutive visits to the criminal defense attorneys in the Capital District Office Park.

In the third scenario, Lerman's issue concerned money. In that case, his trip to the Clearview Office Suites would have been to the financial adviser; his subsequent trips to the Capital District Office Park would have been to the stock brokerage located there.

Pondering the three scenarios, he felt that the legal version was more likely than the financial, and the medical more likely than the legal. Of course, it was possible that Lerman made his four trips for four different reasons, and that his mood changes had nothing to do with any of them. Arranging a handful of facts to form a coherent picture could satisfy one's hunger for order at the price of losing contact with reality.

Still, the medical hypothesis was appealing. Gurney could imagine Lerman noticing some symptom of trouble . . . going to his nearby urgent care facility . . . follow-up appointments with a specialist. Suppose Lerman faced a serious medical issue. How might that news have changed him, changed his priorities? Might it have given him the reckless, nothing-to-lose attitude that the blackmail scheme seemed to require? Might it explain—

His train of thought was interrupted by the sound of a lamp being switched on in the bedroom across the hall, then the sound of Madeleine's approaching footsteps.

"Do you realize what time it is?" she said, standing in the doorway. There was something accusatory in her tone, as though his being up had disturbed her sleep.

There was no light on in the den, and he could barely see her in the moonlight coming through the window.

"I've been thinking," he said.

She made a sound that he took for a sarcastic laugh.

He ignored it. "Suppose Lerman was facing some medical issue, perhaps even dying. Suppose he saw the opportunity to blackmail Ziko Slade as a no-lose proposition. Suppose he imagined that getting his hands on a million dollars and passing it along to his son and daughter would make up for his failings as a father. Suppose—"

"Back up a minute! There must have been an autopsy. Wouldn't it have revealed some medical calamity if one existed?"

"It was a forensic autopsy, not a clinical one."

"Meaning what?"

"The purpose of a forensic autopsy is to determine if a death occurred naturally or unnaturally—and if unnaturally, by what means. If the ME determines that a victim has died as a direct result of his head being chopped off, there's no forensic reason to search for other morbidities. Full clinical autopsies are performed when the cause of death is less clear."

"Can't they dig up his body and search for traces—"

"An exhumation order would have to be issued, and there's no chance that Stryker or Rexton PD would have any interest in that."

63

WHEN HE AROSE THE FOLLOWING MORNING, MADELEINE had already left for the clinic, and his medical theory was being attacked, in the absence of Hardwick, by his own skepticism.

Although the timing of Lerman's last trip to the Capital District Office Park coincided with the beginning of his reported depression, and the formation of his blackmail scheme coincided with his reported emergence from that depression, certain contradictions were casting a shadow of doubt over everything.

While Lerman had recorded three phone conversations with Slade in his diary—specifying the damaging information he had, how much money he wanted, and when he wanted it—Slade insisted he'd received no such calls.

That disconnect demanded that one take sides. Gurney came down, at least tentatively, on the side of Ziko Slade. But if Slade was telling the truth, then Lerman was lying about the phone calls. But why? And what would a medical diagnosis have to do with any of it?

Whenever you're confused, just look at what's in front of you, and take the simplest step forward.

That was the advice of his first NYPD mentor, and it had never failed him. What it brought to mind now was the fear he'd glimpsed the night before on the face of Charlene Vesco. Perhaps he should pay her a visit.

WHEN GURNEY ARRIVED in Garville, gray clouds were enveloping the town in an oppressive gloom. There were no signs of life on Charlene Vesco's street. The vehicles were gone, including the Range Rover. The whole block, with its leafless trees and drab lawns, had a dead look about it.

He parked in front of Vesco's house, walked up the damp brick pathway to the front door, and rang the bell. He could hear the drone of what sounded like a television, but no one came to the door. He rang the bell again, waited, knocked, knocked harder.

The fact that the woman wasn't coming to the door was odd, but not as odd as the silence of the pit bull she'd brought home the previous evening. He walked around to the driveway side of the house. Her car was still there, by the side door. The top half of the door had glass panes. He looked in and saw a short hall leading to a kitchen. The kitchen light was on. He knocked on the door. No response.

He walked to the back of the house, where a series of windows were obscured by lowered blinds. He continued around to the side. The blinds there were raised, revealing a dining room, a small office, and a living room. It was the scene in the living room that got his attention.

It took him a moment to recognize the woman slumped in an easy chair in front of the television as Charlene Vesco. Rivulets of blood extended from her wide-open eyes down her cheeks . . . and from her ears down her neck . . . and from the lower corner of her mouth onto her chest, soaking the front of a pale blue sweater. In the light from a lamp next to the chair, her skin was a sickly white. Her eyes had the dullness that sets in a few hours after death. He started taking out his phone but was stopped by the sight of a second body. A dark gray body on the floor at Charlene's feet. Her pit bull, in a pool of blood.

He went to his car, blocked his phone ID, and placed a call to 911. He gave the dispatcher the address, the location of the body in the house, and its visual condition. He added that it was an apparent homicide and ended the call.

He went back to the window for another look at the room, in case he might have missed something. He noted on a coffee table not far from the bodies a bottle of what appeared to be whiskey and two glasses. That should get the attention of the homicide team.

He returned to his car. In the event that Stryker might be pinging his phone, he drove for several minutes in the direction of Albany before turning the phone off, reversing course, and heading back by a roundabout route to Walnut Crossing.

AS HE BROUGHT the car to a stop in its hiding place in the woods, he was wondering what had been done to Charlene Vesco to produce those unsettling symptoms, and whether the whiskey bottle and the two glasses had anything to do with it.

The blood he'd observed suggested the possibility of a massive dose of an anticoagulant. He considered the idea that it might have been secretly administered in a shot of whiskey but realized that the taste of an amount sufficient to produce such severe effects would have been noticed instantly. It seemed more likely that the chemical had been administered by injection, probably after the woman had been rendered unconscious or at least unresisting—perhaps by a few drops in her whiskey of something less likely to be noticed. That sequence of events, along with the two glasses and her position in the easy chair, suggested that she knew her killer—possibly the occupant of that out-of-place Range Rover.

But why had she been killed? And why in such a bizarre way?

Gurney shivered. The gloom of Garville's weather had followed him home, and his car was getting cold. There was a hint of snow in the air, and before it became more than a hint there were things he wanted to get from the house and bring up to his campsite.

The trek up and down the hill and back across the field to a bedroom window was becoming routine, a routine he found both absurd and necessary. The first thing he did in the house was go to the kitchen sink and let warm water run over his hands to get the chill out of them. While the coffee machine heated up, he got two tote bags from the mudroom and began filling them. In one bag he loaded a loaf of bread, a package of cheddar cheese, a bag of almonds, two bananas, a jar of olives, a large thermos of water, and a container of orange juice. In the other he placed an extra sweater, woolen socks, a scarf, ski mittens, a flashlight, and his laptop with a charging adaptor for the car's USB port. When he finally sat down by the French doors with his coffee, the time on the Regulator clock was exactly 4:00 p.m.

Madeleine had the early shift at the clinic that day and should already be home. As he was frowning at that thought, the security app on his phone produced the distinctive series of beeps that indicated the activation of the camera down on the barn. He moved away from the French doors, went to the kitchen window, and saw with some relief Madeleine's rented red Crosstrek coming up through the low pasture.

She didn't come inside right away. He watched her walking from the car over to the coop. She was carrying the shotgun—rather casually, he thought, as though it had become a natural part of her life. She walked around the coop, stopping to gaze down at the pasture below it, before coming into the house.

"What was that all about?" he asked when she appeared in the kitchen.

She laid the shotgun on the sideboard. "I was getting a sense of where the fence will go."

"Fence?"

"For the alpacas. I asked Jim Smithers to come up and see if it's something he can handle."

"Who the hell is Jim Smithers?"

"The farmer on the road to the village. Did the concussion erase your memory?"

"You mean the old guy with the tilting silo and the ancient tractor?"

Her eyes narrowed, but she said nothing.

"What do you mean—*if it's something he can handle?*"

"The Winklers want to bring the twin alpacas here within the next week or so. The fence will have to be up by then. Obviously, you're not going to do it. I'm hoping he can."

"All this has to happen right now? With everything that's going on?"

"Yes. Right now. I'm not going to postpone my life, just because you refuse to let go of this wretched case."

HALF AN HOUR later, Gurney was arranging things in his campsite tent. He hooked the portable heater up to the propane tank, made room for the contents of the two tote bags by pushing his sleeping bag to one side, and opened a small folding chair that he had brought along. He was planning to stay there for an hour or so, at least until his annoyance subsided. He turned on the heater and adjusted its thermostat to fifty degrees. He settled down into the folding chair and tried to think about something other than his growing conflict with Madeleine.

The subject that finally held his attention was the hematology-oncology group in the Capital District Office Park. Although HIPAA regulations would prevent them from telling him whether Lerman had been a patient, he could at least learn more about the focus of

their practice. Since he was out of range of the house wifi, he decided
to use his phone as a hotspot to access the internet on his laptop.

He went first to the Capital District Office Park website and
checked the list of their tenants for the exact name of the medical
group—Stihl and Chopra Hematology-Oncology Associates. He then
went to their website, where he found extensive bios of Dr. Jonathan
Stihl and Dr. Eliza Chopra. Of particular interest to Gurney were
their specialties: malignant meningiomas, glioblastomas, and lep-
tomeningeal metastases.

All three, he discovered, were deadly forms of brain cancer. For
one of them, survival from the time of diagnosis could be as little as
six weeks—a discovery that fit neatly into his illness-based theory of
Lerman's trips, depression, and willingness to embark on a venture
as reckless as extortion.

Aware of the warping influence of his desire to be right, he decided to test the validity of his theory. He composed an email out-
lining his educated guesses regarding Lerman's trips, his probable
diagnosis, and his motivation. He urged that a full clinical autopsy
be performed as soon as possible on the man's remains—with special
attention to the spinal cord, where metastatic traces of brain cancer
would most likely be found—emphasizing that this could establish
a scientific underpinning for the man's out-of-character moods and
willingness to engage in high-risk behavior.

He addressed the email to Dr. Kermit Loeffler, Medical Examiner, whose contact information he retrieved from the county website.
His hope was that the ME might be interested enough to push for
an exhumation order and influential enough to prevail over Stryker's
likely reluctance. He reread the draft of the email, corrected a couple
of typos, and sent it.

PUTTING THE EXHUMATION ball in Loeffler's court temporarily
cleared Gurney's mind—freeing up space that was soon filled with
questions concerning the demise of Charlene Vesco.

Homicide by anticoagulant was not unheard of, but the few cases he was aware of involved an extended process of internal bleeding. In one instance, the beneficiary of an octogenarian's will had hastened his benefactor's death by increasing his doses of a therapeutic blood thinner, a process that took a period of weeks. The Vesco case was nothing like that. So, what was it?

The howling of a coyote pack broke his train of thought. He put his laptop aside, pushed himself up out of the chair, and closed the tent flap. The howling stopped as abruptly as it had begun. It was dark now, past five o'clock. The only sources of illumination in the tent were the orange glow of the heater and his laptop screen. He eased himself back into the chair, wincing at the stab of pain in the back of his neck, and started an internet search for information about anticoagulants.

The howling began again, followed by the sharp yips of a hunting pack on the move. The sounds seemed to be getting closer, although in those hills it was hard to tell. Then, once more, all was suddenly silent.

Gurney forced his attention back to his search. Most of the articles he found focused on the effects of various types of anticoagulants. Others examined their therapeutic and rodenticidal applications. The final article he came upon listed the naturally occurring sources of these chemicals. At that point his eyes were stinging from the dryness of the heated air in the tent. He was about to stop reading when, at the bottom of the list of anticoagulant sources, he saw two words that produced an instant frisson.

Snake venom.

64

HE CALLED ALBANY GENERAL HOSPITAL TO GET AN UP-date on Hardwick's condition and was transferred to the ICU nursing station, where a female voice asked him to wait a moment.

A male voice came on the line. "Mr. Hardwick's condition is unchanged. Are you a member of the family?"

He recognized the tone of a suspicious cop who was trying without much success to sound friendly. Gurney ended the call and turned off his phone.

After considering the possibility of spending the night in the tent, he decided not to. His annoyance at Madeleine had subsided to the point where he wasn't likely to say anything he'd regret, and another state trooper visitation at that point seemed equally unlikely. He switched off the heater, picked up his laptop, made sure the tent flap was weathertight, and headed down the hill, aided by the faint moonlight coming through the clouds. He took the precaution of taking the long way around the open field, where the overgrowth of weeds would obscure any footprints left in the snow.

When he entered the house, he noted a hint of woodsmoke in the air. He found Madeleine sitting by the fire, book in hand, shotgun propped against the stone corner of the fireplace. She glanced up, then turned her attention back to her book.

He walked over to the hearth and extended his palms toward the fire. The heat made his cold fingers tingle. "Have you eaten yet?" he asked.

"Yes," she said without looking up. "There's some beef stew left in that pot on the stove."

He was starting to head for it when she added, "Gerry Mirkle called a little while ago. She said to tell you that *Controversial Perspectives* is doing a segment tonight on the shooting in Garville."

He grimaced. "How does she know?"

Madeleine lowered her book to her lap. "I explained this to you before. She has an app that notifies her whenever a news report mentions certain names. The *Controversial Perspectives* promotion mentioned yours."

He'd been wondering how long it would take the ferrets at RAM to connect his name to Hardwick's and start spewing out a new set of sensational speculations. Apparently, not very long at all.

The news killed his appetite. Instead of the beef stew, he made himself a cup of coffee. *Controversial Perspectives* would be on at eight. Until then, he'd search for a unifying thread through everything that had happened. He took his laptop and coffee into the den.

The problem with the unifying-thread approach was that it didn't seem that any single narrative could account for *all* the reported facts, since some of those facts directly contradicted others. The most perplexing conflict concerned the three phone conversations Lerman claimed to have had with Slade—calls whose existence the phone company verified—but which Slade denied having received. What possible unifying thread could reconcile Lerman's detailed recounting of the conversations and Slade's insistence that they never occurred?

Gurney realized how much he missed Hardwick's combative skepticism. Although the man could be crude and pugnacious in his opinions, they never failed to contain an element of truth. He had a way of poking at theories that exposed their weaknesses, but rarely, if ever, had the man totally rejected any hypothesis that later turned out to be valid.

In Hardwick's absence, Gurney had the unmoored feeling that he'd been separated from half his ability to get at the truth. But his sense of isolation didn't stop there. As the gap between him and Madeleine grew wider, the more he missed the role she'd played in shaping his understanding of . . . everything.

These ruminations absorbed him so thoroughly that he missed the opening of *Controversial Perspectives*. He connected to the livestream at 8:04 p.m., with Tarla Hackett in mid-sentence.

". . . covering the increasingly contentious and violent aftermath of the murder conviction of Ziko Slade, former drug dealer to the stars."

Jordan Lake nodded. "And the increasingly suspicious involvement of former NYPD homicide detective, Dave Gurney."

"That's right, Jordan. Gurney's involvement has been getting deeper and darker by the day. We've been witnessing a series of bombshells in the case, beginning with the recent suicide of Ziko Slade."

"And followed, just yesterday," added Lake, "by the fatal shooting of two Garville residents by former New York State Police detective Jack Hardwick. The same Jack Hardwick known to be a close associate of Dave Gurney!"

Tarla Hackett leaned forward, projecting a look of angry amazement. "And that's on top of Gurney's direct involvement in the fatal shooting on Blackmore Mountain."

"Exactly," said Lake. "Gurney's connection to one mysterious homicide after another raises serious questions."

Hackett brightened up her expression. "We're hoping to get answers to some of those questions right now—from District Attorney Cam Stryker."

The video switched to a split screen, Tarla Hackett on the left, Stryker on the right. Stryker's black blazer and plain white blouse went well with a smile that didn't come within a mile of warmth.

"We appreciate your taking the time to speak with us this evening," said Hackett.

"Glad to do it."

"Okay, let's get right to it."

Gurney heard Madeleine entering the room. She said nothing, just half sat on the arm of the den couch, giving her an angled view of the laptop screen.

Hackett was saying, "Ziko Slade, convicted murderer of Lenny Lerman, hanged himself in his prison cell. Were you shocked? Surprised? None of the above?"

"Certainly not shocked."

"You saw it coming?"

"Sometimes the pain of guilt drives a person to extreme measures."

"Do you see his suicide as a confirmation of the jury's verdict?"

"Absolutely."

"You personally have no doubt about Slade's guilt?"

"None."

"As you know, Dave Gurney has the opposite opinion."

Stryker's eyes narrowed. "Mr. Gurney has a lot of opinions. More importantly, he has a lot to account for. He's a person of interest in a number of recent homicides."

Hackett nodded. "Jordan and I were just discussing Gurney's links to people who've ended up dead. Any comment on that?"

"Those links are growing. We have reason to believe that he was present last night and again this morning in the vicinity of the particularly vicious murder of Charlene Vesco, a cousin of Dominick Vesco who died yesterday as the result of gunshot wounds inflicted by Gurney's associate, Jack Hardwick."

"Do you have reason to believe that Gurney is now on the run?"

"Yes. Once a decorated detective, now a wanted man."

Hackett flashed a smile of satisfaction. "A final question. If any of our viewers know of Gurney's whereabouts, what should they do?"

Stryker gazed directly into the camera. "Anyone with information regarding the location of David Gurney should call my office at this number as soon as possible."

The split screen was replaced by a close-up photo of Gurney's face and the words, IF YOU KNOW THE WHEREABOUTS OF THIS MAN, CALL THIS NUMBER. After several seconds, this was replaced by live video of Hackett and Lake at their desks.

"Great interview, Tarla."

"Thanks, Jordan. Any closing observations?"

"No observations. Just unanswered questions." He turned to the camera. "What is Dave Gurney? Is he a hero . . . a fool . . . or a murderer? Now, this important message from our sponsor."

Gurney shut down the computer.

"What was Stryker talking about?" asked Madeleine.

"What do you mean?"

"You being in the vicinity of a particularly vicious murder."

"Charlene Vesco."

"I heard her name. That's not what I'm asking."

He forced himself to meet her gaze. "She's the woman who owns . . . owned . . . the tow truck that hit me. She's related to Dominick Vesco, who was on Blackmore Mountain that day and who was almost certainly involved in the murder of Sonny Lerman. I saw her at the hospital last night. I followed her to find out where she lived. This morning I went back to talk to her. When she didn't come to the door, I looked in the window and saw her body. I called 911 and reported it."

"You're leaving something out."

"What do you mean?"

"Stryker called it *a particularly vicious murder.* Meaning what?"

"There was a lot of blood. Some sort of blood thinner may have been involved."

Madeleine's expression hardened. "And now you're *a person of interest in a number of homicides.* I believe those were the words she used."

He said nothing.

"But you won't give it up!"

"How the hell can I give it up? I'm being bashed from all sides."

"If you walked away, the bashing would stop."

"It would be an acknowledgment of defeat. And I have not been defeated! Not by the police, not by Stryker, not by the scum at RAM, not by a dead rabbit, not by a snake in a goddamn gift basket, and not by some piece of shit who attacked me on Blackmore Mountain!"

She gave him that look that went right through him. "It's all about winning? Proving you're right, and everyone else is wrong? That's what matters?"

"My integrity matters."

"Really? Nothing else?"

"Without integrity, there is nothing else."

"You mean, integrity as you define it."

"What the hell is that supposed to mean?"

"Your integrity as a detective. Period."

"That's what I am. It's what I am, and it's what you never wanted me to be."

She opened her mouth as if to reply, then closed it, the set of her jaw tightening.

He let his anger carry him on. "Our marriage was always based on your expectation that I'd suddenly become something else. I wish I'd known about that business with Emma ten years ago. You were ready to leave me because of who I was, because I took my job seriously, and somehow she talked you into staying. Staying, but always with a reservation. Waiting for the magic transformation. Waiting for me to become God-knows-what, anything but a detective. Well, I am who I am, and if that's not what you want, then there's no damn reason for me to be here, is there?"

Madeleine regarded him with a deadly calm. "It's your life. It's your decision."

GURNEY STAYED IN the den through a mostly sleepless night. The moon had disappeared behind the scudding clouds of a fast-moving cold front. The wind was rising, and he could hear it moaning in the chimney at the other end of the house.

Angry and depressed, he felt that he was seeing the reality of his marriage for the first time, seeing that it had always been on the edge of an abyss. No, not an abyss—that was too romantic, too dramatic a notion, a fall from too great a height. On the edge of what, then?

On the edge of dissolving. That was more like it. Dissolving into the cold air of reality. Its solidity and permanence, through thick and thin, in sickness and in health, till death do us part, was an illusion, had always been an illusion. Not even a shared illusion. His own illusion. He could see now that for Madeleine there had always been a condition. It was tolerable for him to be a detective, as long as he wasn't too much of a detective, as long as there were limits, as long as she could believe that someday he'd walk away from his natural profession and turn into something else.

He saw with a sickening shock that what had been holding them together for over twenty-five years were their interlocked fantasies—hers, that he would someday change into the person she wanted him to be; his, that there was something unbreakable at the core of their relationship, something more powerful than their differences, something sweet and good—and *permanent*. But now he saw that this imagined core had been composed of wishful thinking.

These bleak thoughts looped repetitively through his mind as the night wore on, nurtured by the moaning of the wind and by a headache that grew worse as the hours passed.

Sometime between dawn and sunrise, in an exhausted, semiconscious state, he began to dream. He was on Blackmore Mountain in his Outback. Snow swirling past the windshield. The red tow truck looming up beside him. Forcing him sideways off the road. The crash. The truck coming to a stop on the road. Sonny Lerman opening the passenger door, stepping halfway out, laughing at him. Now Gurney was standing apart from himself, watching himself raise a pistol. The pistol firing once, twice. Lerman is thrown back into the truck. Gurney watches himself get out of the car, watches himself approach the truck and look inside. Blood is trickling from the corner of Lerman's mouth, from his eyes, from his ears. But it's not Lerman. Gurney leans closer. It's Jack Hardwick.

Gurney came to with a start. He looked around the den, trying to anchor himself in the reality of the place, the reality of the moment. He pushed himself painfully up off the couch, got his phone from the desk, and called the hospital.

There was no change in Hardwick's condition.

Gurney paced back and forth, flexing his arms, stretching his legs, working the stiffness out of his back, rubbing his cold fingers on his face, trying to put distance between himself and his dream. A shower might help.

To avoid contact with Madeleine, he used the shower in the small upstairs bathroom. As he was drying himself, he caught sight of his face in the mirror over the basin—a haggard face with anxious eyes, the face of a stranger. He hung up the towel and returned to the den.

Later that morning, Madeleine left for the clinic without a word, as though he didn't exist.

As the hours passed, his decision to leave took shape.

Staying with Madeleine at this point made no emotional sense. Besides, Stryker's RAM escalation of his "wanted" status was bound to result in more aggressive police scrutiny of the house and surrounding property, perhaps extending to discovery of his campsite.

He would need a place to go.

He thought of an ideal location.

He called Emma Martin and asked if he could stay for a while at Ziko Slade's lodge.

After the briefest hesitation, she said yes.

PART V

THE VIPER

65

MAKING HIS DECISION AND SECURING A RELATIVELY SAFE destination had oddly taken some of the emotional urgency out of actually making the physical move. In fact, by the time he finally set out for the lodge three days later, a large part of his motivation was the anticipated comfort and security of the place, compared to the inconveniences and vulnerabilities of his hilltop campsite.

That, and the fact that being around Madeleine in these strange new circumstances was disorienting. She had, at least in his mind, become a different person—a stranger who only looked like the woman he once knew. This made the house itself seem strange—as though he were seeing it through glasses that subtly distorted the position of everything.

One of the last things he did before leaving was install the app that communicated with the security cameras on the property on Madeleine's phone. When he explained how the system worked and how the pattern of beeps identified which camera had been activated, she listened with no more emotion than if he were a disembodied voice on an instruction video.

LATE IN THE afternoon of a frigid day, at the end of a three-hour drive, he turned into the pine-shrouded private road that led to

Slade's lodge. The temperature was dropping, a bone-chilling Adirondack wind was rising, and the hemlocks around the lodge were hissing and swaying.

Valdez came out to meet him, a woolen watch cap his only concession to the brutal weather, his smile muted by the sadness in his eyes. He looked years older than when Gurney last saw him. They shook hands, and Gurney offered his condolences for the death of Ziko Slade. Valdez nodded, then led the way onto the porch and into the front room of the house. A fire had just been started in the ceiling-high stone fireplace.

"I recall you like strong coffee," said Valdez in that odd accent that seemed to come from several parts of the world at once. "My preference also. Please sit, be comfortable, while I get it ready."

He had no desire at that moment for coffee, but since it was the man's way of welcoming him, he said nothing. After Valdez left the room, Gurney stepped closer to the fireplace. Slade's tennis trophies were still on the mantel, gleaming in the amber light. They appeared to have been recently polished. The rest of the big room was dustier, less cared-for than he remembered.

The antique pine paneling, wide-board floors, hand-hewn beams, and framed prints of pheasants and woodcocks—all contributed to the image of a rich man's sanctuary and reminded him that Slade's will had made Valdez very rich indeed.

"So," said Valdez, returning with two mugs of black coffee, "what will you do?"

"Sorry?"

Valdez handed him one of the mugs, gesturing for him to take one of the leather armchairs next to the hearth. He settled into the chair across from it before continuing. "Emma believes there's no longer any purpose to solving the Lerman murder. And even though she believes Ziko was murdered, she says it's a waste of time to search for the murderer. She says that justice for the dead is nothing but the poison of revenge. Do you believe this?"

"I believe that she believes it."

"But you are still pursuing the truth?"

"Yes."

Valdez sipped his coffee, his melancholy gaze on the fire. "Maybe Emma is right. Maybe I am poisoned by this desire. If so, then so be it. If someone killed Ziko, they must also be killed. Is that revenge or justice? I don't know. I don't care what the word is. Ziko was my father. A son must respond to the murder of his father."

Gurney said nothing.

Valdez was still staring into the fire. "Do you believe it is the same murderer for Lerman a year ago and Ziko now?"

"I believe the same person orchestrated both murders."

There was a long silence before Valdez turned from the fire and looked at Gurney. "I have told you my heart. What is yours?"

"You mean, why am I still pursuing the Lerman case?"

"Yes."

"Because the official version makes no sense. And because everyone is trying to stop me. The so-called good guys are trying to arrest me, and the bad guys may try to kill me."

A smile crept into Valdez's dour expression. "You don't like people trying to stop you?"

"It makes me wonder what they're hiding."

"What have you discovered?"

"Nothing significant enough yet to vacate Ziko's conviction. But I'm getting closer, and the opposition is starting to panic. Which means the time I have left to uncover the truth is shrinking."

Valdez peered again into the fire. "This *uncovering* . . . this is your motive?"

"My goal."

"There's a difference?"

"My goal is *what* I want, which I'm always sure of. My motive is *why* I want it, which I can never be sure of."

"Meaning that our minds can play tricks on us, yes?"

"Yes."

Valdez sipped his coffee thoughtfully before putting his cup down on the arm of his chair and switching to a lighter tone. "Shall we bring your suitcases in from the car?"

FOR DINNER THAT evening Valdez prepared a stew of cubed pork, sausages, carrots, and white beans. He and Gurney ate in the lodge's dining room, a smaller version of the front room, with its own fireplace.

After they finished, Valdez led Gurney upstairs to the bedroom where they'd brought his suitcases. He pointed out the nearest bathroom and mentioned there was an extra blanket in the closet.

As soon as Valdez went downstairs, Gurney unstrapped his shoulder-holstered Glock and laid it on the bedside table. He put his phone next to the Glock. He slipped off his shoes, loosened his belt, switched off the lamp, and stretched out on the bed—a heavy-timbered four-poster.

Exhaustion and a throbbing headache put him in a nightmarish state, neither asleep nor awake. Every other thought passing through his head was accompanied by the image of Charlene Vesco's bleeding eyes. Since occupying himself with a practical task usually helped, he got up and took out his laptop. After connecting to the house wifi, he got the contact information for the Albany County ME, whose jurisdiction included Garville, and began drafting an email regarding Charlene's death.

He kept it to five brief points: The cause of her death appeared to be a major overdose of an anticoagulant. It was likely administered by someone other than the victim. The intention was evidently homicidal. Heparin-containing snake venom may have been the anticoagulant employed. It was probably administered hypodermically or via the fangs of a live snake.

He assumed the first three facts would be obvious to any competent ME. He mentioned them to create a credible path into points

four and five, which he hoped the ME would find intriguing enough
to pursue. Snakes might not be the ultimate key to unraveling the
mysteries of the case, but then again . . .

He reread what he'd written and tapped Send. With a clearer
mind, he stripped down to his shorts and tee shirt, got into bed, and
soon relaxed into a relatively normal sleep.

Shortly after dawn, he was awakened by a sharp cracking
sound, accompanied by the whistling of a gusty wind. He emerged
from under the bed's warm quilt and went to the window. A large
ice-covered branch was dangling from a nearby hemlock like a partially severed arm.

The screen on his phone indicated it was a minute past seven. After brushing his teeth and showering, he put on a pair of flannel-lined
jeans and a heavy sweater to compensate for the morning chill in the
house.

Instead of going directly downstairs, he decided to take a look
at Slade's bedroom, which he recalled from his earlier visit to the
lodge was the last in the hallway. He opened the door and switched
on the light. The room looked exactly as he remembered it. Like the
trophies on the mantel, it had been kept in spotless condition. He
turned off the light and headed downstairs, imagining that he'd find
Valdez building a fire or making breakfast. Instead, he found a note
on the dining room table.

> I hope you have slept well. There are many foods in
> the refrigerator. The temperature in the house is set
> to rise automatically after 8:00 a.m. I am sorry to be
> gone, but I have business to attend to. I hope to be
> back tomorrow morning. Make this your home. It is
> what Ziko would wish.

There was no signature, no phone number, no indication of
where he could be reached.

66

AFTER A BREAKFAST OF SCRAMBLED EGGS, TOAST, AND coffee, Gurney settled down in an armchair next to the hearth with a second coffee.

Although Valdez's departure and the vague reason he'd given for it seemed odd, it was not unwelcome. It gave Gurney greater freedom to do whatever he wanted, if only to examine the puzzle without interruption in the place where it all began. And to ponder the mystery of Valdez himself.

Perhaps accepting Valdez's surface appearance of being Slade's adoring acolyte was a mistake. Was it conceivable that Slade had been victimized by Valdez?

Although unlikely, it was an intriguing possibility. It might explain one of the case's perplexities—the contradiction between the descriptions in Lerman's diary of the three phone calls and Slade's insistence that he'd never received them. Suppose Valdez had answered those calls, passing himself off as Slade. And suppose, when Lerman showed up to collect his extortion money, it was Valdez who killed him and planted the evidence that incriminated Slade.

That scenario would eliminate a major contradiction, but at the cost of creating thorny new questions. Had Valdez known that he was a beneficiary of Slade's will? If so, how would framing Slade for murder get him closer to his inheritance? Why would he have been answering Slade's phone on those three occasions? And what would his motive have been for pretending to be Slade?

Gurney's excitement at the idea began to fade. However, even if Valdez hadn't killed Lerman, his potential involvement in Slade's prison murder couldn't be so easily dismissed.

It was hard to see Emma Martin as a duplicitous string-puller, coolly focused on Slade's millions, but it was conceivable that Valdez was exactly that. He presented himself as a humble soul, treading a path to Slade-like sainthood. But who was he, really? Where had he come from? And how firm a grip did those roots still have on him?

If Emma was right about Slade's "suicide" having been a concealed murder, and if Valdez had engineered that murder, he would have needed at least one inside accomplice—not just any criminal acquaintance, but a cold-blooded killer under his personal control. The probability of that depended on the unknown facts of Valdez's life. One thing was certain. If the seemingly humble Valdez was behind Slade's hanging, he'd rank as one of the most unnerving sociopaths Gurney had ever encountered.

Then there was the matter of the attack on Blackmore Mountain, the murder of Sonny Lerman, and the gruesome execution of Charlene Vesco. Was it conceivable that Ian Valdez masterminded all of that?

And if not Valdez, then who? Who was the spider who sat in the center of the web? Who was the ultimate controller—the one who had the power to tell the other players what to do—the one who knew why Lerman's head and fingers had to be amputated, what Slade's dark secret was, why Slade and Sonny and Charlene had to be killed?

Something at the beginning of that sequence of thoughts—*the one who had the power to tell the other players what to do*—reminded Gurney of something. At first, it was just a faint echo. Then he remembered where it came from.

He placed a call to Marcus Thorne.

The man answered immediately, sounding busy but curious.

"Surprised to hear from you again. Emma told me Slade's death put an end to her exoneration quest."

"Hers but not mine. There's something from our meeting I wanted to ask you about."

"Talk fast."

"You told me a story about a gem courier who needed money to bail his son out of some difficulty, and he wanted to set up a heist."

"Not just wanted to, he went ahead with it."

"I remember you told me the story to make an interesting point about the importance of a jury's emotional reaction to the defendant."

"Exactly," said Thorne, more warmly now.

The emotional basis of verdicts wasn't the point Gurney cared about, but he knew Thorne did and that quoting him would make him more willing to talk.

"I was wondering," said Gurney in the tone of an eager student, "could you tell me the story again?"

"I'm crushed for time, but . . . alright, short version. It was a major robbery-and-murder case. Prosecution had a seemingly airtight case. A precious gems courier is held up in a parking lot, gets robbed of an attaché case containing three million bucks' worth of emeralds. He gets a punch in the face, and the lot attendant is shot dead. The heist team gets away with the emeralds. But then the courier ID's the heist driver as a guy who'd been following him for a few days. He gives the cops a picture he says he took of the guy on the street. And he gives the cops a plate number for the getaway car. Plate number turns out to be for a car registered to a local scumbag involved in various nasty activities, the nicest of which was fencing high-end jewelry. The scumbag had no solid alibi, and the guy the courier ID'd as the driver turned out to be the scumbag's right-hand man. The DA had a very persuasive case. At this point, I am the scumbag's attorney. The DA offered us a reasonable plea deal, and—given the evidentiary lay of the land, the unsavoriness of my client, and the likelihood of a murder conviction for the dead parking lot attendant—I recommended that he accept it. He refused. He insisted he'd been set up by a business rival, guy by the name of Jimmy Peskin. He gave me a blank check to get to the truth. And I did."

This was the part of the story that Thorne liked, and his pleasure in telling it enlivened his voice. "The real story began with the gem courier's son. The kid had been hired by a top L.A. law firm. But— major *but*—he had problems with gambling, coke, and hookers. His gambling had gotten him into significant debt with a mob guy who was demanding immediate payment or pictures would appear on the internet that would end the kid's career. The kid went to Dad. Dad, desperate to get his son out of trouble, approached a guy whose street rep suggested he might be open to . . . an arrangement. This guy was Jimmy Peskin, major business rival of my client. Dad proposed a jewel heist to Peskin with a fifty-fifty split of the proceeds—providing that Dad incriminate my client by giving the police a false ID of the driver, a false plate number and description of the getaway car, a bullshit story about the driver having followed him, et cetera. Bottom line? Our presentation at my guy's trial incorporated enough of what we discovered about Peskin to create a textbook example of reasonable doubt. In fact, the court reporters found our case a hell of a lot more persuasive than the prosecutor's. One reporter called it a steel-trap indictment of Jimmy Peskin. But, like I told you before, the jury found my guy guilty on all counts, including the murder of the attendant. Because the greatest defense in the world is worthless if the jury thinks your client is a scumbag."

Gurney thought about it for a moment. "So, Peskin agreed to carry out the arranged heist and give the courier half the proceeds, on the condition that the courier tell the police a story that incriminated your client?"

"That's how we explained the framing plot to the jury. But they didn't buy it—for the simple reason that they found my client less appealing than Peskin. You win some, you lose some. Rarely for the right reasons. Fact of the criminal justice system. Fact of life, too. Have to go now, Gurney. Never keep a paying client waiting."

Gurney sat back in the chair, gazing at the dead coals of yesterday's fire. He was pondering what, for him, was the heart of the story—the deal Jimmy Peskin made with the desperate gem courier. Essentially, *I'll stage the robbery for you, if you give the police this phony account of what happened.*

So, the courier got the money he wanted for his son—at the price of perjured testimony, an unjust murder conviction, and a dead parking lot attendant.

I'll do what you want me to do, if you say what I want you to say.

He wondered if that basic quid pro quo could be the template underlying everything that had happened. Exactly what had been done and what had been said in return were yet to be determined, but the structure felt right.

The more he thought about it, the surer he became that there'd been some sort of deal at the root of the affair. A deal that led to six deaths: Lenny and Sonny Lerman, Ziko Slade, Bruno Lanka, Dominick Vesco, and Charlene Vesco. A tremor passed through him at the thought that Jack Hardwick might become the seventh.

The idea of losing Hardwick permanently led to another bleak issue weighing on his mind, his separation from Madeleine.

His departure felt less like a temper tantrum than the inevitable result of a fatal flaw in their marriage. But it was only a feeling. Rational thought on that subject was out of reach at that moment. He told himself there would be time enough to arrive at a clearer vision. If clarity was something he really wanted.

At the moment, he'd rather think about the beheading of Lenny Lerman or the bloody death of Charlene Vesco or just about anything other than the apparent collapse of his marriage.

67

AFTER GETTING A PAD FROM HIS SUITCASE UPSTAIRS AND a third cup of coffee from the kitchen, he took a seat at the dining room table and began making a list—partly of facts, partly of guesswork—to see if a new hypothesis might emerge.

It bothered him that he was turning again to the bogus satisfaction of list-making—a symptom of his isolation and a poor substitute for exposing his thoughts to an intelligent skeptic. But it was all he had. He put his notes in the present tense to make them feel more alive.

> *Lenny Lerman has a problem with his son that he believes money will fix.*
> *He discovers he has a terminal illness.*

An acquaintance tells him about a dark secret in Ziko Slade's past.

With nothing to lose, he sees this as an opportunity for an extortion windfall.

He (like the courier in Thorne's story) approaches a potential partner.

The potential partner agrees to help him, with a condition.

Lenny, like the courier, must make certain statements damaging to a third party.

When the extortion plan comes to a head, something goes wrong, and Lenny is killed.

Lenny's head and fingers are removed.

Bruno Lanka brings the mutilated body to the attention of the police.

Slade is arrested, tried, and convicted, based on physical evidence and Lenny's diary.

The list created more questions than answers.

Might the partner Lenny approached be the shadowy gangster at the edge of the Lerman family? What quid pro quo might that person have demanded in return for his help? Might it have involved Lenny claiming in his diary to have made certain threatening phone calls that he didn't actually make? But if no extortion calls were made— or, to take it a step further, if no extortion plan existed at all—what did Lenny need a partner for?

The notion that the diary might be misleading struck Gurney as an intriguing premise for a new concept of the case. As a private record of Lerman's thoughts and actions, including candid descriptions of his criminal intentions, its credibility had never been seriously challenged. Only the authenticity of his handwriting had been attested to. But if certain entries were lies—

Gurney's train of thought was broken by a flash of light at the edge of his vision. He went to the dining room window, which faced a narrow cleared area next to the house and, beyond that, the forest.

He watched for a long minute without seeing or hearing anything unusual.

As he was turning back to the table, he saw again, out of the corner of his eye, a split-second glint of light. Was it an unwelcome visitor with a flashlight? Or a post-concussion glitch in his optic nerve? This time he watched for a good ten minutes, but there were no more flashes.

The oddity of the experience put him on edge—and resurrected the memory of the first oddity he'd experienced at the lodge, the decapitated rabbit in his car. Both experiences occurred while Valdez was absent, supposedly away on some errand. He could feel the first inklings of paranoid speculation taking hold, and realized he needed to find a way to ground himself.

Although he could imagine the reassurances Emma Martin would give him about Valdez, he decided to call her anyway. It was yet another reminder of how sorely he was missing Hardwick's combative responses to the excesses of his imagination.

"Hello, David. Right on time."

"Sorry?"

"Marcus Thorne just told me about your conversation. He got the impression that you felt you were on to something. Which made me think I'd be hearing from you."

"Did he tell you the gem courier story?"

"He did. But he has no idea how it applies to our case. And neither do I."

"I'm not saying it provides a perfect template for what happened. However . . ." Gurney went on to recount his theory that Lerman might have sought someone's help in a conspiracy against Slade, but the helper then took advantage of Lerman like Jimmy Peskin took advantage of the courier to incriminate a competitor.

"You're saying this individual murdered Lenny, specifically to frame Ziko?"

"I'm saying it's a scenario that fits what happened."

"Are you implying that this individual was a *competitor* of Ziko's?"

"Possibly."

"A competitor in what sort of business?"

"I've been thinking about that. You may not be happy with the answer."

"Don't worry about my happiness."

"One business comes to mind. A business with big money at stake, a business that attracts people willing to commit murder, a business in which Slade had a history of involvement."

Emma's soft voice hardened. "The drug business was part of Ziko's *past*. It was a closed door."

"Is it possible that you might be mistaken about that?"

"Is it possible that one of us is dreaming and that this conversation is not really happening? Many things are possible, but too absurd to consider."

"Okay, let's take drugs off the table and back up a little. If the goal of Lerman's murder was the framing of Slade, which now seems more likely than not, something big must have been at stake to justify all the planning and effort involved. 'Something big' usually means money, power, revenge, or all three."

"I understand, but if this hypothetical framer's goal was to put Ziko in prison, why have him killed?"

"My first guess was to prevent his release in the event of his conviction being overturned. But it could also be that putting him in prison didn't achieve its intended goal, and his 'suicide' was the backup plan."

That comment produced a silence.

Gurney changed direction. "I've been thinking about Ian. Considering his closeness to Ziko, he might be in some danger."

"He's aware of that."

"He doesn't seem worried."

"He's not."

"You don't find his lack of concern . . . suspicious?"

"No."

"You trust him with no reservations?"

"Apparently you don't."

"My experience tells me to follow the money. Ian's multimillion-dollar windfall from Slade's estate could be a significant motive." He didn't mention that the same motive applied to Emma.

She uttered a dismissive little laugh. "Do you really see Ian as an all-powerful crime lord who can reach into a high-security prison and execute someone?"

"A lot of money can buy a lot of influence. And speaking of Ian's money, do you know what he plans to do with his inheritance?"

"He plans to give it away."

"Sounds very generous."

"He's afraid of having more money than he needs. He considers wealth a kind of poison."

"You believe him?"

"Yes."

"Hell of a lot of faith you're putting in a former drug addict."

"He's not the person he used to be."

"You know, not all conversions are what they seem to be."

She laughed. "Of course not. Most are nonsense. Oily righteousness. Bible-waving for ego and profit. The truth is, the deepest conversions are the quietest. They occur when something is seen that wasn't seen before, a profound personal truth. The result is a new gentleness, a sense of the preciousness of life, the importance of service. It's more about listening than proclaiming."

"That's what you see in Ian?"

"Yes."

The certainty in her tone made further questioning pointless.

He thanked her and ended the call.

He wasn't sure what he'd learned—perhaps only that Emma Martin was a lot more confident than he was about Ian Valdez's sainthood.

68

AS HE WAS SITTING AT THE DINING ROOM TABLE, PONDER-ing his phone call with Emma, a wave of anxiety swept through him. He went to the window that provided a view of the forest area where he'd seen—or thought he'd seen—the flashes of light. He waited for several minutes and saw nothing peculiar, but his anxiety continued to grow.

He retrieved his holstered Glock from the upstairs bedroom, strapped it on, then loaded the spare magazine and slipped it into his pocket. In the face of an unknown enemy, it provided only a dubious sense of security, but something was better than nothing.

The downstairs windows had no blinds or curtains, creating a feeling of exposure that made him uncomfortable. He searched the closets for a solution, found some tablecloths, and hung them over the windows in the front room and the dining room, affixing them to the wall above each window with duct tape he found in a kitchen utility drawer.

Looking around at the covered windows brought back a child-hood memory of creating an imaginary fort from a card table draped with a blanket and crawling into it and sitting there in the sheltered semidarkness, entering a world of adventure in which the fort be-came a cave or a teepee or a boat and he was far from home, free to embark on whatever adventure occurred to him. Under that table, under that blanket, in that fort or boat, there was no fear, no arguing parents, only freedom and the future.

A shrill whistle of wind in the chimney brought him back to the present. And the present brought with it a renewed awareness of the precariousness of his position, a sense of loneliness, and the thought of Hardwick on life support.

He got his phone and called the hospital.

No change. Condition critical. Vital signs unstable. The nurse's tone was terse and suspicious. Understandably so, since the patient was responsible for two shooting deaths.

Gurney went from room to room, upstairs and downstairs, checking the window locks and door locks. He started a blaze in the fireplace and tried to relax. He went to the kitchen and made a pot of coffee. He wondered when Ian would return. More critically, he wondered how much faith he should be putting in Emma's opinion of the enigmatic young man.

His thoughts were interrupted by his phone. The screen said it was A. Lerman.

"Hello, Adrienne, I was just—"

She cut him off, the words spilling out. "They've exhumed Dad's body! For another autopsy! How can they do that without my permission? They didn't even let me know—until now—and it's already been done! What on earth is happening?"

"When you say that 'they' exhumed Lenny's body, who do you mean?"

"The pathologist, the one at Slade's trial. It was someone in his office who called me. As a courtesy, she said, as though I had no say in the matter, as though he wasn't my father. And of course it was already done, all after the fact! They sent people out to the cemetery and dug up his grave and the pathologist did an autopsy. The woman who called me sounded pleasant, but it was that awful kind of pleasantness that doesn't mean a thing. Do you know anything about this?"

"In criminal cases a county medical examiner has the right to issue a disinterment order and conduct an autopsy—or a second autopsy—without the consent of any third party. This can occur if new evidence arises, or if there's a well-founded belief that the autopsy will lead to the discovery of evidence sufficient to alter the disposition of the case."

"Does this mean they've discovered something new about Dad's death?"

"I wouldn't be surprised. Remember I told you I was studying the GPS logs of trips he made in the last weeks of his life? Well, it appears that some of those trips may have been to medical offices. In fact, I shared that information with Dr. Loeffler as a matter of course, but I feel blindsided by his proceeding without telling either of us. Did the person you spoke to at Loeffler's office give you any information on the results of the autopsy?"

"No. Nothing. I asked, and she said that the information was being provided to the district attorney's office, and I should check with them. But I have a feeling no one is going to tell me anything!"

"Dealing with these people can be infuriating. But I'll find out whatever I can, Adrienne, and I'll get back to you."

Gurney had no illusions that having prodded Loeffler to perform the autopsy would make him privy to its results. So, some form of subterfuge would be necessary.

He hid his caller ID and placed a call to Loeffler's office.

It was answered by a cool female voice. "Medical examiner's office. May I help you?"

Gurney spoke like a man on an important mission. "This is Jim Holland at the *North Country Star*. We're about to go to press with a story, and we'd like to get Dr. Loeffler's comment on one of the key facts we're including."

She hesitated. "Your name again?"

"Jim Holland—like the Netherlands. I'm assistant managing editor here at the *Star*. I've been in touch with your office before."

"Just a moment."

A minute or so later, he heard the electronic click of the call being transferred. It rang again, once, and was picked up.

"Dr. Loeffler speaking. What's this about?"

"Jim Holland here at the *North Country Star*. We've received some information regarding Lenny Lerman, the murder victim. According to our source, he suffered from an advanced form of brain cancer. Can you provide us with the basic medical details?"

"The autopsy results will be made public in due course."

"I appreciate that, Doctor. In the meantime, perhaps you could simply confirm the details already in our possession."

Loeffler said nothing, which Gurney took as an opening to proceed. "Our source told us that Mr. Lerman's cancer was late-stage and terminal. Are we likely to run into trouble with that description?"

"I wouldn't think so."

"I just want to be sure we're not making any embarrassing medical errors. Our source described the cancer as a particularly aggressive type of meningioma. Can we print that?"

"Not if you care anything about accuracy."

"The *North Country Star* cares a great deal about accuracy, Doctor, and so do I. Which is why I was hoping you'd be willing to put us on the right path."

Loeffler emitted the weary sigh of a professor dealing with a tiresome student.

"Inoperable final-stage glioblastoma," he said and ended the call.

Gurney wasn't surprised by Loeffler's diagnosis. But having his guess confirmed gave his faith in his own hypothesizing a much-needed boost.

The location of Lerman's cancer suggested a possible link to his decapitation. Did the murderer know about Lerman's terminal condition and want to hide it from the police? If so, why? And what role could the finger amputations have played in that concealment?

As Gurney was about to put that last question aside, a possibility occurred to him. The finger amputations might have been designed to create the exact impression that they did—the intent to delay identification of the body. That impression had, in fact, eliminated speculation by Rexton PD and Cam Stryker about other possible reasons for the decapitation.

Gurney felt that his feet were on solid ground, and that gave him an appetite for more progress, along with a more dangerous appetite—for confrontation.

Theorizing about the nature of a crime was a necessary process, but there came a point in every investigation when progress depended on identifying a prime suspect. And there were occasional investigations in which the only way to identify that individual was to provoke him or her into making mistakes.

As he considered how he could apply that kind of pressure to his elusive target, he concluded that RAM-TV—specifically, *Controversial Perspectives*—offered the best opportunity. Their philosophy of provocative insinuation created the right environment for what he had in mind, and they certainly wouldn't object to his presenting supposition as fact.

He found Sam Smollett's cell number and made the call.

She sounded surprised to hear from him, but definitely interested.

He described the kind of interview he had in mind, emphasizing the sensational aspects of what he wanted to share with the RAM audience and its potential for bringing a murderer out of hiding—an event that RAM could take credit for.

"That's fantastic, David! A great counterpoint to our recent interview with Cam Stryker. According to her, you're *a wanted man*." Smollett made that sort of man sound like the world's most exciting commodity. "We'll mention that you're doing the interview from an undisclosed location. A nice touch of cloak-and-dagger. District attorney versus rogue detective. I love it!"

"Sounds good to me, Sam."

"Okay! Let's do it!"

"Now?"

"Absolutely! I'll set up a Zoom call with you. I'll handle the RAM side of the interview. I'll record it all, then edit out my questions, and tonight Tarla and Jordan will ask the same questions, and your answers will come across as live."

"Is that legitimate?"

"*Legitimate*?" She made it sound like a word from a long-forgotten language. "The lawyers can worry about that. More importantly, do you have a black shirt, black sweater, anything like that?"

"Maybe a black tee shirt. Why?"

"Black conveys a tough, no-nonsense attitude. Street-level gravitas. You have any neck or forearm tattoos?"

"No."

"Too bad. Give me your email, and I'll send you the Zoom link. Then go put that tee shirt on."

Five minutes later, having shed his flannel shirt for a black tee, he was at the dining room table, sitting in front of his laptop screen, gazing at a sharply featured female face topped with an auburn brush cut. The smile on the face was animated more by hungry anticipation than by friendliness.

"You look great, David. You ready?"

"Yes."

"Keep that stern edge on your voice. It's perfect. Okay, this is it."

She paused, then spoke in a dramatic newscaster's voice. "Good evening! We open tonight's edition of *Controversial Perspectives* with a bombshell interview with former NYPD detective, Dave Gurney. Gurney has declared war not only on the official version of the Slade murder case, but on DA Cam Stryker herself, who in our last interview described him as a 'wanted' man. So, let's get right to it! Detective Gurney, welcome to *Controversial Perspectives*."

"Thank you."

"You've made it clear you have no faith in the DA's investigation of Lenny Lerman's murder, so you've been conducting your own. What have you discovered?"

"So far, four key facts. One, Lerman had inoperable brain cancer with less than a month to live, which opens the case to other inter-pretations. Two, his diary entries, accepted at face value by the DA, may have been intentionally deceptive. Three, the DA seems hell-bent on blaming the prison death of Ziko Slade on suicide, even though the people closest to him insist he was murdered. Four, the original Lerman investigation team screwed up repeatedly. They missed the significance of Lerman's decapitation; they used his unreliable diary to give Slade a motive for murder; and they've closed their eyes to events that point to a cover-up—such as repeated attempts to stop my own investigation."

"Wow! That's quite an indictment of law enforcement! But I have to ask—why would they hang on to a theory that's as weak as you say it is?"

"Ineptitude. Ambition. Desperation."

"Desperation?"

"A desperate fear of their mistakes being exposed. Mistakes make lousy rungs on the promotion ladder."

"Okay, Detective Gurney, one final question. How close do you think you are to identifying the criminal mastermind behind it all?"

"Very close. But 'criminal mastermind' is not the right description."

"Give me a better one."

"A pathetic homicidal psycho who's about to be taken down."

GURNEY KEPT REASSURING himself that what he'd said was purely a tactical assault, designed to provoke the perp into a self-identifying reaction. But he didn't entirely believe it. There was too much adrenaline in the experience, too great an illusion of power.

Still, it was a defendable approach. Similar approaches in other investigations had paid off. The feelings that went along with it were arguably the natural accompaniments of any aggressive initiative. He resolved to stop thinking about it.

He went to the kitchen and made himself some coffee. Striving for a sense of normalcy, he brought his cup to the dining room table and took down the tablecloth drapes covering the windows. The late morning sun was high enough in the sky to brighten the room, eliminating the need for interior lights and the fishbowl feeling that came with them.

He was just about to take his first sip of coffee when his sense of normalcy was ended by a glimpse of movement in the woods beyond the clearing. He put down his cup and sat very still, peering out into the hemlocks. Again, a slight movement, little more than a shadow a bit darker than the shadows around it, appearing and disappearing.

He slowly pushed himself back from the table, went to the front room, and put on his jacket, but not his gloves. He could handle the Glock better without them. He knew from his previous visit that at the rear of the kitchen there was a short hallway that led to a pantry and a back door—which seemed a safer exit than the more exposed front door. He walked quickly into the woods behind the tool shed and made his way toward the general area where he had spotted the possible intruder.

The forest was cold and silent. The dark mass of evergreen branches blocked the sun that had brightened the clearing, and the ice underfoot made walking tricky. Stopping every few yards to listen, he realized he was getting close to the scene of Lenny Lerman's murder.

Soon he caught sight of the giant pine that served as a forest landmark for Lerman's temporary grave.

Holding the Glock in a ready-to-fire grip, he moved slowly forward.

As he got closer to the gravesite, he noticed some odd little protrusions on its icy surface.

Moving still closer, gooseflesh crept up his back at the dawning recognition of what he was looking at.

Ten fingers, sticking up out of the ground like frozen claws.

69

BACK IN THE LODGE, GURNEY RETREATED TO HIS BEDroom with his Glock, phone, and laptop. Under normal circumstances, he'd call Rexton PD or the nearest state police barracks, report what he'd found, and lead the responders to the site, but these circumstances were far from normal. Announcing his location to law enforcement could result in his being detained immediately at the request of Cam Stryker. With police involvement off the table, his next option would have been to call Jack Hardwick, but just the thought of that now brought a rush of guilt and fear.

He thought about the interview Sam Smollett had recorded with him that morning and wondered if he should call her back with news of his grotesque discovery, but he decided to leave well enough alone. Thinking of the interview reminded him that he'd meant to call Madeleine and alert her to the elevated risk level his verbal attack on the perp might create.

He was afraid she wouldn't pick up, but she did.

"It's me," he said, the affectionate familiarity of it striking an odd note. "I wanted to alert you to something—warn you, actually." He paused.

She remained silent.

"Are you there?"

"Yes."

"I've come to the conclusion there's only one way to end this case—and that's to knock the enemy out of his comfort zone."

"You've identified the enemy?"

"Not yet. Anonymity is part of the perp's comfort zone—being able to pull the strings from the shadows, feel powerful, feel in control. So I decided to hit that comfort zone with a wrecking ball—to create rage and force errors."

"Why are you telling me this?"

"Because I gave an interview to RAM that will air tonight. The interview is the wrecking ball, and the reaction may be explosive. I assume I'll be the target of that reaction, but it might be a good idea for you to request police protection."

She said nothing.

He added, "Poking a sharp stick into a bear's den is not my favorite form of research, but sometimes it's the only way to get a look at the bear."

"You mean, it's the only way you can think of—and since your thinking is so far superior to everyone else's, it stands to reason that your way is the best way. You never question whether your goal makes any sense to begin with—or whether you have the right to expose other people to the fallout from your obsessions."

He bit his lip to stifle the urge to defend himself. "I didn't call to argue. I just wanted to let you know about a possibly dangerous situation and to suggest that you might want to ask the sheriff's department for temporary protection."

"I appreciate your concern." Her flat tone made the words meaningless.

After a few seconds of silence, she ended the call.

He stood motionless in the middle of the bedroom, more baffled than ever by his once close relationship with this woman. Was that relationship actually with her, or was it with his idea of her? Where had that idea come from? Was it based on something real in her? Or was it an artifact of what he needed her to be? Had he, like his childhood self, been sitting in a make-believe boat with a make-believe companion?

His thoughts were interrupted by the sound of an approaching vehicle. He hurried down the hall to Slade's former bedroom, whose windows offered a view of the driveway, and saw Valdez's white pickup approaching the lodge. A minute later, he heard the front door opening and closing and footsteps moving across the front room in the direction of the kitchen. He went downstairs and found Valdez unpacking a supermarket bag.

"I'm sorry to be away so long. Among many other things, an appointment with an attorney. Interesting profession. Everything in writing, because there is so much wrong with people. So much twisting and grabbing and lying. Attorneys, police, locks on doors—all necessary for the same reason."

Gurney nodded vaguely, then waited until Valdez had finished putting away his groceries before speaking. "Something peculiar happened a little while ago."

He went on to describe the event—from the movements he saw in the forest to his discovery under the giant hemlock.

"You have reported this?"

"Not yet. My relationship with law enforcement right now is . . . complicated."

"You're sure of what you saw?"

"Yes."

"You were very close? It was clear? No chance it was something else?"

"No chance."

"How could such a thing be?"

"It seems that the person who cut Lerman's fingers off kept them."

"Kept them for this? To stick them in the ground? Why?"

"One more eerie event to scare me off?"

"You're sure this is aimed at you, not at me?"

"Fairly sure."

"But if you didn't happen to notice the movement, you wouldn't have gone out to investigate. Then what?"

"I suspect further efforts would have been made to get my attention."

"Hmm. So, this person who kept the fingers—he knows you're here?"

"Apparently."

"Perhaps he is still in the forest?"

"I have no idea."

"I must see this for myself."

"Whatever you wish."

Glock in hand, again using the back door, Gurney led the way from the lodge into the woods. Proceeding cautiously over the slippery ground, peering silently in every direction, he eventually caught sight of the landmark pine, and they made their way toward the place where Lerman had been beheaded.

The closer they got, the more perplexed Gurney became. There was nothing unusual about the gravesite. There were no protrusions. Nothing sticking up out of the frozen earth. No claw-like fingers. Nothing.

He stared at the ice-covered ground in disbelief. He stepped closer, holding the Glock in his right hand and with his left using the flashlight app on his phone to examine the shadowed ground. Nothing. Not even any sign that the coating of ice had been disturbed.

Trying to make sense of the situation, he guessed that the fingers must have been set upright on the surface rather than implanted in the earth, allowing for their removal without a trace. Meaning that someone had been watching, making sure he saw them, then taking them away. At least, that was what his rational mind was telling him. But another voice inside him was telling him something else.

Maybe they were never there to begin with. Maybe too much stress and too little sleep too soon after a concussion are taking a toll.

It was an explanation he didn't want to believe. Few things frightened him more than the possibility that he might be subject to hallucinations. Faulty eyewitness accounts of crimes proved time and again that people under stress often saw—and were able to describe in precise detail—things that didn't exist. Add to that stress the disruption of a traumatic brain injury and God only knew how messed up one's perceptions might be.

Valdez eyed the ground but showed no reaction—unless an absence of expression under such strange circumstances was itself a significant reaction.

Gurney pointed to the area where he was sure he'd seen the fingers.

"They were right there."

He heard an insistence in his voice that sounded disturbingly fragile.

70

GURNEY SPENT THE REST OF THE DAY SEARCHING FOR EVidence that would support what had happened. Treating the location around the hemlock as a crime scene, he followed a spiral search pattern, proceeding slowly around the central point in an expanding circle—and then repeating it, expanding it farther and farther into the surrounding forest.

When dusk arrived, all he had to show for his efforts were a sore ankle from twisting it on an exposed tree root and photographs he'd taken of several areas of disturbed pine needles, photographs he then had to admit were meaningless. He deleted them from his phone.

At dinner that evening, Valdez maintained a stolid silence, except for announcing that he needed to make another trip, this time to Emma's recovery center, and would be away until the following day.

"Someone is arriving. I try to make new residents comfortable. It's part of what I do, part of my job."

"Are you a paid for your work?"

The question elicited a rare smile. "I am paid with peace of mind."

After clearing the table, putting the dishes in the kitchen sink, and asking Gurney if he would be alright by himself, Valdez departed in his pickup truck.

Gurney remained at the table, half exhausted and half energized by anxiety. Eventually he got up and double-checked the locks on the doors and windows, upstairs and downstairs, then returned to the table and opened his laptop.

He spent the next hour searching for information on stress-induced and injury-induced hallucinations. He learned a lot, none of it calming. In fact, the more he learned, the more adrift he felt. A flesh-and-blood antagonist could be found, confronted, and defeated. Physical assaults could be parried. Physical evidence could be collected and analyzed. But if the assaults, if the evidence, were only in one's mind, what then?

He shut down his computer and brought it up to his bedroom. The windows had blinds, which he lowered before turning on the bedside lamp.

The sight of the bed reminded him how weary he felt. He lay down on the soft quilt, hoping to put aside, at least for a little while,

the menace of the day. But his mind was still churning with possibilities. Suppose the disappearing fingers were real, after all. Were
they intended to be a confidence destroyer? A paranoia inducer? Or
a distracting jab, setting up a knockout punch? The questions had
no answers. They became increasingly disjointed and led only to an
uneasy sleep and distressing dreams.

The first of these was similar to the Blackmore Mountain one
he had a few nights before. Sleet is pelting the windshield of the
Outback. The red tow truck comes out of nowhere, crashing into
him, ramming him off the road. The truck stops and Sonny Lerman
emerges from it, laughing. Gurney sees himself firing a pistol at
Lerman, Lerman being knocked back into the truck. He sees himself approaching the truck, looking inside. Jack Hardwick's bleeding
eyes look back at him. Hardwick says, "You'll be the death of me,
Sherlock."

The dream kept repeating itself, until it was transformed into
another dream entirely, a dream about Madeleine. When he awoke at
dawn, it was from a dream so sad that his eyes were wet with tears—
yet a moment later whatever caused his weeping had dissolved beyond recall. In its wake was a lingering and irresistible urge to visit
his home.

IT WAS MIDMORNING when he arrived at his secluded parking
spot. The sky was clear, the sun was strong, and ice-melt was dripping from the branches of the evergreens as he made his way up the
steep slope, carrying only his laptop.

Everything at the campsite seemed in order. He opened the tent
flap, got the propane heater going, then went over to the place in the
trees that offered a view of the house and the surrounding property.
He could see the watchers' car down by the barn and Madeleine's
rented red Crosstrek by the asparagus bed. An old blue pickup truck
was parked by the chicken coop, and a man in rough-looking farm
clothes was setting a four-by-four wooden post in a hole not far from

the coop. A dozen or so similar posts had already been set in the pasture below the coop. Additional post holes had been dug every eight feet or so in a loose curve around the far side of the coop. The sight of the work in progress gave Gurney a complicated feeling he had a hard time identifying. Loneliness and resentment were part of it.

He returned to the tent, went inside, and sat in the folding chair—half of him trying to understand his emotional reaction, half of him trying to ignore it. In support of the second half, he opened his laptop and began reviewing his lists and notes, trying to extract a coherent picture from that blizzard of facts and suppositions. But as before, the puzzle pieces refused to coalesce. In his frustration, a radical though occurred to him.

Suppose none of the "facts" were true.

Suppose Ziko Slade had no dark secret, no past encounter with someone called Sally Bones. Suppose Lenny Lerman was never told anything by someone called Jingo. Suppose the calls Lerman made to Slade had nothing to do with blackmail. Suppose they took the form of fake spam calls, calls that Slade would have quickly forgotten. That would finally explain the discrepancy between the phone company's records and Slade's insistence that he'd never received any blackmail calls. Suppose there'd never been any extortion plot at all. Suppose the diary was a pack of lies. Suppose the reason no coherent picture was emerging from the facts was that most of them weren't "facts" at all.

It was a startling notion. But if it was true, what solid ground was left to stand on?

Well, thought Gurney, if one was faced with lies, perhaps the best approach would be to ask, what did the lies have in common? In other words, what underlying truth would they have been designed to conceal?

That notion took him back to Marcus Thorne's story of the gem courier—his lies about recognizing one of the stickup men, about being followed by him, about having taken his picture, about the plate number of the getaway car. One thing they all had in common was that they been dictated to him by a confederate as the price of his cooperation in the phony heist—a confederate with his own agenda.

I'll do what you want me to do, if you say what I want you to say.

If that arrangement were the skeleton of the Lerman case, then the confederate's private agenda was the framing of Slade for a grisly murder by fabricating a motive: the elimination of a blackmailer in order to preserve his whitewashed image. The very motive that Stryker had used so effectively to win a conviction.

The result was not only Slade's incarceration but the demolition of his image as a reformed sinner. Was it possible that both of those outcomes were equally intended? Or even that the latter was more important than the first?

If so, it put the mystery of Slade's prison murder in an interesting new light and took Gurney back once again to Emma's question: *Why, after all the effort of framing Slade for murder, did the perp have him killed?*

All he could think of at the time was the prevention of Slade's release from prison or the possibility that the framing had failed to accomplish the framer's goal. But suppose the goal had been the tarring of Slade's shiny image?

Then the question would become, where exactly was the failure?

Certainly not in the media coverage of the affair, which put Slade in the ugliest light possible, nor in the general public's perception. Media and public alike were more than ready to see Slade as a murdering hypocrite. So, if the goal of image destruction had in some way failed, it must have failed with a much narrower audience—but an audience of enormous importance to the framer.

It was clear that it had failed utterly with at least one person, Emma Martin—whose unshakable faith in Ziko Slade was responsible for Gurney's own involvement. In that context, Slade's prison murder could be seen as a final attempt to defame the man in her mind with a narrative of guilt-driven suicide.

This new way of understanding the case excited Gurney, but it raised a big question. Why would destroying the image of Slade in the mind of Emma Martin be that important? Why would a therapist's opinion of her client matter to anyone else? Under what conceivable circumstances would changing that opinion be worth killing for?

Then, quite suddenly, he realized he'd gotten it all wrong, and the simple truth came to him like a flash of sunlight.

71

HOW COULD HE HAVE MISSED IT? IT HAD BEEN STARING him in the face from the beginning. Maybe that was the problem. It was too obvious.

On the drive from the campsite hill back to the lodge, he went over the details of the case once again—to be sure that his solution could explain everything, from Lenny's beheading to Sonny's shooting to the repeated assaults on his own sanity and security. By the time he turned into the lodge driveway, he was 90 percent sure all the pieces of the puzzle were in place. He realized, however, that understanding what had happened was different from being able to prove it. And it didn't provide a roadmap for what to do next.

He parked next to Valdez's pickup, checked the time—4:05 p.m.— and went into the lodge. There was a fire blazing in the front room fireplace and the scent of cherrywood smoke in the air. Hearing a vacuum upstairs, he went to the kitchen to make coffee. While it was brewing, he returned to the front room, settled down in one of the armchairs by the fire, and tried to figure out the best path forward.

The first decision facing him was with whom to share his new understanding of the case. As he weighed the options, he found himself once again sorely missing Hardwick's aggressive input. It was easy to be seduced by one's own ego-driven preferences when no one was there to point out their weaknesses.

At least he knew better than to visit Stryker and, without proof, present a narrative that undermined her greatest prosecutorial success. Same applied to the Rexton PD and the State Police Bureau of Criminal Investigation, both of which had a stake in the status quo.

There were other interested parties who had a right to know the truth—Howard Manx at the insurance company, Kyra Barstow, Adrienne Lerman, Emma Martin, and Ian Valdez. They also had a right to see the proof. But there was a catch. To get the proof, he'd need to tell the story.

"Lost in your thoughts?"

He looked up and saw Valdez in the doorway. He hadn't heard him coming downstairs, hadn't even noticed when the vacuum had been turned off. Lost, indeed.

"Good way of putting it."

"Something you want to talk about?"

He made a quick, if not altogether comfortable, decision.

"Something I need to talk about. And you need to hear."

His expression as impassive as ever, Valdez sat in the armchair facing Gurney.

Beset with misgivings, Gurney nevertheless pressed forward. "I think I understand what this case has been about from the beginning."

Valdez watched him intently. "From the murder of Lenny Lerman?"

"Starting at least a month before that. It all began when Lerman discovered he was about to die from brain cancer. He had no money, no life insurance, no relationship with a son whose respect he was desperate for, and no time left to gain that respect. He had reached the lowest point of a sad life. In the midst of his depression, something occurred to him—a way that he might still win that son's respect, even perhaps his love. But he wouldn't be able to do it alone. He'd need help—a special favor, the kind of favor a certain distant relative might be willing to provide. The relative was a much-feared man, but desperation emboldened Lenny, and he approached him. The relative agreed to do what Lenny asked, perhaps in part because Lenny was part of the family, however distant, but more importantly, because he saw a way to use the situation to destroy the reputation of someone he hated—Ziko Slade."

Valdez's unblinking gaze grew more intense.

Gurney went on. "The man agreed to help Lenny on the condition that Lenny would pretend he knew something terrible about Slade and was planning to extort a fortune from him. He told Lenny to start keeping a diary, and he told him what to write in it. He told him what to say to his boss and to his son and daughter. He told him how to handle three phone calls to Slade and how to describe them in his diary. He told him to come here to Slade's property the day before Thanksgiving, a day he knew that Slade would be occupied in the kitchen, preparing the following day's dinner. He had an associate meet Lenny here, knock him unconscious, drag him to a secluded spot, behead him, cut off his fingers, partially bury him, and plant all the pieces of evidence that later led to Slade's conviction."

Valdez was sitting rigidly upright in his chair. "This relative of Lenny's, instead of doing whatever favor he'd promised, had him killed as part of his own plot against Ziko. Is that what you're telling me?"

"Not exactly. In fact, Lenny's murder wasn't really a murder at all."

Confusion entered Valdez's eyes. "Not a murder? What was it?"

"The one thing everyone was sure it couldn't have been. Suicide."

"You just told me that an associate of the relative killed Lenny by cutting off his head? How can that be suicide?"

"Because that was the favor Lenny had asked for."

"To be killed?"

"In a way, he was already a dead man. His cancer would have killed him very soon. All he was giving up was another three or four weeks of life, most of which would have been pure misery. Rather than suffer, he chose a quick, painless death—and an opportunity to give his son and daughter a million dollars."

"Through an insurance scam?"

"Because of the terminal cancer, he couldn't get ordinary life insurance, but he was able to get a large accidental death policy. In most of those policies murder is considered an accidental death, but suicide isn't. That's the reason Lenny asked his head be removed— fear that if the terminal cancer were discovered the insurance company would suspect that the murder was actually an arranged suicide and refuse payment."

Valdez nodded slowly. "So, Lenny had nothing to lose and a lot of money to gain."

"Money he hoped would buy the respect of his son, the thing he'd always wanted more than anything else."

Valdez's nodding gave way to growing confusion in his eyes. "It is a strange but believable story of why Lerman was killed. But it tells me nothing of why the Lerman relative wanted Ziko blamed for the murder. What explains such hatred?"

"Fathers and sons," said Gurney, looking into the fire. "Relationships between fathers and sons have been on my mind from the beginning. But I didn't realize until today that a father-and-son relationship held the key to the entire case."

"What does Lerman's relative's desire to frame Ziko have to do with fathers and sons?"

"He framed Ziko because he believed that Ziko had stolen his son."

"What are you talking about? What son?"

"The son who turned his back on him. The son who stepped away from the family, away from the ties of blood. The son who called Ziko Slade his new father."

72

FOR A LONG WHILE VALDEZ SAT PERFECTLY STILL. HE opened his mouth twice, as if to speak, then closed it. Finally, without looking at Gurney, he asked, "How do you know this to be true?"

"It's the only explanation that accounts for everything."

"You have found evidence that he had Ziko murdered?"

"Not yet. But I will."

Valdez shook his head. "There will be no evidence."

Gurney stared at him. There was a strange transformation occurring in him—a kind of hardening of his eyes and posture, a readying for battle. The impression was not of a man putting on armor, but of letting a softer outer layer melt away, revealing the steel beneath it.

"Why do you say that?"

"He is a powerful man with powerful protectors. There is never evidence of what he has done."

"Powerful people can be arrested and prosecuted like anyone else."

"How many international assassins have you arrested and prosecuted?"

Gurney said nothing.

Valdez continued. "There are people high in government and world finance whose reliance on his expertise put him beyond the reach of any ordinary justice system."

"What if I were to go straight to the media and tell the story to the whole world?"

"Your first problem would be his name. He has none. Actually, he has so many, it is the same as none. Dimitri Filker, Gligor Leski, Jurgen Kleinst, Hamid Bokar, Piotar Malenkov, Ivan Kurilenko, Gerhard Bosch. A hundred more."

"And Valdez? Is that one of them?"

"No. Valdez was my mother's name. Everything he owns, he owns in someone else's name."

"What name is on his driver's license? His social security card?"

"He doesn't have either one. Officially, he doesn't exist. But his anonymity would not be your only problem, if you took your story to the media. A direct attack on him could result in your disappearance, or your wife's disappearance, or your son's disappearance. Now, or a month from now, or a year from now. He forgets nothing. Everything must be repaid."

"That doesn't leave me with a lot of options."

Something in Gurney's tone caused Valdez to regard him more closely. "No, there are not many options."

That led to a speculative silence, broken by Gurney.

"What can you tell me about him?"

"Apart from his being an embodiment of everything evil?" Valdez's gaze returned to the fire, his voice now oddly bland. "He's a middle-aged man of average height, soft-spoken. He prefers dark places to bright ones, a genetic defect in his vision. Light is painful to his eyes. He goes outdoors only when his business requires it. He spends most of his time in the shadowy place where he keeps his pets."

"His pets?"

"The lowest level of the house is full of snakes. He collects and breeds them. Constrictors and pit vipers. Many species, with two things in common. They are all deadly. And they can all digest animal bodies, even bones. When they eat their prey, all that is left are a few pellets of hair."

"Sounds creepy."

"More creepy is his excitement watching this happen." Valdez paused, the tiniest tremor in his expression. "Apart from that, he appears normal, just an ordinary man, unremarkable in every way." Valdez paused again. "Except when he eats. He gnaws on his food like a rat."

It took Gurney a while to assimilate all this.

"Is he as wary of you as you are of him?"

"He is wary of everyone. No one can get near him who he has not invited. As for me, he regards me as a piece of his property that he is determined to regain control of. Everything you have said about his attacks on Ziko proves this. I believe you because I know this man. I can feel in my heart that he would frame Ziko for murder, then set up his faked suicide—all to destroy Ziko in my eyes, to destroy my belief that a new life is possible, to make me come back to him. It is the strongest desire in him—to be in control of everything and everyone."

"It may also be his weak point," said Gurney. "It could be our way in."

"Getting in is difficult. Getting close to him is more difficult. Getting close with a weapon is impossible. There are guards. There are metal detectors. There are the snakes. So many snakes. It is not an ordinary house."

"So, it would seem that we need to get an invitation."

"Easy for me. Not so easy for you."

Gurney got up from his armchair and began pacing around the room, in the hope that the movement might give rise to ideas that wouldn't have occurred to him sitting in one spot.

After circling the room several times, Gurney stopped in a far corner, then turned to Valdez. "Suppose you wanted to kill me . . . and make my body disappear. Is that something he'd be willing to help you with?"

Valdez looked up from the fire.

"Possibly. But it's hard to deceive him. Many people have died trying. He enjoys killing people who have lied to him."

"It sounds like disabling his defenses will be like defusing a bomb."

"A bomb with many triggers."

"So," said Gurney, beginning again his slow pacing around the room, "we have to construct a lie that he'd be eager to believe."

AN HOUR LATER, they had agreed on the details of that lie, on a dark favor Valdez would ask for, and on a final risky stratagem that would neutralize the man toward whom Valdez appeared to bear an implacable hatred.

He stood in front of the fireplace, a few feet from Gurney, his phone in his hand.

"I must prepare you for something you may find disturbing. In this phone call, I will be the person I once was, the person he wants me to be again. You understand?"

"I think so."

"You will naturally hear only my part of the conversation, but I will try to say enough so that it will make sense to you." With a tiny tic at the corner of his eye—the only hint of anxiety Gurney could see—Valdez entered a number and waited.

"Yes," he said a few seconds later. "It's Ivan."

Interesting, thought Gurney, wondering exactly when the young man had dropped the "v" and turned the Russian name into a British one.

"That's right," said Valdez into the phone. "I need to talk to him."

He waited. At least two minutes passed before he spoke again.

"Yes, it's me. I've got a situation here. An ex-cop, David Gurney, has been poking around the Slade-Lerman case. He's come to see me a few times. His story at first was that he thought Slade was innocent and was trying to exonerate him. He asked me for some money for expenses. Okay, I thought, I'll give him a couple of grand, see what he can find out. He comes back a week or two later, says he needs five grand. I'm thinking this is bullshit. But I'm curious where he's going with this, so I give him the five, let him think I'm easy. Week later he comes to me again, says there may be a problem. Says he's finding out things that could incriminate me for the murder of Lerman. He says that would also finger me for framing Slade, which is fucking insane. Makes me think my life would be simpler if I never met Ziko Slade. No matter. Water under the fucking bridge. Anyway, after Slade hangs himself, Gurney comes to me and says he found out I'll be picking up nine mil from Slade's estate, and that's going to point the finger at me for sure, but he can make that go away, and all he needs is a hundred grand. But I can see in his fucking eyes that the hundred grand would just be the first bite."

Valdez was silent for nearly a minute, the phone pressed to his ear, his dark eyes gleaming in the firelight.

When he spoke again, it was with a harsh dismissiveness. "No, no, no, it's not all about the money. Listen to me. I don't care about *chasing* money, I don't care about *spending* money, I don't care about how *much* money I have. But someone tries to pick my pocket, I'll cut his fucking hand off. Fucker thinks he can sucker me out of a hundred grand with some shit about protecting me from a frame job? That's one fucking serious mistake."

He was silent for maybe half a minute, listening intently to the voice on the phone, before responding in a less excited but no less menacing tone.

"You ask what's my bottom line? Simple. This fucking Gurney is not what he seems to be. He's no boy-scout detective. He's a god-damn leech, trying to take what's mine. So, I figure his time is up."

Ten seconds of listening.

"Yeah, of course I can handle it."

Another ten seconds of listening.

"I got no problem taking care of it personally. In fact, I insist on it. My finger on the trigger. No other fucking way."

Five seconds of listening.

"What I was hoping was maybe, as a favor, you could help with the disposal."

The phone conversation went on for several more minutes. Gurney gathered from Valdez's side of it that the "disposal" was not only agreed to but that the arrangement would proceed that very night. Valdez would ensure that Gurney would be present at the lodge. Two cars would be sent, one to transport Gurney as a prisoner and one for Valdez.

At the end of the call, Valdez expressed his gratitude for the favor in the tone a humble priest might use to address the pope.

"I HOPE YOU didn't overdo it," Gurney said later as they sat by the fireplace, reviewing the situation and preparing for what was to come.

"Overdoing it is not a problem. He regards such behavior as a sign of fear and respect—acknowledgments of his power. He is God. We are his subjects."

"As his son, you must be a bit more than that."

"True. My special role is to be an extension of him. I am supposed to be his hand. The hand of God, with no will of my own. The greatest sin is to forget that he is God and that I am just his hand. Or perhaps just the finger on the trigger."

"Listening to what you said on the phone, I got the impression you were insisting on being the one with the right to kill me."

"It sounds like a contradiction, but I know how he hears things. He would hear what I said not as a challenge to his power but as an acceptance of my responsibility to deal with someone who has become a threat. My willingness to do what he would wish me to do. You must trust my perception of this."

Gurney's uneasiness was steadily rising—not only because of the increasing role of "trust" in the anticipated events, but because of the impression created by Valdez's persona in the conversation with his father. The possibility that this was the real Valdez was frightening.

"I'm thinking," said Gurney, "that it would make sense to arrange for some law-enforcement backup around his house in the event that we have to hit the bailout button."

"It's not a good idea. He has many police contacts who would inform him the instant any such request was made. It would abort our only chance to get near him. It would also motivate him to deal with you himself, which would put you at much greater risk. We have only one path forward."

That led to a long silence and the most difficult decision Gurney had ever wrestled with—to back out now and hope that a better plan would occur to him, or to take a leap in the dark and trust this man on the basis of little more than Emma's assurance that he was trustworthy.

The decisive moment arrived a little after ten o'clock that night, as two vehicles were making their way up the long driveway to the lodge.

"Okay," said Gurney, taking a deep breath. "Let's do it."

73

AT 1:05 A.M., THE GARVILLE POLICE CAR—IN WHICH Gurney had been transported from the lodge with a hood over his head and his wrists in zip-tie restraints—slowed, made a turn into what he assumed was a driveway, and stopped. He heard the low rumble of a garage door opening. The car moved forward, then came to a stop again. He heard the garage door closing behind him.

The car door beside him opened. A rough voice said, "Last stop. Get out."

The hood was yanked from his head, and he found himself in a dimly lit garage, not far from a glossy pearl-gray Range Rover. The man standing in front of him looked vaguely familiar. Back at the lodge, he hadn't gotten a clear look at his face, but now he was sure he'd seen him somewhere before—the heavily muscled shoulders, the thick neck, the small eyes . . . and then he remembered. Gavin Horst. The shady cop who let him know he wasn't welcome to park on the same street as Lanka's Specialty Foods.

"Hello, Gavin. Any chance you could tell me what the hell this is all about?"

Horst appeared momentarily thrown by Gurney's use of his name. "You asked that three times on the way here. You'll find out soon enough." He pointed to a door in the garage's rear wall. "Walk!"

When they got to it, the door opened and a Horst look-alike holding an extended magazine Uzi stood aside to let them through.

"Straight ahead," said Horst, prodding Gurney in the back with something that felt like the muzzle of a gun.

A concrete-walled corridor led to a recessed door with a keypad on the wall next to it. Horst entered a sequence of numbers and the door slid open, revealing a small elevator with bare metal walls. Horst shoved Gurney into it, stepped in after him, and tapped a button on the wall. With a small lurch, the elevator descended.

From Gurney's sense of movement and the time it took, he concluded that they'd reached a sub-basement level. Horst pushed him out into a room with three concrete walls and one glass wall. Behind the glass wall there was darkness. Opposite the glass wall there was a large wooden desk and chair, and behind that, a closed metal door.

"Go over there," said Horst, prodding him in the back and pointing to a spot in the middle of the floor where two metal rings were embedded in the concrete.

When he got there, the door behind the desk opened and a bony-faced white-haired woman emerged in a flowing black dress, conjuring up in Gurney's mind a fairytale witch. She walked soundlessly toward him, regarding him with steel-cold eyes for a long moment before kneeling and securing his ankles to the metal rings with zip ties.

She stood up and gave Horst a curt wave of dismal. Without a word, he got back in the elevator, the door closed, and Gurney heard the soft whirring of the mechanism carrying him back up to the garage level.

The woman in black went to the door behind the desk and opened it. Three men entered—a linebacker type with an oily black crew cut, black polo shirt, black jeans, and a black Uzi; an unimposing middle-aged man with thinning gray hair, sallow skin, and tinted glasses; and Valdez, who eyed Gurney with an expression of distaste that looked very real. Gurney tried to reassure himself that things were going according to plan.

The man with the tinted glasses sat in the chair behind the desk. Valdez and the linebacker with the Uzi took up positions on each side of him. The man with the tinted glasses spoke first. His speech, like Valdez's, was an amalgamation of accents, predominantly Slavic.

"You are very quiet, Mr. Gurney. Do you know why you've been brought here?"

Gurney took a short nervous breath. "Who am I speaking to?"

"To me, Mr. Gurney. To me."

"Who are you?"

"I am Ivan's father. Now, I ask you again. Do you know why you are here?"

"My assumption is that there's been a huge misunderstanding."

"What has been misunderstood?"

Gurney was trying to sound nervous. It wasn't difficult. "The whole . . . the whole point of my investigation. What it is that I'm . . . that I'm trying to do."

"And what is that?"

"I'm just trying to get at the truth. The case against Ziko Slade had gaping holes in it. I've been looking at the aspects that make no sense."

The man shrugged again. "It made enough sense to convict him."

"Yes, but now even the DA is beginning to have doubts. She believes your son was involved. She may want to pursue a case against him. Slade may be posthumously exonerated. If he is, Stryker is sure to find a new target. Your son could be in real legal jeopardy. But I can help reduce that danger. I'm an experienced investigator. I have important contacts. I can discover the weak points in any case she tries to make, before she makes it. We can be ready. Proactive." Gurney was talking fast, duplicating as best he could the panicky voice of a salesman with nothing but bullshit to sell.

The man nodded. "This readiness—it would cost money?"

"Naturally, there'd be . . . expenses. Time, effort, inducements to key individuals to share information, perhaps an exploration of Stryker's private life. She's not well liked. I'm sure I could buy the cooperation of someone on her staff."

The man kept nodding. "So, quite a lot of money."

"But it would be well worth it. To avoid serious consequences. For peace of mind."

The man smiled. "Peace of mind is important."

"Absolutely!" cried Gurney. "Peace of mind is worth whatever it costs."

"Perhaps you are aware that my son is receiving a large inheritance, so a great deal of money is available. You are aware of this?"

"I . . . yes . . . I heard something about that."

"So, to make it simple, you are saying there is a great danger to my son, which you can protect him from, if we give you enough money. Is that correct?"

"I think . . . that's . . . correct."

"Protecting my son is important to me."

"Of course!"

"A danger to him is a danger to me. The son is part of the father. Part of my body, like an arm or a leg. To lose a son is to lose a limb. This is what a son is. If he is not this, he is nothing. You understand?"

"I think so."

"And you understand that a threat to him is a threat to me?"

"Yes . . . yes . . . I can see that, but . . . what I don't know is why I've been brought here like this."

"Soon you will know. Do you have a hobby, Mr. Gurney?"

"Sorry?"

"A hobby. Something you enjoy, other than what you are paid to do."

"I enjoy what I'm paid to do."

"To protect my son, no matter how much it might cost him?"

Gurney said nothing. He tried to look like a man who couldn't think of a safe answer to a dangerous question.

"I have a hobby, Mr. Gurney. A passion. I want to share it with you." He turned to the man beside him with the Uzi. "Victor, remove the restraints from his wrists and from one of his ankles, so he has more freedom to move."

Striding over to Gurney, Victor pulled a tactical knife from a steel clip on his belt. He cut one of the ankle restraints, then the ones holding Gurney's wrists behind his back. The sudden freeing of his arms sent shocks of pain through his shoulders. He was tempted for a fleeting moment to make a grab for the Uzi, even though that wasn't part of the plan he and Valdez had agreed on, but the odds of success seemed vanishingly small and the knife remarkably sharp. Excruciating though it was, he slowly rotated his shoulders to loosen the muscles cramped from the long trip in the back of the Garville police car.

"Tell me, Mr. Gurney," said the man seated behind the desk, "do you know what a herpetarium is?"

"Not exactly."

"It's a place where serpents live. A wonderful word, 'serpent.' From the Latin word, 'serpere.' It means 'to creep.'"

Gurney could see, even through the man's tinted glasses, a new excitement in his gaze.

Valdez spoke up for the first time—in a softly menacing voice. "The word 'serpent' means also a sly or treacherous person, a person who exploits a position of trust. I wonder, Mr. Gurney, are you a sly or treacherous person?"

"Absolutely not. I believe in putting my cards on the table. I have nothing to hide. I never lie." He was trying his best to sound like a panicked liar.

"You never twist the truth to get what you want?"

"No. That would be lying. And I hate liars."

"So do I, Mr. Gurney. I wonder, have you ever exploited a position of trust?"

"No, never! I'm not a . . . a sneak. I hate sneaks."

"But I think you want to exploit my trust in you."

"No, no, I would never—"

"Shut your fucking mouth! You interrupt me again, I'll cut your fucking tongue out, you piece of shit!"

Gurney blinked in shock. He didn't have to fake his frightened reaction. The explosion of animal fury in Valdez's voice and eyes was all too believable.

When Valdez went on, it was in a voice as chillingly calm as his father's. "I think you only want money from me, while you pretend to want only the truth. You say I am in legal danger, but this danger can be made to go away, if I give you enough money. I think this legal danger is bullshit, but your demand for money is real."

Gurney stayed quiet, letting his expression alone convey fear.

Valdez responded to Gurney's silence with a horrible smile. "It would be good for you to make your confession to me, while there is still time."

Gurney stammered, "I . . . I have nothing . . . nothing to confess."

Valdez shrugged. "I'm sorry to hear that."

The man behind the desk said, "Perhaps he will change his mind. Victor, the herpetarium lights, please."

The guard flipped a switch on the concrete wall, and the area behind the glass on the opposite side of the room was illuminated. Turning toward it, Gurney saw what appeared to be an enclosed jungle. His attention was drawn first to the drooping leaves of the tropical plants, glistening with droplets of water. Then he caught a glimpse of movement on the dark soil under one of the lush plants. A long acid-green snake with ebony eyes was gliding slowly toward a corner of the enclosure where a small tan rabbit was twitching in obvious terror.

"She will swallow it whole, very slowly," said the man behind the desk. "Did you know that rabbits can scream?"

Gurney had a clear recollection of being given that disturbing piece of information by Valdez the evening the beheaded rabbit appeared in his Outback.

His attention was drawn to movements in other areas of the enclosure. He was only a few feet away from more snakes than he'd ever seen in any zoo—snakes of all sizes and colors, moving, coiling, uncoiling, raising their heads, testing the air with their flicking tongues.

"I can see you are impressed, Mr. Gurney. But the best is yet to come." The man opened the center drawer of the desk, took out something the size of a garage door opener, and pointed it toward the herpetarium. The glass wall began rising through a slot in the ceiling until it disappeared. A flood of warm, humid air filled the room with a sweet-rotten smell of decay.

As Gurney watched with increasing alarm, an enormous yellow snake emerged from beneath the rank, dripping vegetation. The creature glided forward, first across the soil of the enclosure, then out onto the floor of the room itself, its massive body moving slowly toward him in a long, loose, S-shaped curve.

"The most beautiful animal on earth," said the man behind the desk. His voice had a purring quality as disconcerting as the snake's approach. "Not only beautiful, but sensitive. She wraps herself around you, and while she is doing that, she is listening. Listening to your heartbeat. She tightens herself around you, focused on the beating of your heart. She hugs you even tighter. So tight you can't breathe. Tighter and tighter, crushing your veins, your arteries. Tighter and tighter until there is no more heartbeat. Until there is only silence. That is how she knows you are dead. The silence of your heart gives you away. Imagine that Mr. Gurney—a creature that listens for your heart to stop, so she will know you are dead. So she can devour you."

As if responding on cue, the gigantic snake reached Gurney's tethered ankle, its weight passing over his foot, as it began to coil itself around his leg. Its weight was as shocking as its scarlet eyes. Its girth was nearly that of a man's thigh.

"What do you want from me?" cried Gurney, easily managing to sound petrified.

"Nothing, Mr. Gurney. Nothing at all."

"This is crazy! I've done nothing to harm you. Nothing!"

"I'm glad to hear that."

As the creature continued coiling itself around Gurney's leg, rising higher, its weight began to affect his balance. As he staggered in a desperate effort to remain upright, he caught sight of a second snake, larger than the first, emerging from under the wet foliage. As it moved toward him, the one that already had him in its grip had risen above his leg and was wrapping itself around his hips. He twisted himself around to face Valdez, Valdez's father, and the linebacker with the Uzi.

"You can have whatever you want! Just name it!"

Valdez's father folded his hands on the desk and produced a

glazed smile. "Peace of mind, Mr. Gurney. That's all. Just peace of mind."

Despite Gurney's frantic efforts to stop it, the snake was wrapping itself around his midsection and moving higher. Valdez was looking at Gurney with a mixed expression of satisfaction and hatred. He leaned down toward his father and said something Gurney couldn't hear. His father continued watching for another long minute before opening the center drawer of the desk and handing Valdez a 9mm Sig Sauer.

Thank God, thought Gurney, who'd begun to fear that the plan he and Valdez had devised would fail. But the key goal had finally been achieved. Valdez was armed and could deal with his unsuspecting father and the man with the Uzi.

But instead of doing so, he came out from behind the desk and, with a vicious smile, walked across the floor to a spot a few feet from Gurney. He slowly raised the pistol with a rock-steady hand until the barrel was on a direct line with Gurney's heart.

Gurney could feel the blood draining from his face as his mind was filled with the horrible, despairing conclusion that the greatest—and last—mistake of his life had been to trust Emma Martin's opinion of Valdez.

Valdez pulled the trigger.

The muzzle blast in the concrete room was deafening.

74

GURNEY STAGGERED IN SHOCK AT THE SOUND OF THE shot. But he remained standing—stunned and confused.

Valdez stared at him, appearing not to comprehend what had happened. He stared at the pistol, then turned to his father with a look of angry bafflement.

"What the fuck is going on?"

The man gestured to the pistol. "Bring it to me."

Valdez walked to the desk and handed it over.

His father ejected the magazine, inserted a new one from the desk drawer, and handed the weapon back to Valdez.

"Try again."

Valdez walked back to his position in front of Gurney and aimed again at his heart. This time, instead of a sadistic smile, he gave Gurney a small nod, then whirled around toward the desk and fired a rapid series of shots, smashing the guard with the Uzi against the wall and his father against his chair, upending it onto the floor.

He pivoted back to Gurney, put a point-blank shot in the head of the giant snake, blowing half of it away, and a shot in Gurney's ankle restraint, severing it. He handed the Sig to Gurney. "Seventeen shot magazine, ten left, you'll need them."

He bounded around behind the desk and grabbed the Uzi from the guard's body, as the door in the back wall was flung open and another Uzi-brandishing guard burst into the room.

Gurney hit him with two center-mass shots just as a third guard appeared in the now-exposed hallway beyond the open door. He fired two more shots, and the man went down hard.

The heavy coils of the partially headless snake were loosening around Gurney's stomach and descending toward the floor, making it possible to step free of them. He backed away from the larger python-like snake that was moving steadily toward him and aimed the Sig at its head.

"Stop!" cried Valdez. "Leave that one alive!"

That made no sense to Gurney, but he had no time to ask why. A large man in combat gear appeared in the hall and was advancing toward the open doorway with an Uzi in each hand. Gurney dove to the floor. The two Uzis began blasting away simultaneously, the rounds ripping through the wooden desk, inches from Gurney's body.

"Marko!" shouted Valdez. "It's me in here, for Christ's sake!"

The man stopped firing but kept the Uzis pointed at the open door. "Drop any gun you have, put your hands over your head, and step out where I can see you."

"Okay, Marko, take it easy," said Valdez in a calming voice. Then he reached around the frame of the door and fired repeatedly into the hallway.

A moment later, the man called Marko was lying on his back, blood pulsing from his throat, the Uzis in his spasming fingers firing into the ceiling.

"How many more guards are there?" asked Gurney, getting shakily to his feet.

"Three more. All upstairs. Trying to figure out what's going on. Making calls for assistance. We've got maybe ten minutes. Watch the hallway, while I take care of something."

Valdez laid his captured Uzi on the desk and dragged his father's body out into the middle of the room. One of the tinted lenses in his glasses was shattered. Blood was oozing from the eye socket onto the concrete floor. His head was less than two feet from the slowly advancing python.

"Jesus," muttered Gurney.

"This is what he has done to many people. It is what he would have done to you. This is justice. I am sorry only that he is not conscious to see what will happen to him. Now, come quickly. They will watch the stairway. We go up in the elevator."

"You know the code for the keypad?"

"Not needed for going up, only coming down."

They stepped into the elevator, Valdez tapped a button on the metal wall, and they started ascending.

"Be ready," said Valdez, holding his Uzi in firing position, aimed at the elevator door.

Gurney checked the magazine in the Sig Sauer and adopted a similar stance.

When the elevator came to a stop and the door slid open, they found themselves pointing their weapons at an empty corridor. Valdez led the way to the garage. The door was open, the fluorescent lights were on, and the Garville police car was gone. Valdez entered first, Uzi aimed at the pearl gray Range Rover. Gurney took up a position to his right.

Valdez pointed to a small metal cabinet on the wall. "Open that and take out the electronic key."

Gurney did so.

"Now, press the Unlock button."

Gurney did so and heard an answering mechanical click from the Range Rover.

"Cover me," said Valdez, "while I check the interior."

He went to the front passenger door, yanked it open, stepped back, then proceeded do the same with the rear passenger door.

"Clear. Now the luggage compartment."

Valdez moved around to the back of the vehicle, and Gurney adjusted his own position.

"There's a liftgate button on the remote. Press it."

Gurney did so.

The liftgate began to open.

A second later, Valdez staggered backward, dropping the Uzi, letting out a shriek.

A long, thin, violet snake had come flying out from under the rising liftgate and was wrapping itself around Valdez's neck.

As Gurney rushed over, a black-clad, wild-eyed woman jumped from the back of the vehicle, hissing, teeth bared, grabbing for the fallen Uzi.

She got her hands on it and began pivoting toward him.

"Drop it!" shouted Gurney.

But the muzzle of the Uzi was rising. He fired three times in less than a second. The 9mm rounds slammed her against the concrete floor.

"Kill this fucking thing!" Valdez's words came out in a rasping, choking rush, as he tried to pry the snake from his throat.

Gurney stepped closer, took careful aim, and blew the snake's head off.

He looked down at the body on the floor—the body of the bony little woman who'd put the restraints on his ankles. Blood was slowly spreading out from her dress onto the garage floor.

He pictured the giant python making its inexorable, hungry way across that other concrete floor toward the head of the Viper.

It was over.

Exhaustion emptied his mind.

He was aware of nothing but the steady beating of his heart.

EPILOGUE

AFTER A BRIEF DISCUSSION, VALDEZ AND GURNEY AGREED to return to the lodge. With Valdez driving the Range Rover, they arrived at dawn. Before heading to bed in a state of physical and mental exhaustion, his back and neck a mass of pain, Gurney asked the question that had been eating at him.

"How did you know there were blanks in the gun he gave you to shoot me with?"

"I knew he would never hand me a live weapon until he was absolutely sure how I would use it."

THE FOLLOWING DAY, Valdez asked how the murder of Sonny Lerman fit into the overall scheme of things. Gurney suggested that his own investigation might have so enraged the young man with the thought of losing his insurance payout that he had gone to Valdez's biological father with his own request for a favor—the elimination of the troublesome investigator.

"But," said Gurney, "he probably considered Sonny at least as troublesome as me, so he tried to get rid of us both by framing me for Sonny's murder, just like he framed Ziko for Lenny's. I'm less sure about the murder of Charlene Vesco. My guess is that she was so shaken by the shooting of her cousin, Dominick, that he doubted her reliability and killed her to avoid further worry."

———

As THE DAY wore on, Gurney commented on the strange absence of anything in the news about the previous evening's bloodbath. "With deadly snakes, dead bodies, and bullet casings all over the place, it has to be the most sensational upstate crime scene in years."

Valdez shook his head. "It will not be in the news. Nothing will be known about it."

"How is that possible? I mean, the gunshots alone . . ."

"The shots were not heard. My father had the house sound-proofed many years ago. There were many sounds he wanted no one outside to hear."

The images that came to mind caused Gurney to fall silent for a long moment.

"And the bodies, the bloody mess—all of that just stays there?"

Valdez shrugged. "When they can't get in touch with him, the people who rely on my father's services will realize something has happened. Cleaners will come. Professionals who deal with special situations. Everything troublesome will disappear. Someday the house will be sold. There will be no connection to him."

"The woman in the black dress," said Gurney. "Who was that?"

"Serena. His sister." Valdez's strained tone implied that there was something sick in the relationship.

Gurney saw no reason to pursue it.

"What do you know about that violet snake she threw at you?"

"That was her favorite. The rarest and most deadly of all. She used to let it crawl all over her body. It was not a comfortable thing to see."

THAT NIGHT, GURNEY sat with his computer at the dining room table and put together a detailed narrative description of the case, omitting only the bloody finale, and emailed it to Cam Stryker. He felt that he owed her at least that much of the truth.

He believed that his relationship with her had reached an uneasy balance, based on the concept of mutually assured destruction. He might be able to win the battle of the Slade case, perhaps even end Stryker's career, if he revealed the full story, including its violent ending. But his own participation in that bloodletting would drag him into a costly and perilous legal nightmare, and he wasn't ready to sacrifice his own life just to destroy Stryker's.

He also sent the case narrative to Kyra Barstow at her private email account, along with a cover note thanking her for her help.

He received no response from either woman, nor did he expect any.

VALDEZ OFFERED GURNEY the use of the lodge indefinitely.

"Stay as long as you wish—a week, a month, a year. Make it your home. I must return to Emma. I'm disappointed in myself. The killing was too easy for me. I found it too easy to be the person I once was."

"You did what was necessary. You saved us both."

"It is not what I did that bothers me. It's how it made me feel. It gave me the excitement of revenge. Emma says to be excited by the blood of an enemy is a sickness."

VALDEZ'S COMMENTS PRODDED Gurney to examine his own feelings about the way things turned out—feelings that were oddly mixed. He had, on the one hand, arrived at a full understanding of the case. He'd managed to fit all the pieces together. The mystery had been solved. As he'd done hundreds of times in his career, he'd figured it out.

But another kind of question remained.

Why had he put the final solution in Valdez's lap?

If the faultless narrative was truly his goal, why hadn't he gone public with it, exposed it to every relevant law-enforcement agency, as well as the media? Why had he taken it quietly to the one person who might be motivated to give him direct access to the man behind it all?

Sometimes confrontation could fill in the missing pieces of a puzzle, but that was not the case here. He'd already put the pieces together before revealing them to Valdez—knowing that Valdez was a route to the Viper. There could be only one motive for confrontation under those circumstances.

A desire for mortal combat.

Had he been fooling himself about who he was? Had he been telling himself that he was a descendant of Sherlock Holmes, applying logic to the messy world of passionate crime—a rational mind in pursuit of the truth—when in fact it wasn't the truth that he was after, but victory? Victory, it would seem, at any cost. At the cost of other people's lives. At the cost of his own marriage. Was there anything he wouldn't sacrifice for victory?

Perhaps he wasn't the Holmes of cerebral solutions, after all, but the Holmes who engaged archenemy Moriarty in a fight to the death at the Reichenbach Falls.

ONE MORNING WHILE Gurney was having breakfast, Kyle phoned to announce that he'd broken up with Kim Corazon, having finally seen the cold and manipulative heart under all that attractive energy. Suggesting in her RAM interview that Gurney was capable of murder provided the final ugly insight into her ambition.

"She's scrambling to finish a book about the Slade case, full of insinuation and conjecture," said Kyle, "and she's using the horrible Thanksgiving event as its selling point to prospective publishers. She doesn't care how that might affect you or Madeleine or anyone else. Her rotten little career is the only thing that matters to her."

GURNEY CALLED THE hospital every evening to ask about Hardwick, but the answer was always the same.

On several occasions, he was tempted to drive down to Dillweed to tell Esti how sorry he was, but each time he decided not to, suspecting that his motive was selfish—to diminish her hostility toward him, rather than to share her burden of fear and sadness.

HIS POST-CONCUSSIVE SYMPTOMS kept coming and going with little rhyme or reason. He could lug heavy armfuls of wood in for the fireplace with no trouble, then be struck by a fit of dizziness or a stabbing headache while scrambling an egg.

TWICE HE HAD the Danny dream, always the same, always leaving him in tears.

On their way to the playground on a sunny day.

Danny walking in front of him.

Following a pigeon on the sidewalk.

He himself only partly present.

Pondering a twist in a murder case he was working on.

Distracted by a bright idea, a possible solution.

The pigeon stepping off the curb into the street.

Danny following the pigeon.

The sickening, heart-stopping thump.

Danny's body tossed through the air, hitting the pavement, rolling.

Rolling.

The red BMW racing away.

Screeching around a corner.

Gone.

SOMETIMES HE HAD an overwhelming feeling that the structure of his life had collapsed, that all the points of reference had disappeared, that everything he'd imagined was permanent had evaporated. One morning, he was looking out the dining room window, watching a curled-up leaf being blown erratically this way and that on the icy surface. He mistook it at first for a small, crippled creature—like himself.

SEVERAL TIMES HE was tempted to go down to the Franciscan Sanctuary and volunteer to regain a sense of purpose, but he never did. And it wasn't just the dog-walking idea that came and went. Whenever he thought of doing anything, he thought of a reason not to.

The only exception occurred after he'd been at the lodge for two weeks. He got the idea that he should drive down to Walnut Crossing, check on the house, talk to Madeleine. He wasn't sure what he'd say to her. Maybe the right words would occur to him during the drive. In fact, nothing occurred to him. Every time he tried to think about it, his concentration dissolved. It was as though his mind had slipped away beyond his reach.

The closer he got to Walnut Crossing, the more pointless the trip seemed. He thought maybe he should just go directly to the campsite, take down the tent, take everything down to his car, drive back to the lodge. But instead of taking the turnoff that would bring him to the back of the campsite hill, he stayed on the county road that led to the town road that led up the hill to his property. He had the feeling that the watchers would be gone, and he was right.

He drove up through the low pasture and parked by the asparagus patch. It felt like everything around him had changed in some way he couldn't identify. He got out of the car and breathed in the cold December air. Madeleine's car wasn't there, and the house showed no signs of life. The fencing around the coop and the alpaca shed had been completed, enclosing at least a half acre of the pasture.

As he walked toward the shed, he heard a low humming, almost a human sound. When he got closer, he realized it wasn't coming from the shed, but from behind it. He followed the fence around the shed and came face-to-face with the creatures making the sound.

Twin alpacas were standing next to an open bale of hay, looking at him. He saw in their eyes an expression that looked like gentle curiosity—along with a sense of peace and contentment.

He wondered if that was what Madeleine was feeling now—a peace and contentment that she'd never felt with him.

A freezing gust of wind sent snow devils whirling across the pasture. He retreated to his car, drove down the town road, and headed north—back to the lodge—determined to figure out who he was, where he belonged, and why he felt so lost.

ACKNOWLEDGMENTS

With the publication of *The Viper*, the Dave Gurney series enters its fourteenth year—an event unimaginable to me when I was sending out that first query letter for *Think of a Number*.

So much of the growth and success of the series, both domestically and internationally, is due to the people I've had the pleasure of working with.

My agents—Molly Friedrich, Lucy Carson, and Hannah Brattesani—are everything a writer could wish for. They are super-smart, super-energetic, and super-supportive.

I feel equally fortunate in my association with the fine professionals at Counterpoint. Dan Smetanka's perceptive questions and suggestions make everything better. In fact, a recommendation he made for *The Viper* has resulted in it being one of the most surprising of the Gurney books. My thanks also to Dan López for his smart edits and improvements in pacing.

As always, I remain grateful to my readers, whose enthusiasm for the adventures of Dave Gurney has been a delightful reward for me, as well as a strong incentive to my creating intricate new problems for him to solve.

And finally, my thanks to my wife, without whose encouragement and patience these books could not have been written.

© Naomi Fisch

JOHN VERDON is the author of the Dave Gurney
series of thrillers, international bestsellers published
in more than two dozen languages: *Think of a Number*, *Shut Your Eyes Tight*, *Let the Devil Sleep*, *Peter Pan Must Die*, *Wolf Lake*, *White River Burning*,
and *On Harrow Hill*. Before becoming a crime fiction writer, Verdon had two previous careers as an
advertising creative director and a custom furniture
maker. He currently lives with his wife, Naomi, in
the rural mountains of Upstate New York—raising
chickens, tending the garden, mowing the fields,
and devising the intricate plots of the Gurney novels. Find out more at johnverdon.net.